Duncan Falco
Boat Service
Ireland's top-se

STRATTON

DUNCAN FALCONER

SPHERE

First published in Great Britain as a paperback original as *The Hostage* in 2003
by Time Warner Paperbacks
Reprinted in 2010 by Sphere
This film tie-in edition published in 2017 by Sphere

1 3 5 7 9 10 8 6 4 2

A CIP catalogue record for this book
is available from the British Library.

ISBN 978-0-7515-7047-2

Typeset in Bembo by Palimpsest Book Production Limited, Falkirk, Stirlingshire
Printed and bound in Great Britain by Clays Ltd, St Ives plc

Papers used by Sphere are from well-managed forests
and other responsible sources.

MIX
Paper from
responsible sources
FSC® C104740

Sphere
An imprint of
Little, Brown Book Group
Carmelite House
50 Victoria Embankment
London EC4Y 0DZ

An Hachette UK Company
www.hachette.co.uk

www.littlebrown.co.uk

To Adele

1

Spinks lay in darkness in the boot of a car eating a cheese sandwich, his chewing and swallowing amplified in the confined, metallic space. He was scruffy, long-haired, unshaven and malodorous. He paused to pick his nose, an enjoyable habit he did not necessarily reserve for private moments such as this, and rolled it until it was dry enough to flick off. He took another bite of the sandwich and continued to chew thoughtfully, blinking in the darkness.

This was the second time he had spent the day in the boot of a car and it was, so far at least, nowhere near as memorable as the first. That was four months earlier, in the middle of summer, and one of the most horrifying days in his twenty-nine years. He was not a particularly large man but whoever had chosen the car that day had given scant thought to his size altogether; they had concentrated solely on the objective and not at all on Spinks's comfort. They could be forgiven to some extent since the whole affair was a hitherto untried experiment and all too hurriedly executed, and Spinks had absolutely no idea what he was getting himself into. He had felt claustrophobic the second the boot was slammed shut and everything went pitch black. It was only when the car trundled through the security chicane and over the sleeping policemen at the main gate to the camp that it occurred to him he should have put something spongy on the bare metal floor to lie on.

The twenty or so mile drive, mostly along country roads, was painful in the dark and cramped space and he spread himself like a starfish in an effort to stop rolling about, but that grew tiring after a while. He imagined all kinds of horrors in the event of a collision, specifically a rear-ender. When the journey ended he thought the worst was over but it had only just begun. What almost killed Spinks was as much a surprise to him as it was to everyone else involved.

His task had been to video the main gate of the Crossmaglen Rangers' Gaelic Football Club on a bright Sunday afternoon as the team prepared to play Dromintree. Crossmaglen is a small town virtually encircled by the border with most of its roads heading directly into the Republic, and certain IRA members of interest who resided in the South were rumoured to be attending the match. It had been a very hot day and the sun's rays gradually warmed the car's metal skin. By early afternoon the inside was like an oven. Spinks later compared it to a prison sweatbox, only his was much smaller, completely without ventilation and prisoners were at least spared a battering journey inside the box over miles of bad road prior to their being baked. He almost passed out with the combination of heat and deteriorating air quality. No one realised how much he had suffered until the car was driven away on completion of the job and the boot opened. Spinks was lying there, dehydrated and hyperventilating, but nevertheless, to his credit, he had stoically completed his task.

On this occasion it was a much bigger boot and he had tailored in an old mattress sponge to lie on. He could roll from one shoulder on to the other if he shuffled around although he still could not stretch out his legs. But more importantly it was now autumn. The previous experience had taught him that one could dress against the cold inside a freezer but there was nothing one could do to keep cool inside a baking oven.

Spinks's excessive body odour was due to the fact he hardly ever washed himself and his clothes even less. He claimed his lack of hygiene was a necessary part of the job. 'If you're gonna be one of 'em, go all the way' was his excuse. It was true that many of the rural indigenous types they operated against made personal cleanliness a low priority, but Spinks was quite alone in his level of dedication. The rewards for his extreme standards for 'blending in' were tasks such as this one, the important criterion as far as his colleagues were concerned was that he worked alone.

He placed an eye in the thin shaft of daylight coming through a small hole in the clear plastic cover of the reverse light where the bulb and socket had been removed. He checked his watch by its tiny light. Six hours he had been here already. The driver had dropped off the vehicle in the middle of the night to avoid being seen, knowing nothing would happen till late morning. It was all part of the necessary security measures, but lying in darkness, with nothing to focus on other than keeping as still and quiet as possible, made it difficult for Spinks to stay awake. He found various ways to amuse himself but these were limited. Farting was one of his pastimes — silent ones of course. He would hold them in for as long as he could, building up their pressure, then expelling them as slowly as possible, without a pause, timing how long he could stretch out the evacuation. Lying in his own stink afterwards was a strange source of amusement to him. He maintained it was unhealthy to hold in farts anyway, even in company, and admitted to enjoying the smell. He believed everyone liked the smell of their own farts and only complained about other people's.

3

He stuffed the rest of the sandwich into his mouth and checked through the spy-hole. He felt around in the darkness for his water bottle as he munched. It did not appear to be where he had placed it by his shoulder. He found his MPK5 short-barrelled sub-machine-gun, with its magazine loaded and ready to fire. Beside it was the stun grenade he always liked to carry. The grenade was not standard issue but having seen them demonstrated by the SAS during a room assault entry while in training he stole one thinking it might be a useful piece of equipment to carry. His 9mm Browning semi-automatic pistol rested under the beam of daylight so that he would know where to grab it if he saw trouble coming.

He extended his search for the water bottle towards his feet and felt it in the lower corner. It must have bounced there during the drive. He strained in the confined space, stretching as best he could, his face pressing hard up against the lid of the boot, until his fingertips finally took hold of the bottle. He pulled it to his chest and took a short breather after the effort. He was overweight and out of shape, which did not bother him in the slightest. When he wasn't on an assignment Spinks stayed in his pit of a caravan listening to Country and Western CDs or sleeping, and if he was not there he could be found in the cookhouse fixing a snack or in the small bar the detachment ran for themselves in their secret camp, sipping on a pint of bitter, which he liked to share with the detachment's alcoholic Labrador, Jenkins.

Before unscrewing the top of the water bottle he took a few seconds to estimate how full his bladder was. His last piss was before climbing inside the boot, over six hours ago. He could sense a little pressure there. A drink might put his bladder over the top. Peeing his pants was not a major issue for Spinks. It would not be the first time he lay in his own urine for hours on end. There was something he found pleasant about the sensation of warm pee spreading around his crotch area. He took a good swig, dribbling on himself in the awkward position, and swilled his mouth to rinse the sandwich down. As he swallowed he placed an eye back into the beam of light to look outside once again and what he saw nearly made him choke. He dropped the bottle, letting the water spill, and scrambled to find the communication prestel that hung out of his sleeve on its wire. He had to summon every effort to stifle a cough so he could whisper into the collar of his jacket where the tiny microphone was stitched.

'Four two Charlie,' he begun, but had to stop to clear his throat again. 'Four two Charlie, he's coming out. I say again, O'Farroll is coming out.'

Spinks kept his eye to the hole with unblinking concentration. From where he was parked he was perfectly positioned to see the front door of the church and the people coming out of it. The church was a solitary, squat, grey construction on the edge of a quiet country road a good mile from the nearest town. All the buildings in this undulating, rambling part of County Tyrone a few miles west of Lough Neagh were grey, or so they seemed. Even the rich countryside that surrounded them had a grey tint. Perhaps it was the dark skies. It rained a lot this time of year.

The church didn't look big enough to hold more than fifty people but then not that many turned out on Sunday mornings these days. Two men in warm three-quarter-length business coats over their Sunday best suits walked out of the entrance, past the tilted, unreadable gravestones and through an opening in the squat stone wall that ran along the side of the road. They stopped to chat while the rest of the congregation, mostly older people, headed to their cars parked on the grass verges.

'O'Farroll and one unknown male static on main outside the obvious having a chat,' Spinks whispered.

A strange noise came from his hidden wireless earpiece deep inside his ear, like a garbled human voice underwater. After a second the words became clear. It was the secure communications system that chopped up the sender's transmission and then sent it through the airwaves all jumbled up to be un-jumbled at the receiver's end. It was said the most sophisticated code-breaking computers would take a month to piece together just one sentence.

'One three kilo, roger that,' said a female voice in answer to Spinks's message.

Spinks kept an unblinking watch on the two men.

The female voice was that of Agatha, who preferred to be called Aggy even though she didn't like either name. In fact, anyone calling her Agatha would generally be ignored, unless that person was a senior officer, of course. Neither name was her real one though. No operators used their real names in case they were ever captured and tortured. It seemed odd to have a truncation of a false name but she hadn't known she would need a secret identity until the day she arrived at the clandestine selection camp. It was all so top secret. Only during that initial processing when her bags and clothes were confiscated and she was stripped and searched did they ask her for a cover name that she would use from that moment on, before she met any of the other recruits, whose identities were also secret, and then for the rest of her time as an undercover operative. If she passed the gruelling four-month selection process, that is. The impatient intelligence officer had given her seconds to come up with a name and she quickly chose Agatha because it was the name of a favourite aunt and then immediately decided she didn't like it. By then it was too late. He had recorded it and gone into the next room where another recruit was being stripped and identity checked. It was Agatha, or Aggy, from that moment on.

Aggy was pretty and in her early twenties. Her face, specifically her eyes, was distinctly feline but everything else about her, her mannerisms and clothes, was masculine. She didn't own a dress and always slouched in an unladylike way; a foot up on her seat or hung over the armrest. Her hands were nearly always in her trouser pockets and she could hardly stand still without leaning on anything close enough that could support her. During selection she kept her hair short and was known as the kid because she was like a pretty young boy. After arriving at the detachment her nickname, behind her back, was much less kind and threw into question her sexual preferences. Considering the profession she had chosen, what she went through to get selected, and what she was required to do, her tomboy qualities were as much an advantage as they were a disadvantage. She was expected to be as tough as any man, do a job that was at one time considered to be exclusively male, but do it as a woman. She was taught and tested as if she were a man, treated with the same level of harshness and brutality one expected of an undercover operative on a selection course famed for its toughness, without any respect for her less robust physique. Then at the end of it she was asked to cultivate her feminine side and was sent out to do the same job as the men but looking and acting like a woman. Her marked failure in the feminine department might have drawn more criticism from some of the hard-line operatives if she did not have such a pretty face. Women were recruited into the job because of a specific need for female undercover operatives; there was no point having one that looked like a man. In fact, many regarded it as manifestly dangerous.

Aggy sat in her dark brown Audi four-door in baggy jeans and black ski-jacket with her trainers up on the dash either side of the steering wheel. The car was tucked into a clearing in a small Scots pine wood just off the road a couple of miles from the church. Beside her was Ed, the crusty, worn-out operative who had dropped off Spinks early that morning. They were waiting for Spinks to cover the meeting, tell them his task was complete and that the church area was clear so that Ed could go back and pick him up. Aggy would drive up the road, drop off Ed a few hundred yards from the church, out of sight of persons or habitats, then he would walk up the road alone, pick up the car with Spinks inside and drive it back to the detachment head-quarters.

It was one of those typical 'long wait' jobs and Aggy was peeved with it, not because of the job per se but with the team selection – or to be precise, Ed. The cover for a male and female operative waiting in a secluded area in a car was usually of the romantic nature. If anyone should happen past they could kiss and cuddle to avoid suspicion: car sex was a very common pastime in Northern Ireland. Ed could not have looked more unlikely as her boyfriend and on close inspection their little off-the-road tryst would have convinced few that they were anything remotely close to passionate about each other. He was gaunt with a potbelly, had a scruffy hombre moustache, and chain-smoked Woodbine roll-ups, a habit since he was thirteen that no doubt contributed to his dried and haggard face, which looked much older than his forty years. Ed abhorred any form of physical training. The last time he ran anywhere was on his selection course eighteen years previously.

As if the differences between him and Aggy were not great enough she found him to be the most boring and obnoxious moaner she had ever met. Out of those eighteen years in the military he had been in the actual field as an operative for six of them. The other twelve had been spent in various administrative posts in the Intelligence Corps, his parent unit. Ed had achieved the rank of sergeant simply because of his seniority in years. It had nothing to do with his abilities, which were limited. In fact, his move through the ranks could be solely attributed to the undercover unit: since he was often away he was assessed *in absentia* and because of the nature of his 'special work' his upgrade was a generous one. He was not a hinge-pin of the unit but as a dinosaur he did have his uses. He was the oldest operative on the books and one of the few who could quite naturally spend hours in a boozy, smoke-filled working man's bar and blend in unnoticed. Unfortunately for Aggy, Ed saw himself as quite the sage and keeper of the undercover wisdom and he never let any of the 'young pups', as he referred to her generation of operatives, forget about all the years he had under his belt.

Ed was as peeved with this particular assignment as Aggy. He was one of the main complainers about women operatives and it did not help matters that he was referred to by other operatives during this particular partnership as the paedophile. This no doubt contributed to his reluctance to cuddle her when the situation required it. They had been forced to embrace three times since arriving just after four a.m. Ed was unshaved, stunk of cigarettes, his moustache was wet with the coffee he continually sipped from his flask, and he held her like she had an infectious rash. One of their cuddles lasted a gruesome fifteen minutes because of a horny couple that had turned up in two cars for an early morning shag.

'They probably think I'm a bloody homosexual,' he

moaned as he held her. He offered his standard complaint more than once that day. 'Weren't any women when I first started this job eighteen years ago,' he would say in his thick Yorkshire accent. 'We made do wi' wigs when we 'ad to . . . Any'ow, I don't know any bloody women ooh sit in a car with their bloody feet up on the dashboard.'

Aggy would simply roll her eyes. It was pointless to even try to argue with him. Spinks's communication was therefore a welcome sign that the task was nearly over and they could dump each other.

'I confirm O'Farroll and one unknown male,' Spinks whispered into his lapel, O'Farroll being the older man. He pushed a button fitted into the rear light module. The shutter of a camera, built into another light, silently clicked, capturing O'Farroll in the wide-frame shot talking with the stranger, and the film rolled on to the next frame. The other man was undoubtedly inferior in rank to O'Farroll, who was the Real IRA's quartermaster and second in command of the War Council. That was a fair assumption since all of the RIRA godfathers were known and it was unlikely a new and superior one would have arrived on the scene without military intelligence finding out.

The stranger laughed at a comment O'Farroll made and then did something that unnerved Spinks. He looked directly towards the rear of Spinks's car for what he felt was a little too long. Every undercover operative had a well-developed sense of paranoia, which they have to learn to control. The two men looked relaxed and jocular as if just passing the time of day, but Spinks, an experienced watcher of people, sensed a definite edge between them.

A few minutes later the stranger did it again. His eyes wandered away from O'Farroll to snatch a glance directly at the back of Spinks's car. Spinks took another photograph

and stared at the stranger, trying to think of anything he could possibly be looking at. A car then pulled up and stopped in the road, blocking Spinks's view of the two men. It stayed for half a minute, its engine running, and when it drove away O'Farroll had gone, leaving the stranger by himself in the road. The man paused for a moment, sliding his hands into his coat pockets. Then as he turned to move away, once again he looked directly towards Spinks before moving out of sight.

A troubled feeling rippled through Spinks. Something inside was tapping out a warning on his nervous system. Experience in this deadly game had taught him to make allowances for his imagination, but there was a limit. He tried to stem the trickle of concern, reasoning that there was nothing he could do that would not blow his cover. Since the lid of the boot was locked, his only way out was to push the back seat forward and climb into the car. If he gave into his paranoia and there was nothing nefarious going on outside, he would blow the mission. If his fears were justified his actions would be validated. If he was wrong, the detachment's bosses would understand but then they would suspect Spinks's nerve had withered, which was not uncommon in this line of work. He could then say good-bye to the extended tour of duty he was hoping for. His three-year stint in the unit was up in two months and he wanted to stay on for another three years. Hell, he wanted to stay on for ever. There was no way he could go back to the regular military, not now, not after life in the detachment, and the thought of civilian life was unbearable.

Spinks came from the Air Force, where he was an ordinary airman, a general duties gash-hand. It was hard enough for him then, having to wear a uniform every day, and keep it clean. He had joined the RAF after he left school because

he could think of nothing else in the world to do, a lost soul with no ambitions or motivations. He was sent on the detachment selection course only because his boss had received a Ministry of Defence circular asking for volunteers for 'special duties' and saw it as a great opportunity to get rid of the disorderly airman. Six months later Spinks was in his new life. To go back to that mundane existence after having been an undercover agent would be impossible. If he had to leave he would go outside and become a civvy, but life would no longer have purpose or meaning for him.

He decided that if there was something going on outside, if there was danger, he would wait until there was no doubt, even if that made it a bit late to do anything about it. Such was the life he had chosen.

Spinks was not a top-shelf operative. Not that there was an official ranking or ratings list. But there was an unofficial one, in the opinions of his fellow rank and file. There were many tales of daring deeds but nearly all were of operatives who had passed into history, some stories even mythical. It was the dream of most undercover agents to have at least one great event that would propel them into that exclusive club of superheroes, but few came even close. One had to be in the wrong place at the wrong time and come through it with some kind of positive result other than having just survived. The hero status thrust upon undercover operatives by the rest of the military minions by virtue of their mysterious and dangerous job was not enough for some. To be a superhero amongst heroes was the dizzy and largely unobtainable height many fantasised about. The more direct route to fame was, of course, through a kill. But one kill did not ensure fame, although it was a good start. Real fame came with multiple kills. Lucky kills didn't count either.

They might even cause an operative to be ridiculed.

But Spinks did not share those dreams, not like that anyhow. He knew his limitations. He would not even imagine being up there with the likes of Stratton for instance, who had several kills; four official since he arrived in the province, but everyone knew about at least two others. Then there were the rumoured countless kills from Stratton's 'other military employment', dozens some said, but no one in the detachment would ever learn the truth about them, not from Stratton anyhow. Spinks did dream of fame. What was unusual was that he had a plan to get himself some. He discovered that after volunteering for the first couple of more unpopular assignments, and carrying them out satisfactorily and without complaint his name was being mentioned in operations meetings and team leaders were requesting him for specific tasks, ones that no one else particularly wanted to do. He had made himself the go-to guy for the crap stakeouts. He had found himself a niche. He had carved himself a unique and positive reputation, which was more than could be said for most. Undercover agents came and went but few were remembered and even fewer talked about by later generations. If an operative was required to be up to his neck in shit to do an assignment, literally, then Spinks was your man.

Spinks suddenly realised he had not given the clear for Ed to come and drive him away. He chastised himself for being so stupid, found the prestel and whispered into his collar.

'One three kilo, this is four two Charlie. O'Farroll is gone mobile towards south. I am clear for pick-up,' he whispered.

Aggy pushed the concealed send button wired into the framework of the car just below her seat. 'One three kilo, roger that. Towards your location now.'

'Four two Charlie,' Spinks acknowledged, releasing the prestel and trying to relax. He figured Ed should take about seven minutes. Then he sensed something, or perhaps it was more like he felt it. It seemed as if the side of the car had been gently brushed against. He tried to extend his senses to the outside of the car. It happened again, a gentle movement against the shell. Spinks hardly breathed, frozen like a rabbit with a snake peering in through the entrance to its hole.

Aggy started the car then to her surprise Ed opened his door and climbed out. 'I'm going to 'ave a piss,' he declared as he emptied the remnants of his cup of coffee down his throat and shook out any drops.

'Now?' she asked, irritated with his timing.

'I'd better 'ave a little sprinkle before I pick up old Spinksy. Long drive back to camp,' he said and casually walked over to the bushes undoing his fly.

'Dick,' she muttered to herself and left the engine running. Not that there was any rush. It was a low-key, relatively relaxed operation, a Sunday morning job in just about every way. Spinks could wait another few minutes. She was feeling short tempered with Ed simply because he annoyed her. She was impatient to be rid of him. There was nothing else on her agenda for that day. She would do her small amount of washing, clean up her tiny room that was barely large enough to take the single bed, desk and wardrobe, then perhaps fit in an aerobic session although she did not feel in the mood just yet. She could check and see if any new videos had arrived, that's if no one else was hogging the TV room. Then she remembered, of course, it was Sunday. The blokes would be watching bloody football all afternoon. There was that long overdue letter to her mother she kept putting off. It wasn't that she had a problem with her mother; it was the letters themselves. They were all lies and getting more and more difficult to write. It was hard for her to think of new things to invent. Aggy's mother thought she was in Germany attached to a tank regiment but Aggy had never actually been to Germany. She could never tell her mother what she really did, not while she was still in the job. Her mother would go daft with the constant worry.

She looked at the back of Ed, who was taking his sweet time. 'Come on, wally,' she muttered to herself.

Spinks could now positively identify a sliding metallic noise against the body of the car. A sudden 'clunk' made him jerk. His breathing became shallow and rapid. Adrenaline pumped through his veins. His hand moved to his gun and he swallowed as he gripped it. His mouth was open to improve his hearing, analysing every sound as his thumb found the safety-catch.

Ed finished his pee, did up his fly with a flex of his knees, and headed back to the car. 'I 'ope Spinsky doesn't think I'm going to stop up the road and let 'im out of the boot and in the front. He can stay where he is, the smelly bugga.'

As Ed climbed in Aggy pulled smartly away, throwing him back into his seat and causing his flask to fall off the dash and on to his lap.

'Steady,' he complained. 'Where's the bloody race?'

In retaliation he produced a tin of tobacco, removed a pre-made roll-up, lit it and puffed on it without inhaling until the car was filled with smoke. She rolled down her window, biting her lip and counting the minutes she had left with him.

'That's tactically unsound, driving with your window open,' he said dryly.

She wondered what she had done to deserve this.

Spinks heard another, louder clink. The car definitely moved. Then one of the doors opened. The car dipped a little on one side as if someone had climbed in. Another door opened the other side and the car sunk a little the other way. He knew it wasn't Ed. Ed would never have gotten into the car or even approached it without warning him over the radio first. Spinks was trying to evaluate precisely what was happening and what he could do about it. His fingers felt the prestel sticking from his sleeve. He realised his hands were shaking. He pushed the button and was about to say something then stopped himself. Whoever was in the car might hear him. He prayed it was just a pair of thugs looking to steal something from it. They would get a shock if they managed to open the boot. He would arrest them even if the mission was blown and it would not be his fault. The bosses would understand that. He held the prestel in one hand and gun in the other, preparing himself to kick the seat in.

The engine suddenly roared to life, two doors slammed shut and Spinks was thrown back as the car screeched away. It must have driven on the grass verge for several yards because it bounced horrendously, tossing Spinks around inside as if he was shooting rapids in a barrel. The gears changed quickly as the car built up speed, returned to the road and swerved as it accelerated hard along it. Spinks lost his prestel and weapon in the turmoil. He searched around for the gun and had just put his hand on it when the car took a sharp corner, bounced over the verge, and slammed him into the roof of the boot. If the lid opened he would be thrown out for sure. He gave up on the gun and found his prestel by following the wire from his sleeve.

'Four two Charlie . . .' he managed to say before being flattened once again into the roof as the car hit another bump. 'Four two Charlie, I'm mobile! The car's been nicked! I repeat, I am mobile and the car's been fuckin' stooooleeeen!'

Ed and Aggy, driving down the road, were momentarily stunned by the transmission. Both reached to press the send button but were stopped by a voice breaking in ahead of them. It was the duty signaller on watch back in the operations room thirty-five miles away.

'Four two Charlie, this is zero alpha, confirm your car is mobile.'

'I'm mobile awright,' Spinks managed to say between severely winding bumps. 'We're goin' like the bleedin' clappers!'

'Zero alpha, roger that,' said the signaller, or bleep as they were affectionately called, and continued as if commentating on a bowls match. 'One three kilo, this is zero alpha.'

Aggy went for the send button but Ed pushed her hand aside and hit it himself. 'One three kilo here. We're still toward four two Charlie's static location, or previous static location. That's not me driving.' The way Ed spoke in his slow, laborious manner, trying to be calm and stating the obvious at such a tense moment added to Aggy's list of Ed's irritating habits.

'There it is!' she suddenly shouted as she recognised Ed's car heading towards them on the other side of the road. As it tore past at speed they could see only one person in front and possibly another in the back seat.

Aggy pushed the send button. 'One three kilo, four two Charlie just passed us from red four to blue seven doing about eighty, possibly two up. I'm in pursuit.'

She hit the brakes slowing the car just enough to throw it into a 'J' turn, which was messy. The driver's side rear wheel spun mud in the verge as she dropped the gear and put her foot down. The engine roared. The car inched forward, finally made traction and screeched up the road. Ed held on tightly throughout the manoeuvre, one hand gripping the bottom of his seat, the other outstretched against the dashboard. His roll-up dropped out of his mouth as his foot pressed firmly into the floor, trying to push down a brake pedal that was not there.

Spinks pushed out with his arms and legs in an effort to stop being thrown around but the heavier bumps did whatever they wanted to him. The MPK5 hit him hard on the head as it made its way around the boot. He made another effort to get a hold of his pistol but it was like trying to grab a leaping fish. There was a wrenching sound and Spinks was almost blinded by the sudden light as the back seat was ripped down. A powerful arm reached in, grabbed him by his hair, and brutally dragged him halfway into the car as they drove at top speed.

'Come on, me little Pink,' the man said in an Irish accent.

The man moved his hand to Spinks' throat and leaned his full weight on to it. Spinks's face swelled as he choked and his eyes filled with liquid and went out of focus as the man kept the weight on him while he searched him. He found the small, flat radio in its harness inside Spinks's jacket and ripped it away, pulling the wires from it. He stuck a large finger into Spinks's ear, dug around and pulled out the tiny wireless earpiece. The man seemed to know exactly what he was looking for and where to find it. He ripped open Spinks's shirt and felt under his armpits and around his body; he undid Spinks's trouser belt, pulled it out as if trying to start a boat engine, and tossed it to one side; he yanked open Spinks's trousers, tearing apart the zipper as he pulled them down to his knees.

'Where is it?' the man shouted as he quickly checked Spinks's bare legs. He brutally turned Spinks on to his front and ripped up his shirt to expose his back, pushing his hand under it to feel his skin up and over his shoulders. He pulled Spinks's underpants down far enough to expose his arse then felt around Spinks's hips. 'Where is it, Pink?' he repeated threateningly. He pulled up one foot after the other and ripped Spinks's shoes and socks off, inspecting each shoe quickly before tossing it away.

He pulled Spinks over on to his back again and gripped his throat, pressing down hard on it. 'You know what I'm looking for, Pink, don't you? Where is it?'

Spinks gripped the man's wrist to try and take some pressure off his throat and shook his head in ignorance of the demand. The man shoved the end of a pistol so hard into Spinks's cheek he shattered a molar. 'Where is it?' he said again. Then as an afterthought, he lifted up Spinks's underpants with the end of his pistol to expose his balls and penis.

'If I focken' find it on you I'll blow your focken dick off,' the man said sticking the gun back in Spinks's face. 'Is that clear, boyo?'

Spinks blinked hard as his eyes came back into focus. It was the stranger who had been outside the church with O'Farroll.

19

2

In the ops room Graham the bleep was in top gear. He was short, hyper, anal and had a mind like a razor. His generation of signallers had to be above average intelligence, not only to operate the latest complex communications systems used by the detachment but also to wire them and several other devices such as trackers and cameras into a covert car from scratch in less than twenty-four hours. Above all they had to be calm under pressure. A good duty bleep in a crisis could mean the difference between life and death for a team on the ground. Graham reached for a row of intercom buttons on a wall and pushed one.

'Boss!' he called out.

While waiting for an answer he talked into the handset on its coiled flex long enough to reach across the room. 'Four two Charlie, this is zero alpha?'

The large speakers on the wall remained silent. There was no answer on the intercom either. He hit another button. 'Boss?' Then into the handset once again, 'Four two Charlie, zero alpha?'

The wall speakers remained silent but a refined English accent came over the tinny intercom. 'Boss here.'

'We have a possible Kuttuc.'

There was no reply from the boss and Graham never expected or waited for one. The boss would be running at full speed to the ops room. Kuttuc was the codename for the most feared event in an undercover operations room in Northern Ireland. It meant an operative had been kidnapped. Every operation that operative was involved in would have to be cancelled. It also had to be assumed everything that person knew about the unit and its operating procedures was compromised. The political mess would then follow. But that was much later. For the operative it meant something more immediate and much more horrific.

Graham grabbed up the phone and held it under his chin while he punched in a number. 'Four two Charlie, zero alpha?' he repeated into the radio handset at the same time. The phone rang in his ear. No answer came over the speakers. Someone picked up the phone the other end and a yawning voice said hello.

'This is Camelot. We have an op Kuttuc in progress. Do you understand what I'm talking about?'

The army clerk in the Army Air Corps headquarters office half a mile up the road had no idea what Graham was talking about, but he could detect the urgency in Graham's voice. 'I don't think I do,' he said, adding 'sir' just to be on the safe side.

Graham instantly went up several notches towards ballistic. 'Then go and get someone who does, preferably your boss, and each second you take is a second off a man's life and if he dies I am going to come down there and personally rip your fucking throat out!'

Graham heard the clunk of the phone hitting the desk, then the clerk's feet as they hurried across the office and out of the door. Graham would do no such thing, of course. He was only a junior non-commission officer, a corporal, but he had learned to sound like he was a Gorgon on the other end of a phone when he needed to. Years of being a signaller, especially in this mystery-shrouded unit, had taught him the power of the anonymous voice shouting down the other end of a communications device. Graham had used the ploy many times and if the person the other end ever asked him to identify himself he would either impersonate his boss, which he could do very well, or simply put down the phone. It was almost impossible to trace a call back to the unit.

A buzzer suddenly went off by the door to the ops room and then sounded continuously as whoever it was kept their finger jammed against it. Graham hit a button on the desk that electrically unbolted the door. Mike the boss hurried in chewing a mouthful of food, having covered the distance from the cookhouse on the other side of the compound in record time.

'Talk to me,' he barked as he went to the large map that covered a sloping desk beneath the operations wall. Under its glass skin, the map contained all data pertinent to operatives, vehicles and locations the det had anything to do with in the Province. He studied the movable markers and wax notations on the glass that gave details of the only operatives on the ground at that time. He was young, fresh-faced and his nickname when he was not in the room was 'the head boy', because physically he could probably still pass for a sixth former. However, the similarities stopped there and anyone not recognising that could find themselves in deep water.

'Spinks's car's been lifted with him still in the boot. One three kilo is in pursuit. They think it's two up. I've had no comms with Spinks for three minutes,' Graham informed Mike, as he handed him the phone and headed for the door, adding, 'The standby chopper chief'll be on the end of that phone any second. Keep calling Spinks – four two Charlie.'

'Where's Stratton?' Mike shouted as Graham left the room, apparently without hearing him. Mike hit an intercom button. 'Steve?'

A few seconds later came an answer, 'Boss?'

'I need you in here right away.'

'On my way,' Steve replied.

'You'll need the rest of your cell.'

'Roger,' Steve said.

Mike hit another intercom button. 'Jack?'

'Yo.' Jack's voice sounded like he was at the far end of a room.

'Get every available bod on the ground towards black seven. We've got a Kuttuc.'

'Right away,' replied Jack immediately and much closer to his intercom.

Mike released the button and paused to think of anything else he could do of greater priority before the dreaded call he had to make. There was nothing else. Then he realised a tiny voice was trying to break through his concentration. It was coming from the phone in his hand. He quickly put it to his ear.

'Yes, this is Camelot. I need the standby chopper now, as in five minutes ago. We have an op Kuttuc . . . That's right. One of our guys has been lifted.'

He pushed down the cradle, released it to get the dial tone, took a deep breath, and keyed a number he was hoping would not be answered. Mike was a captain in the Hussars, his parent unit, and had had to put up with comments about his baby-face his entire career. His looks may not have changed much since he left university but he had matured a great deal during the last three years in this job. When nothing exceptional was taking place he appeared introvert and retiring. None of those characteristics were remotely evident when work got suddenly serious. He had the arrogance one might expect to find in a captain of the Hussars and would go toe to toe with anyone, even superiors, when his blood was up. Two things were guaranteed to bring out the demon in him: incompetence, and anyone trying to screw with his detachment, enemy or otherwise. He had never had an op Kuttuc before. In fact there had only been one Special Forces kidnapping since Nairac, an SAS liaison officer who was lifted, beaten and killed in the mid-seventies. The only det operative ever kidnapped, a couple of years before Mike joined the unit, was from the North Province undercover detachment. He was rescued in the nick of time by sheer luck not long after he had been snatched by the Provos. The main lesson learned from both kidnappings was that every passing second increased the odds against Spinks being rescued.

'Lisburn ops here,' the upper-class voice on the other end of the phone muttered.

'This is Mike at south det, sir. I need to speak to the chief right away.'

'Sounds urgent, old boy,' said the officer.

'It's *very* urgent,' said Mike, this time adding the emphasis that was lacking in his initial delivery.

'One second,' said the officer, reading the urgency.

Mike kept the phone to his ear while his eyes moved to the map and looked at the international border, specifically where it turned closest to the marker that indicated the point where Spinks was kidnapped. The distance was not very great at all.

Graham jogged along the corridor. 'Of course I'm going to get Stratton. Who else?' he muttered to himself in answer to Mike's question as he left the ops room.

Bleeps like Graham ruled the operations room. Naturally, all major decisions had to be made by the boss, but in reality, Graham could handle just about any emergency situation that might arise, and in most cases quicker and more efficiently. Not only was he very proficient, he was aided by a phenomenal memory. Apart from knowing practically every call-sign and frequency the British army used in Northern Ireland, he could remember details of players, their vehicles and number plates, addresses, names, associates . . . the kind of questions operatives asked the intelligence cell over the air all the time and needed quick answers to. It was usually faster to track Graham down and ask him the question first before wading through the database or calling the intelligence cell.

Graham's footsteps echoed on the old tiled floor in the narrow, flaking plastered corridor of the former Second World War Royal Air Force administration building that would have been condemned had the secret unit not taken it over. He turned a corner, arrived at a door, and pushed it open. The room was just large enough to cram in twenty assorted grubby old armchairs all facing a television set on a table at one end, a sagging bookshelf stacked with well-thumbed paperbacks, and at the opposite end to the television, a table covered in a selection of current newspapers. Hunched over a broadsheet on strong, lean arms was a man with long, mousy, unwashed hair wearing an old rugby shirt, his neck sunk between sturdy shoulders.

'Stratton?' Graham said. There was no trace of the familiarity he used when talking to anyone else in the detachment, even Mike the boss, and some of the urgency had gone out of his voice despite the gravity of the situation. He could not help himself. Stratton had that effect on him.

Stratton looked around. He hadn't shaved in several days,

which softened his angular features, and his nose looked as if it had once been broken. His face was expressionless in the way a predatory animal watches humans from within its cage. It was the eyes that fascinated Graham and, for him at least, embodied the character of the man. They weren't manic, nor even piercing. Uninviting, hollow but also penetrating was how Graham described them to his brother, his only confidant on the subject of this extraordinary job. Stratton was like no other man he had ever met. Unlike the rest of the undercover operators, Stratton's parent unit was Special Forces. He knew nothing for certain about Stratton's past, only the countless rumours: veteran of the Gulf War, the Balkans, the drug wars in Columbia, and then there were the rumours about Afghanistan. And that was all before his kills since he arrived at the detachment: four in a year and a half. That was high considering the majority of the operatives had none and only two other men currently serving in another detachment had one each. But Stratton always seemed to be in the right place at the right time, or so it seemed. His success was no doubt helped by the fact that he was always looking for a kill when most operatives were content to merely survive a day's work.

The first kills, only a month after Stratton had joined the detachment, were two unfortunate robbers armed with pistols and threatening to use them on anyone who tried to stop them. Stratton happened to be getting out of his car as the bandits came running out of the betting shop they had just held up and were climbing on to their getaway motorbike. It was all over in a couple of seconds – the time it took Stratton to draw his pistol from his shoulder holster and put two rounds through each of their crash helmets from twenty-five feet away. The robbers were Protestants, not that that was an issue for Stratton. They were bad guys who played with guns and unfortunately for them they ran into someone who didn't.

The other two official kills were the result of an attempted car jacking. Stratton was stuck in a traffic jam in a busy street when a young, inexperienced Provo tapped on his window with the tip of his gun and demanded Stratton get out. Stratton remained cool and noticed the gunman had a partner covering him with a rifle from across the street. As he took a moment to stare into the narrow eyes of his would-be assailant, he saw something else that gave him every confidence he could deal with the situation swiftly and surely.

Stratton climbed out with his arms by his sides and faced the young man, who kept just beyond arm's reach, his pistol held much too tightly in his left hand and levelled at Stratton. The man asked Stratton to hold open both sides of his jacket. If the nervous young Republican soldier caught sight of the pistol in its holster under Stratton's left arm he would ask him who he was. If Stratton didn't answer he was dead. If Stratton answered in his English accent he was dead. It was near impossible to perfect a convincing Northern Irish accent if one was not from these parts and few operatives bothered to try. What Stratton had seen from inside the car, which spurred his confidence and sealed the young man's fate, was that the unfortunate Provo had obviously forgotten that his Browning 9mm semi-automatic pistol was on half-cock. A characteristic of the weapon is that when the hammer is pulled back one click, only halfway back, it is impossible to pull the trigger. To fire the gun the hammer must be pulled back a second click to full cock. The Provo was left-handed – the safety-catch, which is on the left side of the gun, is hard to operate for left-handed shooters and so cack-handers often use the half-cock as a safety device.

Stratton calmly opened his jacket and drew out his pistol. The young Provo squeezed the trigger with all his might but by the time he realised why he could not fire it and moved his thumb to the hammer to pull it back to full cock it was too late. As he dropped to the ground with two bullets through his heart Stratton dropped to one knee to engage the cover man across the street, hitting him in the body with two shots to disrupt his aim, then closing in with an aimed shot to the head to finish him.

Then there were the two rumoured unofficial kills. Graham knew for certain about one of them. Well, pretty certain. He had been on duty that night. The team had been in Warrenpoint on the south-eastern corner of the province doing a surveillance task. When it ended the team made its way back to the detachment. The journey should have taken no more than an hour and a half at that time of night. Graham had asked for a radio check fifteen minutes after the team left the area to make sure everyone was okay. He could tell from the background noise that the operatives were in their cars travelling at speed, all except Stratton, who sounded like he was using his body comms. That suggested to Graham that Stratton was outside of his car and therefore not on his way back just yet. Graham did not dare to ask Stratton what he was doing. That would have required more courage than he possessed.

Twenty minutes after the rest of the team arrived Graham watched Stratton drive in through the main gates of the compound on the security monitor. The following morning the body of a man was found on the edge of the old market square in Warrenpoint. He had been choked unconscious then his neck had been broken. It was Matthew McGinnis, a RIRA sniper known to have shot three police officers and two soldiers and a suspected accomplice in four other killings.

Graham was aware that many of the rumours about Stratton were fiction, but he believed the operative was capable of taking the law into his own hands. Since McGinnis's mysterious death Graham had paid closer attention to Stratton's rare comments about the war against the IRA. There was often a suggestion, if only in his tone, of his contempt for the soft-handed way the judiciary treated the more hardcore terrorists.

'We have a possible op Kuttuc,' Graham said to him now.

Stratton moved quickly but without fuss or change in expression. He lifted a heavy, beaten-up leather jacket off a chair and pulled it on as Graham stepped back to let him pass.

'It's Spinks, four two Charlie,' Graham continued. 'We've lost comms and he's mobile south at speed still in the boot.'

Graham wondered if Stratton ever panicked about anything. He had seen him angry, but never out of control. They headed down the corridor, Graham trotting behind.

'Standby chopper?' Stratton asked in his usual economic way as he turned the corner towards the ops room.

'It should be waiting for you.'

Stratton stopped at a walk-in closet just before the ops room. A wooden framework built on to one wall was divided into compartments, like station baggage lockers without the doors, fifteen of them, one for each operative. He pulled a holdall, full and heavy, out of his compartment.

'The church?' Stratton asked.

'Yes. One three kilo's on the ground in pursuit.'

'The dyke?' he asked.

'And Ed.'

'Doesn't matter which one's driving then, does it?' he said, suggesting Spinks had even less hope.

There was no hint of a joke in Stratton's dry, monotone

voice, but Graham knew him well enough to know it was there and forced a little laugh. Aggy's nickname was generally used when referring to her in her absence, even though the men felt sure she was not, or at least hoped not. No one had gotten to first base with her but most wanted to, even some of those against women in the detachments. Graham did wonder about Stratton and her though. He had watched him staring at her one night in the bar during a piss-up while she was sat with several other operatives across the room.

Stratton took an old SLR 7.62mm semi-automatic high-velocity rifle from the top shelf and a couple of twenty-round magazines of ammunition. Attached to the rifle was a heavy metal object the size and shape of a grapefruit with a wire coming from it that had an electrical adapter on the end. It was a giro steady system designed to keep the weapon as still as possible inside a moving or heavily vibrating vehicle such as a helicopter. Attached to the ejection port of the weapon was a small canvas bag to catch spent shell cases and stop them bouncing around inside the cab. He headed down the corridor to a set of double doors and pushed through them. Graham watched him go then hit the buzzer outside the operations room door.

Aggy was driving beyond her capabilities along the narrow country road lined with stone walls and hedgerows, which she had already brushed against several times, losing a wing mirror on one occasion. An endless stream of comments came from Ed, most of them in the form of clipped or unfinished shouts: 'Don't . . . that!' 'Watch for . . .' 'Easy, EASY!' If Ed were honest enough he would admit that even though they were driving to save Spinks's life he wished she would just stop the car. It was mostly fields beyond the hedgerows on either side of the road. The occasional small wood, farm and row of homes streaked by. They had needed to pass only one car so far, an elderly couple behind the wheel. It had been a tight squeeze, but incredibly they had made it without touching it, although that was when she lost the wing mirror. Ed had raised himself out of his seat as Aggy slipped through the impossible gap between the car and a stone wall.

Spinks's car was still far ahead. Aggy had glimpses of it but didn't feel she was gaining any ground. She was starting to experience that frustrating, useless feeling again. The kind of useless they said she was during the selection course. She knew the constant digs from the instructors were all part of the selection process, designed to test and develop her self-control and ultimately get the best out of her, but she often wondered how true the comments really were. Fast driving had never been her forte. On the course she crashed three cars; in one of those accidents she had cracked a bone in her arm. She was warned that if she wrecked one more car she would be labelled an operational hazard and would fail the course. Her final exercise had involved a high-speed chase deliberately set up by the instructors to test her. She managed to get through it without a mishap but had come close a couple of times. This was the fastest she had driven since that day, perhaps even faster, and she felt much less in control. She kept talking herself through the stages, echoing her fast driving instructor: 'Brake on the straight before the bend, not in it. Hit the corner just a bit faster than you think you can. Balance the throttle through the turn; keep the tyres biting the road. Accelerate on the apex.'

'Towards orange five,' she shouted. Ed appeared not to have heard her, his eyes as wide as they could possibly stretch and locked on to the road ahead. She reached for the send button but he pushed her hand away.

'Keep your 'ands on the wheel! I'll do the bloody comms!' Ed was the most sedate of all the operatives in the detachment in a dreary way – during relaxed working conditions, that is. But car chases held a special fear for him. He hated travelling fast in anything where the speed was beyond the normal design functions. Four-door cars were family vehicles intended for comfort driving, not screaming along narrow country lanes and especially not in the hands of a girl who clearly had no idea what she was doing. His last car chase had been ten years earlier. He had been the tail-end car in a line of four. It had got so hairy he pulled out letting the others go on without him. He admitted during the debriefing that he just could not keep up with the pace. Since then he was given nothing but 'soft' tasks. However, the problem with doing nothing but safe jobs for years was that complacency set in. The true dangers of the profession remained known, respected even, but with time there was a fogging of the grim realities. In the space of a few short minutes Ed was being fully reacquainted with one aspect of them, and that was risking one's own life to try and save another.

Back at the operations room, Ed's voice, the fear in it evident, boomed over the speaker. 'One three kilo, towards orange five.'

The ops room was now a flurry of activity. The intelligence officer, and his two people were busy in the int cell that adjoined the ops room. Two off-duty bleeps had arrived in case they were needed, although if truth be known they were really hanging about to witness this unique event.

'Toward orange five, roger that,' Mike replied into the handset as Graham walked back in.

'Stratton's on his way,' Graham said.

Mike nodded as he pored over the map. The entire province was coded at the major junctions and landmarks, all committed to memory by the operatives even though they had secure communications, just in case that system ever went down and they had to revert back to open comms as in the old days. Graham grabbed a bar cloth off its hook, wiped away the previous chinagraph pencil marks and circled orange five.

'They're heading for Dungannon,' Graham said.

'Probably, but where will they cross the border?'

'If they do.'

'We must assume it for now,' Mike said, scrutinising the thick yellow demarcation line that ran from the top left to the bottom right corner of the map.

'Where's Bill Lawton?' Mike asked referring to the detachment's liaison officer.

Graham snatched up a phone. 'He's at a special branch meeting in Belfast,' he said as he punched in a number.

'Get hold of him. We need at least a dozen checkpoints covered. Tell him to call the Garda before he talks to anyone else. He's to tell them we're concentrating on an area five miles either side of Aughnacloy.'

'Bill Lawton?' Graham asked into the phone.

'He's to call them before he talks to anyone in Whitehall. I don't want to hear from London until this is over . . . How soon can Stratton be at the border?' Mike asked, well aware Graham could handle half a dozen different tasks at once and give them equal attention.

'Twenty, twenty-five minutes,' then into the phone, 'Tell him it's urgent, life and death,' then to Mike, 'Bill's gone tramp around in the building somewhere. Someone's gone off to look for him.'

Mike looked worried, as if trying to see the actual ground on the map beyond the two-dimensional topographical information. 'If he's in a bloody pub I'll have his arse in a sling. The checkpoints will never be set up in time. The army and RUC are too bloody slow.'

Everyone in the room was thinking the same thing. *Poor old Spinksy.*

The Irishman kneeled heavily on Spinks's sternum, searching his jacket pockets as the car bumped along at speed. 'You one of those who don't carry one because you think it's a waste of time? Eh?' He checked the trouser pockets, front and rear. 'Grubby little bastard, ain't ya?' he growled. The man gave up the search and sat back a moment to take a look at Spinks, who lay there like a frightened seal. 'You stink, Pink, so you do,' he said, wearing a look of disgust as he wiped his hands on his own jacket.

Brennan was his name. He was from Dundalk in County Louth. His primary livelihood was armed robbery, cash targets mostly, such as banks, post offices and building societies. He preferred to work during business hours for two reasons: he felt it was the safest time of the day to rob a high street business, and he enjoyed seeing the terrified faces of the people when he burst in wearing his balaclava and armed with a pump-action shotgun or sub-machine-gun. Working for the Real IRA was more of a sideline for Brennan, although he would never admit that to anyone. In fact he described his criminal activities as 'fundraising' to maintain his war effort. He was a Republican to be sure but ultimately he was a mercenary – unless there was glory to be had; enough glory might well tip the scales in favour of doing a job for very little money, although a freebie would have to be exceptionally glorious. Brennan had not done a

34

job for free for the Republicans since his early sectarian executions where he gained the reputation that allowed him to start charging a nice fee. This kidnapping offered both cash and glory. Brennan had been provided with the weaponry and given three thousand pounds, which included expenses, to carry out the assignment. It was well below his normal rate, but the glory of getting a Brit spy more than made up the difference.

The War Council discouraged him from telling anyone about the money he received for his work. Most soldiers were volunteers and worked for a basic upkeep that usually had to be supplemented by a regular job or crime. Some, especially the new, younger members were not paid a penny. If a soldier was sent on a long-term operation, such as a member of a bomb team in England, then the pay was not too bad. But Brennan was given special pay because he was known to get the job done. It was not always pretty, and often a little too brutal for some tastes, but he had a knack for success.

Murder was Brennan's main choice of work. He discovered his penchant for it after he started working for the Provos in his late teens. He liked to do it up close and personal, and the slower the better. If he had the time to get acquainted with his victim, even better. He had no idea if he was to eventually kill Spinks. If it looked like they weren't going to get him across the border then his orders were to execute him. That was his call to make. Ultimately Spinks was to be interrogated. Brennan hoped he would be the one selected to finish him.

'If all your mates smelled as bad as you we'd have no trouble finding them,' Brennan said to Spinks. He reached over into the boot and pulled out the MPK5 and pistol and threw them into the passenger foot-well. As he leaned further in to check for anything else the car went over a bump and he bashed the back of his head hard on the lid. He steamed a look at his young driver Sean as he rubbed the bump, snarled and finished his search. He found nothing else but the empty water bottle. The car then took a corner hard, sending Brennan crashing into the side window.

'You roll this focken car and I'll focken shoot you!' Brennan shouted.

Sean was a cool character and didn't flinch, but he had been warned not to fuck with Brennan. They had never met before the previous evening, when the team was called in for orders and, for security reasons, they had remained in the same house for the rest of the night. All Sean knew about Brennan was what the others had told him before Brennan arrived. One rumour had it that he had once killed one of his own people on a job for incompetence. Sean had long since decided that if they did crash, and if he was able to, he would keep running until he was all the way to America, which was about the only place he could think of where Brennan would not find him.

Whatever the truth about Brennan Sean couldn't give a shite. He had his own job to do and he'd do it how he saw fit. He checked his rear-view mirror. No worries about the car behind; whoever was at the wheel was never going to catch him. Sean slipped down a gear as they approached another tight corner. He decided to be a bit flash and take the tight inside line rather than simply cut the corner. He hooked his front nearside tyre into the small ditch on the inside bend to hold the car tight in the turn and let the back end slip out a little, allowing a faster entry and exit. The trick was to jerk the steering wheel and flick the tyre out of the ditch after the apex. If the tyre didn't eject the car would spin out of the turn and then Brennan would likely shoot him if they crashed.

Sean went through the turn easily and bombed on down the road. He had been selected for this task because he had a reputation for out-driving police cars. In fact his record was one hundred per cent. He often did it just for fun, bombing past a stationary police car in a small town or village and then leading a chase through the countryside until he lost it.

The road straightened out like a rail for at least a mile, with a small humped bridge halfway along it. Sean smiled to himself as he red lined it. His plan this time was to go airborne.

3

Paul Healy sat with a pair of headphones around his neck in the back of an old Ford Transit van opposite an array of jerry-rigged electronics equipment bolted into a basic framework. The gobbledygook sound of the secure communications emitted from a pair of small speakers. Healy was in his early fifties, balding and looked old and tired, like someone who was nearing the end of a long, exhausting journey having discovered halfway through how pointless it all was. Tommy sat watching him from the driver's seat, smoking a cigarette, dog-ends all around his feet. Tommy had been given two specific responsibilities: drive the van, and protect Healy, with his own life if need be. He watched Healy with contempt. There was no way he was going to give his life for that man.

Tommy was suspicious of Healy for no other reason than he was not a member. Tommy didn't have a friend in the world who was not a militant pro-Republican, a member of the Irish Republican Army. Although Healy was Irish Catholic, he was just a hired hand and that made him untrustworthy. If he cared about the cause he would not be taking money. Healy could have been forced to do the job, but experience had taught the organisation that it was far more effective to steal the money to pay for the professional than to steal the professional and threaten him to work for his life. They needed Healy, reputed to be the best in the whole of Ireland at what he did, to be on best form for this job.

Tommy was right to think Healy didn't give a damn about the cause, but Healy had no love for the Brits either, not after what they had done to him. He had only one true lifelong love – solving puzzles. The more complicated they were the greater the challenge and the purer the high if he succeeded in cracking them. He should have been born fifty years earlier. He would have given anything to be a code breaker in the Second World War. He knew everything there was to know about Ultra and the breaking of the German, Japanese and Italian codes. Mathematics and psychology had been the primary skills then; now it was as much about knowing computers and electronics. But Healy had made sure he had kept up to date in that field too. If he had not screwed up all those years ago he could have ended up working for MI6 or possibly even the CIA. But now those ambitions were dead and buried for ever. The irony was that his childhood dream could now be fulfilled only by working for the other side, thugs and morons like these. Terrorists. He had worked for several organisations over the years: Libyans, Palestinians and Iranians. They were pretty much all the same as far as he was concerned. Some were just a bit more insane than others. The jobs were nothing to brag about but at least he made a living doing what he enjoyed and that, surely, was the important thing.

Tommy listened to the unidentifiable sounds coming over the speakers and watched Healy as he concentrated on every transmission and scribbled notes into a large notebook. 'Why do you listen to that if you can't understand a word?' he asked.

'I may not be able to understand a single word, but there's

a lot of information to be gained,' Healy replied as if talking to a child.

'Like what?' Tommy asked, lighting a new cigarette with his old one.

Healy would normally prefer not to get into a conversation with any person who had a single digit IQ, as this one obviously had, but when it came to his work he could talk about it to anyone who would listen. 'Well, there's tone for one,' he said. 'You can hear urgency, or lack of it. You can sometimes tell if it's just casual communication or if it's important, such as an operation. And you can tell, more or less, how many people are on the network. That's quite a lot of useful information in the right hands.'

Tommy stared at Healy unconvinced. 'Sounds like a load of bollocks to me.'

'Which is why you only get to operate that nice big wheel in the front of the van and I get to play with all these little ones in the back,' Healy said with a genuine enough smile. Healy had long since got used to spending his time with thickoes; wherever he worked he always had a driver or bodyguard and it was too much to expect anyone from that stratum to have any intelligence.

Healy first arrived on the scene in the seventies, a cocky, arrogant genius, bragging he could crack any code if he was given the time and equipment and volunteering his services to the IRA. That was in the days before secure scrambled communications. The IRA was willing to take a chance on him and gave him the money, the time and the place in which to prove himself: Belfast. He was as good as his word and within a year had successfully cracked the codes used by Britain's most elite Northern Ireland undercover group, compiling lists of vehicles, number plates, photographs of operatives and the codes for every important location in the province. In the back of Healy's mind he knew there was a good chance he would get caught eventually. In fact, as the prison psychologist said, from the start he really wanted to be caught because he craved the acknowledgement of his genius. After he was arrested he was all too ready to crow to the British, offering to show them how to prevent against any such future technical invasions. Didn't the Americans employ German geniuses after the Second World War? How naïve he was to think they would forgive him, let alone ask him to join them. He never got over the shock of the public trial and the ten-year jail sentence. He was released after six years, a marked man and with any hope of a career in Western intelligence in tatters. If there was any solace he might gain from his circumstances, it was that it was due to his success in breaking the British military codes that the new secure communication system he was listening to at that moment had been introduced.

Another garbled transmission came from the speakers. Healy frowned as he concentrated on it. Then he smiled, nodding in recognition and self-satisfaction as he jotted something down on a piece of paper. Tommy leaned over to read what Healy had written.

'Mary? Who's Mary?'

'It's a voice,' Healy replied. 'Listen to the transmissions long enough and you start to recognise different voices. That was Mary. I'm certain it was. She's been with the detachment almost a year now.'

'How do you know her name is Mary?' asked Tommy, looking confused.

'I don't. That's just the name I've given her.' Healy adjusted some controls on his panel. 'And by the signal strength I'd say she was getting closer.' He then checked his watch, curious about something. 'There's one element missing,' he said, more to himself.

'What's that?' asked Tommy.

'I'd have thought it would be up by now. A bit slow. Which is good, I suppose.'

'What's slow?' Tommy asked, a little annoyed at being ignored.

Healy looked at him as if just remembering Tommy was in the van with him. 'The helicopter,' he said.

Stratton drove at speed along the airbase access road and arrived at a collection of long, narrow single-storey buildings on the edge of an airfield. He screeched to a halt, drawing the attention of the handful of mechanics and service engineers lounging outside on a smoke break. He climbed out with his bag and rifle, passed the servicemen, who watched him curiously, and headed towards a Gazelle jet helicopter parked alone on the grass fifty yards away. There was no sign of the pilot or ground crew.

He opened the passenger door of the sleek four-seater, dumped his bag on the floor in front of the passenger seat, and looked toward the Air Corps buildings. The pilot casually stepped out, wearing the standard green one-piece flying suit, a helmet and pulling on his tight leather gloves. Stratton took off his jacket, removed a shoulder holster from his bag and pulled it on, clipping the tail to his trouser belt. The pilot did not acknowledge Stratton as he walked around the other side of the cab and climbed in with the urgency of someone preparing for a Sunday drive. Stratton had a problem with him already.

'Do you know what an op Kuttuc is?' Stratton asked.

The pilot was a young, cocky lieutenant fly-boy with a condescending smile he reserved specifically for those he considered to be of an inferior class. He had placed Stratton in that category the moment he laid eyes on him.

'Yes,' he replied. It was one of those long, irritating 'yeses' that went up at the end, suggesting the question was childishly obvious. 'One of your chaps has been kidnapped,' he said as if he had been watching too many old Brit war movies. Stratton watched him climb in. The man was digging his own grave, completely ignorant of it.

Stratton checked his pistol and slid it into his holster. 'This kite should've been turning over by the time I got here.'

'I was here as soon as I got the word,' the pilot replied tiredly.

'You're the standby pilot, right?' Stratton asked.

'Obviously,' the pilot said as he flicked switches and pushed buttons in the order on his checklist.

'That means you standby in your kit, helmet at your side, and when the bell goes you sprint like the Battle of Britain.'

The pilot continued checking his instruments, ignoring Stratton. Stratton reached over and took his arm in a vice grip. 'Do you understand?'

The pilot stopped and looked at him, quite horrified by the physical contact.

'Now get this fucking thing airborne,' Stratton continued, releasing the pilot's arm to pull on his heavy jacket.

The pilot continued to check off instruments, glancing at Stratton, unbalanced by his attitude. He was certain Stratton was not an officer and no matter what the urgency he had no right to talk to him in that manner, let alone physically grab him. He decided not to make an immediate issue of it as there obviously was some urgency, but he would certainly bring it up with his CO when they got back. He couldn't give a fig if this ruffian was from Special

43

Forces. Long hair and dirty clothes did not give him the authority to be insolent.

The pilot started the engines while Stratton climbed inside and pulled his door closed. Stratton fastened his seatbelt web, pulled on his headset and plugged the giro-steady device attached to the rifle into the power source on the instrument panel. He placed a full magazine into the magazine breach, rested the end of the barrel on top of the instrument panel and pulled back the cocking leaver, loading the weapon loudly. The pilot glanced at him and the rifle, aware the rifle should have been loaded outside the helicopter and in the sandbagged loading bay as standing orders demanded. He wondered why these people acted as if they could break any rule that suited them.

Aggy flew down the lane in more doubt of her driving skills than ever. The speedometer was hovering around eighty mph. She leaned into a smooth left hand-bend and barely kept her nearside wheels on the road. If another vehicle had been coming the other way the chase would have been over. Ed had squeezed permanent indentations in the base of the seat with his fingers and was fast reaching his breaking point. He pulled on his seatbelt, a defining act since operatives always declined to use seatbelts because it slowed their escape from vehicles if they came under fire.

'We'll do 'im no good if we kill ourselves!' he shouted.

The way Aggy saw it they had no choice. She was not about to give up trying and if she went any slower she might as well stop.

'Crossroads!' Ed suddenly screamed.

She tore right through it without slowing or even looking either way.

'Fookin' 'ell,' Ed exclaimed. 'This is fookin' mad!'

'That was blue six,' she said, trying to sound as calm as she could. Ed only had eyes for the road. 'Blue six, towards green three. Tell 'em!' she shouted.

Ed found the send button and pushed it.

Healy listened to the jumbled communication and checked a device. 'You'd better get ready. Your boys are close,' he said to Tommy.

Tommy ditched his cigarette, craned forward and scanned the empty lane.

The Gazelle raised off the pad a few metres, dipped its nose and accelerated forward, rising at a gentle angle as it gained speed. Stratton adjusted his headset and pushed his mouthpiece close to his lips. 'Straight over the Neagh, south-west. Got that?' he said.

The pilot nodded. Got that, he said to himself. Whatever happened to 'sir'?

'When I give you an instruction, you say understood, or otherwise if you didn't. If you say nothing, I don't know if you've heard or understood.'

The pilot sighed. 'Understood,' he said, making an attempt to convey to Stratton he was not merely a taxi driver.

Stratton pressed a button on the headset cable. 'Whisky one, airborne.'

In the ops room, Graham pushed the transmission button on the desk. 'Whisky one is airborne,' he confirmed. 'One three kilo still has from blue six towards green three.'

'Blue six to green three, understood,' Stratton said. 'Any tracking located? I'm too far to pick up anything yet.'

'No. We won't have anything else in the area to pick up the signal before you get there anyway,' Graham said. 'It's gonna be up to you.'

'Roger that,' Stratton said as he pulled out his map book and studied it.

The Gazelle flew at three hundred feet as it left the land to cross the cold, grey waters of Lough Neagh. Stratton looked below to the water then at the pilot with irritation.

'How long've you been flying, pal?' Stratton asked.

'It's Lieutenant Blane to you. Not pal, understood?' the pilot said, becoming very vexed indeed.

'I asked you how long've you been flying?'

'Long enough.'

'Then get your nose down, drop to ten feet above the water and red line this fucking crate. There's easily another twenty knots in her right above the water.'

'Now don't you start telling me how to fly too!'

'They teach you ground effect in school?'

'Yes.'

'I've got a team-mate right now being driven to his funeral and we're his only hope.'

'It's dangerous to get too low over these waters. The winds are treacherous.'

Stratton cut him off and talked into the radio. 'Whisky one, I've got a chicken shit pilot here. Can you put Mike on.'

There was a silent pause, then, 'Wait one,' came Graham's voice.

After another short pause Mike's refined voice came over the air. 'This is the CO of Camelot. Can you hear me Lieutenant . . . Blane, is it?'

'Yes, sir,' the pilot replied, suddenly a little cautious.

'I'll make this brief and easily digestible. There are only a handful of people between myself and God in this chain of command. If you don't do exactly what the man beside you tells you, and that includes flying underwater if he asks, I promise I will use my considerable power to see you are court-marshalled for disobeying a direct order from me and therefore the Commander-in-Chief. Do you understand?'

'Yes, sir,' the pilot replied, already going red in the face.

'Out,' Mike finished.

Stratton looked at the pilot for the real confirmation that he fully understood. 'Well?' he said.

The pilot could not believe this was happening to him. He had only been in the province two months. So far, all he had been required to do was ferry senior officers to various barracks and carry out the occasional spy in the sky job for one of this lot. Like the rest of his colleagues, he knew the gang from the 'funny farm' were at the sharp end of intelligence gathering, but he regarded them as overrated and that they fancied themselves a bit too much. However, he was also aware they had a lot of clout and that he would be a toilet roll in a napalm fight if he so much as squeaked a word of dissent at them. He firmed his grip on the joystick and pitch controls, dropped the nose and accelerated toward the lapping water.

Graham lowered the handset from his mouth as Mike stepped in from the intelligence cell, reading a file. 'A tad over the top,' he said without looking up from his file. 'And I would never put myself before God . . . Tell Stratton to head for Aughnacloy.'

The two standby bleeps smirked at Graham and received a wink back from him as he picked up the handset. 'Whisky one,' he said into it. 'Head for black seven.'

'Black seven,' Stratton said, his voice, mixed with the thud of the helicopter rotors, boomed over the speakers.

A satisfied grin slowly spread across Healy's face as he listened to the scrambled message. 'Now there's a resonance even you would recognise if you heard it more than a couple of times.'

'That your helicopter?' Tommy asked, his eyes fixed up the lane.

'Very good. That was the helicopter. But I refer to the voice,' Healy said as he adjusted some dials. 'It was a man's voice.'

'You know his voice too, do you?' asked Tommy, somewhat sceptically.

'Oh, yes. I call him Achilles.'

'That's a grand name you've given him.'

'He's someone you wouldn't like to cross swords with in a hurry.'

'That a fact?' Tommy said contemptuously.

'I've heard his voice only a handful of occasions. On two of them someone died . . . two of yours.'

Healy hit a replay button on a tape recorder and played back Stratton's last transmission a couple of times. The garbled sounds echoed through the van. 'Yes, that's Achilles all right.'

Tommy glanced over at Healy, disliking him even more following his reference to the dead as 'yours' and not 'ours'. A car zoomed down the lane like a jet, passing in front of the van from right to left, the tail wind rocking the lower branches of the trees that reached over the road.

'That was Sean,' Tommy said quickly.

'Mary is not all that far behind,' said Healy.

Tommy started the engine and craned to look back up the road in the direction the car had come from. He tapped the steering wheel with his fingers, a little nervous about this next phase, but anxious all the same to get it done.

He suddenly saw Aggy's car no more than a couple hundred metres away, the bushes whipping in its wake. 'Here she is,' he said as he put the engine into first gear and nudged forward a little, the nose of the van just poking from the small clearing in the wood. He needed to time his move perfectly. He could not afford for her to ram him and put him out of action. His orders were to get away and over the border as soon as possible. More to the point, he had to get Healy and his equipment back into the south.

When Aggy's car was eighty yards away Tommy gunned the van forward and forced the creaky old vehicle on to the lane to show her his rear. Healy watched anxiously out of the dirty back window as Aggy's car slammed on the brakes but continued to close at a rapid rate of knots, fishtailing in the narrow lane. He grabbed hold of the seat in case she hit them.

It was obvious to Aggy and Ed the instant they saw the van pull out that this chase was over for them. The instantaneous subconscious question for Aggy was: how badly was it over? Ed already foresaw the absolute worst. Aggy's mind raced to process what little information she had. Her hands turned the wheel just enough so as not to cause them to roll immediately. They missed the back of the van on Ed's side by inches and headed at an angle for the hedge. The slight verge served as a ramp to tip the front up and the car left the lane. It hit the hedge halfway up, punching out a chunk of it and shattering the headlights as they sailed through. The car was airborne for a few seconds before nosing hard into a freshly ploughed field. The frame bent on contact and the windscreen cracked all over. Aggy locked her arms on the steering wheel and rocked like a crash dummy on contact with the earth, her face enveloped in the airbag. The rear wheels hit earth and the car slid sideways for a short distance, shuddering over the ruts to finally come to a steaming stop.

Healy looked back at the car as they drove down the lane. He watched it until they were out of sight. 'Bye bye, Mary,' he said.

Tommy glanced at him and shook his head.

* * *

Aggy and Ed sat for a moment without moving. Ed had his hands over his eyes as if refusing to look, or perhaps he was praying.

'You okay?' she asked.

'Fuck off . . . Don't speak to me for a moment, okay?'

She accepted he needed some release time and checked all about them through the windows. There was no sign of anyone. She felt for her gun. It was still in her shoulder holster.

'How come my fuckin' airbag didn't go off?' Ed finally asked.

'You don't have one on your side. That's where they put the radio scrambler.'

'Fuckin' brilliant,' he said.

She pressed the button below the seat. 'Zero alpha, this is one three kilo, check?'

'Zero alpha, send,' came Graham's voice from the ops room.

'We're out of it,' she said. The words came out like a pathetic confession of failure for all to hear.

Stratton received the message with his usual calm acceptance and quickly moved on. He studied the map, considering the possibilities. The obvious one – and the one he would go for – was that the kidnappers planned to take Spinks directly over the border and into the South. Keeping Spinks in the North would remove the high risk of being stopped at a crossing point, but then they would remain under the RUC and army's nose. If Stratton was wrong and the kidnappers stayed in the North, there was still a chance of finding Spinks alive. If they made it over the border, Spinks was a dead man for sure. Time was the crucial factor. It would take precious minutes for the army and police to set up roadblocks on every crossing, especially the small lane crossings in the countryside, minutes they might not have.

Water from the Neagh sprayed the bubble glass as the helicopter roared across the lake barely five feet above it. Land the other side was in sight, but they were still too far to know if Spinks had played his ace card, the only card he probably had left.

Brennan sat in the rear of the car, his pistol levelled at Spinks, while keeping an eye on the road ahead as they entered the town of Dungannon at a normal speed.

'Nice and easy,' he said. 'Let's not draw any attention.'

Sean was annoyed with the obvious advice. He took the constant flow of petty orders as a show of nerves on Brennan's part, not what he expected from a man who was as hard and experienced as he was reputed to be. Sean drove into the town and before heading up the steep hill toward the city centre he turned into a housing estate.

'There it is,' said Brennan. 'Pull in behind.'

Sean slowed the car and parked behind a van in the quiet street. Brennan leaned closer to Spinks's face with his pistol shoved in his stomach and made his words as clear and murderous as possible.

'We're now going to change vehicles. If you try to run, I'll shoot you, you Pink bastard. If you make a fuss and lark about, it won't matter because we own this street, but I'll batter the livin' shite outta ya anyway for not doing what you're told. Understand?'

Spinks nodded.

'I was ordered to deliver you alive. No one said anything about bits of you bein' missing, okay?'

Spinks believed him.

'Pull yer trousers on,' Brennan said.

Spinks shuffled on his back and pulled up his trousers and clipped them together. He tried to fasten the zip but it was broken.

'Don't worry about your shoes and socks. We'll get you a nice pair of comfy slippers when we get to the hotel,' Brennan said with a grin. 'Nice and slowly now. The driver's going to get out, open your door, and I'll follow you out.'

Spinks pulled his shirt closed to cover his exposed chest and stomach. Brennan nodded to Sean, who opened his door and climbed out. He looked around and up and down the street. The windowless wall of the building behind him was covered with drawings of Republican flags and slogans. There was a handful of people about, someone returning from shopping, an old woman walking a dog, a couple of housewives chatting over garden fences, children kicking a football the far end of the street. Sean opened the rear passenger door.

'Nice and easy,' Brennan reminded Spinks.

As Spinks started to sit up he felt spasms of pain in several parts of his body, damage caused from the ride and where Brennan had roughed him up. He supported himself on his arms, pushing himself upright so he could drag his legs around and move them out the door ahead of him. His right hand slipped off the seat and into the boot where it touched something metallic jammed under the seat. The stun grenade. Spinks stalled for a second, his mind flying through the possibilities. He knew it was a slender chance, but he also knew that if he ended up wherever this thug was taking him it was the only one he had. There was still the ace to play, but he couldn't use that while this bastard kept so close an eye on him. This might give him the opportunity to play that last card, if he could only get to it. When the kidnap scenario had been discussed in training all the emphasis was placed on avoidance. Once the operative was in the enemy's clutches it was pretty much accepted the game was to all intents over. 'Take your chances early,' was the advice they always gave.

'Move it,' Brennan said impatiently, prodding Spinks with the gun.

Spinks lost hope at the sight of the gun barrel and decided the idea was suicide. He let his hand leave the grenade as he squeezed his legs past the back of the front seats. But, suddenly, he felt like a drowning man letting go of his lifebelt. He knew he had to take the risk. He had absolutely nothing to lose. He pushed his feet round to the door and fell back to let his hand find the grenade once again. It was jammed under the seat, but the right way around. He could feel the ring. He slipped his finger in through it, but then Brennan grabbed him viciously by the throat.

'Move your bloody arse!' he growled, his spittle hitting Spinks in the face.

The threat only served to remind Spinks how much he had to go for it now. He knew they were in Dungannon. He had recognised the town immediately. This monster grew only stronger the closer they got to the South. 'I said move it!'

Brennan released Spinks who pulled himself upright. As he did so he pulled the ring clean from the stun grenade. There was a distinct and audible 'ching', a metallic sound he knew well but which, he hoped, Brennan and Sean would not. It was the actuating arm flying off under released pressure from the detonation spring, which in turn allowed the plunger to strike the cap that would start the sequence.

The explosions were rapid and immediate, noisy and bright, like a giant firecracker, dozens of bangs in succession, non-injurious but frighteningly loud, with particles of blinding, burning magnesium to add to the effect. The smoke and cacophony filled the car, one of the small charges going off inches from Brennan's face. Brennan jerked back in immediate fear, dropping his gun to cover himself. The weapon designed to create instant confusion had done its job perfectly.

Spinks pushed out of the car and, crouching low, his bare feet hit the ground. He rolled forward and shouldered Sean backwards, throwing him to the pavement, then mustering all his grit and determination he ran with every ounce of strength he could pull from his legs. He slammed one bare foot in front of the other, ignoring the pain as the soft skin on the soles of his feet were slashed open in the first few paces. He was moving, but, it seemed, hardly at all as if he was running through molasses. The explosions behind him would not last long. Five or six seconds perhaps.

He turned off the pavement, ducked between the van and the car, and ran on to the street.

People looked towards the noise, looked at Spinks, his jacket and shirt flapping open, his bare feet. Spinks kept running, hard as he could, gaining a precious yard with each step, arms beating the air. Yet more misfortune befell him when the clip holding his trousers together snapped and they started to slip. He grabbed them with both hands and kept on going, but it upset his rhythm, slowing him as the crotch dropped closer to his knees and shortened his stride. He pulled them up a few inches and speeded up again.

Then he felt something dig into his crotch, under his balls, something sharp. He knew what it was and suddenly feared losing it. He reached into his underpants, still running hard, his fingers digging beneath his testicles. He touched it. At that same instant something flew out of his body, out of his chest just below his left shoulder. It felt hot and it burned. It flew ahead of him. It was a length of blood. He felt a hard whack on his back, behind where his chest burned, a brutal thump, like a rock hitting him, or a hammer blow. His mind acknowledged a loud bang somewhere behind him, a boom.

The force of the blow toppled him forward. He tried to keep his feet under him as he tipped by increasing his stride but it was no use. His head dropped lower than his hips, the road suddenly all he could see, He released his trousers and reached out with his left hand, his right jammed awkwardly inside his underpants, but the hand crumpled on contact, unable to hold his falling weight. His face hit the tarmac and scraped along the rough surface, taking the flesh from his forehead, his nose, and gouging his lips and chin. His gut hit and he bounced a little and rolled on to his side and then his back. He skidded a few more feet then lay there, breathing hard, dazed, commanding his limbs to get going. They beat the air as if he were running, but he could not coordinate them, the ground gone from beneath them.

Suddenly arms grabbed him and he was rolled on to his front. A hand pulled him up by his hair, another grabbed his collar, choking him, while another grabbed one of his arms. He was dragged forward in this position, his toes scraping along the road, taking the skin off to the bone.

He reached the back of the van, its doors open. He was raised quickly up and inside, then dropped into something, a trunk, or large box. He looked at the blurred faces above him, but only for an instant before a lid came crashing down inches from his face and it went black. There were more bangs in quick succession as doors were shut, and then the vehicle's engine started up.

Spinks lay, rocking, in a dark, confined space once again. His shoulder started to burn as if it were on fire. He let out a moan, then a cry for help. All he could hear was the engine and the whine from the axle beneath him. It was his worst nightmare come true. Every operative's worst nightmare. The unthinkable was happening to him. He was the one. It did not seem possible, even as he lay there. They had talked about it, the recruits together, during breaks in training, or at night in their beds, and sometimes at the bar in the camp after a few beers. It was like a ghoulish fairytale, the kind of horror that could only happen to someone else.

Spinks started to cry. His life flashed in front of him, with plenty of time to see the details. Life was not so meaningless, even the old days, the boring pointless days of his youth. He wanted to live. And he would, for quite some time he expected. But every second of that would be horror. The stories of what they did to captives were unthinkable. If they could slowly torture to death one of their own, what would they do to him, a British spy, a hated undercover man?

Tears rolled off his face into his ears. His chest shook with painful heaves as his fear took hold. He scratched the top of his coffin. His nails broke. He didn't care. He scratched and pushed with his feet as he cried. But it was no good. His coffin was too strong. He gave up the effort and just cried. He wallowed in his nightmare for a few moments more, and then even that was too exhausting to maintain. He eventually lay there, quietly, listening to his breathing above the sound of the engine. He moved a hand to touch the burning pain below his shoulder. It was wet. He felt under his shirt and found a small tender hole in his flesh. Images of his run and fall came back to him. He could see the scene more clearly now than when it happened. He was in Dungannon. They were still in the North. Then he remembered his ace.

Despite the intense pain in his chest, Spinks twisted

himself in the confined space so that he could manoeuvre his arm down into his underpants and between his fatty legs. He reached under his balls to where it had moved and felt its hard plastic edge. Brennan had thoroughly searched for it but had stopped short of Spinks's most dank nether regions. Had it remained where Spinks originally placed it, loosely in the front of his undies, Brennan might have found it when he pulled them down. He gripped the miniature transponder in his fingertips and carefully pulled it out.

4

The Gazelle left Lough Neagh behind and headed south-west for the border. It climbed just high enough to pass over a line of high-tension power cables then dropped majestically to rooftop height again, still going flat out. The pilot was concentrating too hard now to be distracted by the rollicking he had received from the thug beside him and Camelot's commanding officer. He was doing what he had been trained to do for all those months in Germany not more than a year ago. Fast and low. He was good at it too. Had Stratton not been so rude and perhaps stroked him a little he might not have been so wet about it. He decided to show this brute a thing or two about flying.

Stratton checked the map even though he knew the area well. After following the M1 for a short distance they cut a line for Aughnacloy, leaving Dungannon a few miles to the right of them.

'Give me five hundred feet,' Stratton ordered. The pilot mumbled something that sounded like 'five hundred' and complied, adjusting the pitch just a little and the framework shuddered and the thud of the rotor-blades deepened as they took a larger bite out of the air. The increased g-force was perceptible as the slender craft ascended then levelled out.

'That's the border, along there,' Stratton informed the

pilot, making sure he knew exactly where they were.

'I'm aware exactly where the border is,' the pilot replied curtly.

I'll bet he is, thought Stratton. Air Corp pilots from his unit had inadvertently crossed it on a number of occasions. One idiot had even flown to the town of Monaghan, ten miles inside the Republic, thinking it was the Northern Irish town of Armagh. He actually landed on the heli-pad of the police station and climbed out and waved at some officers before he realised he was very much in the wrong place. Since that day pilots were warned their careers would be over if they so much as skimmed the border.

The pilot turned well before the frontier and cruised north-west and parallel with it. Stratton could see a combined army and police checkpoint forming below on the main road to Monaghan. It was the smaller roads that worried him. He made out an army foot patrol heading across fields toward the border. For the umpteenth time he checked the signal tracking device attached to the craft's control panel in front of the co-pilot seat. Where the hell was Spinks's marker?

Spinks held the small device in front of his face. He could not see it, but it helped him, memory wise, to locate the small switch on its side. He had tested it that morning, as he always did prior to heading out on to the ground, before he positioned it in the best hiding place he could think of. He was often reminded of its existence when the corner of the device dug into his testis and required an immediate adjustment. Otherwise he usually forgot about it. It was just another piece of equipment operatives carried and only a last-resort device in the event of the improbable. He could forgive it for all the discomfort it had given him in the past three years because that bastard who shot him had not found it. Now his only prayer was that it actually worked.

He clicked up the tiny switch with his nail. A pinhead-sized LED light blinked in the darkness. It was working, apparently. He rested it on his chest and exhaled heavily, and as he did so a sharp pain shot through his chest and shoulder to remind him of his injury. 'I've been shot,' he said to himself, as if fully realising it for the first time. 'I've been fucking shot and kidnapped, shot and kidnapped!'

Stratton saw the red light flash the instant it came on. A burst of excitement raced through him as he tuned the tracker. All the lights on the panel began to flicker as it warmed to the signal. A gradient of tiny bead-sized lights indicated the signal strength was low but readable, and a single larger one at the bottom of the panel indicated it was behind them.

'Turn around,' he said quickly to the pilot. The pilot responded and banked the Gazelle steeply one eighty degrees. 'Whisky one, I have a signal. I repeat I have a signal towards yellow four.'

The words conveyed the rush of excitement straight into the operations room and the tension rose sharply. Mike beat Graham to the handset and snatched it up. 'Roger, whisky one, towards yellow four. All stations, towards yellow four. Stay off the net unless it's an emergency, out.'

The intelligence team hurried in from the int cell just to watch. That's all they could do now.

The phone rang. Graham picked it up. 'Ops,' he said quickly and listened to the voice the other end. 'It's Bill Lawton,' he said to Mike.

Mike was engrossed in the map and allocated a small part

of his concentration to the call. 'What has the Gardaí said?' he asked.

'Did you hear that?' Graham said into the phone. Bill had and rattled off an answer. 'He said they're sending as many people to the border opposite Aughnacloy as they can spare,' Graham relayed.

'What about London?' Mike said as Graham aimed the phone at him, then back to his own ear for the reply.

'The boss took care of that,' Graham said into the phone. 'He hasn't heard anything, as in Bill hasn't heard anything,' he said to Mike. 'Bill thinks they're going to leave it up to us.'

'That means they don't have a clue what to do,' Mike said. 'Fine. Anything else?'

Graham listened for a moment. 'Okay,' he said and put the phone back into its cradle. 'No. He'll be on the end of this phone if and when he's needed, and he said good luck.'

'Save it for Spinks,' Mike muttered as he started pacing a small area, keeping his eyes on the map but not really seeing it now. His ears, and just about everyone else's eyes, were glued to the speaker on the wall. It was all up to Stratton now.

Aggy stood outside her wrecked car in the field listening to the transmissions. She and Ed were more or less forgotten about and unless they called up on the radio with a problem it would remain that way until this was all over. Ed was in the car smoking a roll-up. He was his old, calm self again and already spouting suggestions as to how and what the ops room should be doing. Then she heard the Gazelle and her thoughts left everyone else.

She walked further out into the field, hoping to see it beyond the trees across the road. It sounded close. When the

Gazelle did come into view it was further south along the wood than she expected, the direction and distance of the sound deceiving as always. It was about half a mile away, black against the sky and going like a rocket. She'd heard his voice over the radio and knew he was in it. Perhaps he would see her. It would pass across her front, maybe a bit closer than it was now. He would know where she was and that she was all right. Then she wondered who she thought she was kidding. He wouldn't be thinking about her, let alone worrying if she was in one piece. It was too much to expect he might even glance in her direction. There was no way of knowing what was on that man's mind no matter what the situation. Often she caught him looking at her but never once had she seen anything in his eyes that gave her encouragement. A hint of desire or even a thin smile would be nice, but there was never anything remotely like interest, it was just as if he happened to be staring in her direction.

At that moment his only thoughts would be of what he loved most and did best. She wasn't worried about him nor did she fear for him, not even slightly. Her feelings about him might well be confused but she was sure of one thing: there was hope for Spinks while he was up there. Stratton gave everyone that kind of feeling. When he was part of your team, on an op, when his calm, strong voice came over the radio, you knew you were on a winning team. She wondered if it was nothing more than simple hero worship she felt for him. She would follow him into hell itself if that were where they had to go. He was larger than life and there was no one else she had ever met who made her feel that way.

Stratton stared unblinking at the direction indicator as the light went to the right, then flickered to the top, then to the left. He spewed instructions to the pilot, trying to keep the top button lit, which meant the signal was dead ahead. 'Left a bit, left . . . straight. Don't go any lower. Stay at five hundred. Left a little more. Straight.'

He checked his map. A line drawn through their location and in their exact direction went above the border, but only just. That meant Spinks was still in the North. He glanced over his right shoulder at a field half a mile away. Near the edge, just beyond the skirt of the wood, was a car a few yards from the road, in a field. A figure was standing alone beside the car, looking up at the helicopter. He watched for a moment longer then went back to the transponder receiver.

Brennan sat in the front of the van beside Sean at the wheel. They were out of the town, in the countryside. Two other men were in the back, sitting on the trunk, which was the only other object in the van. They were middle-aged, red-faced, weathered, as if they had spent their entire lives digging roads in the open air. The van pulled to a stop at a crossroads.

'Straight over,' said Brennan.

'I know where I'm going,' said Sean, aware he was playing with fire. Any backchat to Brennan was to take your soul in your hands. Sean wasn't even sure why he had said anything other than it was his nature to be outspoken and arrogant. Perhaps the danger had got his blood up and he was feeling like a fight. Brennan wasn't the only one capable of a bit of madness, especially behind the wheel of a vehicle.

'I don't give a fock what you know. Just do as I say, when I say it and without lip,' Brennan barked. 'This isn't a focken test to see if you know your way around. If we were walking through your focken house I'd still be telling you where to go. Lippy focken bastard.'

Brennan was aware he was not as cool as he normally was on a job. He had done a lot worse than this, but he felt more nervous than he could remember. His eyes were everywhere, inside every passing car, in the air, beyond the hedgerows. Every mile closer to the border increased his unease as well as his excitement. But his fear of failing was greater than his fear of battle. That was engraved on his soul from a lesson he learned early in life. He was sixteen when he did his first kneecapping but he had to wait until he was twenty-one before he could carry out his first execution. It was on his birthday and he'd had a few drinks, not that he needed any such courage. The boyos had arranged it as a surprise coming-of-age party. The victim was a sixteen-year-old Protestant they had pulled off the street and driven to a remote rural spot. The teenager was the son of a prominent member of the Ulster Volunteer Force, who was earmarked for persecution and then death.

Brennan would never forget it. Not because it was his first kill but because it wasn't. He bungled the task, even though he did everything as he had been instructed. He had placed the barrel of the gun in the centre of the boy's forehead, pulled back the hammer, looked into the boy's eyes, uttered some farewell piss-taking comment, and slowly squeezed the trigger. Brennan had not been instructed to make such a meal of the pre-shoot chat. Lengthening the agony of his victim with his tormenting banter was a torture he decided on only at that moment. When he pulled the trigger, the gun fired, and the explosion sent the bullet through the boy's head and out the other side. The feeling Brennan experienced the second the bullet boomed from the barrel amazed him. He felt like a god. When he pulled the pistol away from the boy's skull he was fascinated by the wisp of smoke coming out of the entry point. Brennan remembered rubbing up some of the black powder burn around the hole with his finger and dabbing it on to the end of the boy's nose as he said to him, 'Rest in peace.' Brennan and his friends then left the boy twitching in the grass and went back to the pub.

But the boy wasn't dead. The lad was discovered a few hours later by a farmer walking his dog and rushed to hospital. The doctors couldn't understand how he had survived such a wound, let alone with all of his faculties until they discovered the bullet had been fired at such an angle that it had travelled inside the skull along the bone precisely in the crease that separates the two halves of the brain, and missed the cerebral cortex before popping out the back. Brennan was ridiculed, but it was a lesson he vowed never to repeat.

There was one thing that niggled Brennan about this particular kidnapping, an edge he had not experienced before. He had worked against the Paras, the Marines, the RUC's Special Branch and had had a brush or two with the SAS, but he'd never come up against Pinks before, although he knew all about them. They made him more nervous than all the other Brit units. The SAS were bad enough but the Pinks were different. If you were going to be ambushed in the middle of a job it would likely be the SAS and every Republican soldier knew that if they walked into an SAS ambush it was pretty much over, and definitely so if there were no RUC around to make sure they didn't finish you off if you were wounded. The SAS were murdering bastards and carried handcuffs just for show. But the Pinks were worse for one important reason: they were in a unique position to play the game with a different set of rules to all the others – their own rules.

Pinks took the law into their own hands. That or they were under the command of some bastard in MI5 or 6 who gave the orders. It wouldn't have been directed from the Brit government. The IRA had long since scared that lot into abandoning any kind of unofficial revenge killings. The politicians no longer had the backbone for that kind of game, especially now that they were part of the European Union. The only Brit unit that could plan and carry out an execution independent of any authority, with a high degree of confidence that they would not be discovered, were the Pinks. What made this all the more dangerous for Brennan was not so much that the Pinks could carry out a murder but that it seemed they were only too willing to risk illegally utilising the technology and resources of the Brit army to do so. They worked in a minefield, between the IRA and their own government. An autonomous execution squad. He knew that not all the Pinks were up to playing this high-staked game and that those who did risked their careers. But the fact remained, if you bloodied a Pink it wasn't over just because you got away with it. You were a marked man for as long as there was one of them around willing to take revenge, and they had a lot of resources at hand to track you down. And Brennan had one of them in a box in the back of the van! Kidnapping one was the greatest wrong you could do them and they would want revenge. Brennan was not over the border yet and could breathe easier only when he was, and even then, afterwards, he would not be safe.

Fuck 'em, he said to himself. This was war. Brennan could handle it. The immediate problem was getting this one home and to the interrogators. If the RUC or army stopped them they could have a bit of a fight if there was the opportunity, and if it looked like Brennan might not win, all he had to do was give it up. The worst that would happen was jail.

But if the Pinks got to them before they passed over the border that was a different story. It would be a fight to the end for someone. That made it the most exciting game he had played yet, and Brennan was up for it. If he beat them, if he got one of them home alive, he would be a legend in his own lifetime. He looked around at the two men in the back.

'Where're your tools?' he growled.

The men pointed to a sack on the floor.

'What focken' good are they there? Put 'em in your hands, you stupid bastards.'

One of them picked up the sack and pulled out two American M16 assault rifles. He handed one to his pal.

'Load 'em and put the safety-catches on, for Christ's sake! Don't they teach you morons anything at that school?'

'Army,' Sean suddenly warned. They all instantly looked ahead through the dirty windscreen.

A convoy of four army Landrovers headed towards them on the other side of the road. They passed by at speed, each loaded with soldiers. Sean kept an eye on the wing mirror, watching until they were out of sight.

'Anyone catch what regiment that was?' Sean asked.

'Who gives a fock. Take the next right,' snapped Brennan.

Sean turned right into a small lane. 'About a mile to go,' he said, wondering if that, too, would offend Brennan. But Brennan was concentrating too hard on the road, fields and sky to take any more notice of what Sean had to say.

'Only thing we need to worry about from here on is a foot patrol,' Brennan said.

'Or an eagle flight,' added Sean, referring to a common army practice of dropping patrols off in the countryside using helicopters.

'There's the gate,' Brennan said, pointing up ahead. Sean

slowed, turned and stopped in front of a five-bar wooden gate that led into a field. Brennan hopped out and opened the gate. Sean drove through, stopping long enough for Brennan to leap back in.

'Stay on those tracks. Come on, come on, move it,' Brennan said, getting impatient.

Sean set off again, following a pair of tractor ruts across a lumpy field. Brennan sat forward in his seat, looking in every direction. They passed through a gap in a hedge into another field. 'Two football pitches and we're home,' he said.

Everyone could see the spindly hedgerow up ahead that was the Irish border. The van dipped and creaked in the ruts and when Sean skidded and slid a little he braced himself for a bollocking but instead it seemed Brennan was already in a celebratory mood. 'Don't break the van after all that, Sean me lad,' he said in a fatherly tone. 'Easy does it now.'

Sean dropped down a gear and drove with more care, composing himself in readiness for the victory cheer as the border inched closer.

Sean was the first to think he heard it, then Brennan detected a dull throbbing sound. About the same time they knew their ears were not deceiving them, a helicopter thundered in an arc across their front, low to the ground, its rotors facing them, pulsating loudly as it banked steeply to head around to their rear. Sean swerved hard in reaction, the van's tyres digging into the soft earth. Everyone was ramrod straight with tension. Brennan grabbed Sean's collar violently as he yelled: 'Go! Go for it, you focker! Go!'

Sean lost traction as he hit the accelerator too hard and the van fishtailed. He brought it under control and drove over the ruts and dips towards the spindly hedge now a football field away.

★　★　★

As the helicopter came around the rear of the van, Stratton looked down on it like a hawk eyeing a rodent scurrying for its life. He grabbed a thin wire that ran across the cabin door, the emergency release cable, and yanked it hard as he booted the bottom of it. The door flew off its hinges and flapped to the ground in the downdraught and the wind tore inside the cab. Stratton turned in his seat so that he was facing outside, rested a foot on the skid below the edge of the door, and hung as far out as his seatbelt would allow so that he could comfortably fire the rifle down at a steep angle.

He gripped the SLR tightly into his shoulder and shouted into his mic, competing with the downdraught from the rotors. 'Keep my side facing the van! . . . Did you hear me?'

'Yes,' the pilot replied, although he was distracted by something else that greatly concerned him.

'Move up. Keep just ahead of the van!' Stratton continued as he raised the barrel so that he could look along its length and sit the target on the end of it.

The pilot dropped the helicopter's nose a tad, lost some height, putting it at house-top level, and moved up alongside the van.

'Ahead, ahead!' Stratton called out, indicating with his right hand to push forward. He wanted to be further in front to get a clear shot backwards at the driver, but the pilot was not moving the way he wanted him to. 'Ahead I said, damn it!'

The pilot inched the Gazelle forward, bringing the front windshield of the van into view. Stratton brought the weapon site to his eye and aimed, the gyro-steady device helping to keep it almost magically solid in his hands. The van suddenly swerved and headed on a course beneath the chopper, the steeper angle making it difficult for Stratton to get the shot. 'Right, damn it! Right!' he shouted.

The pilot pulled steeply to the right and then banked left to expose the front of the van to Stratton once again, but his agitation was growing. 'What if you hit your own man?' he shouted.

Stratton composed himself to shoot. 'Not unless he's driving,' he muttered as he took first pressure on the trigger. Stratton could clearly see the two men in the front. The driver glanced up at him. 'Steady,' Stratton said.

Sean took his eyes off the gap in the hedgerow he was aiming for to snatch a look at the man hanging out of the helicopter aiming the rifle directly at him. He swerved left and right, but his options were limited if he wanted to get into the South.

'Go for the gap!' Brennan yelled, anxious to be over the border.

'Shoot him!' Sean yelled back.

'You're nearly there. Drive, you bastard!'

Stratton held the sight on his target. The instant he squeezed the trigger and fired the helicopter banked hard over and turned away. Stratton couldn't believe what had just happened. He snapped around expecting to see some catastrophic reason why the pilot had changed course, but there was nothing.

'Why'd you turn away?!' he shouted.

'That hedge was the border.'

'What?' Stratton yelled in utter disbelief.

'I'm not going over the border,' the pilot said firmly. He had lost every fight with Stratton till now. But this time he had the law on his side, both international and military.

'Get back in pursuit of that van,' Stratton said dangerously.

'I will not.'

'You will not be held responsible.'

'Who do you think you are?'

'You're sending a man to his death because of a piece of airspace?'

'Call it what you want. I can't go over that border and that's final. Those are my standing orders and I suspect they're yours too.'

'Do you have any idea what they will do to that man?' Stratton said, disgusted with the pilot.

'You won't win this one and there is no one with the authority to make me cross it, not you or your god of a commanding officer.'

'If it's games you want to play we can do that,' Stratton said as he pulled his pistol from his holster, shoved it between the pilot's legs, and casually fired. The bullet smashed through the seat and into the bulletproof sheet that lined the floor. The pilot's heart leaped into his throat and he might have jumped out of his seat had he not been strapped into it. Somehow he managed to keep hold of the pitch and joystick as the helicopter lurched and dipped. Stratton maintained his enraged gaze, waiting for the pilot's decision.

'You're crazy!' he yelled.

'And you're gonna be dickless in five seconds and it won't end there, trust me,' Stratton said as he moved the end of the pistol into the pilot's crotch making him flinch.

'You're truly insane,' the pilot screamed, as much in pain as in horror.

'If it helps . . . The guy in that van is worth a dozen of you. I've been in enough of these crates to know I don't need you to land it.'

'You'd go to jail for the rest of your life!'

'Why? We got shot down and you got burned to a crisp.

71

Why would I go to jail? No more talking. You have three seconds to turn in pursuit of that van. Two . . . one . . . '

When the high-velocity bullet smashed through the windscreen just as the helicopter peeled away, Sean thought he was a dead man, until he heard Brennan scream and saw the blood shoot from between his fingers where he was holding his leg. It had passed cleanly through, missing the bone, but had taken a fair bit of meat with it. It took a second for the pain to reach Brennan's brain and tell him that he was in fact the one who had been shot.

When the others realised the chopper had pulled off they couldn't believe it at first. Brennan was too distressed to notice until they tore through the hedge and were over the border. Sean was shouting that the Gazelle had gone and the others looking out of the back window acknowledged it. Brennan found the Gazelle in his wing mirror still in the North and turning away from them. Despite the ferociously burning pain in his thigh he grinned as the others broke into a rapturous cheer.

'The bastards are staying in the North! The bastards are staying in the North!' he shouted, not quite believing his own eyes. He tore several strips of cloth from his shirt and bound his leg tightly to stem the flow. The sight of their powerful enemy held at bay from the chase as if by an invisible barrier was anaesthetic enough. They screamed obscenities at the helicopter and celebrated, clapping their hands, stamping their feet, and banging on the crate that Spinks was inside as if it were a drum.

Sean beamed as he swerved the van from side to side in the field. Brennan patted his shoulder with a bloody hand. 'Well done, laddy. Well done! That was fantastic driving. Focken fantastic driving. You'll go down in bloody history today, fellah, that's for sure. You all will,' he shouted.

Sean stuck his finger in the bullet hole in the windscreen. 'That was focken close.'

'Focken close? It got me, didn't it, you bastard,' Brennan said.

The others burst into laughter, a release of tension more than anything else. Even Brennan saw the funny side and laughed.

'I knew they wouldn't jump the border,' Brennan said. 'I focken knew it. That's why I pushed you to drive on, me lad. I knew they wouldn't come over, the chicken shit bastards.'

'For a while there I thought it was a focken Pink,' Sean said.

'Fock 'em if it was or it weren't,' Brennan said. 'We'll take on the Pinks, the SAS, whatever they want to throw at us. They'll have to come over the focken border to get us now though. And good luck to 'em.'

Everyone cheered the statement. Brennan grinned as he kept a wary eye on his wing mirror. He was too long in the tooth not to know that they were home free only when they got to the rendezvous and the Pink in their trunk was handed over. Not a moment before. He reached out of the window and moved the wing mirror around until he found the helicopter, no more than a tiny black splodge flicking in and out of the mirror as the van bounced along. While the others laughed and relived the last hour he suddenly felt there was something not quite right about the image. It didn't look as if it were getting any smaller. Perhaps it was just hovering. His smile started to wane as the image appeared to be growing larger, little by little, second by second.

He leaned forward to get a closer look at the mirror, praying he was wrong. But he was not. The helicopter was coming on, full bore towards them, nose tilted down like a raging bull at full charge.

Brennan stuck his head out into the wind to look back. The others continued celebrating, unaware, except Sean who sensed the change in Brennan and saw him looking back. He glanced in his own wing mirror and his smile quickly dropped from his face.

'It's coming back,' Sean said. The two singing men in the rear did not hear him. 'It's coming back!' he shouted at them as he put his foot down and the van accelerated across the field towards a distant hedgerow.

The silence in the operations room was almost painful. Everyone in the detachment's small camp had found their way into it: bleeps, the intelligence cell, the ops officer, the second in command – even the cook, mechanic and detachment storeman had crept in and remained at the back to watch and listen.

Mike leaned over the map board, waiting. The last transmission they had heard was Stratton saying 'I have', which simply meant he had the vehicle that contained Spinks in sight, or to be precise, the one that contained Spinks's transponder. That meant, in Stratton's case at least, that he was going to do something to stop it. There was no point interrupting him just to ask what exactly. There was nothing any of them could do to help anyway.

'How close are our cars?' Mike asked quietly, referring to the other operatives who had scrambled from the camp to get to the area.

'A good ten minutes away,' Graham said.

That meant they were well out of the race. Mike tapped the perspex sheet that covered the entire map with his wax pencil, beating out a meaningless rhythm as he thought. 'How long since his last transmission?'

'One minute twenty seconds,' Graham said.

Mike stood up and folded his hands across his chest as if holding himself together, afraid his anxiousness would burst out. But he could not keep control any longer. He picked up the handset and pushed the button on the side of it. 'Whisky one, zero alpha, sit-rep?' he said.

Everyone glanced up at the speaker, but it remained silent.

'Whisky one, this is zero alpha, sit-rep?'

'I have,' Stratton said, his voice suddenly booming over the speaker, making the cook jump which in turn caused the mechanic to do the same.

Mike and Graham looked at each other, both thinking the same thing. Stratton had said 'I have' a while ago. They wondered why nothing had changed in that time.

'Location?' Mike asked, doing his best to contain a tension he had never experienced before.

There was another long silence. Mike suddenly felt uneasy.

'Whisky one, what is your location?'

'We're going into the green,' was Stratton's calm reply.

The uneasy feeling rippled through the room.

Mike lowered the handset. The second in command and ops officer watched him, wondering what his next move would be.

Mike thought long and hard on it. It was obvious what was happening. The van was over the border with Spinks in it. He was not about to consider telling Stratton to cancel the pursuit. Even if that were an option, which in this case it was not, Stratton would ignore him anyway. A border excursion was nothing compared to losing an operative. Mike was the kind of officer who stood by his men in a fight. If he was not going to order Stratton back, it therefore meant he supported him. He might as well start right there and then.

'Get me Lisburn ops,' he said calmly to Graham. 'And get Bill Lawton standing by. We might as well start patching this up with the Irish right away.' All Mike could now hope for was that Stratton tied it up as quickly and neatly as possible and without taking the battle all the way into Dublin.

'The road, the road!' Brennan yelled, pointing to a gate in the hedge a hundred yards ahead. Just beyond it was another hedge running parallel that indicated there was a road or track in between. Sean steered a gentle arc, adjusting his angle so that he could crash through the gate and enter the lane without slowing. The gate looked sturdy, but nothing was going to stop them now.

He hit it hard, smashing through it and destroying the headlights, and turned sharply on to the narrow lane, sliding just a little and bashing the far hedge with the flank but without losing much pace.

The Gazelle came on in pursuit like a relentless hunter. It banked hard over and levelled out to the right side of the van, no higher than a goalpost off the ground, and started to push ahead. Sean snatched a glance at it. This was useless, he thought. They were stuck in the lane like it was a bowling alley with nowhere to go but straight ahead.

As the Gazelle inched closer Brennan watched the man in the left seat of the cab leaning out with a rifle in his hand. He could see him more clearly now, his civilian clothes, straggly hair, unshaven features, and he was looking directly at Brennan as he raised the rifle to his shoulder.

'Pink,' Brennan said under his breath. 'Focken Pink!'

Brennan leaned out the window and fired a long burst, almost losing his gun to the hedges crashing past as Sean tried to manoeuvre as best he could in the narrow lane. The two men in the back held on to anything they could as the van lurched heavily, Spinks's crate sliding from one side to the other. One of the men fell on to his back while gripping his M16 and accidentally loosed off several rounds that ripped along the roof in a line barely missing Brennan's head. But Brennan was too caught up in the desperation of his position to direct his madness at them.

'What do we do?' screamed Sean.

Brennan seemed frozen, watching the man in the helicopter.

'Brennan?' Sean shouted.

'Drive! Just keep driving,' Brennan shouted back.

'We could run in four different directions. They couldn't get all of us,' Sean said.

Brennan shoved the end of his gun barrel at Sean, glaring at him with manic eyes. 'You stop this van and I'll blow you to focken pieces,' he yelled.

Sean got the message loud and clear.

Stratton held the rifle tightly into his shoulder and looked down through the sights. A bullet skimmed the bottom of the Gazelle. Another creased the glass bubble, causing a crack that spread to one of the corners, but Stratton did not move from his purpose. The pilot flinched but he was more frightened of Stratton's wrath should he veer off course than anything else.

'Steady!' Stratton called out. After a short pause, he squeezed the trigger four times in quick succession.

The first round spat through the windscreen and hit Sean in the chest; the second in his gut; a third passed through his neck; and the fourth flew between him and Brennan and into the crate Spinks was in. Sean slumped forward in his seat like a puppet with its strings cut as a jet of blood from his neck spouted around the cab. It squirted Brennan in the face as he grabbed the steering wheel and shoved Sean off his seat and against his door. The van tilted sharply as it mounted the embankment and scraped along the hedge. Brennan did his best to straighten it out, gripping the wheel with both hands. Sean's feet were twisted and jammed under the dash, keeping the accelerator full against the floor. Brennan managed to manoeuvre it around a tight corner, hugging the outside hedge, and he might well have completed the turn successfully had it not been for the large boulder jutting from the outside hedge that had without doubt been there many thousands of years and was not about to give an inch to a van travelling at speed. And it didn't. The front of the van collapsed like a bag of crisps and abruptly stopped but the contents continued on at the same speed. Brennan and Sean went through the windscreen and punched into the hedge as though it were a safety net. The two men in the back flew the length of the van and slammed into the front seats. The crate followed close behind and near flattened one of them between it and the seat, his bones snapping like firewood.

The Gazelle turned sharply close to the ground and the rotors thundered as it circled the wreck tightly.

'Land!' Stratton shouted. 'Quickly!'

Brennan lay in the hedge, dazed and bloody. He fought to regain control and tried to move, but it seemed impossible to get his limbs to obey him. Contact was finally made and he moved his legs in search of firm ground below. He turned in the hedge and saw Sean lying beside him, mangled and very dead. The field was within reach just ahead and he grabbed the thorny branches around him and pulled himself forward. Every part of him ached and he waited for the shot of pain from somewhere in his body that would tell him a part of it was broken. As his senses regrouped he could hear the helicopter and the memories of the most recent events flooded back. He increased his efforts to pull himself on. The pain was dull and all over, but nothing appeared to be broken.

He wiped some blood out of his eyes and reached out of the hedge and down to touch the ground. He dug his fingers into the soil and pulled himself further forward, rolling out of the thicket on to his back and allowing himself a few precious seconds to breathe before forcing himself on. As he turned on to his front to push himself up his hand fell on to something metallic. His sub-machine-gun. He willed himself to his knees and picked it up in his battered, shaking hands, then he winced in pain. His leg. He'd forgotten he'd been shot right through it. But the urge to survive took over and he forced himself to take a step. His leg almost gave way but there was enough muscle left to support him.

He saw the helicopter hovering above the field the other side of the lane and shakily aimed his gun towards it and then lost his balance and almost fell over. He steadied himself, got the gun on aim, and squeezed the trigger. But it wouldn't fire. He checked the safety-catch, almost dropping the weapon. He pulled out the magazine, checked it for ammunition, and pushed it back home. He cocked it, aimed, and pulled the trigger once again. It fired, and on fully automatic!

Stratton had already unclipped his seatbelt and was leaning well out of the cab as the helicopter pulled up into the hover ten feet above the ground. At the sound of the gunfire he jumped, ripping the giro-steady cable from the consul. He hit the ground and jammed the rifle into his shoulder, searching for a target as the helicopter backed away from the fire.

Stratton saw movement beyond the hedge near the van

but he was not about to shoot at anyone he could not positively identify.

The Gazelle landed not far behind him, its rotors remaining on full revs. Stratton ran forward, reached the hedgerow a few yards behind the van, dropped the rifle, and took out his pistol. He eased through a gap in the hedge and stepped down on to the lane. It was all very quiet but for the hiss of steam from the van's engine. Stratton paused to tune his senses and then cautiously headed to the front of the van. He saw the windshield smashed out and Sean lying in the hedge. In the field just beyond a sub-machine-gun was lying in the grass. Stratton eased forward, eyes everywhere, and reached through the hedge to feel the gun's barrel. It was hot. He then heard what sounded like a snapping stick some distance away and stood on the front bumper of the van so that he could see over the hedge. In the distance a man was limping heavily away.

Stratton stepped back down into the lane and made his way to the rear of the van. One of the doors had popped open on impact. He looked inside. There was some movement and the sound of strained breathing. Stratton climbed in to find the two Irishmen broken and bloody against the back of the seats. The one sandwiched between the crate and the seat was motionless and judging by the unnatural position of his head, twisted three-quarters of the way around, it looked as if his neck was broken. The other lay in an awkward position unable to move, watching Stratton, his every breath a painful effort. Stratton aimed his gun at the man who was in too much pain to care and remained staring at Stratton. A noise came from inside the crate that was lying on its side. Stratton ignored the broken man and pulled the crate over so that the lid was upright. He noticed the bullet hole in the top and its corresponding exit point in the side. He unlatched the lid and opened it expecting to find Spinks seriously damaged.

Spinks lay tightly inside the cramped space squinting up at Stratton, adjusting his eyes to the light, as frightened as he was hopeful.

'You okay, Spinks?'

Spinks blinked hard as the images came into focus. He knew that voice.

'Stratton?'

'Can you walk?'

'Stratton,' he repeated, still afraid it was some kind of hallucination. 'Tell me it's really you.'

'It's me. Are you hurt?' Stratton asked, then noticed the blood on Spinks's jacket and crouched to get a better look. 'You've been hit.'

'They shot me,' Spinks said.

Stratton raced through his options if he couldn't move Spinks, none of which were good. This had all been about saving Spinks and there was no point doing anything that would put his health in jeopardy having got this far.

It was as if Spinks had read Stratton's mind. 'Where are we?' he asked.

'In the South.'

'Then we'd better get going,' he said as he raised his hands, gripped the sides of the box, and started to pull himself up. A pain shot across his chest and Stratton quickly grabbed him.

'Easy,' Stratton said.

Spinks took several short breaths. 'I can do it,' he said then pulled himself once again until he was sitting upright. Stratton inspected the entry and exit points high on his chest. 'As bullet holes go, they're in an okay place.'

'That's good,' Spinks said, attempting sarcasm. He then

braced himself for a major effort to stand with Stratton's help and climb out of the box. His knees almost gave way as they took his full weight but Stratton held him. Spinks pushed them straight. 'I'm okay,' he said. 'I'm okay.'

Stratton helped Spinks out of the box beside the broken man lying on the floor of the van, watching them.

'What about 'im?' Spinks asked.

'What's your name?' Stratton asked the man.

'O . . . O'Kelly,' the man said, catching his breath.

Spinks wondered if Stratton was going to kill him. He wouldn't be in the least surprised if he did. That didn't mean he knew Stratton well enough to know he'd do it. Quite the contrary. He didn't know Stratton well at all, but the rumours about him left one in doubt as to his true character.

'Looks like he's paid a price for today,' Spinks said, hoping that if Stratton was into executing the bloke he might change his mind. It wasn't something Spinks was into, even after what he'd been through. He wasn't a murderer.

The man's eyes started to glaze and his breathing suddenly grew shallower, and then it stopped altogether.

Spinks stared at him with no sign of remorse or celebration. It was simply an event.

'Come on,' Stratton said and helped Spinks out of the van. They shuffled to the gap in the hedge and Spinks glanced back at the front of the van.

'Fuckin' 'ell!' he said. 'Good thing I was in that box.'

As Stratton helped him through the hedge he grabbed up his SLR and they made their way across the field towards the waiting Gazelle. The short walk helped Spinks's circulation and he could almost support himself by the time they reached it.

'I knew it was you. I fuckin' knew it,' Spinks said. 'Soon

as I 'eard the shootin' I said to myself, that's Stratton that is. Then we 'it a fuckin' wall.' Spinks chuckled until the pain made it difficult to laugh any more.

Stratton helped him into the back and laid him down on the bench seat. As he climbed into the exposed front passenger seat the Gazelle lifted skyward and turned North.

Stratton put on his headset, positioned the mic in front of his lips, and pushed the send button. 'Zero alpha, whisky one. I have four two Charlie. He has a gunshot wound but he's gonna be okay. I'm towards your location.'

A cheer went up in the ops room. Mike picked up the handset. 'Roger that, whisky one,' he replied. 'Any other casualties?'

'Two, possibly three dead, unconfirmed. At least one escaped.'

'Understood,' Mike said. 'See you when you land.' Mike put down the handset and sat back in his chair, looking a little spent. 'Send a tow to pick up one three kilo,' he said to Graham.

'Already on its way,' Graham said. 'Nice one, boss,' he added, grinning. 'Not a bad ending, all things considered.'

Mike wasn't feeling particularly celebratory. His thoughts were elsewhere. There was something he had queried the moment Spinks had been kidnapped but had pushed to the back of his mind. 'This one is far from over . . . We've at least one major problem to figure out now.'

The second in command and the intelligence officer glanced at each other, unsure what Mike could be referring to.

'If you mean the border excursion, I'd take that any day over a kidnapped operative,' the int officer said.

'That's not what I'm talking about,' Mike said. 'This problem is even more serious than Spinks being kidnapped.'

The others looked at each other, unaware what that could possibly be. Mike saw the vacant look in their eyes and lowered his voice so that only they could hear.

'Spinks's kidnapping was a set-up from the start. It was elaborate, well planned and executed, and they almost got away with it. You don't put something like that together in a few hours or overnight even. They knew he was going to be outside the church in the trunk of that car long before he arrived there. We planned that operation less than two weeks ago and it was known only to a handful of members in the detachment and military intelligence. No one in the RUC or regular army units knew about it . . . So how did RIRA find out?'

The ops officer and second in command went thoughtfully quiet.

5

Hank caught glimpses of England through the clouds. His first sight of the old world was fascinating but it also increased a feeling of uneasiness that had been slowly growing deep within him. Not that it was unusual for Hank to get nervous about anything that could drastically affect his career. But this was different. He was heading into the complete unknown and, what was truly new for him, doing it on his own.

When his commanding officer first told him six months ago that he was on the shortlist for the job he was jazzed, but when it was made official a couple of months later he began to feel apprehensive. Up until then he had not allowed himself to think of all the things he would have to deal with, but confirmation brought a myriad concerns, not all of them work related. He had four months to get organised and his first problem was what to do with the house for the two years abroad. He considered selling it, but when he suggested that to Kathryn she went nuts, ranting about how much time and money they had spent getting it just right. Hank knew her horrified reaction was not just to do with the house. He pulled back from selling it and placed an advertisement on the Navy website newsletter offering it up for rental. Kathryn tried to fight that option too. She said the thought of complete strangers living in their home revolted her. Hank totally refused to leave the damn thing empty for two years while still paying the mortgage. She gave in but it was only the start of his Kathryn-related problems.

Janet and Helen, their five- and six-year-old girls, were another concern. He wondered how they would find moving to a new country and a foreign school even though, thankfully, their initial reaction was 'cool'. Marty Whelan, the guy Hank was replacing, turned out to be a great help. Marty, who had a wife and child, had gone through everything Hank was about to and assured him all would be fine and that in no time at all they would be settled in. He reminded Hank that the posting with the Brits was a couple of decades old and that most of those who had gone before him had been married with kids and managed okay. Hank knew he was getting too strung out about the move and blamed Kathryn for much of his stress. She was by far his biggest problem at the moment. He was afraid this trip was going to test just about every aspect of their relationship. The problem was she did not want to go to England and her reason was deep-seated, family and historical. She hated the English and everything about them. Not that she had ever known a single English person or even been to England before. She had been brought up to hate them.

The captain's voice filled the cabin announcing that there were twenty minutes before landing. Hank pushed his fingers through his short, brown hair. He had not slept a wink on the flight even after four beers and four Jack Daniels chasers. He prided himself on being able to sleep anywhere, anytime, wet or dry, on rocks or feathers, but the combination of the new appointment and family concerns was more than he had ever had to handle at any one time before. He finally decided the best way to deal with Kathryn's issues was to ignore them. This trip was about his career and not her problems with the English. He was going to spend two years with the Special Boat Service (SBS). If he did well he could look forward to a promotion to E8 on his return. That promotion was the true source of his concerns. Without it, and it was not guaranteed by a long shot, he could look forward to three or four more years max in the Navy and then it was civvy street. The very thought depressed him. His dream was to be a lifer but it all hinged on how he was going to get on with – and impress – this foreign Special Forces outfit that his own American one was originally based on.

He had received several briefings on what to expect and how to comport himself. The two organisations were related, i.e. both were Navy and played in the water, though not exclusively, but they were also quite different. Americans gave the impression of being more laid back than the British, and in most cases that was true, but the SEALs were in fact a much more rigid structure and more traditional than the SBS. The SEALs were also far wealthier. The SBS had seen more action in the past few decades and boasted a greater number of successes, but Hank was not intimidated by that and proud to be a Navy SEAL.

He knew that if he wanted to return home in two years with an outstanding report he was going to have to impress. The issue was not if he could achieve his goals, but how. He had seen action in the Gulf War even though that was an overall disappointment for the SEALs, who were hardly utilised. His team had retaken a small oil platform in the Persian Gulf to prevent the Iraqis from destroying it, but there had been no resistance and it was basically a formality. He had also been part of the team that liberated the US embassy in Kuwait, but that was just a show for the press, roping down from a helicopter on to the roof while journalists, who had been there days before, filmed the event from outside on the street in a somewhat carnival atmosphere. Somalia was a little more hairy for him but he missed out on the bigger engagements. Afghanistan had looked hopeful but ended up another disappointment. As usual, it seemed, he arrived too late to see the best of the action. It was always about being in the right place at the right time and he never was. Two years with the Brits, however, did not necessarily mean a break in those possibilities. There had been rumours of previous exchange officers seeing action with the Brits, and not just in the Gulf or Afghanistan. He would just have to wait and see how true that was.

Hank checked his daughters were belted into their seats beside him and glanced over at Kathryn the other side of the aisle. She always looked pretty to him, even when she was stressed and unhappy. Her auburn shoulder-length hair shone like it had just been washed. It fascinated him the way it always seemed to fall perfectly into place. But her eyes looked tired as they stared ahead at nothing and there was a slight frown across her forehead. She was still annoyed at having to travel economy class. That was tough, he thought. The overseas allowances made this a good money trip and he was not about to squander it on an expensive upgrade. It annoyed him the way she had no respect for money. Hank's philosophy was that of a Special Forces soldier: economy and planning, but despite his insistence he reckoned he lost as many fights with Kathryn as he won. The two things he regretted giving into most were the house and the car, both more than they could sensibly afford. It irked him every time he thought of the size of the combined monthly payments. Now the damned car was in storage for two years while they continued paying for it.

He went back to the view out of his window, his thoughts gravitating once again to his new posting. He had no idea what he would be doing once he arrived in Poole town. In some ways, coming to England would be like starting over. That was one of the big pluses for him. Making friends was not a problem. He liked to work hard and party harder, which had been as much a part of his problem as it was his charm. The plan for this trip was to hold off in the party department until he was more familiar with the guys. It was a matter of record that Hank could make an ass of himself when drunk, which was why he almost lost out on getting the promotion he needed to qualify for this job. But this trip was as much about public relations as maintaining the good rapport they had with their cousins over the pond. Hank had learned that his boss had based his final decision on the conclusion that Hank might just fit in with the Brits quite well; after all, the Brits liked their beer too.

'Mommy,' Helen said, leaning into the aisle. 'Are we nearly in England?'

'Yeah, sweety. We're nearly in England,' Kathryn replied, wishing her little girl wasn't so excited. The nose of the plane dipped a little to lose height.

'Pinch your nose and blow into your ears the way we practised it, honey,' Kathryn advised. 'You too, Janet.' The two girls pinched their noses and blew repeatedly, their little cheeks puffing out.

'I felt a pop, Mommy,' Janet said.

'That's good, honey.' Kathryn glanced at Hank, who was still staring out of the window, absently rubbing his palms. She wanted to put her hands on his and tell him he was going to do just fine, but she couldn't. He may be worried about the next two years, but so was she. She resented him for not understanding her needs. While he was doing his job she was looking forward to two years of hell.

Kathryn stood in the arrivals lounge between two trolleys piled high with suitcases, and Helen and Janet parked tiredly on top of them. Hank had gone outside to look for Marty, who was supposed to be meeting them. Kathryn was tired and wondered how long it would take to get to wherever they were headed. She had no interest in looking at a map of the country and knew nothing about where they were going, how far it was, or even in what part of England it was situated.

She looked around the crowded terminal at the people, races she had never seen in the flesh before and languages she could only guess at. She heard American voices and craned to search for them. They were easily spotted: a loud, well-fed group in crisp, colourful clothes; retired couples from Texas or Arizona she guessed. She watched as they shuffled towards an exit that promised the coach terminal.

She was really here, she thought. Goddamned England. It was numbing. There was not one single positive aspect of being in England and no end of negative ones. Leaving the house had been unbearable. She hated the people they had let it out to: a lieutenant from SEAL Team 4 on the West Coast and his snooty Californian wife. The woman made it obvious it was beneath her status to rent a house belonging to a mere chief petty officer, but as she kept saying, much to Kathryn's irritation, 'there simply wasn't anything to choose from' implying Kathryn's house was a last resort.

Saying goodbye to her friends was almost as bad. The day they left for the airport it should have been her turn to host the wives' get-together. Hank had accused her of being petty when she moaned about it but it represented all that was important to her. Her social life dominated everything. Most of her friends were Navy wives and young mothers. There was always a birthday party, a baby shower or picnic to attend or plan. Every weekend someone was having a barbeque. She never went shopping alone; a phone call would always find at least one wife to come along and turn it into a day out. Her women's group was probably the most important event for her. And at the centre of everything were, of course, the children.

Standing there in the arrivals lounge, thousands of miles from all of that, Kathryn felt as if she had been ripped out of her life by the roots. She had even delayed packing to the last minute, hoping and praying the trip would somehow fall apart. Never in her life had she considered coming to England. It irked her even more to think Hank was actually keen on it. His parents were also of Irish descent. Maybe not second generation like hers but what was the difference? When she tried to talk to him about it all he would say was, 'They ain't at war with you.' 'Tripe' her mother called his comment. 'The war was against the Irish, and we're Irish,' she insisted. Hank said Kathryn was using the Irish thing as an excuse and that it was her friends she really didn't want to say goodbye to.

Kathryn ultimately gave in because Hank had threatened to quit the SEALs if she didn't go with him; it was a married and accompanied draft and he would not have been able to go without her. She had never seen him so angry as when she first refused. She thought he was going to wreck the entire house when he came home drunk later that night. If he quit the Navy they would have had to leave Norfolk for him to find work anyway. She had her doubts that he would have carried out his threat but she didn't want to take the risk. He was capable of doing crazy things at times. Hank tried to console her with stupid comments such as it wouldn't be quite so bad once she made new friends. He just didn't get it. She didn't want anything to do with the English. She was realistic enough to know she could not avoid the other wives completely but she was not about to get pally with any of them. The girls would obviously make friends at school. They would want to bring them home. The mothers would then want to come in for their cups of tea and no doubt ask endlessly stupid questions about what it was like in America. There would be birthday parties and sleepovers. The more she thought about it the more it worried her that she could not keep it up for a week, never mind two years.

'Mommy? I wanna drink,' Helen said, looking as if she was close to falling sleep.

'You're gonna have to wait, honey.'

'But I'm thirsty.'

'Daddy has all the English money.'

Kathryn saw Hank moving nimbly through the crowded hall towards her. A man she vaguely recognised was following him. He must've been six three or four, at least a couple inches taller than Hank.

Hank arrived a little out of breath and grabbed one of the trolleys, turning it in the direction he just came from. 'Hold on, honey,' he said to Janet, then to Kathryn as he started to push off, 'We gotta hurry. Marty's parked in a no-waiting zone.'

'Hi,' Marty said with a carefree grin as he arrived and took charge of the other trolley, but in nowhere near the rush as Hank who was already heading off.

'I told Hank we don't need to rush so much,' Marty said in a lazy, mid-western drawl. 'They ain't so crazy here 'bout parkin' out front as they are States side.'

'Comin' through here,' Hank shouted to people blocking his way.

Kathryn plucked Helen off the trolley Marty had hold of, forcing a smile for him, uncomfortable as she usually was with strangers. 'I'm Kathryn.'

'We met a couple years back at an open day,' Marty said. 'My wife's name is Kate.' Marty was broader than Hank and had a farm-boy quality. He was almost handsome.

'I remember,' she said. 'I'm sorry but I don't remember your wife. Kate, did you say?'

'Yeah,' he said. 'I'd only just dragged her out from Kentucky that week. She was shy about meetin' new people back then.'

Kathryn decided she liked Marty and his slow, confident way of talking and moving.

Hank looked back to check on their progress. 'Come on, honey. Otherwise the car'll get towed,' he shouted.

Marty politely indicated Kathryn to go ahead. She wondered how well Marty knew Hank. They seemed quite opposite in character. She took Helen's hand and moved off in pursuit of her husband.

By the time Marty approached the entrance to the M3 motorway, seatbacks had been adjusted for maximum comfort, pillows were made from clothing and everyone was settled in for the drive.

''Bout two hours should see us into Poole, maybe more if this jam doesn't clear,' Marty said.

'Is the traffic always this bad?' Hank asked as they crawled along the three-lane highway sandwiched between a truck and a double-decker bus.

'There was a bomb scare on one of the bypasses a couple hours ago. That's why I was late. We'll be past it soon.'

'Bomb scare? Who would that be?' Hank asked.

'RIRA probably. They've been stepping up their attacks on the mainland lately.'

'RIRA?' Hank asked, having never heard the term.

'The Real IRA. That's what they call themselves. They're one of the new groups since the ceasefire.'

'They're all IRA though, right?' asked Hank.

'I guess. You've got the official IRA, the old original outfit, and then the Provisional IRA. Anyhow, they're supposed to be having a ceasefire. Then there's a group called the Continuity IRA, which are pretty much like the Real IRA. They're made up of guys from PIRA, the Provos that is, who don't agree with the ceasefire. But then the Provos were originally formed back in the seventies or sixties by guys who thought the IRA in those days weren't putting up enough of a fight. Basically not a lot's changed as far as most of the Catholics in Northern Ireland are concerned. They still want the Brits out.'

'So why don't they just leave?' Kathryn said, almost to herself, not really wanting to get into a conversation on any subject.

'Problem is the Protestants want to stay British and there are more of them than Catholics and they've got most of the power and money . . . Funny thing is the Brits first sent troops into Northern Ireland to protect the Catholics from the Protestants. The first Brit soldier killed was by a Protestant, or was it the other way around? Yeah, I think the first guy the Brits shot was a Protestant. Maybe it was both. Anyhow, nothing seems to have changed, like I said. Except of course since the September eleventh thing. Terrorism, even in Ireland, doesn't get the same support it did before the towers were hit.'

'What about the English terrorists?' Kathryn asked.

94

Hank rolled his eyes.

'How's that?' asked Marty.

'Haven't you ever heard of the famine?'

'The famine?' Marty asked.

'That was when the English tried to wipe out the whole Irish nation,' she said.

'Sorry. History ain't my thing,' Marty said, eyeing her in the rear-view mirror. He grinned. 'You ain't gonna be too popular round here with sentiments like that.'

Kathryn stared out of the window at the traffic, as if she gave a damn.

Hank knew where Kathryn was coming from and kept quiet.

'What's a bomb scare, Mommy?' Helen asked, sucking her thumb, trying hard to stay awake.

Hank leaned around from the front passenger seat and tucked the blanket up under her chin, snuggling her in. 'It's when people try and scare other people, honey. You warm enough, cuddles?' Helen nodded as her eyes spent more time shut than open.

'Anyone wanna grab a coffee or a bite?' Marty asked.

The little girls were already asleep. 'I'm okay. You okay?' Hank asked Kathryn.

'I'm fine,' Kathryn said, checking her watch.

'Dinner in Poole it is, then,' Marty said.

Kathryn did a quick calculation and decided that the wives' monthly get-together finished about four hours ago.

Three hours later they arrived in Corfe Mullen, a town a few miles inland from Poole, and pulled into a cul-de-sac in the middle of a large residential area built on a collection of hills. The adults climbed out leaving the children fast asleep. Hank and Kathryn stood on the pavement and looked up at the modern bungalow built on a sharp incline. It looked clean and maintained but nothing spectacular.

'I hope it's okay,' Marty said, worried Kathryn wouldn't like it. 'You can always change it,' he added.

Kathryn had no enthusiasm whatsoever. The driveway, just long enough to fit a car, was very steep and led up to a garage connected to the house. The garden wrapped tightly around the front and the entire building fitted snugly in between the houses either side with very little room to walk between them.

'What do you think, honey? It looks fine to me,' Hank said.

'It looks fantastic,' she said dryly.

'If you don't like it we'll grab a hotel, for Christ's sake,' Hank snapped. 'They have hotels in this town, don't they, Marty?'

Marty remained neutral.

Kathryn pulled a bag out of the vehicle. Marty held out the keys for Hank. 'The small one's the front door, the long one's the back. Why don't you dump your stuff inside and we'll head round to my place. Kate's got a real Southern home-cooked supper waiting for you guys. We live a couple blocks up the road. We've got a couple beds set up for you and the kids for tonight.'

Kathryn smiled politely at him in thanks, appreciating Marty's kindness.

Hank took the key as Kathryn headed up the steep incline. 'What time are you going to the base tomorrow?' he asked.

'You don't have to come in till next week,' Marty said. 'Take your time. Get settled in.'

'I'd like to get into it right away.'

'You're not scheduled to meet the boss till next Wednesday.'

'Maybe you can show me around, if you've got time.'

'If that's what you wanna do,' Marty said, seeing Kathryn waiting impatiently at the front door for Hank to open it. 'That's what I'm here for,' he said as he grabbed a bag and headed up the drive.

Hank was getting annoyed with Kathryn's attitude but told himself to stick to his guns and let her deal with her problems. He had a job to do and bright and early tomorrow was day one.

6

The morning was crisp and fresh as Marty drove Hank through Hamworthy, a small borough of Poole on the water, past the Yachtsman pub and up a hill flanked by homes shoulder to shoulder. Hank was having a yawning fit but did not let his jetlag hamper his enthusiasm. He had not been able to get to sleep before three a.m. and felt unusually tired when Marty woke him up at eight with a cup of coffee. When they left at eight-thirty Kathryn and the children were still fast asleep.

Hank was fascinated with the differences between his country and this one, from buildings to clothing, cars, shops, even the signposts. They passed one that indicated they were headed toward Rockly Sands Holiday Park.

'That the sea?' he asked catching a glimpse of yacht masts and an expanse of grey water between the houses.

'The harbour,' Marty said. 'Supposed to be the largest natural harbour in the world, or maybe in Britain, I forget which.'

'That a fact?'

'Most of it's too shallow for big boats – too much mud. Biggest goddamned mosquitoes you ever seen down on the south side. New SBS recruits get to sit in the bushes the first night and day wearin' nothin' but shorts and a T-shirt. Man, they get eaten' alive. It's the start of their hell week, like our buds.'

The road levelled out at the top of a hill. 'These houses are officers' quarters.' Marty indicated left and right like a tour guide. 'Those over there are for regular ranks.'

They passed a column of soldiers running along the road.

'Are those SBS guys?' Hank asked.

'No. They're regular Marines. The camp's mostly SB but there's a bunch of regulars: sailors, army, admin, cooks, transport, stuff like that . . . SB don't run in columns of three.'

They reached the end of the houses and a field large enough to fit four rugby pitches appeared on the right, the other side of a high-security fence. Beyond the field, three hundred yards away, was a cluster of buildings, nothing taller than three storeys. 'That's the camp,' Marty said.

Hank studied the base with interest as they drove parallel to it.

They turned a corner towards the main gate. Two Sea King Navy helicopters came into view, parked at the far end of the playing fields.

Marty pulled the car to a stop at the main gate, where an armed sentry wearing a green beret moulded to his head and combat clothing stepped out of a cubicle in the middle of the road to check his identity card. Hank watched another sentry the other side of the road waiting alongside a mirror lying face-up on wheels with lights attached in case he was needed to check beneath the vehicle.

'Hank? ID,' Marty said.

'Oh, sorry,' Hank said as he quickly searched for his ID. He pulled it out of his wallet and handed it to the guard, who checked the photo then Hank's face.

'Get used to my ugly mug,' Hank said with a grin. The guard remained expressionless as he handed back the card and signalled his partner to raise the barrier. Marty gave the guard a wave and drove slowly into the camp and along the main road that headed through the centre of the building complex.

They passed hangars, administration buildings and a flag-pole in the middle of a small green where the Union Jack lay motionless at the top. Hank looked down the side roads beyond the buildings that lined the main road, catching glimpses of lines of vehicles that included large jeeps camouflaged for desert with twin heavy calibre machine-guns mounted in the back. At the end of one road he saw several sleek, camouflage speedboats on trailers, also with twin machine-guns mounted behind the cockpits. The road curved to the right leaving the main hub of the camp behind and headed towards another, smaller collection of buildings, all looking quite new with several more under construction.

'A few years back SB only had a small piece of this camp. Now they damn near own all of it.'

'Are all of SB based here?' Hank asked.

'Hell, no. They're spread about the country like hen shit. They're always goin' or comin' back from somewhere.'

'A lotta missions?'

'Yeah. A lotta ops I guess.'

'What kinda ops?'

'Well, you know how it is. They're pretty secretive, obviously, just like us.'

'They don't tell you what's going on?'

'Well, depends what they're doing but you won't feel like an outsider,' Marty said, trying to find the right words. 'They've always made me feel at home, if you see what I mean.'

'So you get to know what's going on?' Hank asked, not catching Marty's attempt at subtlety.

'It's kinda like, well ... I'm not officially supposed to

know everything they get involved in, but . . . well . . . you virtually live on top of each other, and this ain't exactly a big organisation. I mean, like they're about a quarter our size. So you're gonna hear things you probably ain't supposed to. And they know that. It's kind've understood that what- ever you hear you keep under your hat, as they say.'

Hank nodded.

'The boss is a pretty cool guy – Colonel Hilliard,' Marty continued. 'You won't see much of him though. He spends most of his time in London or checking out operational areas.'

'What kinda stuff are they doing?' Hank asked.

'A lotta stuff.'

'Like what?'

Marty shrugged, reluctant to say any more. 'They go every- where.'

'Like where?' Hank persisted.

Marty sighed. 'They flew two minis out to South America last week, for instance.'

'Mini-subs?'

'One day a team's packin' jungle stuff, the next another's loadin' up arctic gear.'

'You get to go on any ops?'

Marty drove into a car park with a handful of cars in it and pulled into a space. He killed the engine and remained in the car, taking a moment to compose a reply. 'It's like this, Hank . . . We're over here to exchange knowledge with these guys and maintain a working relationship. As far as ops are concerned we're only supposed to get involved in things that come under NATO or the North Atlantic treaty – joint Anglo-US stuff, okay? Like Afghanistan and the Gulf, for instance.'

Hank nodded.

'If other stuff comes up, if you happen to be in the room when it's mentioned, you just shut the fuck up and stay in the background.'

'What kinda stuff?'

'Come on, Hank.'

'What's the problem? You said I'm gonna hear about it anyway. What kinda stuff?'

'Hank.'

'What am I, some kinda spy?'

'There's nothin' in particular. I'm just generalising here. Sometimes you run across something that ain't nothin' to do with the US.'

'You saying you get involved in these things sometimes?' Hank pushed, sensing there was room to dig a little deeper.

'I never said that.'

'But are you saying that? Come on, Marty. I'm gonna find out, right?'

Marty was reluctant to disclose any more detail but Hank was not going to let him off the hook easily. 'Okay. Yeah. Things can happen.'

'You get involved in ops.'

'Yeah. It's possible under the right circumstances to get involved in some ops. It pretty much depends on the situation, how you get on with the guys, the team boss especially. But generally there's no way. It'd be too risky if anything went wrong.'

'So how would you get on an op – just for instance?'

'Jesus, you don't give up, do you?'

'I'm just asking.'

Marty sighed. 'Well, supposing you were on an exercise with a team somewhere – the Far East for instance, and the balloon went up.'

'What balloon?'

'It's just an expression. Supposing there was a sudden real op emergency and you just happened to be with the team that had to respond. Maybe they can't leave you where you are or they can't get you back to the UK. So they take you along. They ain't technically supposed to, but there isn't much anyone can do. You're kinda stuck with 'em.'

Hank thought about that for a moment. 'So . . . you done anything like that?'

'I've been on a couple of short ops.'

'Like what?'

Marty shrugged. 'Stuff.'

'Come on, Marty. It ain't like we're on different sides,' Hank pleaded. 'I'm not gonna say anything to anyone, for Pete's sake. It's your job to let me know what goes on here.'

'I went on an op to Columbia.'

'Drugs?'

'Yeah.'

'But that's joint Anglo–US ops anyway.'

'Yeah, I guess.'

'What I'm talking about is, you know, other stuff. Their stuff,' Hank persisted.

'If I did I wouldn't say.' Marty was beginning to feel uncomfortable. Hank was about to complain, but Marty cut him off. 'Hey, look, Hank. You gotta respect the job, okay. There's a trust thing going on here.'

'What's the big deal? So what if you went on an op with these guys. I'm just interested, that's all. Christ, if you think I'm gonna blab it all over town then fine . . . '

Marty exhaled tiredly and gave in. 'I was on that Sierra Leone job last year against the West End boys.'

'No shit,' Hank said, impressed. 'You see any action?'

'I ran a couple re-supplies to the OP dive teams sitting in the river below the enemy camp. It was interesting. We

103

were outnumbered about twenty to one most of the time.'

'Were you there when the shit went down?'

'I was on the edge of it. We bagged a couple runners. I got to shed some lead.'

'You bagged someone?'

A smirk grew across Marty's face. 'I gotta strike.'

Hank gushed enthusiasm. 'Damn, that's great, man. You fucken bagged a motherfucker.'

'Yeah,' Marty said, grinning.

'That's fucken cool,' Hank said, momentarily lost in a daydream, suddenly wishing he had been on the last exchange instead of Marty.

'It was a good op, well planned and executed. One of the guys leapt out of the water just as the Paras and the SAS were flying in on the choppers, ran into a hut and took out six of 'em in one go.'

'No shit! Six?'

'That was nothin' compared to how many one team waxed at the jailbreak in Afghanistan. It must be some kinda record for an SF team.'

'I know. I was there,' Hank said.

'You were there?'

'Two days after it was all over . . . Where were you?'

Marty looked suddenly pissed off. 'At the friggin' airport, picking sandflies outta my butt. Sweet FA went on down there while the rest of the guys were running around Tora Bora rackin' up the rag-heads one after the other.'

They both sat in silence for a moment, depressed at their missed opportunities.

'Some guys get all the breaks, don't they?' Hank said. 'I always feel like I'm the one who gets left out, you know? I'm not lucky that way. It's like I don't push it enough.'

Marty nodded in sympathy. 'Yeah, sometimes you've gotta

make it happen,' he said as he opened his door. 'Let's go take a walk about.'

'Shit, I'd bust a gut to see some action while I was here,' Hank said.

Marty paused to look at him. 'Part of it is up to you. If they think you're a dud they'll leave you on the sidelines.'

Hank flashed him a look. 'Why would they think I was a dud?'

'All I'm saying is, don't push anything on to these guys. Let the marriage happen at its own pace. Okay? For sure you'll spend the first year in a training team taking selection courses, laying on demos, giving lectures, stuff like that. Then maybe after that they'll put you in one of the squadrons for some cross training.'

'Why would they stick me in a training team for a year?' Hank asked, not overjoyed at the prospect.

'It's what everyone does. I did a year before I joined M squadron. Training team is the best place to learn how they operate in general. It's cool. You'll enjoy it.'

Hank shrugged, trying to adopt a philosophical attitude.

'Trust me. It's a lotta fun,' Marty added, then offering him further consolation, 'Sometimes training team is the only team around and if an op comes along they can find themselves suitin' up.'

Hank nodded, looking a little more pleased about that. 'What are the negative things?' he asked.

'There's always negative things,' Marty said. 'They don't have the same cash flow we do. They're kinda poor compared to us. You lose a piece of kit for instance and you're paying for it if you don't have a good story. Can't just walk into the store like back home and say give me another.'

Hank shrugged. He could live with that.

'Come on,' Marty said, opening the door. 'It's a good

105

time to take a look around. A lot of the guys are away.'

As they headed across the camp Marty pointed out various buildings: the gymnasium, swimming pool, officers' and seniors' messes, the climbing towers and headquarters complex.

'You enjoyed your time here?' Hank asked.

'Yeah, pretty much. I'm lookin' forward to getting home though. I think Kate's gonna miss it more than me. She was hardly in Virginia a few months before we came here so she never made a lotta friends. After two years she's made a bunch of friends here.'

Marty glanced at Hank, something on his mind. 'Everything okay between you and Kathryn?'

Hank shrugged. 'Yeah,' he said.

'I don't mean to pry,' Marty said. 'Moving countries, especially with kids, can be tense.'

Hank glanced at him, wondering if he should give Marty an explanation for the day before. 'She'll settle in. She doesn't like being away from home.'

'I only asked because it's kinda important you don't have any problems on the home front. I mean, she's as much a part of the team as you are in a way. They hold the wives in pretty tight here. They're encouraged to support each other, especially when the guys are away. If a big op goes down they haul them all into the camp and brief them as much as they can. The guys can sometimes be away for months without being able to call home and what with the job being on the dodgy side . . .'

'Dodgy?' Hank asked.

'Dangerous. You'll pick up a lotta new lingo here too. We may speak the same language but I gotta tell ya, when I first got here I didn't understand half the goddamned things some of the guys said. They've got Scottish guys, northerners, cockneys. And they've all got their own slang. For instance, if you hear someone call out "septic", that means you.'

'Septic?'

'Septic tank – Yank. Cockney rhyming slang. They like to take the piss.'

'Piss?'

'Yank your chain. It's the way they are. At first I thought they didn't like me. Then I noticed they did it to each other just as much.'

Marty led Hank through a square that separated the accommodation buildings from the main galley complex. 'What I was saying about Kathryn though,' he went on, 'she's gotta be able to stand on her own feet. If you go away for a couple months it ain't gonna be cool if she's bangin' on the RSM's door asking where you are or wanting to go home 'cos she's unhappy.'

'She'll be fine. We've talked about it and she knows why we're here. She was just tired. I'm pretty sure the tough part's over with – that was getting her here.'

'Hey, Marty,' a man called out from across the square and made his way towards the two men.

'What's hap'nin', Dolesy?' Marty called back, then quietly aside to Hank, 'This guy's head of land ops training. A good guy. He may be your first boss.'

Doles arrived and shook Marty's hand. 'When's your leaving run?' he said in a light Scottish accent.

'Friday. You here for it?'

'Free beer, you kidding? I'll be there, pal,' he said with a grin. Doles was squat and strong with tough, chiselled features.

'This is Chief Munro. He's takin' over from me. Colour Sergeant Doles.'

'Pleased to meet you,' Doles said, offering his hand.

107

'Hank,' Hank said, shaking his hand firmly.

'Gotta run. Catch you later, Marty. Good to meet you, Hank. No doubt I'll be seeing you around,' he said as he headed away with a wave.

'Friendly guy,' Hank said.

'Yeah. Most of the guys are. I've gotten to know a lot of 'em pretty well. We do the barbeque thing quite a bit, stuff like that. Their kids play with ours – you know. Just like back home. And going away can be pretty fun too. These guys like their beer . . . From what I hear about you, you should get on like a house on fire. They can party when they want to.'

'That's not quite so true these days,' Hank said, playing it down. Marty didn't comment further.

They arrived at a large hangar at the top of the camp.

'This is C squadron hangar,' Marty said. 'They're away at the moment.'

He pushed open the heavy sliding door and went inside. The cavernous space was divided into several areas. Dozens of individual equipment storage cages lined one wall, racks of diving suits, underwater breathing apparatus, gas bottles and high-pressure pumps lined another. Several nine-cell parachutes hung from the ceiling and half-a-dozen snow-mobiles were parked in a corner beside various boxes of arctic equipment, tents and camouflage nets. Another area was home to a variety of specialised climbing equipment: harnesses, helmets, folding ladders and ropes, all neatly organised. Another stack of shelves contained communication and sundry electronics devices. A flight of stairs led up to several offices on a platform, which ran along one side of the hangar like train carriages.

'Upstairs are the boss and sergeant major's office, briefing room and ops room.'

'You worked here?'

'The last six months.'

'How many of these hangars do they have?' Hank asked.

'A few, all around the country.'

The main door opened. They turned to see a man walk in carrying a heavy backpack over one shoulder and a holdall in his other hand. It was Stratton. He ignored them as he walked to a cage, opened it, threw his gear inside, slammed the door shut, and headed back the way he had come.

'Who was that?' Hank asked.

'He arrived a couple days ago. I don't know him.'

'Man looked a little pissed.'

'I overheard some of the guys talkin'. He just got back from Northern Ireland. Something went wrong on an op and he was the fall guy, something like that. It was one of those conversations you overhear and don't ask about.'

Hank nodded and looked around the hangar. 'Like ours but smaller,' Hank said.

Marty checked his watch. 'You like tea?' Marty asked. 'Hot tea with milk and sugar?'

'Can't say I've ever tried it that way,' Hank said.

'Get used to it,' Marty said as he headed back to the main door. 'It's mandatory around here. You have to drink a cup every morning after your workout and it's the only drink you'll get when you're on the job.' Marty led Hank outside, closed the door, and walked across a small square towards a set of squat buildings. 'Nine a.m. is teatime every morning in the dive team. Just about every SB guy who's in the camp will show up there. It's a kind of unofficial daily meeting place. Which reminds me. I guess I should tell you some useful phrases you're gonna have to get to know, such as "the tea's wet".'

'The tea's wet.'

'Right. That means the tea is ready.'

Hank nodded. 'Tea's wet,' he said.

'If you're lucky you are known as a jammy bastard, as in jam.'

'Lucky?'

'A jammy bastard.'

'Jammy bastard,' Hank repeated.

'That's right. A knobber is like a wanker.'

'You're losing me.'

'Sorry. A wanker is a jerk.'

'Wanker is a jerk. Gotcha.'

'And so is knobber.'

'Knobber, right. And wanker.'

'Wanker and knobber, right. And a sporny-eyed waz-zack . . .'

'A sporny what?'

'That's team speak – maybe a tad advanced. Forget that for now. Kip means sleep: get some kip – go to sleep.'

'Kip,' Hank said.

'But if you're a kipper, you're a stinkin' two-faced dried fish . . .'

'Are there many of these?' Hank asked.

'Hundreds.'

'Oh, boy.'

'You'll get 'em,' Marty assured Hank as he led him into the diving equipment building and to the tea boat where a dozen SBS operatives were already partaking in a hot cuppa.

7

Kathryn stood outside Rushcombe infant school, a tidy establishment of some four hundred pupils set in the middle of residential Corfe Mullen. She was watching Helen and Janet walk towards the main entrance, each holding the hand of a teacher. Helen looked back and waved. Kathryn returned the wave and smiled but her smile faded as soon as the girls were out of sight.

The children had been very enthusiastic about the whole idea of a strange new school while they ate breakfast that morning, asking Kathryn endless questions. Kathryn had felt quite the opposite about it, however, and had not been able to sleep much the night before. Now that she was alone she felt even worse. It was as if she were without a purpose. Life, or what there was of it, would begin again when she picked up the children in the afternoon.

As she turned to walk back to her car she heard a woman's voice calling after her.

'Mrs Munro? Mrs Munro? . . . Kathryn?'

Kathryn stopped and turned around to see a neat, conservatively dressed woman in her mid-thirties beaming a smile and heading towards her energetically.

'Sorry to shout. I wasn't sure it was you at first,' the woman said. 'I heard you talking to your children before they went into school. We don't get too many Americans around here. It is Kathryn, isn't it?'

'Yes,' Kathryn said, quite coldly and without a smile.

'I'm Joan.' The woman continued to beam and held out a hand.

Kathryn took it limply. 'Are you a teacher?' she asked.

'Oh, God no. Sorry, I should've said. I'm the RSM's wife – RSM of the SBS. That's regimental sergeant major to you. Gosh, I don't know what the US Navy's equivalent would be. Master Chief I think. Anyway, he's the boss of all the non-commissioned officers. I arranged your accommodation and also the school for the girls.'

Kathryn nodded. 'I see. Well, thank you,' she said, wondering how she could get away without being obviously rude. The truth was Kathryn was not an impolite person and much as she had convinced herself she did not like these people she could not bring herself to openly show it.

'That sort of leaves me doing a kind of equivalent job amongst the wives,' Joan continued enthusiastically. 'How's it been, settling in?' she asked.

'Everything's fine,' Kathryn said, wanting to get away.

'I would've popped round to see you sooner but I thought I'd give you a couple of weeks to find your feet. I know how it is, moving to a new country. Dave – my husband, that is – and I did two years in Australia with the Australian SAS. It takes a bit of getting used to, but it'll seem like you've been here ages in just a few months.'

Kathryn wanted to say that it felt like a life sentence already.

'Don't worry about your girls. They'll be fine. I've instructed the headmistress to call me, as well as you of course, if they have the slightest difficulty settling in.'

'That's very kind,' Kathryn said, looking over at her car. 'I should be getting on. I've still got a pile of things to do.'

'Of course . . . Any time I can be of help, please let me

know,' Joan said, following her for a few yards. 'I just wanted to touch base and introduce myself.' Then remembering something she stopped and reached into her pocket. 'Oh, this is my phone number. If you need anything at all just call, any time. Perhaps we can get together during the week for tea.'

'Perhaps,' Kathryn said, taking the note and forcing one last smile before turning away. 'Bye.'

'Bye,' Joan echoed. She found Kathryn's reluctance to chat curious, but put it down to shyness and walked away in the opposite direction.

Joan was the first of the enemy to break through Kathryn's defences and have a conversation with her, brief though it was. Kathryn wished Joan had not been so damned pleasant. In the past two weeks Kathryn had succeeded in avoiding several wives who had tried to make contact. She didn't answer her phone unless she absolutely knew it was Hank or was expecting a call from the States, and never returned any of several messages she had received inviting her to take tea. Kathryn wished she could be much harder and tell them to their faces that she was not interested in socialising. But it was unnatural for her to be hurtful to a stranger who had done nothing to deserve it, even being born English. In fact she was experiencing an internal conflict, part of her wanting to reconcile this national hatred she had been brainwashed with since childhood. She knew there was some truth to Hank's accusation that her unhappiness had nothing to do with the English and that it was all down to being away from home and her friends.

She opened the car door and immediately cursed herself as she slammed it and walked around to the other side where the steering wheel was. She wondered how long she would keep doing that.

* * *

Hank sat in the Land Tactics Training Team office, his feet stretched out in front of him on a desk. He was dressed in his crisp, ironed, green Navy SEAL fatigues, his name stencilled in bold black letters over his left breast. He was reading a lecture pack, one of a pile of manila folders stacked beside his shiny, black leather calf-length boots. To get a better look at the diagram on an overhead projector transparency he raised it up to the crisp, morning sunlight coming in through the large windows that took up nearly the whole of one wall. The other three windowless walls were covered in various maps and collages ranging over a plethora of military subjects, such as land navigation, booby-traps, explosives formulas and survival techniques. The team was responsible for the training of all things to do with Special Boat Service procedures out of water. Seated at the largest of the three desks, writing a report, was Colour Sergeant Doles; Corporal Bob Clemens sat at his desk by the window reading a newspaper and sipping a mug of tea. It was all very quiet and sunny. The diagram Hank was studying showed several star formations – the Plough, Cassiopeia and Orion – and indicated how to use them to locate the North Star.

He placed the transparency back in the folder, put the file on top of the pile he had already looked through, and took the next one from the larger pile he had yet to read. This next pack was well used, the tattered folder barely holding together at the corners. He thumbed through the introduction on the subject of explosive linear cutting charges and turned to a sheet with a list of various mathematical formulas for plastic explosives. Hank sighed. Mathematics was not his best subject.

'Do I have to memorise all these calculations?' Hank asked Doles.

'No. You just have to be able to teach 'em,' Doles said in his soft Scottish twang without looking up.

'Just teach 'em, Hanky boy, just teach 'em,' Clemens echoed loudly in an American accent, also without looking up from his newspaper.

Hank stared at Clemens, a square-jawed, powerfully built rugby enthusiast, wondering if the man disliked him or just specialised in a witless version of the so-called dry British humour. It seemed to Hank that every time Clemens said something to him it was in a condescending Texas accent, and a very bad one at that. And why Texas? Hank wondered. He was from North Carolina, and Clemens from somewhere in south-west England, a 'janner pig' as Doles often referred to him.

Hank took a quiet break from the lecture packs and looked through the windows. Autumn had taken a firm grip and the air was moist. The slight breeze had a whiff of rotting sea vegetation that suggested the wind was coming from the south where the beach was only five hundred yards away. The training office, which was quite small considering its responsibilities, the subjects it covered and the various training aides that needed to be stored in it, was situated in a small, mature-conifer wood about two acres in size near the back gate of the camp. Just outside the office, intertwining and connecting over a dozen of the tall pine trees, was a Tarzan course of ropes, wire ladders and cables. It was originally built for the maritime anti-terrorist teams years ago when they were first formed. The men had used it in their daily workout ritual to maintain a high degree of upper body strength and endurance in preparation for the endless training exercises around the world scaling oil platforms and large ships. As the maritime teams grew in size and expertise they moved to a more spacious, purpose-built location.

The Tarzan course passed into the hands of the training team, who retained its nickname 'the pain pines' and used it to beast the SBS selection courses, and any other military personnel for that matter, foreign or otherwise, who visited the unit to get a taste of how it operated.

The team, just the three of them at the moment due to a shortage of operatives and a quiet period as far as training was concerned, ran together every morning at eight o'clock for several miles and always finished with a round of pull-ups and dips and sometimes a couple of shifts up the thirty-foot ropes. The workouts were generally relaxed affairs with nothing too strenuous, which was the norm for training teams, although on occasion the competitive spirit raised its head and a run ended in a sprint finish. It was up to the individual to maintain his fitness and it was dimly looked upon if a reasonable standard was not maintained. Hank fitted well into the team fitness wise. Over five miles he was faster than Clemens but not as fast as Doles, who was lighter on his feet. Clemens was about equal with Hank on the ropes, where they could both manage five arms-only shifts up the thirty-foot lengths without a rest in between. It was in the swimming pool or the old quarry lake on the heath half a mile away that Hank had them both beat. He was a powerful swimmer and thrashed them easily over any distance including under the water.

Doles was only just past his peak in SBS terms. That meant he could get involved in all aspects of operations except the more strenuous activities such as climbing oil platforms. He was a swimmer-canoeist grade one and qualified to instruct and supervise every aspect of operational training, including diving, climbing, explosives and weapons. Clemens had been in eight years and could be described as reliable with stacks of enthusiasm when focused. He was preparing for his own senior instructor's course at the end of the year, which would eventually qualify him to run his own team. Hank was disappointed when he learned he was to be on the same course, a comprehensive, intensive four months of lessons and supervisor training. It would no doubt be useful and he'd learn something but he didn't think it would help his promotion prospects back home; more importantly, it would take a good size chunk out of his time in the UK, which he thought could best be spent in an operational team.

Hank lowered his legs from the desk and flexed his knees. They ached a little and were stiff from the morning run, which he put down to the cold, damp weather he was not used to.

He was feeing bored and wondered when the team was going to start some work. He had done nothing since joining but read lectures and SBS standard operational procedures, go on long drives to get acquainted with the various local training sites, and do a couple of dives in the harbour to keep his diving minutes in date. It was an unusually quiet period according to Doles. The next SBS selection course was not due to start for another two months and the team was waiting to find out what they would be doing until then. Doles suggested Hank lap up the peace and quiet while he had the chance. Once the work started he would have very little down time. Hank didn't particularly care about having little down time. He was here to work and that's what he wanted to do.

The door opened and Lieutenant Jardene leaned inside. 'Sergeant Doles,' he said in his usual calm, polite manner.

'Sir,' Doles replied, looking up from his writing but not standing.

'Step outside a minute, would you?' Jardene asked.

Hank liked Jardene. He had one of those toffee-nosed

Brit accents that most of the officers had. Rumour had it he had the education and pedigree to go all the way up. Apparently his father was an army brigadier and his older brother a navy commander. Jardene was fit, fresh faced, direct and intense to talk to, not that Hank had had many conversations with him. Jardene was in overall command of SBS training and therefore Hank's direct boss. He was the first to welcome Hank to the team with genuine enthusiasm and said how much he hoped Hank would gain as much from his stay as he gave. It made Hank feel even more determined to do well.

Hank watched Jardene and Doles through the window. Jardene was doing most of the talking while Doles nodded with a look of deep concentration. Whatever they were talking about looked important.

The conversation lasted no more than a minute and on completion Jardene headed away. Doles opened the door and leaned in. 'Bob,' he said and indicated for Clemens to come outside. Clemens had also sensed something was up and moved quickly. Doles closed the door behind him.

Hank watched Doles talk with the same intensity as Jardene. After a few minutes Clemens walked briskly away. Doles then stepped back into the office and sat back down at his desk.

Hank lifted another lecture pack off the pile, put his feet back up on to the desk, and thumbed through the pages, although he was unable to concentrate on them. Something was in the air and he wanted to be included but he knew that he had to act as if he was politely keeping his nose out of it. If they wanted to include him, they would.

He flicked through the lecture pack notes but could not keep from glancing over at Doles, who was leafing through a file. Doles seemed to find what he was looking for, jotted something on a notepad, tore out the page and left the room.

As Doles walked away Hank got up and went to the window to watch him. Doles headed up a well-worn path through the trees and out on to the road that lead to headquarters.

Hank went back to the desk and slumped into his chair. He tossed the lecture pack down, a tad frustrated, impatient to get involved, and flexed his legs, searching around the aching kneecap for the source of the pain. He checked his watch. Lunch was in an hour. If no one returned in another thirty minutes he decided he would head over to the mess.

He thought about giving Kathryn a call, looked at the phone on Doles's desk and changed his mind. He had nothing new to tell her anyway, that's if she even answered the phone. He knew she was screening her calls in case a wife telephoned. Her attitude was beginning to irritate him. He blamed her mother, whom he never got along with, not from the first time Kathryn had brought him to the family home in Boston. He considered her to be an overbearing bully who thought far too highly of herself. But even though she no longer had a direct influence on her daughter the damage was already done. Hank could only hope Kathryn would find one English person she liked enough to start turning her around. The growing instability between them worried him. He had hoped the atmosphere might have mellowed but things were as bad as the first day they arrived in England. It seemed a long time ago since they were at peace with each other. And it wasn't all her fault. He'd been under a new strain of pressure the past few years; he'd reached that point in his career when the future was uncertain. The pyramid of promotion was getting narrower and more guys were competing for fewer jobs. Those left on the sidelines

119

could count the days to civvy street. Hank had tried to put it out of his mind but the pressure was on to lay on a damn good performance with these guys.

Doles walked past the window and stepped back into the office, followed a few seconds later by Stratton. Hank recognised him from that first day in the hangar with Marty. Stratton did not acknowledge him and joined Doles to pore over one of the many maps pinned to the walls.

'They said we could use area "A",' Doles said, following the boundary line of a piece of countryside with his finger.

'We'll also need "E",' Stratton said, pointing to an adjacent expanse of land. 'I need the town.'

'When I asked about those areas they said 22 were using E and F.'

'I need E and the connecting road to A,' Stratton insisted, jabbing his finger on a circular road that ran through both of the areas. 'Call 'em and tell 'em we need it.'

'But they're just going to tell me the same thing.'

'Did you say the magic word?'

'No, because I don't know the magic word,' Doles said with a hint of sarcasm.

'Op Phoenix.'

'Can I use that over the phone?'

'Use the secure phone. Look, we have priority. Trust me, we'll get anything we want on this one.'

'But you don't know what it's about.'

'No, but I know who it's from,' Stratton said.

'Then they know what it's about. I mean, Phoenix was put together today, right?'

'They won't know. But when they make the confirmation call to DSF they'll be told to give Phoenix priority. You know what the SAS are like. They always get upset when we get the big jobs instead of them. You'd think they'd

120

be used to it by now.' Stratton headed for the door. 'I'll get a stores list to you by this afternoon,' he said as he opened it.

'Oh, Stratton?' Doles said, remembering something. 'Be handy if I could sort out accommodation soon as poss. Got any idea on numbers?'

Stratton did a quick calculation in his head. 'There'll be eight from M. Clemens, you and me, that's eleven, plus two drivers, a cook and a storeman. I want to use the bashers in quadrant A. Once we get into the camp we're pretty much staying there, okay?'

'And you don't know how long for.'

'Nope.'

'That might be a problem if—'

'The magic word,' Stratton interrupted with a smile, one old friend to another. He winked and then left.

Doles sat at his desk and scribbled some notes. 'I like magic words,' he said to himself.

Hank had been watching and listening but went back to thumbing through the lecture pack as Stratton left. Doles paused to look up at Hank as if just realising he was there. His gaze lingered on Hank while he thought about something. Hank looked up at Doles, who remained staring at him. Hank went back to his file, wondering what Doles was thinking. Doles picked up the phone and dialled a number.

'Sir. Doles here,' he said. 'What do you want to do with the attached rank? . . . Yeah.' There was a long pause while Doles listened. Hank also waited for the reply, hoping he was the attached rank in question, even though he had no idea what for. 'We've got odd numbers at the moment. He'll even them up,' Doles said. 'That would help for some of the serials.' There was another pause as Doles listened. 'No reason why it should be a problem,' he said. Then after listening

121

for a moment longer he said with finality, 'Okay,' and put down the phone.

Hank kept his eyes fixed on the lecture notes, waiting for Doles to say something, but he was silent for what seemed an age. Hank became anxious that it wasn't him they had been talking about.

'Hank,' Doles said finally.

Hank looked up with an expression of nonchalance. 'Huh?'

'The team's on a warning order to move in less than twenty hours. We're joining another team from M to beat up for an operation. The boss said if you want to come along for the training phase it's okay by him.'

Hank shrugged. 'Sure. Sounds great.'

'It's an isolation. Do you know what that means?'

'Once we go in no one comes out or communicates with the outside world till the op's completed.'

'After the team is debriefed on completion.'

'That's fine by me.'

'Don't you want to know how long it could be for?'

'No . . . When the job's done, I guess.'

'What about the wife and kids?'

'Not a problem.'

Doles liked the answer. 'We leave tomorrow morning,' he said. 'All you need to bring are civvy clothes. No military stuff whatsoever: watch straps, things like that. You'll need your ID card. No smart clothes. Jeans and T-shirt routine, things you don't mind getting damaged. There'll be laundry facilities. You can tell friends and family you're going to Scotland on an exercise for a couple of weeks. That's what your wife will be told if she calls the camp. Bring some beer money in case but you won't need much else otherwise.' Doles checked his watch. 'You might as well head home for the day. Bob can take care of stores by himself. Be here by seven for a seven-thirty departure.'

Hank picked up all the lecture packs and put them back in the filing cabinet. 'Can I ask where we're going, or do I wait 'n' see?' he asked.

'I can tell you where the training camp is. It's in Wales. The actual op location is secret. I don't even know where it is or what the job is.'

Hank nodded as he picked up his cap and smoothed the starched edges. 'I haven't been to Wales,' he said.

'Hank?' Doles said, stopping him as he reached the doorway. 'You're only going for the training.'

'Whatever,' Hank said with a smile. 'Just glad to be doing something.'

'I think you'll enjoy it.'

'I look forward to it. See you tomorrow,' Hank said as he closed the door.

As he headed through the wood towards the car park, Hank felt uplifted, despite Doles's assurance he would not get on the op itself. He had been in England just two weeks and was already going on operational training. That wasn't a bad start, he decided. Who knew where it could lead?

8

Hank sat in the second of two unmarked Range Rovers as they crossed the Severn Bridge in close file and passed into Wales. Doles sat in front alongside the driver, in a thick arctic duvet jacket. Apart from Clemens and Doles, Hank didn't know the other three operatives in his vehicle. In fact the only other person he knew was Stratton, who was in the other Rover, although he had not as yet exchanged a word with him. The men's personal baggage, all military backpacks and holdalls, were stuffed into the back of each Rover. Whatever equipment they needed for the training was apparently already at the secret camp they were headed for, the unmarked stores lorry carrying food, weapons and ammunition having left Poole before dawn.

Everyone had been pretty quiet throughout the trip, most sleeping. Hank had stayed awake. He was sticking to his game plan of staying in the background, remaining the grey man. He had overheard that the mysterious camp was named Ilustram and was designed and built for Special Forces use only. Its location was classified. The team was hoping to get at least a week of intensive training in before individuals were selected for the mission. Whatever that was he still had no idea. He suspected most of the others didn't know either. If they did then it was down to their 'need to know' – and Hank did not need to know. There was no sense of excitement.

A short distance after the bridge the vehicles turned off the motorway and on to a minor road that cut through the countryside. Hank was content to take in the sights; the scenery became quite beautiful as the road began to meander, shadowing the course of a river that followed a wide valley.

An hour after leaving the river valley, as Hank started to nod off, the Rover came to a stop. He looked up drowsily to see that the front vehicle had halted at a barrier outside a guardhouse and he shook off his tiredness. A civilian police officer was talking to Stratton through the passenger window. Hank looked around, wondering if this was Ilustram. They were still in the countryside, surrounded by trees, with fields visible beyond. A hundred yards or so behind the guardhouse was a cluster of new office-style brick buildings. A high-security fence stretched in opposite directions from the guardhouse barrier. There were no signs to indicate that it was the entrance to an army camp.

A minute later the police officer raised the barrier and waved the vehicles through. Hank looked into the guardroom as they passed it and saw several more policemen inside. If it was a military camp, he wondered, why were there no soldiers on guard?

The Rovers passed through the neatly manicured complex where half-a-dozen cars were parked in front of the buildings. There was no sign of life. A few hundred yards the other side of the complex the new tarmac road gave way to a dirt track and they headed into open countryside.

They followed the security fence for a mile before veering away to drive through wide open fields.

As they approached a small wood Hank saw the outline of several three-storey buildings within it. They were plain concrete structures resembling unfinished office blocks that had been on fire recently. There were no windows, doors or wooden frames in any of the openings. A couple of battered cars parked off the side of the track leading to the buildings were riddled with bullet holes.

Further on, the other side of the road, a dozen men were dressed in black assault clothing, all armed with submachine-guns and wearing chest harnesses. Gasmasks hung from their hips. Beyond them, surrounded by a high earthwork, was a civilian passenger aircraft that looked like it had not been airworthy for many years. Scorch marks surrounded many of the doors and windows. More armed men were exiting the aircraft down a ladder. The men by the road watched the Rovers as they passed.

'There's old Geordie Marshal,' Clemens said.

'G Squadron,' said Doles.

SAS, Hank thought. The SBS didn't do aircraft and there was only one other SF unit in the country that did. Hank watched them through the back window until they were out of sight.

A mile further on a handful of long, narrow brick huts in parallel rows came into view. They looked as if they had been built during the Second World War. Hank recognised the unmarked truck parked alongside the end hut as the stores wagon from Poole. The Range Rovers pulled off the track and parked behind it.

The men stepped out, stretching and yawning, some lighting up cigarettes. Hank stepped out and took in the scenery. It was a bright, cloudless day with a slight chill in the air. Some trees dotted the immediate area, otherwise it was open fields in every direction. He thought he could hear gunfire in the distance carried on a breeze that suddenly picked up and rustled the brittle leaves on a nearby pair of oaks. As he focused on the sound he was interrupted.

'Listen up,' Doles said in a raised voice as he climbed out

the front of his vehicle, holding a clipboard. Everyone stopped talking and faced him. 'This is building one,' he said, pointing to the first building on the road. 'It'll be the admin staff basher and stores. Building two, the next one over if you hadn't guessed, is the galley. Building three, SBS accommodation. Four is showers and heads.' He checked his watch. 'Time now is ten twelve. Let's get everything unloaded. Sort out your beds. Grab a brew and muster here for twelve-thirty ready to go.'

'What's the first serial?' one of the men asked.

'If you don't interrupt, Jackson, I'll get to it.'

Someone nudged Jackson in the back. 'Yeah, shut it, Jackson,' a voice said playfully.

Doles moved right along. 'Today will be pistols and SMGs on the range. Before dark the aim is to fit in some car and van drills. Lunch will be nosebags. Dinner whenever we get back.'

Hank observed the men as Doles spoke. Most of them seemed young, between twenty-two and twenty-six he guessed.

'There'll be no specific teams,' Doles continued. 'Those will be nominated as and when required. You'll draw weapons at . . . eleven?' he said, looking directly at the quartermaster for confirmation. 'You keep your pistols with you until we leave here. They will be on your person at all times and, gentlemen, they will remain loaded with one up the spout, even when you're asleep. I don't need to warn you that any NDs – that's negligent discharges for our non-English speaking guest – and you will be looking for a new career. The serials will be worked out day-by-day, hour-by-hour if need be, so remain flexible. Keep your shit together, move like greased lightning when you're told to, and I don't want to hear any stupid questions. Are there any questions?'

There were none.

'Clemens?' Doles continued. 'You'll look after Hank and familiarise him with any kit and routine he's not au fait with.' He then shifted his gaze to Hank. 'You happy with everything so far?'

'Not a problem,' Hank said.

'Good.' Then louder to everyone, 'Back here twelve-thirty, weapons cleaned and ready to go.' Doles walked over to Stratton, who was standing alone across the track, and the two men walked away.

Hank faced Clemens, who was looking directly at him, wearing one of his weird, big-mouthed smirks whereby he let his unusually long tongue protrude from his mouth to touch the tip of his nose. 'Come on, Hanky boy,' Clemens said. 'Let's git yarll kitted up and on the trail.'

Hank wondered if Marty had been given a jerk like Clemens when he first arrived.

The packs were tossed out of the back of the Rovers and everyone grabbed their own and headed for the accommodation building.

Inside the squat hut it was one long, cold, damp room with a concrete floor and narrow metal beds spaced out along both sides, each separated by a grey metal locker. On a table by the entrance was a stack of clean sheets, pillowcases, blankets and pillows. Hank took Clemens's lead, grabbed a set, and followed him in to the room.

'Grab any pit you want, Hanky boy,' Clemens said, tossing his pack and bedding on to a bed.

Hank took the bed opposite and dropped his pack on the floor. He opened the circa WWII locker, which was empty but for a couple of twisted wire coat hangers hanging on a bent rail.

'Hank?'

Hank looked around the locker door at Clemens, who was holding up what looked like a large tube of toothpaste.

'Know what this is?' Clemens asked, tossing the tube to Hank. Hank looked it over but did not recognise the chemical contents. He shrugged at Clemens.

'Last time I was here everyone caught crabs, from the beds, or the sheep shagging after hours. I suggest you have a good scrub down with that stuff before you go home otherwise the missus will wonder where you've been.' Clemens flapped his oversized tongue and grinned as he winked at Hank and went back to sorting out his kit.

Hank placed the tube in his locker and looked down at his stained and lumpy mattress. He had slept on worse. He detected movement outside the metal-framed window above his bed. It was Stratton and Doles in the narrow gap between the buildings. They were talking. Stratton sensed Hank's stare and looked at him. Doles also noticed Hank and the two men moved on. Hank had the distinct feeling they had been discussing him.

The vehicles left the buildings at the precise time Doles had stipulated, with everyone aboard. The shooting range was another secluded spot surrounded by fields and pockets of woodland. Hank climbed out along with the others and helped carry the boxes of ammunition through the entrance.

It was a rudimentary construction with no buildings inside other than a simple concrete shelter to house the boxes of ammunition and targets in the event of rain. It was an open-air, rectangular arena with an entrance wide enough for a vehicle to drive through. The sides were steep earth embankments down to a knee-high sandbag wall all around the inside. It was designed so that targets could be placed and engaged anywhere within it. The embankment curved around the entrance so that bullets could not escape through it unless, obviously, fired into the sky.

'Listen up!' Doles commanded as he walked into the range. 'Load up your pistol magazines only. Grab a target and find yourself a space. Some of you may not have shot close-quarter pistol in a wee while. This first practice is to shake the rust off and get the feel of your weapons. Start off with some dry drills, then in your own time I want you to practise drawing from your holsters, single-handed as well as two-handed; standing and kneeling, no rolling around on your backs or bellies unless you've been shot; empty magazine and reload drills; close-quarter techniques holding the weapon into the body. All firing positions will be static and no further than three metres from your target. No firing on the move. All shots will be double-taps, no leaping about, and be mindful of the persons beside you. Any questions?' then without waiting half a second for a response, 'Carry on!'

Hank tagged on behind the others, picked up a box of 9mm rounds and selected a figure eleven target: a man-size torso papered on to a thin wooden board with a stick nailed to the back. Everyone selected their own small area of embankment; Hank chose a far corner and headed across to it. He stuck the target into the earth, just behind the low sandbag wall, placed the box of rounds on the sandbag wall, and removed the Sigmaster P226 9mm semi-automatic pistol he had been given by the admin sergeant from the leather shoulder holster he was wearing under his jacket. He released the empty magazine, took two more from a quick-release hip holder, and proceeded to load them. Within a few minutes Hank was dry practising: drawing his weapon from his holster and coming up on aim without firing to get the feel of it. It had been several months since Hank last held a pistol.

'No shooting from the hip, Hanky boy,' Clemens called

out from a few yards away, grinning like a moron. 'This ain't the OK Corral, pardner.'

Hank ignored him and carried on practising a double-handed technique from the draw. Satisfied, he cocked the weapon and pushed it firmly into his holster. No one else had started firing yet. Hank didn't mind being the first. He felt comfortable enough and was a competent shot with a pistol. He relaxed his shoulders letting his arms hang loosely by his sides, composing himself. A sudden and deafening boom made him flinch as the man beside him a few feet away fired off two rounds in quick succession. The shock was painful to Hank's ears and he cursed his own forgetfulness.

''Urt yer ears, Hanky boy?' Clemens cackled.

Hank walked back across the range to the stores shelter and picked up a pair of ear defenders. By now everyone else was firing as he placed them over his ears and went back to his stance. With everyone wearing rugged civilian clothing it looked more like a terrorist training camp than a Brit military one.

Hank lined up in front of his target, composed himself once again, drew his weapon, fired a double-tap, and replaced the weapon into the holster in a smooth action. He didn't feel a hundred per cent comfortable but that was to be expected. His actions would be smoother after he had emptied a few magazines. Hank had been brought up with guns. As a kid he regularly went hunting with his buddies, often camping overnight, shooting squirrels, rabbits and prairie dogs. He drew again, quicker this time, and fired another double-tap into the target. He felt a little better and closed his mind to the activity around him as he drew and fired again.

★　★　★

131

By the time Hank had emptied two boxes of ammunition a car screeched into the range and came to a dusty halt in the centre.

'Cease fire!' Doles shouted as he climbed out. 'Anyone here not done car drills before?'

Hank looked around. No one else had a hand raised. He raised his. Doles nodded to him and addressed the others. 'We'll start with two-man drills, then when everyone's gone through we'll go to four-man,' he said. 'Choose your partners. Hank, you hang back until everyone else has gone through then you can jump in with Clemens, okay? Nice and easy first time please, gentlemen,' he said louder, addressing everyone. 'Control, control, control. Make sure you are clear of the man in front of you before you raise your weapon. Take down all the targets and place a cluster of three or four along the back wall,' he said pointing to the far end of the range. 'I want to see you driving in at speed. When you hear gunshots it means you have been engaged. Halt. Debus, and engage your targets. Clear the vehicle soon as you can: remember the vehicle is the initial focus of incoming fire. I'll give you a ceasefire and the next couple take it away. We don't have much time and we have a lot to get through. Oh, yes, and anyone puts a hole in this car it's a fifty pound fine, understood? Except you, Jackson. I'll take a hundred quid for each hole you put in one.'

'Understood, Colours,' Jackson said as everyone else laughed, sharing a joke Hank was not party to.

'First pair, let's go!' Doles shouted as he clapped his hands.

Targets were grabbed, a handful was placed at the far end in a bunch, and everyone headed to the back of the range except the first two operatives, who jumped into the car.

'In case you didn't notice, Dolesy is real sensitive about putting holes in cars,' Clemens said to Hank with a grin as

132

they stacked the used targets. 'A couple years ago there was about fifty of us up 'ere doing car drills and Jackson was sent back to the HQ to pick up another car. God knows how but the idiot somehow went and picked up Doles's thinking it was one of the company training cars. Dolesy was on another part of the range at the time. No one realised the cock-up till the next day when Dolesy went to get his car to head on home. There were about fifty bullet holes all over it.'

Jackson overheard Clemens and joined in the conversation, grinning. 'He went fuckin' banzi,' he said. 'I 'ad to 'ide in the bleedin' woods till he left.'

Joe, the tallest of the operatives and one of the youngest, chimed in. 'Wasn't he stopped about five times by the cops on the way home?'

Clemens chuckled. 'Yeah. He must've looked like he'd just been in a bank robbery or summit.'

'His missus went nuts en'all when she saw it,' said Jackson. By now others had joined them to revisit the story, adding and embellishing what they knew. Hank found himself in the middle, looking at each person as they talked, laughing with everyone else.

Brent, a well-spoken southern English boy, added what he knew. 'Doles had no end of trouble trying to get it fixed. None of the repair shops would touch it for less than fifty quid a hole or something like that.'

'And what about his wife though,' Jeff said. Hank had to listen carefully to understand everything this young operative said in his northern accent. 'She kept driving it since they had no other car and everywhere she went she was having to explain what had happened to it.'

'He eventually sold it to a skinhead,' said Clemens. 'The bloke actually came up to Dolesy and asked him how much he wanted for it. He thought it was brilliant.'

As the story grew in richness Hank went from grinning to laughing as loud as anyone else. It felt good. It seemed a long time since he had last laughed out loud.

'You want some advice, Hank. Don't do any car drills with Jackson,' Jeff offered.

'And if you do,' Joe added, 'make sure you're in the back. He's a dangerous bastard.'

'Piss off,' said Jackson.

'You won't see anyone else rushing to be his partner,' said Brent.

While the serials took place and couples swapped to take their turn in the car, Hank was engaged in one conversation after another, answering questions about SEAL operatives some of the men knew personally and swapping stories, only pausing to watch when the car flew into the range and the occupants leaped out to shoot at the targets. For the first time since arriving in the UK the ice was starting to break for Hank. Much as he wanted to remain the grey man, he could not contain the born extrovert within him for long. If he ever wondered why he wanted to stay in the military, it was times such as this that reminded him why: he revelled in the company of soldiers. This most natural and rewarding fellowship was a mystery to many men and all women. It transcended borders and nationalities; Hank was American to be sure, but he knew he was going to feel at home in England with these men.

Hank lay in bed that night feeling tired but not sleepy. It had been a good day. They had returned from the range well after dark and supper had been late. There was little in the way of interesting conversation during the meal. Everyone seemed tired. Most people thinned out to their beds soon after to read or sleep. The clouds that had covered the sky throughout the day had gone without unloading their moisture and the moonlight flooded in through the bare, cobweb-laced windows.

Hank was thinking about the day's shooting and how much he had enjoyed it. Clemens had thrown him a curve by asking him to drive on his first four-man serial. But Hank was a competent driver and won a 'well done' from Doles after he stopped the car with a handbrake turn that placed its flank square on to the targets allowing the front and rear passengers on that side to open fire immediately. Even Clemens had warmed to him as the day went on and had virtually ceased talking to him in a Texan accent, and when he did, it no longer sounded as if he was trying to jive him.

As Hank drifted off to sleep he wondered what Kathryn was doing and how the girls had got on with school that day. He wished he could have spoken to her and told her about the day's events. He pulled the blanket tighter around him, feeling the chill as his body cooled. He thought about getting up to fetch an extra blanket but decided he would put up with it for the time being. He wondered what the next day might bring. He was sure that whatever it was, he would do as well as the best of these guys. It was the most confident he had felt since arriving in UK.

The following morning, after breakfast, the operatives were driven in the two Rovers to another part of the vast training area. Hank had expected a workout before starting the day but with breakfast at six and a six-thirty a.m. move it had not been practical. During breakfast he noticed no one else had shaved and he was also the only person in a clean shirt. Everyone seemed to be wearing the same scruffy clothes they had worn the day before. As soon as he finished

135

his meal he went back to his locker and put on his old clothes.

As the Rovers pulled to a stop on the dirt track Hank could see Stratton waiting up ahead beside two civilian cars. Any speculation as to what this next phase of training could be was met with shrugs of ignorance. They had been told to bring nothing, other than their loaded pistols of course.

The vehicles slowed to a stop and everyone climbed out. The clouds had returned and it had rained briefly during breakfast, filling the air with the rich smell of earth. The men gravitated towards Stratton.

'Close in,' he said, keeping his hands in the pockets of his old leather jacket, his collar turned up against the slight breeze, which was noticeably colder than the day before. 'I call this next phase character drills. It's simple and straight-forward. You will be in pairs, driving in this vehicle. One pair at a time will drive off from here and follow a course that has been set out for you. The car will be returned here on completion of the journey and the next pair will head off. Everyone will take part. The scenario is this: you are undercover operatives in Northern Ireland. You're heading across country to carry out a recce. You do not have commu-nications with headquarters or anyone else. In the car is a sketch of the route you will follow. It's not a complicated route. Anyone who gets lost shouldn't be in the boy scouts, never mind the SBS.'

Hank noticed the difference in the men when Stratton addressed them. No one made a comment or looked anywhere other than directly at him. Stratton had charisma for sure, but there was something else. It was not just that he was the team leader, or that he was intolerant of anyone not paying full attention. There was something about his demeanour, the way he moved and the way he looked a person in the eyes. When he spoke you listened. Hank felt there was still something else though. He couldn't put his finger on it, but if he were pushed to describe what he felt he would have to say there was a darkness about Stratton.

'You'll cover a distance of approximately two miles,' Stratton continued. 'Drive normally, as you would without attracting undue attention to yourselves. During the journey there will be incidences. You will react to them as a member of Her Majesty's internal security forces. At the end of the day, undercover operatives, special forces, whatever your job description, you are officers of the law and must abide by the rules that apply to every other member of the internal security force working in Northern Ireland.' Stratton handed a sheet of paper to Brent. 'Those are the driving pairs in the order they will follow. I don't expect any questions because I've given you all the information you need. First pair will depart precisely on the half-hour . . . in eleven minutes.'

Stratton climbed into one of the Rovers and the two cars drove away up the road.

Everyone crowded around Brent to find out who they would be with.

Clemens left the huddle and joined Hank. 'You're with me,' he said. 'We're last.' Hank could not be sure but he thought Clemens seemed nervous.

The first pair was gone some forty minutes before the car returned, driven by one of the Rover drivers and otherwise empty. He parked it, turned off the engine, climbed out, leaving the keys in the ignition, and without a word walked away across an open stretch of ground towards a line of trees, through which he disappeared. Everyone noticed the car had a few extra dents on it. The next pair climbed in and drove away up the road. The three remaining pairs sat back and waited.

An hour and a half later, after another pair had gone, a different vehicle arrived, driven by the other staff driver, who dropped off four brown paper lunch bags. Clemens took one and handed another to Hank, who was sitting under a tree across the track.

'You ever do any civvy stuff like this?' Clemens asked as he sat down on the grass and made himself comfortable.

'Nope,' Hank replied as he looked inside the bag.

Clemens squinted inquisitively into his bag, took out a sandwich bound in cellophane and unravelled it. He inspected between the slices, looked unimpressed, closed them and took a big bite from it.

The circuit car returned and the staff driver climbed out and headed for the wood, again without saying a word. The last pair before Hank and Clemens put their lunch in their pockets, climbed in and drove away.

The earlier breeze had dropped off and the heavy grey clouds had made it perceptibly darker. Hank wondered if they would dump their load or move on. He tuned in to the sounds around him: the birds, the wind, the gentle rustling of small critters in the undergrowth . . . and Clemens chewing.

'You married?' Hank asked him.

'Na. I'm a fag,' Clemens said, quite seriously. He then spat out something that apparently should not have been in his sandwich and checked inside to see what it was.

Hank was unsure if this was another of Clemens's dry witticisms. Clemens glanced at him long enough to wink. 'Relax, Hanky boy. I'm pulling your plonker. You'll 'ave to come round for dinner when this is over and meet the missus and kids.'

Hank nodded, feeling sure the offer was a genuine one. After all, Clemens had not said it in a Texan accent. 'Sure,' he said. 'How many kids you got?'

'Two. Boy, girl. You've got a couple, ain't ya?'

'Two girls.'

'What kind of food do you like? You one of them fussy types? I know how you Yanks are. Got to be organic and no microwave stuff and non-fat and all that.'

'Not us. We eat just about anything, I guess,' Hank shrugged. 'We're a meat and potatoes family. Barbecues. Stuff like that.'

'I like cooking Italian. I like to think I'm a bit of a gourmet,' Clemens said, deliberately pronouncing the 't'. Any form of upper class affectation was anathema to Clemens, and that included pronouncing French correctly. He tossed the rest of his sandwich away. 'Only pusser can cock up something as simple as a bleeding cheese sandwich,' he said tiredly.

'Pusser?' Hank queried.

'Pusser means Royal Navy.'

Hank nodded. 'You going on this op?' he asked.

'Hope so,' Clemens replied. 'We won't know who's going till the brief. That's if it's still on by the time we're ready to go. I've been on so many standby-to-go's I've lost count. Two months ago we got as far as hovering over a cruise ship near Iceland, just about to leap aboard because some fuck-pig was threatening to hijack it and shoot the captain when we pulled off because the dick'eds finally noticed all the bloke had in 'is 'and was a friggin' water-pistol . . . Knobbers.'

Hank nodded as he opened his own sandwich to inspect it. It looked like a slab of luncheon meat in margarine, made in two seconds flat. He closed it and took a bite anyway. 'Is it up to Stratton who goes?' he asked.

'Na. He'll put his suggestions to ops. I expect the ops officer'll probably agree with 'em though.' Clemens pulled a sausage roll from his bag and smelled it. 'I'd like to know what the op is,' he added, biting half the roll off in one go. 'I just hope it's not two weeks in a fucking bush watching some farmhouse. That's one thing about this job that bores the shit out of me. I've done more ops up to my nuts in kak watching sweet fuck-all for weeks at a time than I can remember.'

Hank wished he knew more about the Northern Ireland thing. From what he had gathered so far it was probably closer to police undercover drug ops in the States than anything the US military did.

'What's he like?'

'Who, Stratton?' Clemens asked. He shrugged. 'I don't know him all that well. I've never been in one of his teams before. He's one of those who flits around a lot.'

Clemens dumped the other half of his sausage roll. 'Who can fuck up a sausage roll?'

'Pusser?' Hank asked.

'You got it, pal. It's the hardest course in the Royal Navy, a cook's course. You know why?' he asked rhetorically. 'Because no bastard has ever passed it.' Clemens gave one of his idiotic chuckles as he dug an apple out of his bag. 'I bet they've even fucked up this apple,' he said, polishing it on his sleeve. Clemens took a huge bite and continued talking as he munched. 'He's probably one of the most experienced seniors we have. He's done ops in just about every theatre. Got an OBE, MBE, BEM . . . one of them. Don't know one from the other myself.'

'That a medal?'

'Yeah. He got it for some job against the Ruskies, I think. A few years ago now. Cold War stuff. Went into Russia off a sub and brought some MI6 character back. He was also at the jail break in Afghanistan, lucky bastard.'

'He was there?' Hank asked.

'Yeah. From what I heard they shot over four hundred Taliban.'

'I got there the day they left,' Hank said.

'That right?' Clemens asked.

'Sure were a lotta stiffs.'

'He's a bit of a cold bastard.'

'How's that?'

'Can't you tell?'

'The guys seem to like him.'

'That's because he's got kills, hasn't he? Everyone likes a man who's had a kill. You're a member of the club if you've got blood on your 'ands in this business.'

Hank could detect a bit of envy in Clemens's voice.

'And Stratton isn't just a member; he's the bloody president. Isn't it the same with your lot?'

'Sure,' Hank said. 'Everyone likes a kill on their record books.'

Clemens looked at him as if trying to read into his eyes. 'You in the club then, Hanky boy?' he said in the Texan accent.

Hank wondered what the accent change meant.

'We gonna start swapping war stories now, me old janner pig?' Hank asked, trying out the Devon accent for the first time and sounding more like a Pakistani.

Clemens gave him a blank look that Hank was unsure of.

'I ain't got any,' Clemens said, taking another bite of the apple.

Hank was about to admit he did not have any kills either but decided to keep it to himself. He was aware that his comment made it seem like he had and preferred not to talk about it. If Clemens asked, Hank would tell him, and if he did not, he would let Clemens think otherwise.

They finished their lunch in silence, both men beginning to feel a little apprehensive about the upcoming mystery drive.

When the car arrived they stood up as it came to a halt in front of them. The staff driver kept to his dumb routine and trudged his familiar route towards the wood.

'I'll drive,' Clemens said, climbing in. Hank got into the passenger side. 'You map read,' Clemens ordered as he started the engine. Hank reached for the safety-belt behind him but it was all tangled up. 'No safety belts,' Clemens said. 'You didn't wear any yesterday, did you?'

Hank remembered. Clemens put the engine into gear with a crunch. 'Piece a shit car,' he grumbled. 'You set?'

Hank checked the map, which was nothing more than a photocopy of a hand-drawn sketch. 'Straight for half a mile then right at a T-junction,' he said. 'I guess this means a wooded area,' he asked, showing it to Clemens.

'Looks like it.' Clemens revved the engine then eased his foot off the clutch and the car set off.

Clemens kept the speed at thirty miles per hour and they bumped over a cattle grid through a gap in a hedgerow and came to the T-junction.

'Right,' Hank said and they followed the road into a wide firebreak.

'Keep your eyes skinned for anything and everything,' Clemens said looking in all directions. He adjusted the rear-view mirror to check behind.

Hank's apprehension had increased, helped on by the tension in Clemens. 'If we get ambushed, do we return with live fire?' he asked.

'You do whatever you want, buddy-boy. Whatever you

want. But I have a feeling that whatever happens it won't be so realistic that you'll have to blow someone away.'

Hank eyeballed the door handle, memorising its location and action. He moved his seat back as far as it would go to give himself maximum room to manoeuvre and jump out if need be. The road took a gentle bend to the right and the wood opened out a little more on both sides. Hank searched the darkness behind the front line of trees as Clemens maintained a steady speed.

'We must've done a mile by now,' Clemens said. 'Something has to happen soon.' Then seconds later he called out. 'Up ahead, up ahead!'

Hank's eyes snapped to the front. Clemens pushed on the brake and stopped the car.

They stared ahead in silence as the engine ticked over.

A hundred yards to their front a car was lying on its roof just off the road, with a thin wisp of smoke curling skyward from the buckled engine compartment. They turned in their seats, checking in all directions for an ambush. Hank noticed his heart rate had quickened. Clemens looked unsure what to do.

'Something's gonna happen,' he said. 'Something's gonna happen real soon.'

They continued looking and waiting but nothing else materialised.

'How 'bout reversing outta here?'

'Where to?' Clemens said, checking his rear-view mirror for the umpteenth time. 'Stratton said follow the road and complete the circuit. That's what we have to do.'

It soon became clear nothing was going to happen while they remained in their current position. Clemens depressed the clutch and eased the engine into gear. 'Bollocks,' he said. 'Let's go 'ave a look.'

They moved off and slowly approached the wreck. 'Something'll happen here, you know that, don't you?' Clemens said, more to himself, licking lips that had suddenly gone dry.

As they drew closer they could make out two bodies lying in the grass beside the car. It looked like a man and a woman. They were face down and motionless.

Clemens stopped the car as they drew alongside the upturned wreck, keeping the engine in gear and a foot on the clutch, ready to speed off if a threat showed itself. They maintained their vigilance in all directions, but the two bodies were of the greatest interest. Clemens could make out bloodstains on the woman. Then the man suddenly moved, slowly, and groaned as if in great pain.

'He's moving,' Clemens said.

Hank craned to get a look past Clemens. 'Shouldn't we see if they're okay?' he asked.

Clemens was in a quandary, checking in every direction and then returning to the bodies. 'I don't know.'

The injured man made an effort to crawl but did not have the strength. 'We either check 'em out or we move on,' Hank said. 'Seems kinda strange to just drive on though.'

'Okay,' Clemens said, coming to a decision. 'I'm gonna get out and take a look.' He padded his gun in its holster through his jacket as he opened the door to make sure it was there, placed his feet on to the dirt track and stood up, every move preceded by a quick check around.

Hank felt vulnerable in the car alone and climbed out his side leaving the door wide open in case he needed to dive back into it. Clemens took a cautious step towards the bodies that were in a slight dip. Hank walked around the back of the car where he could get a better look at the bodies, still checking in all directions as he moved. He touched the butt of his gun inside his jacket to remind his hands where to go quickly if need be.

Just as Clemens leaned over the injured man to get a look at him, three men with balaclavas over their heads and aiming sub-machine-guns leapt from the trees right in front of them. 'Don't move! Don't move!' they shouted. At the same time the injured couple sprang to their feet holding pistols they had concealed under their stomachs. The woman was a man in disguise. Three more hooded men charged from the trees the opposite side of the track to close the trap.

Hank jerked around to face them. A shot of adrenaline rushed through him as the screaming ambushers closed in aggressively. His overriding personal directive to be proactive took charge and he went for it, his hand jerking under his jacket towards his holster, but a burst of machine-gun fire ripping up the ground at his feet froze him, the loudness and impact a warning of the sheer destructive power of a bullet.

'Move and you're focken dead! I'll focken kill you, you bastard!' the man who fired yelled. Hank put all further thought of movement out of his head. There was something chillingly real about this.

'On your knees! On your knees!' Another shouted, prodding Clemens with his gun barrel. They were talking with Irish accents.

'On your knees!' one of them yelled with finality and levelled his gun at Hank's head.

Hank and Clemens lowered themselves on to their knees where they were then harshly pushed to the ground, their backs knelt on, and weapons jammed into their heads. Hank was unprepared for the level of brutality. A hand grabbed the hair on the back of his head and rammed his face into the dirt.

'You fockers are dead,' one of the men standing between Hank and Clemens growled. He placed his foot on Hank's back and put his weight on it. 'You hear me, Yanky? Your focken goose is cooked.'

The wet soil chilled Hank's face. It was an effort to breathe with the weight of the boot on his back. The attackers then became silent and motionless, as if they were robots at the end of their current program and waiting for their next command. Hank heard someone step from the bushes and trudge through the grass to stop close by his head.

'Let 'em up,' said a man. Hank thought he recognised Stratton's voice. The boot and hand lifted off him and he could take a full breath.

Hank got to his feet wiping his face and spitting dirt from his mouth. He glanced at Stratton, then at the others, who kept their balaclavas on. Clemens got to his feet, looking annoyed but kept his glaring eyes aimed at the ground.

Stratton nodded to the ambushers and they stepped back and cleared their weapons.

'Hank,' Stratton said, as if nothing of any consequence had happened. 'Your turn to drive. Continue the route. Get going.'

As Hank walked around to the driver's door his jaw throbbed and he wondered if he'd cracked it. He climbed into the car and moved his mouth from side to side. If it wasn't it was badly bruised, but he could live with it. He wouldn't show these guys he was in any pain if he could help it.

'On you go, Clemens,' Stratton said.

Clemens gritted his teeth, ignored the dirt stuck to his face and walked around to the passenger side. He climbed in and slammed the door. Hank started the engine and drove slowly away from the scene. He adjusted the rear-view mirror and watched Stratton talking with the ambushers.

Clemens wiped the dirt from his face and spat some out of his mouth.

'Who were those guys?' Hank asked.

'SAS fucks,' Clemens said angrily.

'I guess we were meant to ignore the accident and drive on through.'

'Hindsight's a beautiful thing,' Clemens said curtly. 'Act like poxy internal security officers is what he said. That's what we were supposed to be, right? So you don't drive past a bleeding traffic accident with people lying half-dead in the bleeding road, do you? A load of bollocks, that's what it is!'

'What were we supposed to get from all that?'

'Fucked if I know,' Clemens said.

Clemens sat back and stewed in his anger, staring down at his feet like a kid who wasn't going to play any more. Hank decided to leave Clemens to himself. If something else happened on this little adventure it would be in Hank's hands anyway. He assumed that was why Stratton told him to drive.

The track curved gently to the left along the wood. Hank checked the mirror and caught a last glimpse of Stratton walking away from the SAS ambushers until the wood blocked any further view.

Hank concentrated on the road ahead. They arrived at a junction and he stopped the car. Clemens still looked too irritated to get involved, so Hank reached down beside his feet and picked up the map. After comparing it to the surroundings he took the right turn.

Hank felt surprisingly relaxed as he drove, not as nervous as he was at the start, as if being thrown to the ground and stomped on had cleared the tubes a little.

The track turned the corner of a wood and crested a

slight rise. As they headed down the other side a small town appeared in front of them. It looked strangely out of place, as if a large square had been neatly carved out of the centre of a city – streets, buildings, the lot – airlifted, and then deposited in the middle of the countryside. The sight was enough to make Clemens snap out of his gloom and sit up and stare at it. It was surreal. There was no sign of life in the town. It was grey and characterless, a dense urban block in the middle of open countryside, unloved or cared for.

'Toy town,' Clemens said. 'I didn't know they had one here.'

'What's a toy town?' asked Hank.

'It's usually used for troop training – a city environment. Purpose built. There's a huge one in Thetford the army uses before going over the water. They put on riots and snipers, stuff like that . . . The regular army doesn't come in here so this is obviously for SF only. You'd better slow a little.'

Hank slowed to a crawl as they approached the edge of the town and the first few buildings. The dirt track turned into tarmac and widened to the width of the main street that ran down through the centre of the collection of concrete and brick structures on either side. Clemens was back to full alert now. He pulled out his gun and checked it.

'We can expect to come under fire,' he said. 'Look out for pop-up targets in windows and doorways. If we do, stop the car, get out, find cover, and then we'll cover each other to a safe location. Watch out for friendly targets, woman carrying babies, stuff like that.'

Two-storey houses lined both sides of the street, interspersed with the occasional local shop. It reminded Hank of an ugly version of Disneyland in so far as everything one expected to find in a town was there but superficially. There were signposts, a phone booth, lampposts, dustbins and a bus stop. The street and pavements were littered with bricks, chunks of concrete and broken bottles. Several cars were parked sporadically along both sides of the road, all wrecks, and many burned out and without wheels. It looked as if a serious riot had recently taken place.

'Your gun cocked and loaded?' Clemens asked.

'Yep,' Hank replied, his hands tense on the wheel. He steered carefully along the main street, nice and easy, eyes everywhere, avoiding the larger lumps of rock and concrete. It all felt so confined. The street seemed narrow even for English towns and the houses appeared to be closer at the tops as if they leaned in over the street. An attack could come from just about anywhere. There were dozens of doorways and windows, most of them broken or missing altogether.

Fifty yards into the town a bottle floated through the sky as if out of nowhere and smashed on the street beside the car. Hank maintained the steady speed. Seconds later another bottle smashed close by followed by several more. They flew from the buildings either side of the car as it passed. One hit the car and Hank speeded up. Bricks and lumps of concrete then joined the bottles. Hank drove faster as they headed towards a collection of wrecked cars arranged like a chicane, forcing him to swerve in between them.

Several men appeared, running from the houses, and pelted the car with stones and pieces of wood. A couple ran up and whacked it with sticks and kicked it. Hank drove as fast as he could, threading the obstacles in the narrow street without hitting them. A Molotov cocktail struck the road beside the car and flames splashed against its side. More rioters appeared up ahead. There must have been thirty or forty, shouting and yelling and hurling missiles.

As Hank screeched out of the chicane he put his foot fully down. The flames bubbled the paint on the car before they extinguished. Then several yards ahead Hank saw a woman running down the pavement pushing a pram. She looked panicky, as if trying to escape the riot herself. The final obstacle was two cars parked either side of the road leaving a narrow gap for him to squeeze through. As he closed on the gap, the woman running down the pavement suddenly tripped and fell and the pram wheeled from her grasp and on to the road. It rolled straight into the gap between the parked cars. Hank took his foot off the accelerator as his mind considered his choices: swerve and go down the right pavement and hit a bus stop, take the left pavement and try to squeeze past several lampposts, which looked unlikely, or slam on the brakes and hit one of the parked cars. The problem with all of those options was that they meant coming to a stop, and that meant having to deal with the rioters.

There was of course another option, an unthinkable one at any other time and place. But somehow this was all so different. He was supposed to be an undercover agent. His life was in danger, and the life of his partner. Ahead was a pram with supposedly a baby in it. Self-preservation meant something else. It was not just about one's life. It was war.

Hank ran out of decision-making time and slammed his foot down hard on the accelerator. The car bore down on the gap. Clemens instinctively reached for the dashboard and sunk in his seat. Hank hit the pushchair square on and it left the ground like a football in a penalty kick. Something flew out of it and arced back towards the windshield. It was flesh-coloured. A baby. It slammed into the windshield, cracking it, then rolled over the roof. Hank kept his eyes on the road ahead. Clemens looked back to see the doll bounce on the road and its head fly off. A few seconds later they emerged from the grey, desolate structures back into the countryside and on to a dirt track once more as if it had all been a bad dream.

Clemens exhaled deeply and relaxed in his seat as the worst of the tension left him. 'Nice one,' he said. 'Notch one dead baby up to Hank.'

Hank was in a kind of mental limbo. For a split second back there, just after the collision, he thought he had done the right thing, and now it seemed all so completely wrong. He wondered what he could have been thinking choosing the pram. This wasn't a war they were in, not really. Stratton said they were effectively police officers. Cops don't plough through babies to get away from rioters. 'Shit,' he mumbled to himself.

'I reckon that just about sums up our day,' Clemens said, sounding relieved that he was not the only one who had cocked up.

Hank stood under a pair of old oaks watching the horizon, behind which the sun had long since dropped, leaving only a faint glow. It had turned colder with the coming of darkness but he could not be bothered to go to the room and put on a sweater. The day's events continued to eat at him. He looked back at the building that served as the galley. The lights were on and the moving silhouettes behind the opaque windows told him supper was being dished up. He didn't feel particularly hungry and he was in two minds whether or not to eat anything at all. He remained confused. There had been no debriefing from Stratton at the end of the exercise. They had returned to the huts after the serial without so much as a hint of what the point of it all had been. If he was wrong he wanted the chance to explain why he had done it, or at least hear what he was supposed to have done.

Hank began to doubt if these guys were all they were cracked up to be. Then again, maybe he was taking it more seriously than he was supposed to. Maybe they would find out later. He decided to eat and trudged back across the track towards the galley.

Just about everyone was inside having supper. Stratton sat at a table with Doles, both eating in silence. Hank had a sudden urge to go up to him and ask what he thought about the day's activities. But he decided against it. He would play it the Brit way, whatever that was exactly. He picked up a plate, scooped up a steak, some mashed potato and cabbage, took a knife and fork out of the cutlery box and headed for the back of the room where there was an empty table.

Clemens was sat with several others and as Hank passed he heard his name mentioned.

'. . . and Hank not only went for the bloody thing, he accelerated right into it.' Clemens laughed in his croaking manner, his mouth wide open, and his huge tongue sticking out. He showed no guilt on seeing Hank. 'Ain't that right, Hanky boy? You railroaded that pram and that kid right into fucking space.'

Some of the men were amused but others were not.

Hank paid no heed and sat at the empty table and placed his food down. He was finding it easier to ignore Clemens. The guy had a big mouth.

Hank sawed at the steak with the blunt knife without much effect and then gave up and dug into his pocket for his penknife. The blade cut through the meat with ease but his teeth faired little better than the cutlery and his bruised jaw soon ached with the effort of chewing it. He tried a mouthful of mashed potato, which was obviously powder and water, and decided he would have to be a lot hungrier than he was to get through this particular meal and pushed it away.

Across the room Stratton got up, placed his dishes in the tub and headed out of the room. Hank grabbed the opportunity, picked up his plate and cutlery, and headed between the tables towards the entrance. He scraped the food into the trashcan and dumped the plate and tools in the tub.

Hank stepped outside in time to see Stratton walk around the corner. He hurried up and closed on Stratton's back. 'Sergeant Stratton,' Hank said.

Stratton stopped and turned to face him. 'We don't call anyone by their rank when in civvies,' he said.

'Right,' Hank said, suddenly wondering if this was a good idea. Stratton seemed to be in a serious mood. Hank was then suddenly unsure how to begin.

'I, er . . . We haven't officially met . . . Hank Munro . . . chief,' then with finality, 'Hank.' He held out his hand. Stratton shook it.

'Sorry I never said hello earlier. It's been a bit crazed.'

'Hey, that's okay,' Hank said, shrugging. 'I know how it is . . . I just wanted to say that I appreciate being invited along.'

'Always a pleasure to play with our cousins from over the pond,' Stratton said.

Hank smiled appreciatively then got to what was bugging him. 'Look, I just wanted to ask you about today—'

Stratton cut him off. 'You can come to prayers,' he said.

Hank was thrown by the odd comment. 'Prayers?' he asked, as if he had not heard correctly.

'Orders. You weren't in the galley when it was announced. The operational briefing. Building one.'

Stratton headed away. The briefing, or prayers as Stratton

called it, was a complete surprise to Hank. The op was happening and he had been invited to the O group. If nothing else it was an indication he was still okay on somebody's list.

Several of the guys passed Hank and after they had all entered building one he followed.

It was the same as all the other buildings: one long cold brick room with a concrete floor and a small toilet in a cubicle near the entrance. The only furnishings were a dozen metal chairs spread in a double semi-circle halfway into the room, facing a table and lectern. Behind these were several boards propped on chairs and draped in black cloths to cover what was on them. All the windows were cloaked in the same heavy black cloth. Two men were waiting at the far end behind the table and lectern: Lieutenant Jardene and a man Hank had never seen before. They were dressed in civilian clothes, a little smarter and more tasteful than the men, and their hair was short and neat.

'Sit down, please, gentlemen,' Jardene said. Hank waited until everyone was seated and took the last chair, pulling it further back from the others, feeling like an intruder perhaps and subconsciously trying to remain as invisible as possible. Stratton and Doles entered, closing the door.

'Everyone here, Stratton?' Jardene asked.

'Yes, sir,' Stratton replied, standing behind Hank. Hank half looked over his shoulder to see Doles leaning against a wall, holding a pen and notebook. Hank then noticed everyone else had a notebook. He cursed himself for not being in the galley when the warning order for the briefing had been given. It was little things such as this, not having a pen and paper when he needed one, that irritated him about himself.

'We received the green light for operation Phoenix only

a few hours ago,' Jardene continued. 'This is Captain Sumners from military intelligence. He's going to kick off with a brief background to the operation. Needless to say, everything you hear in this room will not be discussed outside of it.' Jardene's eyes rested on Hank's for a second, as if impressing upon him that he was aware he was in the room, that it was no mistake, and that the rules applied to him as much as anyone else. Hank felt a rush of importance.

'Gentlemen,' Captain Sumners said in greeting. 'Two months ago one of our intelligence operatives was captured by members of the Real IRA in County Tyrone. It was a well-planned operation that almost succeeded.' Sumners glanced at Stratton who remained poker faced. 'RIRA did not just happen upon the operative by chance. They knew precisely where to find him and when.

'Many of our successes against the IRA over the years have been due to informants within the terrorist organisation itself. It is no secret that the IRA has had its own informants within the RUC and army, and even inside army intelligence at lower levels. The notion that they could penetrate the higher levels of our own military intelligence has always been considered improbable . . . A year ago we learned from a reliable source that there was very possibly a well-placed RIRA spy, or mole if you like, within the ranks of our military intelligence. This not only encompasses MI5, 6, A4, etcetera, but also the various intelligence cells of our military units. The informer who provided this information did not have any more details to offer, other than RIRA had gone to great lengths to protect this highly placed and valuable source.

'Initially, many at MoD treated this information with scepticism. Today, it is looked upon with serious concern. There are many tactics employed to catch a spy. Luck plays a great part, often a chance encounter seemingly unrelated and setting the hunt into focus. That's pretty much what happened in this case.

'RIRA has enjoyed a strong intelligence relationship with the ALG, the largest of the Algerian terrorist organisations. The ALG has its sympathisers within French government, military and intelligence services. We believe our RIRA mole communicates with his or her handler through one such ALG spy who is a member of French counter intelligence, DST . . . Don't worry if any of this loses you. It's only background.'

Sumners removed the black sheet from one of the boards. On it were several pictures of a dark-complexioned man in his forties, some taken with surveillance cameras, others official passport photos.

'Serjo Henri,' Sumners went on, indicating the pictures. 'I won't go into any of his details other than his appearance and VDMs, visual distinguishing marks that is, since it isn't important to this operation, but suffice to say we believe Henri is the link between our mole and his RIRA handler. In case anyone is wondering why a RIRA mole inside our military intelligence should need to go through an Algerian spy working for French military intelligence, the simple answer is it makes it devilishly difficult to discover or intercept communications. It is safe to assume that Henri is nothing more than a go-between and knows nothing about what he delivers either to the mole or to RIRA.

We have been watching Henri for the past six months and have discovered how he receives invitations to take secret meetings. We're certain the trigger that tells him a meeting has been called for is a code of some sort stuck on to a lamppost. It's not uncommon to find small ads on lampposts in Paris and he obviously knows what to look for. He quickly removes the code, which he can do almost without stopping. We've never seen one of the codes as he's very thorough about disposing of them. We think they indicate a prearranged location and a date and time. Henri lives and works in Paris and he takes a walking exercise along various streets in his neighbourhood several times a week. He passes dozens of lampposts, any one of which might hold the invitation, and since it isn't possible to watch every lamppost in the centre of Paris twenty-four hours a day, every day of the year, we can't catch them that way.'

'Who's been carrying out the surveillance?' Stratton asked.

'A couple of our embassy staff. Up until now it has not been a high enough priority to mount a full operation, and there are other reasons I'll get to later, which will also explain why I'm briefing you lot instead of one of our own teams.'

'Have you covered any of the actual meetings yet, sir?' asked Doles.

'No. The two embassy staff members have done well but they are not trained surveillance operatives.'

'Then how do you know the lamppost triggers are for meetings?' Doles persisted.

Sumners was a patient man and used to having questions fired at him since so much of his work was piecing together bits of a puzzle. 'We haven't actually covered any meetings, as I said, but we've housed Henri at a couple just to prove our theories. In both cases Henri picked up his trigger in the afternoon, on a lamppost as I have described, and then he went to a café the following morning. Different cafés, but in the two cases we observed he sat outside, then after a while he went inside, presumably to meet his contact. Without a proper surveillance team and technical support we wouldn't even attempt to cover the actual meetings inside.'

Brent put up his hand. 'Sir, so how have you tied Henri to the mole?'

'By cross-referencing sightings with events in the past we've been able to make some conclusions. Obviously, one must be careful about one's deductions, but like doing a cross-word, there are certain answers to clues on which one must depend to support others until they can support themselves. On three occasions Henri's actions have coincided with events in Northern Ireland. An example is his movements five days before the intelligence operative was abducted in Tyrone. Henri picked up a trigger for a meeting, which he took the following morning in a café. When he left the café half an hour later he caught a taxi. One of the attachés just happened to have his car nearby and managed to follow him – to the airport, where he boarded a flight to Dublin. We had a man waiting for Henri at the other end. He followed him on a train to Dundalk where he left him. This meeting tallies with a report from RUC special branch. Four days later the detachment's operative was snatched. We believe Henri met with our mole in the café that day and was handed information that led to that attempted kidnapping.'

'How many of our people knew the operative was in the car?' Doles asked.

'We've obviously covered that route in great detail. The orders for that operation went to London a week before it took place. There are a fair number of people who could have had access to the file in the Lisburn office as well as London. An investigation in that direction would not be worthwhile for a number of reasons.'

Sumners paused for a moment to check where he was on the board. 'Right. Let's move on to the op. Yesterday afternoon Henri was seen picking up a trigger from a lamp-post a mile from his apartment. If past habits are anything to go by he will attend a meeting somewhere in Paris tomorrow. We can only hope it will be with our mole, and if not, someone who can take us to the next step in finding him . . . Are there any questions before we get on with the operation orders?'

There were none. Sumners deferred to Jardene, who pulled the cover off the other large board to reveal a detailed map of a section of the centre of Paris. Dotted around the map were photographs of specific streets and locations in that area.

'The ground is central Paris,' Jardene begun. 'Specifically a triangle formed by the Place de la Concorde, L'Opéra and the Louvre. It's a somewhat upscale part of the city, a lot of shops, businesses, very much a tourist area. Henri lives in a small apartment over a shop, here in Rue Shebal. In the past his meetings have been within two miles of his apartment. He prefers to walk or use public transport. He likes to practise anti-surveillance techniques often but he doesn't move very quickly and if you keep a good team formation you should have no trouble with him. Your mission is to house him at the meeting and then cover it with audio and visual recording systems.'

Hank sat listening with interest as Jardene spent the next hour going over every detail of the operation. When Jardene revealed the individual tasks Hank hoped that, despite it being a long shot, his name would be mentioned, but it was not. When Jardene got to the final phase of the orders, naming the command structure from top to bottom, Hank's name failed again to make the list. Hank remained philosophical. There had been no chance of him going on the op from the beginning, but hoping had not done any harm.

'Are there any questions?' Jardene finally asked the room at the end of the briefing.

'Sir,' said Jackson putting his hand up. 'Why us? I mean, we're not as good at surveillance as the det is. Why not use them or A4?'

Jardene looked to Sumners.

'Yes, I was going to mention that, wasn't I?' Sumners said. 'Since we have no idea who the mole is – my suspicions lean more towards MI5 – we want to do this out of house. We doubt the IRA has infiltrated your lot. It wouldn't make much sense since only a handful of SBS and SAS operatives work over the water these days and therefore spend little more than a fraction of their careers working against the IRA.'

'Why did we spend the last few days rehearsing shooting and fast driving if we're not going to be armed or use vehicles?' Doles asked.

'That was my decision,' said Jardene. 'It really couldn't be helped since we had no idea what the operation was until this afternoon. All I knew was that it was RIRA related. I assumed that meant we would be going over the water and so I thought it best to brush up on some basics until I knew more. But you have all had surveillance experience and Stratton has commanded dozens of such operations. You may be a little rusty but I have every confidence you will come up to scratch.'

'What about the French?' Jackson asked.

'What about the bloody French?' someone replied sarcastically, to a few chuckles.

'That's a good question actually,' said Sumners. 'The French will not be informed of this operation. For a number of reasons we will be keeping this strictly a UK intelligence op. For all intents and purposes you are on vacation in Paris. That's why you will be using cell-phones only for communications. Normally you would stay in the embassy for a day to be processed and qualify for diplomatic immunity. But obviously we do not have enough time for that. Technically what we're doing is quite illegal and would cause a diplomatic storm if it got out. There must be no risks taken. If this operation is blown the repercussions will go all the way to the top.'

'Exactly why aren't we telling the French?' Doles asked.

'We don't trust the bastards, that's why,' Clemens answered.

Sumners interrupted the laughing. 'First of all, we don't particularly want the French to know we have a mole. And if they found out that one of their own intelligence officers was working for RIRA and the ALG they might close him down immediately to avoid any further embarrassment. Henri is our only lead. We're prepared to take the risk to keep him operational.'

'Any more questions?' Jardene asked. After a moment's silence, he continued, 'This is not a difficult operation. I must impress upon you not to be overconfident though. If at any time you feel you have been overexposed you must pull off.'

'I would rather lose the mouse for another day than let it know there's a cat in the house,' Sumners added.

'Right then,' Jardene said. 'Pack any kit you will not need and leave it in building one. It'll be taken back to Poole. You should be home by tomorrow night after a debriefing back in Poole . . . Dolesy.'

Doles took his cue and stepped forward to address everyone. 'Okay. Stores, transport, timings. Be in building six in thirty minutes. You'll be given cell-phones, spare batteries, hand chargers and expenses money. Brent. You're the tech man on this one. When I've dished out the phones and money we'll go through the audios and cameras. Any questions? That's all. Oh, and the expense money is for meals and transport only, not beer, Jackson. You give back what you don't spend, and no receipts, tough titty, you pay out of your own pocket.'

'Jock bastard,' someone mumbled, followed by some laughing as the men headed for the door.

'You better believe it,' Doles said.

'Oh, and I suggest you clean up – wash and shave – you're tourists not farm labourers,' Jardene called out.

Hank waited for everyone else to file out. Sumners and Jardene remained to huddle over the map and discuss the operation further. He thought about asking Jardene what he should do with himself but decided against interrupting him and left the building.

He stepped out into the chilly night air. The stars were clear and bright as the night before. Stratton was talking with Doles at the far end of the building. Hank headed to the edge of the compound a few yards away to look out over the countryside. Doles finished his conversation with Stratton and headed away.

'Hank,' Stratton called out. Hank looked over at him. 'You been to Paris?' he asked.

Hank walked casually towards Stratton with his hands in his pockets. 'Nope,' he said.

'I suppose you don't speak French.'

'First time anyone's ever asked me and the first time I wish I did,' Hank said with a smirk.

Stratton smiled thinly. 'Always a lot of American tourists in Paris,' he said.

There was something in Stratton's tone that caused Hank's hopes to skyrocket. 'Wish I was one of them tomorrow,' he said.

'Maybe you should be.'

'How would that work?' Hank asked, remaining as matter of fact as he could.

'You got your passport?' Stratton asked.

Hank's hope sunk again. 'No,' he said.

'Navy ID?'

'Sure.'

'That'll do. You stick with me, okay?'

'Okay,' Hank said.

'Put your kit with the rest of the baggage for Poole and I'll see you at the vehicles,' Stratton said and walked away.

Hank could not help grinning. First thing was a quick wash and shave, then put on that clean shirt he'd brought along. He walked briskly to his basher. Things were not bad at all, he decided.

9

Four hours after leaving Ilustram Hank was sitting on the Eurostar and heading through the Channel Tunnel. He was boxed in between Stratton opposite, staring out of the window into the darkness, and Doles beside him, with his feet up on the seat beside Stratton. They were the only operatives in this carriage. The others were spread about the rest of the train in ones and twos. Only two civilian passengers shared the carriage and they were at a far end.

The three men had hardly said a word to each other since they left the training camp. Doles had nodded off for most of the journey in the van. Hank felt tired, but not enough to sleep just yet. He was aware Stratton had not slept either and wondered what was on the man's mind. He had the feeling something was troubling him; perhaps it was the responsibility of the operation. Hank was tempted to start a conversation but couldn't think of a way into it, past that invisible wall, which discouraged anyone from getting too close.

But Doles seemed to be close to Stratton. They had a connection of some kind. Hank thought about striking up a conversation with him instead. Doles had the potential to be quite the chatterbox. Hank still had difficulty understanding his Scottish accent though, and when he did found him to be quite opinionated, or perhaps it was just the forceful way he talked. The man had a habit of talking at you rather than with you. But Hank felt it would only be a positive thing to get to know him better, and indeed all of the men, including Stratton. As he pondered what he might open with, Doles beat him to it.

'Long time since I was in France,' he said without looking at Hank. 'It was during the Falklands war . . . Christ, I was still a single man in those days. Seems like yesterday.'

'You were in France during the Falklands war?' Hank asked, curious.

'Aye. Bastards were sending Exocets to the Argies even after that lying turd Mitterand promised Thatcher he wouldn't send any more. And he bloody well knew it because his bloody brother was chief executive of the company that made the bloody missiles.'

'What were you doing there, or can't you say?'

'Christ. It was more'n two decades ago . . . They were shipping the Exocets across France and through Italy and then loading them on to Peruvian merchant ships that would then deliver them to the Argies. We were minutes from blowing one batch of missiles to hell when Thatcher called us off. She had a change of heart about taking the war into Europe. Bastards wouldn't even give us the frequencies of the Exocets they sold to the Argies either. As far as I'm concerned the fucking frogs sunk our ships and killed our sailors as much as the Argies did.'

Hank thought he understood most of what Doles had said. One or two more heavily accented words had escaped him but he'd got the gist of it. Hank knew very little about the Falklands conflict and even less about European politics.

'And to think those bastards were Scotland's allies against these Sassenachs for hundreds of years,' Doles went on,

165

nudging Stratton with his foot at the word 'Sassenach'. Stratton raised an eyebrow at Doles then went back to looking into the blackness. Hank wondered if Stratton liked Doles or just put up with his familiarity. He started to wonder if Stratton had a family, brothers and sisters, and what he was like with his folks.

Doles nudged Hank. 'You Americans don't like the French much either, ain't that right?' he asked.

'I don't know any French people myself.'

'They were all that stood between you lot still having a Union Jack for your national flag. I don't understand why you and the French aren't big pals. Strange bloody lot if you ask me. Mind you, can't expect much else from a race that'll eat anything that bloody moves. Ain't that right, Stratton?' Doles said, nudging him with his foot again. Stratton's only indication that he heard Doles was a slight smile.

Doles mellowed as his thoughts drifted to another time and place. 'My first girlfriend was French. I met her a week before my SBS selection course. She was an au pair for a Rupert and his wife on the officers' married patch just across the field from the camp. I met her on Hamworthy beach. She was absolutely, staggeringly fucking gorgeous. A bloody ten if there ever was one.' Doles smiled as he pictured her lying there.

'What happened to her?' Hank asked.

'A couple weeks after passing selection they sent me to play games in Central America. I was gone six months. I couldn't write to her of course. It wasn't cool to write to a girlfriend while on ops . . . When I got back to Poole she was gone. The officer she worked for had got a draft to 45 commando up in Arbroath and took his family with him. She didn't go with them. I heard she waited around in Poole for a couple of months. She would go to the guardhouse about once a week and ask to speak to me. I don't know if she even knew I was out of the country. Maybe she thought I didn't want to speak to her . . . Anyway, then she left town and went back to France, I suppose.'

'You never saw her again?' Hank asked.

'Yes,' Doles said. 'Once. About ten years after. I was walking up the steps into the pictures in Bournemouth with the missus and our two wee boys. She was coming out with some bloke. She recognised me right away and smiled, just a little . . . Great smile she had . . . No one else noticed but me and her. I looked back at her as she walked up the road, and she looked back at me.'

Doles drifted into silence.

'That's a pretty sad story,' Hank said.

'See, Stratton. Hank was touched. Not like you, you cold-hearted bastard.'

'Wait till you've heard it a dozen times,' Stratton said.

'If it hada worked out you could be daddy to a couple of French kids by now,' Hank said, emphasising the irony.

'She wouldn't have married him once she really got to know him,' Stratton said.

'Is that right? And what does that say about my missus?' Doles asked, acting as if he had been insulted.

'You're Anne's only flaw.'

'Bastard,' Doles said, without malice. 'What's your excuse for being single, then?'

Stratton went back to staring out of the window, as if Doles's comment had cut the conversation dead. Hank was aware some kind of exchange had just taken place between them.

Stratton got to his feet and they watched him walk down the carriage and into the head.

'Did you say something to piss him up?'

'Piss him off, not up. No. I just raked up some old stuff that's all.'

'Would I be right in guessing woman problems?'

'Depends how you look at it. He was almost married once.'

'Almost?'

'Quite a few years ago now. She was a fine lass. A nurse in Poole. Sally. A lot of fun . . . They were a great couple, ideal, know what I mean? Or so it seemed to everyone else anyway. They must've been together some four years I think . . . Four or five . . . Anyhow, something about the job started getting to him, inside his head. We used to hang out a lot. He was my best pal, you know what I mean? Anne and me, Anne's my wife, and him and Sally would get together at least once a week. Then he started to change, didn't want to hang out any more . . . Anyhow, one day Sally just up and left while he was away on a job somewhere. They had a nice little cottage together out in the sticks. When he came back she was gone. No letter, fuck all . . . Smart as he is I don't think he's ever quite understood why.'

'Do you know why?' Hank ventured.

'He got himself fucked up . . . He started thinking too deeply about things to do with the job. He forgot to stay detached I think.'

'No chance of him getting back with Sally?'

'No. She's gone. She got frightened . . . Anyhow, he's not ready for anything like that. He's got to straighten some things out.'

Hank was intrigued. 'A woman can change a man,' he offered.

'That's true,' Doles said.

Stratton exited the toilet and came back to his seat.

Doles stood. 'I think I'll have a wee piss m'sel,' he announced and headed up the carriage.

168

Stratton went back to looking out of the window in silence. Hank decided this was as good a time as any to ask the question that had been niggling him.

'Stratton?'

Stratton didn't acknowledge him at first. 'Stratton?' Hank repeated.

Stratton looked at him as if he had just woken up. 'What?' he said.

'The driving exercise. When I ran into that buggy. Was I wrong? It's been kinda bugging me – the buggy thing.' Hank smiled at his childish play on words, despite Stratton's blank look.

'What do you think?' Stratton asked.

'Tell you the truth I ain't sure. I did what I thought was right at the time. Then afterwards, the guys . . . well, I got the impression I'd screwed up, you know. Be kinda nice to know what you think.'

'Would you do it again under the same circumstances?'

Hank thought about that a moment. 'Let me ask you this first, if you don't mind . . . Why'd everyone have to do those tests?'

'Why'd you join Special Forces?' Stratton asked.

'I wanted to be a soldier and I wanted to be the best of the best,' Hank replied.

'You sound like a commercial,' Stratton said.

Hank knew his answer was on the pathetic side but he did have a deeper, more meaningful one when in a serious mood. 'I think a lotta guys don't really know what they're getting into when they join Special Forces. There's no way you can truly know what it's about till you join. Then you find yourself doing things you never imagined, no matter how much you'd heard about it before. For me, it's not just a job. It's a constant struggle to prove myself, and not only to myself, to the guys I work with. You know what I mean?'

'Not really,' Stratton said.

Hank felt that Stratton knew exactly what he meant even if it wasn't how he felt about it. It was like a snub. Hank was suddenly unsure if he liked Stratton at all. The guy didn't seem to have any respect for him.

'Why'd you join SF?' Hank asked.

'I joined the Marines first because I had nothing else to do at the time. By the end of training I was disappointed. I looked at the guys I'd passed out with and thought I was better. Since I was stuck in the mob for a few years I decided to see what SF had to offer.'

'What do you think about the job?'

'It has its moments.'

'Did it teach you anything about yourself?'

'I learned that I like working by myself. Sometimes I get the chance.'

Hank decided he and Stratton were worlds apart. Hank liked being in a team. The team ethos appealed to him. He did enjoy the feeling of self-importance when he did small tasks alone but that was not what Stratton meant. Stratton meant he didn't like working with people. There was a big difference in this business. Hank decided that's what it was about Stratton, the shield around him. He was a lone wolf, nothing more complex than that.

'So?' Hank continued. 'What about the test? You never answered my question.'

Stratton was staring out the window again. 'It wasn't a test,' he said. 'There are no exercise solutions.'

'Then what was it all about?'

'It was an opportunity for you to take a look at yourself. You can only do that under pressure. That's when you know who you really are.'

'So, there is no answer?'

Stratton looked into Hank's eyes a moment then leaned forward. 'It was a question, Hank, but not one I can answer for you. Every SF operative thinks he has a right to be in the job because he passed some tough selection course. But some of us are not as qualified as we like to think we are. Some of us don't have what it takes and don't know it because we don't often get the chance to find out who we really are, and when we do it's sometimes too late. You ran into that pram and killed a baby instead of yourself. You know a little bit more about yourself today than you did last week. That's all.'

'But I wouldn't have done that back home, not in a normal day in my life. When I hit that buggy I was on ops.'

'Hank. I don't give a shit.'

Stratton sat back, ending the conversation. Doles returned, took his seat, and checked his watch. 'Should be on the ground nicely for eight. Even have time for a spot of scran before the stake-out.' He took a deep breath, exhaled, and closed his eyes as if the ritual was enough to set him off to sleep.

Hank was thinking about what Stratton had said and was still unclear if the man approved of what he had done yesterday or not. Stratton closed his eyes. Hank decided Stratton was the kind of guy no one got to know very well. He was in a different place to anywhere Hank had ever been or was likely to go.

The train burst out of the tunnel and Hank looked at the French countryside for the first time. The light was only just starting to creep over the horizon. He thought of Paris, what it looked like. All his images were from movies and all contained the Eiffel Tower. He closed his eyes. He would see Paris soon enough, but as a spy, kind of. That was neat.

None of the guys back home had been a spy in Paris. His thoughts went back to the buggy and the baby flying out of it and he was confident he'd done the right thing, as far as military logic was concerned. But would he really have killed himself had it happened in civvy-street? he wondered. He truly couldn't say. Hank decided that Stratton's little exercise was bullshit. He didn't believe he knew himself any better because of it.

10

Bill Lawton stood at the open French windows of his room on the fourth floor of La Concorde Hotel, overlooking the narrow Rue Cambon. The buildings lining the tight little street were tall and slender and stood compacted together. Bill was hidden behind the white net curtain that flowed from the ceiling, far enough back into the room to see the street below without being seen from the offices opposite.

Bill had been in this hotel once before five months earlier. He had had the same view of the street but from the room above. It had been summer then. Now it was wet and the wind that gently billowed the curtains brought a chill with it. The room was on the tatty side, with its cheap furnishings and artwork, pale grey paint covering old patterned wallpaper. But it was clean, discreet, a four-minute walk to the Place de la Concorde in one direction, ten minutes to the Louvre in the other and two minutes to the Métro.

Bill could clearly see the circular tops of the four empty tables on the patio outside the small café almost directly across the road. He checked his watch. His overnight bag was packed and lying on the bed, his tweed jacket and Barbour beside it, ready to go. He felt the knot of his woollen tie and adjusted it for the umpteenth time, the only outward sign that he was nervous. He was no stranger to perilous rendezvous and had been in far more dangerous situations without feeling this edgy. But there was a distinct difference this time. Driving alone into bandit country in Northern Ireland to meet an armed IRA tout on the man's home turf was fraught with danger, but on those occasions Bill was supported by a sophisticated intelligence network and a small army of Special Forces operatives on the other end of his emergency standby radio. On this particular rendezvous he was completely alone.

He forced himself to take a deep, relaxing breath and began to pace the room. Each time he reached the window he glanced down at the café tables; they remained empty. Everything was fine, he assured himself; there was plenty of time.

He went through the schedule once more, chiefly to maintain his calm. As soon as the meeting was over he would hail a taxi on the Rue de Rivoli at the end of the road no more than forty seconds walk, take it directly to Charles De Gaulle airport thirty to forty minutes away depending on traffic, and hop on a British Airways shuttle to Heathrow, any one of five or six that would get him to London before the end of the day. He had tonight and tomorrow of his three days' leave remaining before he had to catch a flight to Aldergrove airport, where a duty driver would take him back to his office in Lisburn Army camp. But most important, and the reason he needed to be back in London no later than six that evening, was that he had a dinner date.

Just the thought of it was a distraction for several reasons, good and bad. The main downside was that she was officially out of bounds. He was a commissioned officer in Her Majesty's Army and she was a corporal, or at least he assumed she was. She was too young to be a sergeant. She might even be a private. Anyhow, she wasn't an officer. If his superiors found out about the tryst he would be in deep water – fraternising with non-commissioned ranks was a serious no-no in his regiment. But she was beautiful and his hunger to sleep with her from the moment he had laid eyes on her had overridden every other concern. Imagining her naked body entwined about his almost made him forget he was in France, never mind what he was doing here. This was to be their first date. He did not expect to discover her flesh the first night; he suspected she was going to be a difficult catch to land altogether. He wondered if she would see him two evenings in a row, the two nights he had left on leave. After that it might be impossible. Two nights might do it though. If not, no matter. She was going to be worth the wait, he could feel it.

Bill had known her for several months although he had talked to her only on a handful of occasions. His job as liaison officer between Northern Ireland army group headquarters and the commander of the southern intelligence undercover detachment meant he had little reason to communicate directly with the field operatives. He linked the detachment with the rest of the intelligence community and brought in whatever relevant information he could dig up. It was rather like being a public relations rep at times, which suited Bill down to the ground for he had the gift of the gab and for making friends. The detachment was a couple hours' journey from his office and on his frequent official visits he usually grabbed a quick cup of tea and a bite in the little cookhouse. Sharing a table with an operative or two was inevitable, which is how he first met her. He had fantasised about her from that first day and under the normal circumstances of the job that was as far as it would have gone. To ask her out on a date would have been unthinkable. Undercover operatives didn't go out on dates in Northern Ireland and rarely had any kind of relationship with anyone outside of the small, secluded detachment.

Which is why he could not believe his luck when he saw her boarding the same flight as his from Aldergrove to Heathrow the day before he flew on to Paris. As coincidence would have it both were heading home for a few days' leave, and it seemed as if fate had truly intervened when he saw that the seat beside her was empty. The forty-minute journey was enough to have her laughing and enjoying his company. Bill was not strikingly handsome, which he saw as an advantage. His predatory intentions were well disguised and might not have been so if he was good looking. He was attractive but in other ways. His manner appeared passive and his charm and wit natural as they stealthily infiltrated their target. By the time a woman was aware of his intentions she had developed some of her own.

Bill had no time to waste on this occasion. If he had not asked her to dinner before she left Heathrow to catch the Underground into London he might never have another chance. He sensed she was genuinely keen when she accepted and gave him her telephone number. She seemed the type of woman who knew clearly what she wanted as far as men were concerned. He wondered what her real name was. She didn't look like an Aggy. To be sure she didn't look like an undercover operative either. Of all the female agents he had seen in his three years in military intelligence it was not much of a compliment to say she was the best looking since few of them were even attractive to him. Although she never dressed to impress it was obvious that she had a well-proportioned and athletic body. Needless to say, he was looking forward to the evening immensely. He had to remember when telephoning her, if he talked to her mother, Aggy's cover story was that she was stationed in Germany. He wanted to call her there and then to confirm the date, but he would have to wait until his plane landed.

His thoughts were brought sharply back into focus as he spotted a man and woman sitting at one of the tables outside the café.

The man was supposed to be alone; Bill would not reveal himself otherwise. The high angle made it difficult to confirm it was his man, although he had the same colouring and seemed the right age. Bill had met him twice before and would recognise him if he could get a reasonable look. He needed the man to raise his head just a little more. If it was him, the fact he was accompanied was a warning signal. Bill didn't even want to think about that until he was certain.

The man looked up as the waiter came out of the café to take the couple's order. Bill was relieved to see it was not his meeting. He checked along both sides of the street. A man was lingering on a corner by a lamppost smoking a cigarette. Bill quickly scanned around and then came back to the man. He watched him for a few minutes, occasionally checking elsewhere. The man then took a broom from a doorway and began sweeping the gutter. A street cleaner. Bill stepped back into the room as another bout of paranoia rushed through him. He was experienced enough to control it but could not suppress the fear of the risk he was taking. He had asked himself the same questions at least once a day for the past ten years: what was he doing? Why was he risking absolutely everything for it? But asking himself these questions was part of the game of assurance Bill played with himself. He was ninety-nine per cent certain about what he was doing. Well, ninety-eight perhaps. He reasoned that the doubt represented his moral obligation to question his actions. He checked his watch. Sixteen minutes to ten. He would give his meeting till exactly ten o'clock. If he did not show, Bill would head for the airport.

11

Hank sat beside Stratton in a café, at a table in the back where it was gloomy and unpopulated. He had not seen the rest of the team since they arrived at Gare du Nord, and then a couple of them only briefly before they disappeared in different directions. Stratton seemed to know this part of Paris well. He had given the taxi driver the name of the street in what sounded to Hank like fluent French, and then on arrival he led Hank down several back streets directly to the café, all without consulting a map or notes.

Hank checked his watch. It was quarter of ten. He was on his third cup of coffee, having polished off a sandwich jambon and was considering another. He decided to wait until Stratton finished his, although that didn't look as if it would be any time soon. He'd taken just two bites and the rest was getting cold on his plate. The front of the café was doing a fair morning's trade, the waiters moving quickly about delivering coffee, croissants and toasted sandwiches; he and Stratton could remain where they were for hours without drawing undue attention.

Stratton had not said a word since they'd left the train. Hank had no inclination to talk either, at least not to Stratton. That was too much like hard work. He wondered what Stratton was like socially, whether he drank and hung out with the guys in bars. Hank was sure Stratton didn't dislike him. He felt his coldness was a combination of the pressures of command and that Hank was still a stranger, not to mention a foreigner.

Hank looked around at the people in the café with curiosity, the way they dressed, how they talked to each other, their body language. He noted the things that made them different from Americans, how they communicated with their hands and facial expressions for instance. A flush of contentment passed through him. He was actually enjoying himself, as if he were on holiday. Everything was being paid for, he had no responsibilities, no worries concerning the op, and he was with the ground commander himself, which meant he didn't even have to think, just follow. He would have preferred being more involved in the operation, of course, part of an actual surveillance team, not just a spectator, but all in all he was having a very pleasant time.

Stratton's cell-phone vibrated in his pocket and he buried the earpiece in his ear, checked the caller ID and pushed the receive call button.

'Go ahead,' he said as he took out a street map that was neatly folded to display a couple of square miles just north of the river, with the Louvre bottom centre. 'No one can make that call but you,' he said. 'If you think you're warm, back off. The rule is, if in doubt, get out.'

Stratton disconnected and studied the map as he hit a number; he then talked calmly into the small mic in the wire that dangled from his ear past his mouth. 'Alan? Where are you?' he asked, then listened a moment. 'Dave thinks Henri might have made him. He's pulling off. Move up to the south-west corner of Place Vendôme and support Jeff. Henri should be entering the square in the next two minutes . . . The Ritz, that's right.'

Stratton disconnected and scrutinised the map. His phone

vibrated again and he checked the caller before hitting the button. 'Go ahead,' he said and listened for a few seconds. 'If he goes left or straight, leave him. If he goes right or doubles back, you have to take him, but don't get burned.'

There was a long pause, then he confirmed what he heard: 'He went left toward Vendôme, is that correct? . . . Okay, out.'

Stratton hit the end button and then a memory dial button. A few seconds later his call was picked up. 'Jeff? . . . He's towards you from the north entrance, understood?'

Stratton disconnected and hit another memory key quickly. 'Brent? . . . He's into Vendôme . . . That's right. Hold your position.'

Stratton ended the call and stared ahead as if in intense thought, but he was waiting, holding the phone, expecting it to vibrate any second. It took a couple of minutes before it did.

'Go ahead,' he said and listened for a moment, then suddenly looked annoyed. 'You're bunching. You can't get that close if you're in support . . . I don't care how crowded it is. That's two more we've lost now.' Another pause to listen, then: 'No, I'll do it. Call Brent and Doles. Tell them I'm covering the church at Barres.'

And with that, Stratton pocketed the phone, stood up and tossed money on to the table. 'Let's go,' he said with urgency and Hank quickly followed him out of the café.

They moved along the street at a brisk pace. Hank walked beside Stratton when he could but he had to repeatedly step back to let oncoming pedestrians pass on the narrow, busy pavement. Stratton walked like a dart with fixed determination. Hank had to run around a parked car at one point to catch up with him. He felt as if he could be hit by a grand piano falling from the roof of one of these buildings and Stratton would just keep on walking. They turned a corner into another equally busy street lined with shops. Hank wanted to know where they were rushing to but chose not to ask. Then, as if Stratton had heard him, 'Henri did a double-back behind a group of people leaving a shop. Jeff was following too close and got burned. So did Joe who was backing too closely.'

'He knows they were following him?'

'No, but if he sees either of them again he will.'

'If he's doubling back maybe he already thinks he's being followed.'

'Not necessarily. Doubling back is a standard anti-surveillance move. Anyone who's been in this game long enough checks who's behind them just about every time they take a walk, on or off duty. Recognise anyone behind us?'

Hank wasn't sure if Stratton was kidding or not. He looked back as they walked and checked the dozens of people behind them. Parked cars were crammed along every inch of pavement both sides of the street. Stratton side-stepped through a gap between two and crossed the road. Hank looked forward again, saw Stratton was over the road and hurriedly caught up.

'We're not as good at this as we should be,' Stratton continued when Hank came alongside him. 'Six experienced guys could do this task all day without getting burned. We've already lost four.'

The phone went again. Stratton didn't break stride as he answered it. 'Yes.' He listened for a moment then: 'Okay, that's good. Move out of the area. Your day's finished.'

Stratton disconnected and speeded up a little. 'Jeff now thinks that when Henri did his double-back he was actually doing a pass of the meeting point. He just doubled back again past a café. That's twice he's passed it. Odds are we'll house him there any minute. We're gonna have to cover one end of the street while Brent moves to the other until Henri goes static and the rest of the team can move into position.'

'How far?' Hank asked.

'Rue Cambon. Just around this corner.'

They continued at a brisk pace to the next junction where an old church took up one corner; it was built back from the road so that the corner itself was a small open square, a relief of space from the claustrophobic streets. Stratton crossed into the square and stopped on the corner where Rue Cambon continued on its narrow course for a couple more hundred yards towards Rue de Rivoli. Stratton studied the street, which was comprised of shops, a couple of bars and a café. Hank kept behind him, looking around, trying to act natural, seeing if there were any familiar faces, friendly operatives or otherwise. A pretty woman in sexy tight pants walked by and looked at him, oozing lasciviousness. He realised he was staring and quickly looked away. And then he could not resist looking back to watch her shapely rear. When he turned back Stratton had gone. A rush of panic popped inside his chest before he caught sight of Stratton heading down Rue Cambon and he sped off to catch up.

Stratton reached the next crossroads, the last before Rivoli a hundred or so yards away. Hank moved in behind him and took a peak up the street. He could see a small café on their side of the road with a couple of tables outside. Across the street from the café was a sign that read 'La Concorde Hotel'. Stratton stepped back around the corner and hit a key on his phone.

'Brent? He's at one of the outside tables of the café, opposite La Concorde Hotel . . . That's right . . . Let me know when you're set up and we'll pull back.'

Stratton checked around the corner once again then stepped back. 'Henri's at the café,' he said to Hank. 'With a bit of luck it's the rendezvous. Brent's going to get a covert camera visual from inside the bookshop on the corner.'

Hank nodded and stepped back out of view of the café. This was fun. He was in the thick of it and buzzed by the prospect of watching a meeting between a French intelligence officer spying for the Algerians and a Brit military intelligence officer spying for the RIRA. Out of the blue he thought about Kathryn. He hadn't spoken to her for almost a week. If everything went well he would see her and the girls before the end of the day. All the team had to do now was video the Brit when he arrived and record the meet. If he got here in the next half-hour they could be home by early evening. He must remember to pick up a couple bottles of French wine, some expensive stuff. Kathryn would like that. Perfume of course would be much smarter. He would try and make love to her tonight, see if he could mend some bridges. It had been three weeks since they last rolled in the hay. He wanted very much to get the relationship back on track. All it needed was some extra effort and understanding on his part to smooth things between them.

He checked his watch. It was five minutes to ten.

Bill pulled on his jacket without taking his eyes off Henri below. He had seen him arrive a moment earlier and watched him now sitting there, calmly reading a newspaper. He knew nothing about Henri other than he worked for French intelligence. He suspected Henri's sympathies were with Algerian freedom fighters, unless he was doing it for money, but he doubted that somehow. It was a certainty Henri had no interest in the Irish cause. Bill wondered what Henri got out of this. Perhaps the Republicans were providing his people with training; they were, after all, the world's number one terrorist organisation when it came to small-team tactics. Like Bill, Henri would gain nothing of material value. They were both doing it for their cause, two nationalities, two separate goals, but everything else they had in common: spies, operating alone, deep within the enemy's ranks, everything to lose if caught, including quite possibly their lives. It was no secret among those in the business that uncovered spies never reached the courts and the attention of the media if it was at all avoidable. And not just because of the embarrassment factor. That was the least important reason. Uncovered spies could continue to do damage even when incarcerated. It was preferable that they mysteriously disappeared or died in an unfortunate accident, the important criterion being they could no longer communicate in any way shape or form. It was unofficial, of course. Those kinds of requests from upon high were never committed to paper. They needed to happen nonetheless. And it had to be kept secret – the kind of secret that was never revealed to the general public, ever. Bill understood it all too well and would be the last person to complain about the logic of it. When the IRA uncovered a tout within its ranks it meant interrogation followed by execution. Bill had such an execution order in his parcel of information for Henri to pass on to his handlers.

Most of the details in the pack involved operations the undercover detachments were mounting and the locations of recent wiretaps and secret observation posts, but it also included the names of two informers within the IRA's command structure. Bill was sentencing those men to death. Like Bill, they knew the risks they were taking. Indeed, it was possible that one day it could happen to him. And there was the problem for him. Like the sword of Damocles, it was difficult to live with that aspect of the job hanging over him and getting more dangerous each time he provided information. Either because of that danger or simply because he was getting older and wiser, life was becoming more precious to him.

In recent months Bill had grown increasingly concerned with the way the RIRA command was using the information he provided. There was always a danger that if they mismanaged the information it could send up flags as to the possible existence of a spy within British military intelligence. That would release the hounds. The RIRA command was sometimes sensible about allowing the detachments some successes against them so as not to arouse suspicion, but not often enough in Bill's mind. The favoured ploy was to continue certain operations RIRA learned the Brits were aware of. It was like a pantomime of terrorist activity to keep the watchers occupied while RIRA conducted the real operations elsewhere. The incident that triggered Bill's alarm bells was the bungled kidnapping attempt of Spinks. He was concerned that RIRA's obsession with capturing a Pink would tempt them to push the envelope a little too far. Bill blamed himself as much as them though. It was a warning to him that despite his importance he had to take more responsibility for his own security. Included in his package for Henri was a criticism of that kidnapping operation, his fears of information mishandling, and a request that he be allowed to hibernate for a while, years perhaps. If they did not agree he would consider imposing it himself. They couldn't do much about it. He was an ace in a game where RIRA had so few. But taking charge of his own destiny like that had its dangers. There were those who might not be very understanding.

Bill reached for the window to close it before leaving the room. As he did so he happened to glance down the street. What he saw made him lunge back into the room in utter horror. Fear ripped through him. His breathing quickened as his heart rate soared. Nausea overcame him and he barely managed to hold the vomit down.

He stood there for several seconds, trying to regain control. He could have been mistaken.

He moved around to the far side of the room and then, with his back flat against the wall, he stood on tiptoe to look out on to the street. His view was obscured by the balcony and he inched from side to side until he could fit the road junction between the window frames in the door and the rails.

There was no mistaking it. It was Stratton.

Bill watched Stratton move back around the corner and out of sight. The horrific implications made him giddy with fear. His immediate thought was that Stratton was here to kill him. It would make perfect sense. He knew Bill by sight and he would want revenge for Bill's part in Spinks's kidnapping attempt. Bill knew only too well that Stratton was a killer. There were his four official kills, but then there was McGinnis, the IRA sniper, who was found with a broken neck in Warrenpoint the night Stratton was there with his team. There was no proof, of course. But the tout on the border near Bessbrook Mill was different. Bill knew it was Stratton who was responsible because Bill had been there that very night; he couldn't say anything because he wasn't supposed to have been. Bill was spying on a meeting between an RUC Special Branch detective and the very same tout. Bill did not know who the tout was at that time, only about the meeting and his existence and he wanted to find out his identity. But unbeknown to Bill, Stratton was also watching the meeting. When the Special Branch officer left, Stratton followed the tout a few hundred yards and killed him. At the time, Bill could not understand why Stratton had killed a tout who was effectively working for the Brits. It was only several months later that he learned the tout had not only been trying to squeeze more money from the Brits for his information and threatened his Special Branch handler with his life, but had also been behind a series of killings of Brit soldiers on shore leave. They were lured to an apartment by his accomplice girlfriend and then murdered. One airman was found dead with his throat slit and his testicles cut off and placed in his mouth. As far as Bill was concerned the bastard deserved everything he got. What truly peaked his curiosity was whether Stratton was acting on his own or working for King Henry. King Henry was a metaphor borrowed from the occasion when Henry II, speaking in anger, commented that the country would be best served if Thomas à Becket were gotten rid of, whereupon four of his knights, who had overheard, rode off and killed him. The point of the metaphor being it was not a direct order, merely a whim from on high.

Bill was afraid he had made Stratton's dreaded hit list.

He grabbed his stuff and hurried to the door. But he stopped in his tracks. Something about the scenario did not add up. He forced himself to consider the facts calmly. Things may not be quite as they appeared and an overreaction could be disastrous.

To begin with, it was possible that it was a coincidence and Stratton was on holiday or on a completely unrelated job. Bill quickly threw out that notion as ridiculous. Stratton had been looking up the street, towards the café, partly concealed around a corner. It had to be assumed he was trying to get a look at the café and therefore Henri without being seen. If Stratton knew Bill was in the hotel he would not have exposed himself. Stratton was far too good an

187

operative for that. Bill knew him by reputation only, although of course he had seen him several times on his visits to the detachment. Bill felt confident enough of Stratton's professionalism to conclude that if Stratton wasn't watching the hotel then no one was. Stratton was watching Henri in the café, which would support the supposition that he was not alone and part of a surveillance team. Bill contemplated the possibility that they did not know he was the person meeting Henri. If they were suspicious of him he would have been placed under surveillance and followed from London and they would be watching the hotel. The fact that it was Stratton down in the street supported this conclusion: they would never have sent anyone Bill would recognise. If they did not know Bill was meeting Henri then they did not know who was. But did they know there was a spy in MI5 who reported to Henri, a French spy? And did they know Henri was reporting to the Real IRA? That was a leap to assume, but nonetheless it should be considered.

Bill went through the points again to make sure there weren't any gaping holes in his logic. He was satisfied. Now he had to consider what his next move should be. Obviously he had to get away and back to London, but he could not leave the hotel and risk bumping into Stratton. Stratton was out front, but there was no rear exit to the hotel. The back opened out into a courtyard in the centre of the block and the exit from the courtyard was Rue Cambon, virtually smack opposite the café. Bill then considered Henri. He should contact him somehow. That might help both of them. Henri would leave the café and draw the team away from the area. It would also give Henri an opportunity to escape the country and avoid a nasty interrogation that might produce a description of Bill.

Bill checked to see if Henri was still seated outside the

café. He was. Bill searched the desk drawers and found the telephone directory. He glanced through the window to check the spelling of the name on the front of the café and then found the number. He felt for his cell-phone in his pocket and stopped. That would be stupid. He couldn't use the phone in the room either. Any landline phone in Europe could be traced to another. But he knew how to use a phone and chill the trace. There was always a risk, but the present situation made it acceptable. He went to his door, listened a moment, then opened it to check the landing was clear. He stepped into the corridor, pulled the door behind him without closing it, and went to the stairs that spiralled for several floors in both directions. Someone left a room above, closed a door and walked across the corridor and into another room. Bill quickly and quietly moved down the carpeted steps to the floor below and paused again. Beyond an arch was the reception. Against the wall on Bill's side of the arch was a public payphone. Bill moved to it, staying tight around the corner out of sight of the receptionist who was sitting in a chair with his head at counter level reading a maga-zine. Bill lifted the receiver, placed a coin in the slot and dialled the number.

It rang for a moment, then a man's voice answered.

'Bonjour, monsieur,' Bill said. His French was slow but workable. 'Je voudrais parler avec l'homme qui est assis devant votre café. C'est très important, s'il vous plaît.'

The voice asked him to wait a moment. If the call was traced it would be impossible to say who could have made it, as long as Bill remained unseen, that is. At the worst all they would have was a description. Unless they knew they were looking for Bill it would do them no good.

'Come on, for fuck's sake,' Bill mumbled, willing Henri to get off his arse and go to the phone.

'*Oui?*' came Henri's voice.

'It's me. We can't meet,' Bill said, and then before Henri had a chance to say anything or hang up, Bill continued urgently, 'Listen to me carefully. You are being watched at this very moment by British military intelligence. Do you understand?' Bill could imagine Henri's shock as he digested this information, with all its horrendous implications. If he had a family, he didn't any more. If he had a house, it was gone, as were all his possessions. If he wanted to escape he could never contact a friend, lover or family member ever again without running the risk of capture or even assassination. In one sudden bolt out of the blue, life, as he knew it, was over.

Henri did not answer but Bill knew he was still on the end of the phone. He could hear him breathing.

'Henri? Do you understand me?'

'I understand,' he said, sounding quite calm.

'One of them is standing on the first corner as you turn right out of the café on your side of the road. He is six feet tall, early thirties, strong build, wearing a camel-coloured coat and dark trousers. Do you understand?'

'Yes . . . And you?'

'I don't know yet,' Bill said.

'Good luck to you,' Henri said after a pause.

'And you too.'

The phone went dead. Bill replaced the receiver and carefully checked the receptionist was still in his seat. He then hurried back up the stairs, into his room where he closed the door. He went to the window and looked down on to the café. Henri walked out and stopped on the pavement. He calmly buttoned up his coat, turned to his right and walked down the street.

★　★　★

Stratton, around the corner, was unaware that Henri had left the café. His cell-phone vibrated and he answered it. It was Brent warning him from inside the bookshop that Henri was foxtrot towards him and in fact approaching at that very moment. Stratton instinctively turned his back to the corner and kept the phone to his ear as if innocently pausing in the street to have a conversation. Hank had no idea what was going on and was looking around at the variety of architecture that surrounded him. Henri arrived at the corner and stopped, as if deciding which way to go. He casually glanced over at the man on the phone with his back to him, who matched the description Bill had given him. His eyes then flicked to the man beyond him who was looking up with apparent interest at the tops of the buildings across the street. Henri turned his back on them, crossed the road and headed away.

Stratton turned to see Henri walking away. He hit a key on his phone. 'He's towards the Place de la Concorde. Did you see him with anyone?'

Brent quickly explained about the waiter and that he had not seen anyone else, although he could not see inside the café from his location. Brent's immediate concern was what Stratton wanted him to do next.

'Standby,' Stratton said and paused to think. Several questions presented themselves: what did the waiter want? Had Henri suspected he was being followed and cancelled the meeting? Was the stop at the café another anti-surveillance move? Could he now be on his way to the actual rendezvous?

Stratton focused on Henri. If the Frenchman suspected he was being followed they had blown it anyway. If not, Stratton wanted to house him. The solution was a straightforward one at that point. 'He's heading west on Mondovi, which will bring him out on Rivoli, north-east corner of

Place de la Concorde. Cover it,' he said to Brent on the phone then disconnected. If Henri gave the slightest hint he knew he was being followed Stratton would pull off. Henri would walk them around all day otherwise.

'Hank,' he said and Hank gave him his full attention. Stratton indicated the only man walking away up the street across the junction. 'That's him,' he said.

'Henri?' Hank asked, surprised.

'Follow him. Stay well back. The road turns left at the end and leads to Rivoli, the main street. He can't go anywhere else except inside a building. If he enters a building, carry on past and memorise the location. Don't be obvious. Act natural. Wait for me on Rivoli. Got it?'

'Got it,' Hank said, a ripple of excitement passing through him.

'If for some reason I or no one else hooks up with you on Rivoli we'll meet back at the café where we had breakfast. You remember where that is?'

'Yes.'

'Go,' Stratton said, and Hank set off.

'You're just a tourist,' Stratton added as Hank headed across the junction to put himself on the opposite sidewalk to Henri.

Hank gave a thumbs-up without looking back, his eyes focused on Henri.

Stratton watched them both for a moment. Henri was halfway to the corner.

Stratton then set off along Cambon towards the café. As he walked he punched a number key on his cell-phone.

'Brent. Hank has him on Mondovi. Call Clemens. He should be somewhere on the Place de la Concorde. Henri should be on Rivoli in less than a minute.'

* * *

Bill had seen the man with Stratton head off after Henri and then watched Stratton walk directly below his window and enter the café. A few seconds later Stratton stepped out and continued on towards Rivoli. Stratton was probably checking on the faces in the café in case they ever came up again and was now off to join the pack following Henri. Bill picked up his coat and bag and left the room.

Hank kept as far back from Henri as he dared; he was concerned about getting caught by one of his double-backs. This street, unlike all of the others they had been along so far, was practically deserted, probably because, except for a restaurant on the outside bend of the corner, it was purely residential. Hank was the only other person in the street and Henri would see him if he stopped and turned around. Hank decided if that happened he would simply keep on going and head into the restaurant.

Just as Hank set firm his contingency plan, Henri crossed the road and headed directly for the restaurant. Hank slowed down, quickly formulating a new plan if Henri went inside. Henri stopped outside and faced the menu in the window, his back to Hank.

Hank stopped. He didn't want to pass Henri if he could avoid it. He had just a few seconds to think. He was outside an apartment block with a glass door that led into a lobby. Hank stepped into the doorway. If Henri doubled back, Hank would head into the lobby and up a flight of stairs he could see until Henri passed.

Henri appeared to read the menu for a moment before continuing on towards Rue de Rivoli.

Hank waited until Henri had passed out of sight beyond the corner before leaving the doorway; he walked up to the restaurant as if to inspect it himself while casually looking down the street. Henri was halfway to Rue de Rivoli. Hank set off after him.

Henri raised something to his ear as he walked. It was a cellular phone.

Stratton turned the corner of Rue Cambon on to Rivoli, passed the bookshop Brent had been inside, and made his way west under the ornate stone arches that covered the pavement on this stretch of road. It was densely populated with shoppers and tourists, who milled sluggishly, in tune with the heavy traffic that crammed the wide, four-lane Rivoli. He headed on towards Rue de Mondovi, where Henri was expected to exit from any moment, but there was a press of bodies filling the distance to that junction.

Hank watched Henri reach the end of Mondovi and enter the multitudes on Rivoli as if passing through a wall like a ghost. Hank speeded up and stopped at the edge of the crowd. He scanned in all directions for a sign of Henri but there was none. Directly ahead of him, the other side of the broad sidewalk, he caught a glimpse of a subway entrance and steps dropping below street level. He looked around once more, this time hoping to see one of the team, again without luck. Stratton had told him to wait at the end of the street but Hank wondered if he knew about the subway. If Henri had gone down into it and no one had seen him Hank would be expected to check. There was nothing to lose and everything to gain. If Henri wasn't there he would come back and wait as planned.

Hank pushed through the cross traffic and headed down the steps.

The density of people in the confined tunnel, shuffling in both directions, made it difficult for Hank to move any quicker than the flow. He twisted and sidestepped, pausing only to avoid full-on collisions. He reached a row of metal doors and pushed on through and down a sloping corridor, which suddenly opened out into a crowded hall. He stopped on the edge and looked around, eyes locking for a second on to anyone who resembled Henri before moving on. Then he saw him, slipping a ticket into a turnstile, removing it from a slot the other end and passing through.

Hank hurried to the ticket windows and chose one that had just two people waiting in front of him. Money he told himself and dug into his pockets to find some notes. Ignorant of the cost of a ticket he chose the largest bill and clutched it, willing those ahead of him to hurry up. He checked over his shoulder and caught a glimpse of Henri heading down a tunnel the other side of the stiles. When he looked back there was no one between him and the ticket window. A man attempted to step in front of him but Hank barged him aside. The man spat something in French but Hank ignored him and faced the ticket person behind his window.

'Uhh, anywhere. Your furthest journey,' Hank said quickly.

The man in the ticket office shrugged and responded tiredly in French but was not forthcoming with a ticket.

'The end of the line, okay, buddy? I just wanna go for a ride.'

The man shrugged again, this time with his mouth and jaw in a deformed expression that appeared to signal he was baffled.

'Look, pal. Just give me a friggin' ticket to anywhere, okay. Anywhere, for chrissake!'

Hank looked back at the turnstiles and considered jumping them, but there were doors the other side that activated only with the use of a ticket – he wouldn't get through. Then a woman in the line behind him explained something in French to the ticket officer, who shrugged again, rolled his eyes and punched several buttons. Two tickets popped out of the machine. Hank shoved his bill under the window, grabbed the tickets, and hurried to the turnstiles. The ticket person called out after him but Hank was too focused to think about his change.

Hank put the ticket into the slot in the turnstile. It popped out the other side and he snatched it up and pushed through the doors.

Hank hurried along the tunnel, threading past the people like a slalom, and came to a sudden stop where it divided into three more tunnels with signs advertising different destinations.

'Shit!' he exclaimed.

He chose one, ran to its mouth and looked into it. Dozens of people were strung out along its length, the end disappearing in a bend. Hank felt frustration welling up in him. People pushed passed him to enter the tunnel. He was about to turn back to check another tunnel when he caught a flash of what looked like Henri at the far end. He wasn't sure if it was the Frenchman, took a second to make a decision and went for it. He moved quickly along the tunnel, bashed into more than one person without apologising, and hurried on.

He arrived at a flight of stairs and hurried down them. A short tunnel at the end led on to a crowded platform. He remained on the corner, standing on tiptoe to search the sea of heads. A train burst out of the tunnel beside him and the brakes screeched as it slowed to a stop. The doors opened and he saw Henri step into the centre doors of a crowded carriage.

Hank pushed his way along the platform to the closest end of the same carriage and jumped in as the doors closed.

The train started off and entered the tunnel.

Hank craned his head to catch a glimpse of Henri, who was standing in the middle holding on to a rail, staring ahead. He looked calm and relaxed.

Hank felt sweat trickling down his temples. A woman beside him watched him. He wiped the sweat away with the sleeve of his jacket and she looked away.

Hank took stock of the situation and considered what he had actually achieved by this spontaneous piece of activity. It was quite probably a pointless exercise since he had no phone – not that it would work in the métro anyway – no map and he had no idea where he was, and once off the train couldn't follow Henri by himself even if he had that equipment. The smart thing to do was to get off at the next stop and find his way back to the rendezvous point. He decided that was what he would do.

He glanced through the glass door beside him that led through to the next carriage and to his surprise there was Clemens looking directly at him. Clemens gave him a quick smirk.

Hank never thought he'd be pleased to see that ugly face. He looked in Henri's direction then back at Clemens. Clemens nodded. The train suddenly popped out of the dark tunnel and into a brightly lit station. It came to a stop and the doors hissed open. Henri remained where he was. People got on and off, the doors closed and they moved off again. Hank checked Clemens was still in the other carriage.

Hank settled down and made an effort to relax. He dropped his shoulders and rotated his head a little to ease the tension. The carriage between him and Henri was crowded and he didn't feel exposed. The next move would be Clemens's.

The following stop a seat became vacant beside Hank and he took it. From where he was sitting he could just about see Henri's legs, and Clemens's.

The train stopped several more times. At Bastille Henri stepped off. Hank followed and watched Henri move with the crowd towards the exit at the end of the platform. Clemens passed him and he tagged along behind. As he walked up a flight of stairs a man brushed passed without a look. It was Brent. Hank felt even more comfortable and settled into the rear of the surveillance snake. All he had to do was keep Brent or Clemens in his sights.

Henri did not leave the métro station and instead led them through several tunnels to another platform, where a train had just arrived. Hank saw Brent step into a crowded carriage and so he chose the one behind where he could see him through the connecting doors. He couldn't see Henri but that responsibility was no longer his.

Two stops later, at Gare d'Austerlitz, Brent climbed off the train. Hank followed him along several tunnels and up an escalator that led out into daylight. Brent turned a corner several yards ahead of Hank. When he caught up to it a short corridor led to a row of swing doors across the far end. Hank pushed through and found himself in a cavernous hall crowded with people, small shops and rows of ticket counters. It was a mainline station and the platforms were beyond a long row of double doors the other side of the hall. Hank had lost sight of Brent and stopped to look around.

A hand grabbed his arm. Hank jerked around to see Clemens.

'Where's Henri?' Clemens asked quickly, eyes searching anxiously.

'I don't know,' Hank said. 'I haven't seen him since we changed trains on the subway.'

'He's doubled back, the slippery bastard. This place is a fucking maze. What about Brent?'

'I lost sight of him when he turned into here.'

'There's another platform level below. Through that way,' Clemens said, pointing at an archway. 'I'll check the platforms on this level.' And with that he moved off across the hall.

'Clemens,' Hank called after him, but Clemens didn't hear or chose to ignore him and kept on going.

Hank didn't like this. It was all beginning to feel out of control. He wished Stratton would turn up and take charge. What was he supposed to do if he did see Henri? He had no form of communication. Clemens was wrong in sending him off by himself. Last time it made sense. Stratton had given him clear instructions. His gut instinct this time was to ignore Clemens. But then he would be in a negative position come the debriefing. If he went off alone this time at least he could blame Clemens. He headed in the direction Clemens had indicated and through the archway that led to a descending escalator. He skipped down it and into a grimy, grey, concrete hall with a low ceiling, much smaller than the main station and not nearly so crowded. The combination of supporting pillars throughout and various foyers offering such items as flowers, magazines and tourist paraphernalia gave it a labyrinth effect and obscured visibility of most of the hall. Hank made his way through it, checking in all directions. Then he caught sight of Henri heading up an escalator the other side of a row of ticket turnstiles.

Hank looked back the way he had come, hoping to see the others, but he was disappointed. He searched for his tickets as he approached the stiles and pulled them out of his pocket. He had no idea which of them would work, if any. There were no doors on this barrier and he could jump over if he wanted to. He shoved one of the tickets into the machine and the turnstile sprung open.

Hank pushed on through and headed for the escalator.

It took him up on to a long, open-air platform with tracks on both sides and a handful of people hanging about. Dirty brick buildings occupied the centre and Hank walked to the corner of the nearest one and checked along both sides of the platform.

Hank didn't need to search for long. Henri was halfway along one of the platforms, standing near the edge in full view. Hank stepped back behind the building and looked towards the escalator, hoping to see Brent or Clemens appear.

A train pulled into the station. When it stopped the doors automatically opened and Henri stepped inside. Several people emerged from the escalator but there were no familiar faces.

It was decision time again. Hank didn't feel comfortable at all about getting on the train this time. It could be going to Poland for all he knew.

A door klaxon sounded. It was now or never. His instincts called out for him to stay put, but something else ordered his legs to get moving and jump on board as the doors closed.

It was a double-decker carriage with only a handful of people aboard. There was no sign of Henri, but then he had climbed on the other end. Hank hoped some of the guys were on another part of the train but somehow he didn't think that would turn out to be the case this time.

He walked up the steps to the top deck and moved along, holding on to the rails as the train slowly left the station lurching from side to side. He stretched to peer down into the far end of the lower deck, where he caught a glimpse of Henri.

Hank sat down where he could see the side of Henri's head if he leaned forward but where Henri would not be able to see him if he looked up.

The train cut through the city. Hank checked his watch. It was ten forty-two. He calculated that he could afford to stay with Henri for an hour. If Henri got off he might follow him for a bit, or simply go on to the next stop and catch a train back the way he had come. If Henri was still on board in an hour Hank would get off anyway and back-track to the rendezvous point. He had a list of the team's phone numbers in his pocket and would call Stratton and report where he last saw Henri. Hell, out of the whole team he was the only one who had kept sight of him. Even if he didn't see Henri make a meeting he might still get a pat on the back for trying.

Hank was content with his plan and watched the backs of buildings as they sped past. An endless scrawl of graffiti seemed to run in one long connected strip of fractured colour on both sides of the track. The stations were much further apart than on the métro. At the first stop, ten minutes later, an elderly woman got on and sat the other side of the carriage from Hank. He leaned forward to see if Henri was still there and saw him talking into his cell-phone. The doors closed and the train shunted off again.

As the train pulled into Juvisy, twenty minutes later, Henri remained in his seat. A handful of people got on and a man took the seat directly facing Hank. He was squat, broad shouldered and powerful looking, muscle-bound but not sculptured like a professional bodybuilder. He was naturally hard, a product of strong genes and a tough occupation, a labourer, Hank decided. A thick scar tracked from his right eye down to his throat and his hands were huge and calloused. Hank wondered where he was from. His hair was jet black and his skin tanned and weathered. He was dressed in a worn, cheap, ill-fitting suit and a pair of seasoned, black work boots with white parachute cord for laces. The man sat quietly, unmoving, looking straight ahead, like a troll. Only once did he look at Hank with his slow, large, expressionless eyes and when Hank looked at him he turned away.

As the train pulled out of the station someone sat behind Hank. Hank casually turned to look back but not enough for his peripheral vision to catch sight of whoever was behind him. The elderly woman was still seated opposite clutching her handbag. Hank suddenly felt uneasy. He reasoned it was a combination of being alone in a strange country under strange circumstances and heading further away from the city. He looked at the station map above the window and saw the next stop was a place called Savigny sur Orge. Hank had a rethink of his plan and decided to get off at Savigny and head back to the city. He could do no more on his own and felt he should never have gone this far.

Ten minutes later the train started to slow. The track ahead was curved and Hank could see the small station. As the leading edge of the platform passed the carriage he checked the sign. It was Savigny. He leaned forward to check on Henri and saw he was on his feet and standing at the door. Hank stopped to rethink again: should he just let Henri get off, give him time to head along the platform, then when he was out of sight get off himself? Or should he wait until the next stop? What the hell, he thought. As long as Henri did not see him it couldn't do any harm to follow him for a bit. He was still twenty minutes short of the hour deadline he'd given himself.

As the train slowed Hank sat back to wait until it had

stopped completely and allow Henri off the train. Suddenly a powerful arm wrapped around his throat and yanked his head back over the seat so brutally Hank thought his neck was going to break. He could barely breathe, his eyes bulging as the flow of blood was restricted. He grabbed the arm but it was like a block of oak. Then a blow as if from a sledge-hammer slammed into his gut. The gnarled man opposite was on his feet in front of him and cocking back his huge fist for another punch. Hank kicked out but the squat man kneeled on Hank's crotch and powered his fist into Hank's chest with such force it cracked several ribs. The arm around Hank's neck released him, but only so that it could grip Hank's head, turn his face towards the window and slam it into the coach frame. Hank saw stars and felt consciousness slipping away. The blow was repeated and blood splashed across the window. Another blow struck him in the gut and he felt the strength drain from him. His brain was closing down communications with the rest of his body. He could see the bloody window frame move away from him once more, then close in again at speed. There was a loud crack and everything went dark and silent.

The train stopped and the doors opened. Henri looked up to see the two men drag Hank from his seat and along the aisle past the elderly woman, who could do nothing, but watch in utter horror. They pulled Hank down the stairs, took an arm each and lifted his limp body out of the train. The biggest of the men, the one who had been seated behind Hank, lifted him easily on to his shoulder and together they walked casually down the platform, Henri in front, sombre as an undertaker. The handful of people in the station took little notice or couldn't care less about what appeared to be a drunk being carried home by his workmates.

No station staff were on duty at the turnstile as Henri

led them through. The two powerful men followed, each pausing to slide his ticket into the machine and push on through.

They trooped down a flight of steps into a short, litter-filled tunnel, which led out to a small car park in the centre of the sleepy town. They walked to a van that looked as if it had seen many miles over many years. The squat man opened the back; Hank was thrown on to the dirty floor and the door was closed. Henri climbed into the passenger seat and the squat man into the driver's seat. A moment later the van was driving out of the car park. The large man in the back rolled the unconscious Hank on to his front, took a length of cord and tied Hank's wrists together. He looped the line around Hank's neck, pulling on it so that Hank's arms bent further up his back, and then bent Hank's feet back and tied the line around his ankles. Hank lay trussed up better than a turkey, blood bubbling from his mouth as he breathed, the rest of his face bloody from the gash across his forehead. The large man sat back on a box, produced a packet of non-filter Gitanes from a pocket, lit one and handed it to the driver. He lit another and offered it to Henri, who declined with a polite wave. As the two men puffed on their cigarettes, filling the van with smoke, Henri opened his window.

12

Bill Lawton cracked open a miniature whisky and poured it into the plastic cup, over ice that had not had time to melt before the first double had been drained. An overactive imagination was keeping him from convincing himself that he was not blown. Thirty-three thousand feet below he could see the coast of England from his window at the back of the British Airways 757. The thought they might be waiting for him in Heathrow had almost changed his mind about catching the flight, but he concluded that if they knew about him they would have nabbed him right away to avoid the risk of letting him slip from their grasp. But then again it was possible they might have wanted to watch him to see if he led them to anyone else.

Before checking on to the flight Bill had pondered his pitifully few options if he did choose to run. The Republic would not be a wise option. There was nowhere in that country he could start a new life. He didn't know who his handler was. It was someone high up obviously, but there were dozens to choose from. Going over to the Republic was the last thing Bill wanted to do anyway. What with the new relationship the Irish Government had with Britain in the fight against terrorism he would be as unsafe there as in England. He had enough money to fly to some foreign country, South America for instance, buy a car or motorbike and head into the hills, perhaps literally. But the fact that he still had access to his money indicated they did not know about him or at least were not ready to pull him in. He had gone to a cash dispenser in the airport and had drawn out the maximum he could from his bank account and two credit cards. If they did want to pull him in the first thing they would have done was block his money sources to impede his attempt to escape.

If he did decide to run the obvious location was North America. It would be the safest civilised location before settling for a shack in the middle of some godforsaken jungle or outback. But America had problems for him too. That vast country would only truly be a safe haven under the protection of one person in particular, the man who got him into all of this in the first place, but the very thought of meeting him again filled Bill with bitter resentment. Bill told himself to forget about running, for the time being at least. The powers that be did not know the identity of their RIRA spy yet and doing a runner would point the finger straight at him. It would be wise to plan to run eventually but for now he had to carry on as normal and use the time to organise it properly. He would gradually liquefy all his assets and then at the right moment quietly slip away. It would help if he knew whether or not Henri had escaped. That would aid his assessment of the situation with regard to the time he had. But then again, even if Henri had been caught, Bill doubted he would give them an accurate description of his British contact. Henri had the appearance and manner of a hardened vet, one of the old school. It would make sense, in the light of Bill's value, that his handler employed a middleman who was worth his salt.

Bill assessed how difficult it would be for military intelligence to track him down based on their knowledge that their spy had quite likely travelled from the UK to Paris within twenty-four hours of the meeting. A check of all the flight listings wouldn't do them any good since he was travelling on a false passport, and that was assuming he had flown between Paris and Heathrow. As far as they knew he might have travelled by train, ferry, car or caught a flight from one of half-a-dozen locations in the UK – with the option of as many carriers – to numerous European airports prior to arriving in Paris. Their only real hope was to wait for him to rear his head again, but he wouldn't. After the scare he had today his spying days were over. Even his handlers would have to concede that one.

He repeated the words to himself. 'It's over, over at last.' He could finally justify pulling out of the game he felt he had been manipulated into like a fool from the beginning. 'That fucking bastard of a priest,' he spat with intensity, unaware whether he'd actually said the words aloud. He looked over at the man across the aisle, who was still looking out of the window. He made an effort to calm himself down again.

He thought about being able to live a normal existence without the constant threat and worry of life imprisonment or assassination. But there might also be a price to pay for closing shop. There were some who would be angered by it. A lot of hopes were riding on him. It all depended on what the godfathers would say and how they would react. Surely they could figure out for themselves that it was over for him.

Of course, *he* wouldn't, *Father fucking Kinsella!* That bastard wouldn't let Bill off the hook quite so easily. He would happily leave Bill to be squeezed dry until he was caught and fried. Kinsella would interpret Bill's end as invaluable publicity for the cause. The press would be all over it. Bill would be touted as the most successful and highly placed

IRA mole within British military intelligence in the IRA's history. Father Kinsella would of course communicate to Bill how sorry he was, but privately he would see it as Bill's final and greatest contribution. 'The fanatical bastard,' Bill uttered as his blood started to boil once again. Then he sensed the man across the aisle look at him. Bill was thinking out loud. He drained his beaker and warned himself to calm down.

Bill considered the pros and cons of playing the godfathers along. He could try the extended vacation approach, asking for a hibernation long enough to ensure his identity was safe, several years for instance. But that was not something Bill really fancied trying. It would be like a 'buy now pay later' deal. The fact that he would have to start up again eventually would always be hanging over his head. And Father Kinsella would not forget to wake him up again. Bill was his greatest success and he would milk the glory to the bitter end – Bill's end. How could a priest become such a manipulative bastard? Bill wondered. And why had it taken him so long to figure it out?

Bill could feel himself getting worked up again and needed a distraction. He took the duty-free catalogue from the pouch in front of him and flicked through it. What about tonight? he thought. Should he still see Aggy?

He looked up to see a stewardess approaching and he hit her with that Irish smile of his, which automatically appeared whenever an attractive woman looked at him.

'Excuse me,' he said. 'What do I have to do to get something from this catalogue?'

'You ask me, sir,' she said, returning his smile. 'What would you like?'

He pointed to one of the perfume bottles on the page. 'What's this one like?'

'It's the most expensive.'

'Then I'll take it . . . and have one yourself.'

Her smile widened to show a set of perfect teeth. 'It doesn't suit me,' she said. 'But thanks anyway.' Her eyes lingered on his beyond the boundaries of normal service requirements. 'I'll go and get that for you,' she said and walked away.

Bill leaned into the aisle to check out her shapely calves and bottom. Life was such a wonderful thing, he thought, and he had so much to lose. It was far too optimistic to be planning a normal life just yet but Bill was a flagrant romantic and the contemplation was irresistible. Sadly even a beautiful bottom such as that could not rid him of his fears. The black light of death was searching for him, he could sense it. He had been an idiot and he hated himself for it as much as he hated that bastard. He truly was the reluctant spy. He thought back to when he got into this crazy game. It had been a long, slow, process spanning several years. The truth was it went beyond the time of the priest, all the way back to the beginning. But that's why the priest chose him.

William Lawton had not always been his name. He was two years old when the Lawton family took him in. It was not uncommon for a Catholic baby to be adopted by a Protestant family. Children aren't born with religious, political or racial beliefs and the Lawton family did not mind where the child came from as long as it was the Celt side of Anglo-Saxon. His legal father was a copyright lawyer, born and educated in Northern Ireland and employed by a partnership that had offices in Belfast and London. The family had houses in the centre of both cities and even though his father spent most of his time in the Belfast office his mother preferred London, not least because it meant getting out from under the marshal law that governed the Province. By the time Bill was a teenager she had become entrenched in her only true interest – and the main reason she wanted to live in London – her charity organisation. She would be out of the house from dawn till late on her never-ending quest to feed and clothe the poor children of the world, which is what led to Bill boarding at the Royal Hospital School near Ipswich at thirteen years old. The school was a grand old institution and strongly associated with the Royal Navy, enforcing upon its students traditions such as parading most Sunday mornings before church in full dress uniform, brass band and rifles included. The school was equally enthusiastic about rugby, and even though he did not make head of house or captain of the first fifteen, his two foremost ambitions at the time, Bill had to say at the end of his five years at the school that he had enjoyed every one of them. He saw his parents on average once every couple of months for the first few years and by fifteen started spending more of his half- and full-term breaks with friends or travelling. For the last two years he spent all his vacations, apart from a couple of days around Christmas, roving alone, mostly across mainland Britain and occasionally France. He preferred travelling by himself for a number of reasons: none of his friends shared his specific historical interests; he was a spontaneous sightseer, jumping on and off trains as it suited him; but most importantly, he had learned how much easier it was to meet girls when alone.

He had never ventured into the Irish Republic for no other reason than he had not developed an interest in Irish history; his trips were generally motivated by his interest in a place. He was not particularly intrigued by politics or religion but would describe himself as a Loyalist or a Protestant if pushed. He bore no ill towards Catholics and like most people his age on the mainland he did not particularly care what the Troubles in Northern Ireland were about and wanted to see the bombing and the fighting come to an end.

Bill was eighteen and on his summer holidays prior to starting university when his curiosity about his origins grew enough to motivate him to explore them – as long as the process wasn't too time consuming. Bill was not necessarily interested in meeting his birth parents; if anything he was inspired once again by his fascination with history. His prime area of interest was eighteenth- and nineteenth-century European history, specifically the French revolution, the British industrial revolution and America's formative years up to the First World War. He hoped his own family history would reveal itself to have played some part in those times but he was not expecting much. He had no idea how his life was to change with the discovery of his ancestors, or one in particular.

It was his father who, respectful of the young man's inquisitiveness, furnished him with the information that set the investigation in motion. He dug up the old adoption papers, which showed Bill's birth parents to be John and Mary Meagher. His father was not completely sure about all the facts but he believed they were both killed in a traffic accident. Bill was a competent researcher and looked forward to the challenge of uncovering more. It did not take him long to discover his parents had died on a Saturday afternoon in Enniskillen, County Fermanagh, Northern Ireland. John and Mary Meagher were originally from Tipperary in the Irish Republic and had left it five years before Bill was born to move to Ulster to take over the small farm John had inherited from an uncle. When John and his wife died, the farm, which was not a particularly successful venture, was taken over by relatives who owned adjacent divisions of what was originally one large concern.

Bill's research failed to produce a location where they were buried and so he decided to visit the farm in the hope of finding out more. It turned out the family that had taken over the farmhouse were distant cousins and they informed Bill his parents had been killed in a head-on collision with a drunk driver and that their bodies had been sent back to the Republic for burial. The cousins showed little enthusiasm in helping Bill. In fact they were down right inhospitable. They were unimpressed that Bill had come all the way from London that day and did not even invite him into the house for a cup of tea, conducting the entire conversation on the doorstep. The last thing Bill asked before leaving was if they had any photographs of his parents. They did not, and with that they closed the door on him. Bill felt embarrassed and confused by their hostility and it was only on the bus back to the family home in Belfast that it dawned on him that it was possibly because of his accent. He might have been born a Catholic, and a Meagher, but as far as they were concerned, he was now an English Protestant, kin or not.

With a month left of his holidays he decided to get this little investigation over and done with. The following day, equipped for no more than two nights on the road, he made the journey by train and bus to Southern Ireland and the village of Kumrady, several miles north-east of Limerick. On seeing the delightful setting his immediate thought was why his parents had ever wanted to leave. Enniskillen was not a patch on this place.

It was early afternoon when he arrived in the village. His plan was to have a look around the place his parents were born and raised in, find the grave in the church cemetery, utilise any spare time looking for their family homes and be on his way in time to get back to Limerick by early evening so that he could find a B&B for the night and return to Belfast the following day.

It took him a while to find the headstone, not that he had rushed in looking for it. Cemeteries fascinated him. The headstones transported one into the past, revealing the names of people who had actually lived, pure history that could pinpoint a precise day in the story of mankind. Within the confines of this one tiny cemetery, in the space of an hour or so, Bill found people who had been alive during the French revolution, the Peninsular War, the battle of Trafalgar and the Russian revolution. A high point of the day was finding two men who, it could be deduced, left the village when they were young, died somewhere in America in 1867, and were then shipped back to the place of their birth to be buried. Bill wondered how they had both come to die at the same time, and how they had enough money to pay for their bodies to be shipped all that way back to their little village.

When he did find his parents' grave the first thing Bill tried to imagine was how they had looked to the world; the little things: how they had acted, laughed, talked, what they did with their everyday lives. Now that he was here, standing above them, the urge to know more about them grew stronger. A sadness washed over him but he couldn't think exactly why. Perhaps it was nostalgia. He'd had pretty much everything he needed growing up and never felt deprived of anything, and he had hardly thought about them for more than a few seconds in all those years let alone missed them. For the first time in his life he felt a personal loss. He wondered how much like them he was, or which of them he was most like. His mother was twenty-three when she died, just five years older than he was now, and his father twenty-seven.

Bill leaned back on a nearby tree, lost in thought, unaware of a man approaching from behind, slowly making his way through the cemetery from gravestone to gravestone, reading each in turn. As he came around the tree he almost bumped into Bill, startling him. Bill noted the telltale white collar under the man's tweed jacket. He was well mannered and acted most humble, as one might expect of a priest, however his appearance made him look more like a navvy; he was large, with heavy bone structure, powerful hands and a bull neck. He apologised for disturbing Bill but instead of leaving him to himself, as one might expect in a place such as a cemetery, the priest was intent on striking up a conversation. He was an American with a strong New England accent and introduced himself as Father Kinsella, on holiday from Boston and visiting relatives for a few weeks. His first question to Bill was what was an Englishman doing in an Irish graveyard. When Bill explained he was actually Irish and that his parents had come from the village the priest grew noticeably warmer towards him. At first Bill felt trapped by this friendly but overbearing character. This was a private time for him and now that it had been interrupted he wanted to beat a polite retreat at the first opportunity and be on his way. But Father Kinsella wasn't ready to move on. He explained to Bill his fondness for reading gravestones, especially in Ireland, although the East Coast of America, specifically the central region, was particularly fascinating when it came to Irish headstones. He described how he once spent a two-month vacation following the trail of the famous 69th, an all-Irish Brigade that distinguished itself in some of the greatest battles of the American Civil War. He asked Bill if he knew that more than forty per cent of all foreign-born enlistments into the Union Army during the Civil War and about seventeen per cent of its entire strength were Irish.

Bill did not. Father Kinsella knew his Irish history as well as any professor and was very passionate. He confessed that the names and dates on the headstones transported him back to times and places in America's history and also Ireland's often dark and troubled past. When Bill admitted he knew little of Irish history Father Kinsella did not hide his disappointment. In fact his animated expressions of horror initially amused Bill, though he had a feeling it might be unwise to show it.

'What's your name?' Father Kinsella asked with an intimidating look, which once Bill got to know him, he realised was not nearly so intimidating. 'I ask because there are very few Irish names that don't have some history attached to them . . . Go on,' he pushed. 'Tell me it and I bet I'll tell you a story about one of your ancestors that you didn't know.'

Bill could see himself getting stuck here all day. He tried to summon the courage to tell this priest he needed to be on his way, but he had to admit there was something interesting about the man. Perhaps it was the enthusiasm he had for history and the way he animated every swell of passion with majestic movements of his hands and exaggerated facial expressions.

'Meagher,' Bill said. It was a conscious decision to choose Meagher and not Lawton, even though he felt a tinge of guilt. But Meagher was, after all, his rightful family name and it was no point listening to anything Father Kinsella might have to say about Lawton since it was not truly his own. Bill was not prepared for the extraordinary reaction Father Kinsella expressed when he heard the name. His mouth opened and remained in that position for a few seconds, eyes wide and staring, like a large frozen grouper.

'Did you say Meagher?' he asked.

'Yes,' said Bill.

'M-E-A-G-H-E-R?' he spelled.

'That's right,' Bill said, then pointed at the gravestone a few feet away. 'That's my mother and father's grave.'

Father Kinsella looked at the gravestone, the sight of which only fuelled his look of astonishment. 'By God,' he said. 'That's truly amazing.'

'Why's that?' Bill asked.

'Meagher was the name of the Brigadier General who commanded the 69th Irish Brigade I was just telling you about.'

He quickly studied Bill, then his surprised expression turned into a frown. 'Are you telling me you're a Meagher and you don't know anything about your family name?'

'I only found out a few days ago,' Bill said in his defence. 'My parents died when I was young . . . I was adopted.'

The priest's frown melted, but not entirely. 'You should still know enough about Irish history to know the name Meagher,' he said and took a closer look at the gravestone.

'I was adopted by a family in Belfast.'

'What's their name?' he asked.

'Lawton.'

Father Kinsella looked around at him. 'That's not an Irish name,' he said, almost accusingly. 'You were adopted by an English family?'

'Northern Irish,' Bill said.

'Protestants?'

'Yes.'

Father Kinsella took another look at the gravestone. 'Well, that explains why you don't know anything about your Irish ancestors, I suppose. I'll forgive you for now. But by God you'd better start learning.'

'Yes, I will. I'm sorry,' Bill said, unsure why he felt the

need to apologise, but Father Kinsella nodded, accepting it as if it should have been offered.

The priest turned to the gravestone and took a closer look in silence, and then he reached out and touched it, running his fingers slowly across the lettering with some reverence.

'And you've never heard of Thomas Francis Meagher?' he asked.

'No,' Bill said.

'There should be a statue to the man. Probably will be one day. You ever been to Waterford?'

'No.'

'That's where he was from. He would be, let me see . . . He'd be your great, great, great, possibly great grandfather.'

'How could you know that?' said Bill.

'Know what?'

'That that particular Meagher was an ancestor of mine?'

'If you're a Meagher from the county of Tipperary then you're a descendant of the O'Meaghers of Ikerrin,' he said. 'Do you want to hear a little about him?'

Bill felt he already knew enough about the priest to suspect this might take a while. 'I don't have a lot of time,' Bill said checking his watch.

'To hear about your own ancestor?' Father Kinsella said, the frown starting to reappear. 'Where're you staying tonight?' he asked.

'Limerick.'

'How're you getting there?'

'Bus,' Bill said.

'I'll drive you. How's that? Save yourself some money too, and time you can spend learning something valuable.' Before Bill could respond, Father Kinsella started to head off. 'Come on,' he said, and Bill followed him out of the graveyard like an obedient Labrador. Nobody had led him by his nose so easily in his life.

It was a bright, fresh day and as they crossed the stream that ran past the village on its way to Lough Derg and the River Shannon, Bill was taken back to another era. By the time they reached the rental car he was absorbed in everything the priest had to say. And it was not just history, it was Bill's history.

The stewardess arrived with Bill's perfume and he paid her in cash. He smiled distractedly, his thoughts elsewhere, wondering if it was as early as that first day in the cemetery that Father Kinsella decided to commandeer Bill's life and make him a martyr for the cause.

13

Stratton stood alone in a room on the top floor of the British Embassy, looking down on the brightly lit city across the river, the tip of the Eiffel Tower, its silhouette outlined by thousands of white light bulbs, just visible above the Grand Palais. Beyond the gardens hundreds of red and white car lights shunted along the Champs Elysées.

But Stratton could see none of this. All he could see was the crowded Rue de Rivoli of that afternoon. He thought he had seen Hank through the crowds, standing and looking about, and then he was gone. Stratton went to the spot and searched around, filtering the sea of faces passing him, the countless people moving in all directions, but there was no sign of Hank or Henri. He called Clemens and then Brent, whom he knew were in the area, but when he heard the automated message responses, it was evident they were out of signal range, which could only mean they had entered the subway and were underground. He called several other operatives but no one had anything to report. For the next few minutes he continued calling Clemens and Brent in the hope they had surfaced somewhere else around the Place de la Concorde, but after a while it became apparent they had taken the métro. When Clemens finally called him from Gare d'Austerlitz, Stratton chastised him for letting Hank go off on his own. When he had not heard from Hank for several hours, though it seemed a long shot and perhaps ludicrous to even contemplate, the word kidnap crossed his mind. It would have been his immediate concern had they been in Northern Ireland, but not Paris at eleven in the morning. Now, ten and a half hours later and still no sign of Hank, he knew in his gut that the bizarre possibility was true. The rest of the team were still on the streets checking the likely places he might turn up, searching hospitals and police stations for their 'lost American friend'.

The door opened behind him and Stratton focused on the reflection in glass; Lieutenant Jardene was standing in the doorway.

'Anything?' Jardene asked, knowing that if there was Stratton would have said so.

Stratton had his cell-phone in his hand. 'No,' he said.

Jardene let the door close behind him and entered the spacious office. 'I can't fucking believe this,' he said. It was the first time Stratton had heard him swear.

'He's been lifted,' Stratton said.

'I still think it's too soon to jump to that conclusion,' Jardene said.

'He's been lifted,' Stratton said again.

Jardene was not in denial, but it was his responsibility to remain optimistic. 'We'll have to tell the French soon. They'll have to know . . . We'll need their help in finding him.'

Stratton's phone vibrated and he raised it to his ear. 'Yes?' he said and listened for a moment. Jardene watched Stratton's eyes, looking for any sign of good news even though he knew the man well enough to know his expression would give nothing away. Stratton would tell him they had found Hank alive and well or brutally murdered in the same casual manner.

'Okay,' Stratton said to the caller. 'Stay there until you're recalled.' He thumbed the end-call button, pocketed the phone and said nothing to Jardene.

'London's going bloody apeshit,' Jardene said.

Stratton could sense something accusatory in his tone. Or perhaps he was being overly sensitive to the inevitable. The first question they would ask was who the ground team leader was. His name would have been the first that they cursed. Screw them, he thought. They couldn't be any harder on him than he'd been on himself.

'I wouldn't want to be in the boss's shoes when the call is made to Washington,' Jardene said. 'The Yanks'll go through the roof . . . God, it doesn't even bear thinking about. American Special Forces operative unofficially working for the Brits kidnapped while on illegal surveillance operation in France, and technically against the IRA.' He couldn't believe it himself. 'The implications just go on and on. We can always tell the French to sod off and pipe down but the Americans are going to want someone's head on a pike.'

And shit rolls downhill, Stratton thought. He knew where a good part of the British shit would ultimately settle though. Around Hank himself. He would be buried in the stuff, especially if he wasn't able to defend himself. London would wriggle all it could to focus much of the blame on poor old Hank, despite the fact he should not have been on the ground in the first place. The head most likely to roll in the unit itself was Jardene's. He was the officer in command. Stratton would get dragged over the coals at the court of inquiry as the ground supervisor, but at the end of the day he was a field operative. It was one of the advantages of being a non-commissioned officer when commissioned ranks were on the ground. They got the glory that came with success – and the crap that came with failure. Jardene had been in the embassy throughout the op and therefore as good as in the field. He didn't interfere with the ground op because he trusted Stratton, not that there was anything he could have done to help direct the operation anyhow. His experience of foot surveillance was virtually zero. If an operation came up next week somewhere in the world and Stratton was available he'd probably be on it. Life would soon be back to normal for him apart from the occasional dig from other operatives. It would not be long before it became an amusing story; such was the sick humour of the service. But it would be a serious bump in Jardene's career. Jardene undoubtedly had dreams of commanding the squadron one day. He was capable enough. But if there was competition for the post, what happened today might be the foot to kick the chair out from under him. The Yanks would not forget and might even be offended if the officer who lost one of their boys became CO of a unit they considered a sister.

'What do you think happened?' Jardene asked eventually.

Stratton shrugged. 'Henri sussed us.'

'When?'

'At the café. He wouldn't have gone there if he'd twigged before. He would have ran as soon as he smelled us.'

'Then the café was the rendezvous?'

Stratton nodded; he was certain of that. If you're twigged on the walk you don't stop for a coffee and let the enemy gather its forces. You take them away from your objective, keep them strung out, and you fly the first chance you get. Henri flew, the first chance he got, which was at the café. He went from there directly to the métro, the best place to screw with communications and to thin out any followers. If he flew from the café, that meant he twigged at the café.

'Was he playing Russian, do you think?' Jardene asked.

Playing Russian referred to the way the Russians liked

222

to carry out anti-surveillance. Stratton had worked against them in London more than once. They were the hardest in the business to follow because they often sent a tag to shadow the hare. Jardene was suggesting that Henri had a partner experienced in surveillance who followed him from far enough back with the specific task of watching to see if anyone was following him. If he detected any suspicious behaviour his job would have been to warn Henri off.

'It's possible,' Stratton said.

'But you don't think so.'

'We were so god-awful I thought Henri would twig us on the first leg to the café. But he didn't, otherwise he wouldn't have gone there and risk exposing his contact. A half-blind tag would've seen the shambles and called him long before he reached the café.'

'I see,' Jardene said.

'It doesn't look as if Henri used a tag in the past since up until now he's been followed by just two tails. A tag would've seen that.'

'Right,' Jardene said, accepting the argument. Then he voiced a notion. 'Unless the tag had comms problems and couldn't contact Henri until he was at the café.'

Stratton didn't say anything. Jardene knew he was reaching. 'I know it's far-fetched but it could have been something like that.'

'And maybe Henri got a call from his doctor and found out he had cancer . . . Keep it simple. Save the complicated hypothesis for your memoirs.'

Jardene flashed him a look, then thought better of telling him not to be so insubordinate. Stratton was right anyway. There were a thousand possibilities. It had to be kept to the basics otherwise the thread might be lost.

'You don't think there was a tag, then?' Jardene asked.

'No.'

'Then Henri became suspicious at the café. How?'

Stratton would have loved to know the answer to that.

'No one did a pass,' Jardene added. 'How did he know? . . . ' he trailed off to himself. He paced the room to help him think but it wasn't working. He was feeling the pressure and preparing himself for what was to come. He checked his watch. 'Hank wouldn't go to the American Embassy if he ran into trouble, would he?' Jardene asked.

'He's not stupid,' Stratton said. 'He knew he shouldn't have been on the ground with us. He did what he did to try and save the day and because he was the only one in the right place who could. It wasn't his fault. It was mine.'

'He might still turn up,' Jardene said, trying once again to believe in his own optimism. 'Let's just pray he does.' He headed for the door. 'I expect London will call us in soon, before they talk to the French. We'll get everyone together here first, then I expect we'll head back as soon as we can and debrief.'

Stratton continued looking out of the window and did not acknowledge he'd heard. Jardene left the room.

Stratton went back over the day once again. He pictured Henri sitting outside the café looking calm and relaxed. Brent saw the waiter come out and speak to him, then moments later Henri followed him back into the café. A few minutes after that Henri flew from the area taking the team with him. Henri must have learned he was blown when he left the patio and went inside. Stratton was certain if he questioned the waiter he'd find out that Henri had received a telephone call. It was the caller who warned Henri he was being followed. Someone who knew about the meeting was watching the café and the surrounding streets. That someone in all probability was the actual contact. Stratton would ask for a trace on the call, as soon as the French were brought in and had calmed down enough to co-operate, but he didn't expect to gain much from it. Anyone involved at this level of the game would know how to make a 'safe' call. A public phone, or a sterile mobile. Stratton had been hard on the team and didn't in truth think they had been all that bad. They had been bunched and clumsy at times but quick to react if they felt Henri had glanced at them even once. Stratton was the one in the street nearest the café. Him and Hank. They were the ones most likely seen. Whoever it was probably walked straight past them, became suspicious and watched them. Then after seeing them hang about the corner they blew the rendezvous. That had to be it, or something like it.

Stratton felt suddenly drained. But it wasn't just the day's mess that was weighing heavily. It was the feeling that something was unravelling inside of him. He was tiring of his life as it was. He felt like bits of him had broken off over the past few years and he didn't like what was left. The day rattled him on more than one front. The one area in his life he remained confident in was on the ground, on an operation, but today had proved that there were limitations. Perhaps it was being in a team. Operating alone had become his work of choice. There were signs that he had grown much more reclusive. It was only too obvious in the way he reacted to others and the way they acted towards him. Another danger sign was he didn't care about what his colleagues thought. The work used to have a purpose for him but it had grown blurred over time. The spirit of team ethos he liked to champion in his earlier days appeared to be lost to him now.

He could not remember when it all began to go sour. It wasn't because of Sally. He had forced that relationship, thinking it was what he wanted or needed. When she left he felt no remorse. He didn't miss her. Perhaps she knew he wouldn't, which was why she left. No one knew how he felt, not even Doles who liked to think he knew Stratton so well. The stubborn Jock know-it-all would remain unconvinced no matter what Stratton said.

He wondered where it would end. Perhaps when he no longer had something to aim for. If that was true, what was he aiming for now? The cracks were already starting to appear. For the present at least he could concentrate on finding whoever was responsible for Hank's abduction. They were tied to those who tried to kidnap Spinks, and the spy was tied to them all. He was the key. There was still more to be had from this day than he had found, he knew that. He had come within inches of the spy and there was a clue out there as to who it was. But then there was a clue to every mystery in the world somewhere. Stratton only cared about this one.

14

Aggy sat alone in a restaurant at a small table set for two, with her back to the wall. Positioning herself so that she could watch the door and where no one could come up behind her was a habit she had developed since working over the water. She was feeling uneasy. Not because of the dinner date but about the way she was dressed. She was wearing a silk T-shirt and no bra under a small, tailored leather jacket, and a short skirt, all newly bought that afternoon. She'd given it the once-over in the hall mirror before stepping out of the house but that was while standing still. When she saw her reflection walking towards her in a shop window, she realised how provocative she looked. The T-shirt clung to her breasts, accentuating her nipples as they bounced with a freedom that left nothing to the imagination. Add to that her short lycra skirt riding up her thighs – it was far too feminine a look for her. She didn't do sexy. If she'd had the time she might have gone back home and changed.

She pulled the sides of the jacket together to cover her breasts but as soon as she released them they fell back open and her breasts poked out again. She couldn't sit holding her jacket closed all night. She considered not turning up but then dismissed that as cowardice. Bill might get the wrong message. She didn't know him very well but sensed he was a bit of a tomcat. Her plans were dinner, maybe a bar or club afterwards, but nothing else, not that she was worried about him getting out of line. She was more than capable of taking care of herself.

She sensed a young man at the bar a few feet away looking at her. A quick glance at him and her immediate thought was had she seen him on the street while walking to the restaurant? Perhaps he had followed her. She looked at him again, catching his eye. He smiled and his eyes moved down her body and beneath the table, where he had enough of an angle to see her legs disappearing into her short skirt. She looked away and pressed her knees together. Why do women wear short skirts? she wondered. They're so impractical.

She checked her watch and looked at the entrance. Bill was late. Tardiness was one of her pet hates. She considered how much quieter Covent Garden was tonight than the last time she had been to this part of town. But then it was summer, when it was daylight until gone ten and filled with tourists and shoppers. Now it was dark and cold. Aggy didn't mind either, not since joining the detachment. She had changed in many ways over the past year. The most noticeable, according to her mum, was how much she had mellowed. She still had a temper but the job had taught her to keep it holstered. Tolerance was what she had acquired, and not just with people. She had learned to endure harsh conditions such as bad weather and discomfort. As for darkness, being out in it alone, she had developed a weird kind of attraction for it. It had taken several months to actually feel comfortable walking by herself through a wood in the middle of the night. There was something predatory about it that fascinated her. She wondered if she had stirred some primeval instinct. Before the selection course she hadn't done a night exercise period, never mind alone. The instructors did not take such risks with women recruits; the aim was not to discourage them since so few applied for the job. Her very first night task was not only on her own but on an actual operation to re-supply an observation post in South Armagh. It was her second week on the job and not the kind of task a female operative was normally employed to do. But all the men were otherwise engaged and the ops officer wanted to test her. If she screwed up they would know her limitations.

After being dropped off by car in a quiet country lane she walked a mile and a half across fields and through woodland to the rendezvous point with one of the operatives, who had been in the field for days. On completion of the drop she continued on another memorised route for a mile to a different location, where she met the car again, driven by the ops officer himself, and they returned to the base. The gun she always carried helped her confidence but within a few months she felt she no longer needed even that psychological comfort, although she would go nowhere outside the camp without it. She had learned the key to operating alone at night was to control the imagination and understand the tricks the eyes could play.

As she took another sip of her sparkling water the man at the bar got off his stool and came over. He stopped quite close to her. 'You waiting for someone then?' he asked.

She looked up at him tiredly. 'Yes,' she said as if the answer was a glaringly obvious one.

'He late or are you early?'

She wondered why he assumed it was a he.

'Or is it a woman you're waiting for?' he added. 'Must be. That would make more sense. I mean, I couldn't imagine a bloke being late for a babe like you.'

She telegraphed her disinterest as best she could but he remained, undeterred. She couldn't understand why he was unable to sense how much she wanted him to go away. It never failed to surprise her how some men could not read such obvious vibes.

'If he doesn't turn up, can I buy you dinner?'

'I can afford my own dinner,' she said.

He grinned. 'Great. Maybe you can buy me dinner then.'

What a tit, she thought. Are there girls who actually tolerate morons like him?

She looked up at him, about to tell him to get lost, when a figure moved in behind the man. It was Bill, with a smirk on his face. The smile was for her but she did not respond. The man suddenly sensed Bill's presence and looked around. Bill kept the grin while shifting his focus to the man.

'Hi,' Bill said. 'We'll have a couple of menus. And while you're at it get us a nice chilled bottle of Sancerre. You do a pretty good '96 for fifteen quid, or you did a couple months ago.'

'I'm not a waiter,' the man said with an attitude, not easily intimidated.

'I'm sorry,' Bill said with clear insincerity, looking over the man's clothes with a critical eye. 'I thought you were.'

They stared at each other, Bill's smile unwavering, but his eyes had hardened.

'Would you mind excusing us then, pal?' Bill said. Men have different ways of sending out a warning signal. Some use body language, a tensing of the shoulders, clenched fists, a scowl, the placement of feet for balance. Bill's warning was in his language, but it was not obvious. Those who knew him well enough would advise caution when he used the word 'pal' in such a way. The man sensed Bill's confidence but he was not entirely unfamiliar with situations such as this and was not about to let himself be stepped on. He was pissing on another man's territory, which disadvantaged him, but he nevertheless stared into Bill's eyes long enough to retain his machismo honour then looked back at Aggy, winked and walked away.

Bill's grin spread further across his face now that he finally had her to himself.

'How're you doing?' he said and leaned down to kiss her cheek. But she turned her head to avoid it and all he got was a clumsy kiss of her ear.

It stalled him. 'I'm a naturally affectionate person,' he said, making an excuse for his forwardness. 'I kiss everyone hello and goodbye.' A flush of embarrassment remained in the air between them as he sat down. 'It's getting chilly, don't you think?'

His smile had no effect on her.

'Bit cold in here too . . . Anything wrong?'

She looked at her watch. The penny dropped and he checked his own.

'I'm sorry I'm late. I really am. I'm not normally a tardy person. I've been rushing around like a March hare all day. So many things to do and people to see, and then the bloody tube train broke down and I was stuck with a dozen people in the tunnel for ten, maybe fifteen minutes.'

'You're twenty minutes late,' she said.

He looked wounded. 'I swear if you knew the mileage I'd put in today you'd understand. When I finally got home I had the fastest shower I think I've ever had in my life. I left my place at the run and practically got dressed on the tube.'

She wasn't impressed.

'Look,' he said, and stuck his feet out and pulled up the ends of his trousers to expose his socks: one black, one brown. 'Odd socks,' he exclaimed. 'And that's not all. As I was putting my shirt on I was hopping on one leg at the same time pulling on my underpants and I think I put one of my feet through the little slit that's in the front because they're god-awful tight and there's a whole bunch of extra material at the back.' He leaned over to lower his voice. 'When I'm walking I think it looks like I've shit myself.'

She tried hard not to smile.

'Please forgive me,' he pressed his case. 'It'll never happen again. Let's start over.' He reached into his jacket pocket, pulled out a small gift-wrapped package, and placed it on the table in front of her. She looked at it and then at him.

'It's perfume. Good stuff, so I'm told.'

'I don't wear perfume,' she said.

'It's not for you, it's for your mum,' he said, adjusting smoothly.

She smiled, catching the adjustment. 'Thank you.'

'You look absolutely gorgeous,' he said and peered around the table to get a full look at her. 'My God. She has legs too. I've never seen you in a skirt before.'

'I can't remember the last time I wore one. At school, I think.'

'I'll tell you something. If those old fogies back at you-know-where could see you now there might be a few shut faces. I've heard the complaints that you don't look feminine enough. They must be a load of old fruits, that's all I can say.'

'They think I'm one.'

'No way,' he said, although he had heard that.

'They call me the dyke.'

'Well, I think some of those boys have spent far too long cooped up in that little camp with no one but each other for company.'

'How do you know I'm not?'

'If you are I'd have to say I'm flattered you think I'm the one who might turn you around. And I'd also have to say you've chosen wisely.'

'You think highly of yourself.'

'Is it true then? Are you a dyke?'

The waiter came over and handed them menus. 'Can I get you a drink?' he asked.

Bill ordered the Sancerre, his favourite Loire, and the waiter left them.

She hadn't answered and so he pushed on. 'You don't care to defend your sexuality either way then?' he asked.

'Is that all you're here for?'

'Well, I'd be a liar if I didn't admit it was your beauty that got me interested in the first place. And yes, I would like to have sex with you before we get married.'

His forwardness fell on stony ground, which was a bit of a blow but his own fault. He had not stuck to his tried and tested theory to first get a woman talking about anything, then find their humour and get them laughing. Only then, when the temperature was right, steer the conversation to sex or a related subject that led to bodily contact. He was in a bit of a hole and had to get back on track. But before that he had to establish whether or not she was a lesbian.

'I believe that when a man sets eyes on an attractive woman for the first time, and vice versa, the first question that pops into his head is, could this be the woman I want to spend the rest of my life with? Is she the one? Sometimes you get your answer the second she opens her mouth – bad teeth or something like that. But if you're not put off you continue to get to know her, moment by moment, day by day, until she shows you something about herself that you could not live with. And of course, if you don't find anything about her that you could not live with, then she's the one for you.'

Before he got to the end of his little thesis, he felt like he was drowning in his own bullshit. From the way she looked at him, he realised this was not a theory to placate Aggy. 'Maybe that's too simple,' he said, still wallowing. He knew that if he was going to get out of this now it was going to be with her help.

'Would you still sleep with a woman who didn't meet your expectations?' she asked.

'Yes. Having sex is a completely different thing. Most men would sleep with any woman whether he liked her or not, if she was physically attractive enough.'

'And if you met a woman who was good enough to spend the rest of your life with and she jumped straight into bed with you, how would that affect her rating?'

'You mean, before she got to know me?'

'Yes.'

He grinned. 'Alas, one of my biggest problems is my frankness and general honesty . . . So, yes, I'd have to say it could adversely affect her qualifications.'

'You'd respect her less?'

'I could only truthfully know that the next day of course, after I'd weighed everything in my mind, but probably.'

'Why?'

'I'd always be wondering if she might jump into bed just as quickly with someone else.'

'What if she did it because you meant nothing to her?'

This was all wrong, Bill thought. They were talking about sex all right, but not in the way he'd anticipated. 'I'd feel used,' he said, trying to inject some fun into it.

'And how do you feel about me?' Aggy asked casually, without humour.

234

'So far, I'd spend the rest of my life with you,' he said without his usual smile.

'So I shouldn't even think about sleeping with you, unless I didn't want to spend the rest of my life with you?'

'No, you shouldn't,' he said. 'Would you sleep with me if I didn't want to spend the rest of my life with you?'

'No,' she said.

'Then we're settled,' he said, grinning, wondering if they had arrived back on firm ground.

She sipped her water.

'I can't believe none of them have hit on you – the guys in the detachment,' he said.

She shrugged as she picked up the menu and perused it.

'There's not one that you fancy then? Not even a little?' he asked, almost desperate to know if she was heterosexual. He might even welcome news that she had slept with one of the men at this point.

She glanced at him over the menu, wondering whether to tell him her more private thoughts or not.

'Not that I'm worried about competition,' he added. 'I wouldn't do anything such as get him transferred to another detachment, he said lying through his teeth.'

She smiled ever so slightly. 'There was one,' she finally admitted. 'But he's already left.'

'That's a pity,' he said. It was a relief, not that the man had left, but that one had existed in her life.

'He wouldn't have been any competition anyway.'

'Why's that?'

'It was a one-way street. I don't think he fancied me.'

'You didn't go out with him then?'

'No. I don't think we ever said more than two words to each other that weren't work related . . . Like I said.'

'Maybe he was a fruit.'

'I doubt you would have said that to his face.'

'Tough guy was he?'

'I don't think Stratton had a sense of humour about that sort of thing. I'm not sure he had a sense of humour at all.'

Something inside Bill rocked at the mention of the name. The unbreakable smile looked unsteady for a few seconds. He cleared his throat.

'Do you keep in touch with him?' he asked.

'We weren't in touch when we worked together. I'm not sure why I mentioned him,' she said, although that was not true. She wanted to let Bill know she was not a lesbian.

'Why do you think you fancied him?'

She shrugged. 'I don't know. Why do you fancy anyone?'

'You like that kind of man?'

'What kind is that?'

'He's a bit of a heartless killer, by all accounts.'

'I'm not sure how true those stories are and I don't think he's heartless.'

'Everyone else does. The way I understand it is he likes killing people so much it's not only part of his job it's his extra-curricular activity too.'

'People like to make up stories about guys like Stratton.'

Bill was sticking the knife into Stratton for a number of reasons, jealousy only one of them. He wondered if it would affect her feelings for Stratton if she knew how true the stories were. But women were strange that way, he reminded himself. They loved rogues. Bill' had made a lot of mileage out of that one himself.

'Can we not talk shop any more?' she said. 'I have one more day off and I don't even want to think about work . . . I almost didn't meet you tonight because of that.'

'Then not another word about it,' he said.

The waiter arrived with the wine and after he poured

them a glass each they ordered. Bill chatted away, doing most of the talking, which he did not mind. Besides, Aggy was a good listener and he was making her laugh. Which was something she'd done little of in the past year.

'What do you do to amuse yourself in your downtime back at the det?' he said, then quickly, 'Oops, I said the "D" word.'

'It's okay. Let's face it, it's our life. It's hard not to talk about it. How about best efforts?' she said.

'Best efforts . . . It is an unusual business we're in,' he said. 'Hard to ignore we have such unusual occupations.'

'I was walking down Oxford Street this morning, mostly window shopping, when I found myself doing anti-surveillance.'

'Not a bad idea looking as delicious as you do. How short is that skirt? I've been praying you'd go to the loo soon so I could get a look at it.'

She stood up and put her hands on her hips, mimicking a model's flare.

'Turn around,' he said.

She pretended to be irritated by the attention but did as she was told and turned around one way, and then back the other.

Bill looked at her perfect breasts, slender hips and tight, rounded bottom with X-ray eyes, 'Jesus,' he mumbled to himself. She sat back down and he continued staring. 'You know, it would not be such a good idea if you dressed like that over you-know-where. You'd attract far too much attention.'

She sipped her wine. 'The last thing you need in that job. That's why I try and look like a boy. They want me to look feminine, but they're wrong. I wouldn't last a week.'

He was enjoying her more and more, mainly because he

never expected her to be as sharp as she was.

'I read mostly,' she said. 'In my spare time. Books.'

'Books,' he said. Another nice surprise. 'People don't read enough books these days. I read all the time.'

'What kind of books?' she asked.

'Non-fiction. History.'

'Just non-fiction?' she asked.

'Pretty much. Unless it's a fictional character set in a factual setting.'

'Like what?'

'*Lord of the Rings*. Noddy.'

'Idiot,' she said, laughing. 'You can't stay serious for more than a few seconds at a time, can you?'

'I am Irish, remember. But you should know that the Irish joke a lot to hide how serious they truly are.'

'You don't seem Irish.'

'And how does an Irish person seem?'

'I mean you've only got a faint accent.'

'I spent most of my youth in England.'

'Your accent's nice. It has soft edges.' She looked into his eyes, growing warmer towards him.

'Thank you,' he said, staring back at her.

The waiter arrived and placed their meals in front of them.

'That was good timing. My heart was tearing at me to lean over and kiss you.'

'You'll get gravy on your shirt.'

'I might just walk across the bloody table if you look at me like that again.'

She suddenly felt it was moving too fast and pulled back a few bends in the road.

'Is it difficult for you . . . fighting your own people?' she asked, then wondered why she did. It was a stupid question.

'My own people?'

'I didn't mean it to come out quite like that. Forget I said it.'

'I know what you mean. I think the Catholics have a valid argument.'

'Do they?'

'They weren't always at war with the Brits, you know,' he said. 'Before the IRA there was the IRB: the B stood for Brotherhood. They were non-militants and had quite a few admirable characters among them.'

'Like whom?'

'There were loads of 'em.'

'So tell me.'

He smiled at her inquisitiveness. 'Okay. Have you ever heard of Thomas Francis Meagher?'

'No.'

'Right then. I'll tell you a little about him. Now you're sure you want me to bore you to death with a bit of Irish history?'

'I like history.'

'That's all you had to say. Okay. Let me see. Thomas Meagher . . . He lived around the time of the great famine. Do you know when that was?'

'Somewhere in the eighteen hundreds?' she asked, guessing.

'More than what most people know. And you know that was when the Irish wanted to become independent?'

'Kind of.'

'Kind of,' he said rolling his eyes good-humouredly. 'If you're going to go to war against them you should at least have the decency to know what it's about.'

'That's why I'm asking.'

'Better late than never, I suppose . . . Well, the British

239

didn't want that and so they planned to weaken the country by exporting as much of the food as they could to England, leaving hardly anything for the people to eat but potatoes. You know about that?'

'Kind of.'

He took a mouthful of food and a swig of wine before continuing. 'Okay. Then a mysterious blight arrived in Ireland that wiped out the potato, pretty much the only food there was to eat, and over a million of the population died. There are some people in the Republic who still believe that blight was a bit of British biological warfare.'

'No, I don't believe it.'

'I said some people believe it. There's no evidence it's true.'

'I can't believe we'd do that.'

'Well, maybe not, but they did refuse to lift a finger to help the starving families and continued exporting as much food as they could out of the country. That's when a secret society known as the Young Irelanders was formed and they led the great rising of 1848. Have you heard of that?'

'No.'

'Well. Thomas Meagher was about your age at the time and he went around giving speeches stirring up anti-British sentiment. He was arrested along with several others for putting up barricades in Tipperary, the rising came to an end and Meagher and his pals were all tried and sentenced to be hung, drawn and quartered.'

'Just for putting up a barricade?'

'Well, they'd done a few other things, but not much more than that. There was an informer in their ranks who told the British that they were up to all kinds of revolutionary things.'

'A tout? Some things never change.'

'Right,' Bill said. 'Well, there was an uproar and Queen Victoria stepped in—'

'I've heard of her,' she interrupted.

'I'm impressed,' he said. 'Well, the old girl decided to change the nine men's sentences to life in prison in a penal colony in Australia. Now, I said there were some great Irishmen in those days, didn't I? Well listen to this. All nine of those men escaped within a few years and you won't believe what they then went on to achieve.' Bill leaned forward in a conspiratorial manner. 'One went on to become Prime Minister of Australia . . . '

'Prime Minister of the country he was sent to spend the rest of his life in prison?' Aggy said.

'Yes. Charles Duffy was his name.'

'That's amazing.'

'I haven't finished yet. Another became Governor General of Newfoundland. Another became Attorney General of Australia, another Minister of Agriculture and President of the Council for Canada, another a prominent New York politician, two served in the United States Army and both became Brigadier Generals, and Thomas Meagher became General of the 69th Irish Brigade, one of the most successful and feared units in the American Civil War on the Union side, and later he became Secretary of State and acting Governor of Montana. What do you think about that then?'

'That's amazing,' she said again sincerely. 'I mean, that's unbelievable.'

'There you go. And that's just a handful of great Irishmen.'

'Tell me some more.'

'Get a book.'

'No, go on. It's interesting. How did Meagher escape?'

'From Australia?'

'Yes.'

'Well, he was a brash adventurer, and a very honourable man. He wrote a letter to his district magistrate and simply told him he intended to set himself free because he did not respect the law that imprisoned him. But he didn't run off right away. He waited until the magistrate had received the letter and sent the police after him. As they arrived at his house to arrest him he galloped away, lost them, hopped on to a boat and sailed to New York City.'

'What happened then?'

'I'm not going to spend the entire evening talking about the history of Ireland.'

'Just Meagher. What happened to him next?'

Bill sighed and looked at her with a mock frown. He was truthfully enjoying telling her the story. 'Okay,' he continued.

'Wait a minute. Where are we? I mean what year?'

'The 1860s. When the American Civil War started the Irish Americans had little interest in fighting at first. When Meagher arrived in America he continued his struggle for the freedom of Ireland and became a prominent leader within the IRB. That's when Abraham Lincoln stepped in and made a deal with him and other members of the IRB to get the Irish to fight in the war. Meagher saw it as a way to raise an army to eventually fight the British. He agreed to fight on the Union side if Lincoln agreed that after the war his men could keep their arms. And basically, that's what happened, and a great deal of credit for the winning of the American Civil War had to go to the Irish soldiers who fought in it.'

'But how could the Irish attack the British from America?' she asked.

'They invaded Canada.'

'No way,' she said.

242

'They did. After the civil war Meagher's army was allowed to camp along the Canadian border. The idea being that if the Irish could invade Canada they could use it as a barter to win home rule in Ireland.'

'Wait a minute,' she said with a chuckle. 'The Irish actually invaded Canada?'

'Don't laugh too soon,' he said. 'They invaded it and more than once. The most famous fight was the battle of Ridgeway, where they actually routed the British.'

'No.'

'Well, to be honest, it wasn't a British army as such. It was a garrison. And it wasn't quite like any of the big battles of the Civil War, but people were killed and the British were routed. Unfortunately the Irish couldn't hold on to the land and they were kicked out a few days later.'

'What happened next?'

'Lincoln was assassinated and the new President, Johnson, turned against the Irish, or at least no longer helped the cause, and it all went downhill from then on.'

'That's astonishing.'

'Do you want to hear something else some old Irish Americans believe?

'What?'

'Well, they believe the British killed Abraham Lincoln.'

'Now you're totally bullshitting me.'

'I didn't say it was true, I just said there are those who believe it. What is true is that there was no love lost between the Brits and the Yanks in those days. They were always close to having another war with each other. Don't forget the Brits were helping the Confederate army defeat the Union at the time. And they also knew Lincoln was helping the Irish and had made a deal with them that would help start a war in Ireland. And Lincoln also had his eye on Canada and wanted to link Alaska with the rest of North America.'

'My God.'

'Exactly. There, now, is that a story or what?'

'What happened to Meagher?'

'Ahh, funny you should ask because that's another interesting part of the story. Before the last invasion of Canada, which was nixed by another bloody British spy – the guy who actually planned the invasion for the Irish, would you believe – Meagher, was, as I've said, made Secretary of State for Montana and became acting Governor. Not long after he mysteriously disappeared off a paddle steamer one night. His body was never found.'

'But there are those who believe it was the work of the dastardly British,' she said, mimicking him.

'Are you making fun of this?'

'I'm not, really. I think it's great, well, you know what I mean.'

'Actually that just so happens to be true.'

'There's evidence?'

'No. But there are those who believe it.'

'Why would the British want to kill him?'

'Maybe they were settling old scores. Or perhaps it was because Montana is on the border of Canada and Meagher was planning another invasion. No one will ever know. And that's it. No more stories about Ireland, not tonight anyway.'

'Did he have any children?' she asked.

'Why do you ask that?'

'Just wondered. We don't have any Meaghers on our players list.'

'Maybe there are one or two running about under different names,' he said, aware that was not the smartest thing to say, even in jest, but it was harmless enough with Aggy.

'It does make you think though, doesn't it? Maybe we are wrong,' she said.

'That it does.'

'And then they put a bomb in a pub or blow up a street full of innocent people just for the publicity and you realise they're not right either.'

'As far as they're concerned it's a war. In war civilians suffer along with the armies.'

'Do you think Meagher would've done something like that?'

'Of course not. But who knows what he would've done if he'd been born today.'

'I don't see any honour in it,' she said.

Bill kept quiet.

'What do you think you'd have done if you'd been born Catholic? Would you have joined the IRA?'

'No,' he said, avoiding her look.

'You joined the British army.'

'And I'll be happy when I'm out of it.'

'You're leaving?'

'That's the plan.'

'When?'

'I don't know exactly. Soon I think.'

'Why?' she said as she took a mouthful of food.

'Had enough. Getting a bit bored. I have time enough for another career.'

'Doing what?'

'I don't know yet,' he said and stood up. 'I have to go.'

She looked up at him, confused. 'Oh?'

'To the loo to sort out my bloody underpants. I've been sitting on my balls since I got here.'

She laughed and covered her mouth. His eyes lingered on her, enjoying her, then he leaned down to kiss her on the cheek. She allowed him to.

'That's just my hello kiss you owe me. You're a beautiful girl, and do you know what I wish from you?'

She looked into his eyes, afraid he might say something that would spoil the evening.

'I hope to God you'll tell me your real name soon because I can't stand Aggy.'

She grinned as she watched him walk away towards the toilets, shifting a lump in the back of his pants. Her smile remained even after he was out of sight.

15

Kathryn sat on the couch in her living room staring into space. She couldn't remember ever having been this bored. The room was as sparse and unwelcoming as the day they had moved in, as was the rest of the house. The plain walls and mantelpiece were empty and not a picture or ornament to be seen. She had brought over some framed family photos but they were in a box in the garage. Kathryn had done nothing to make the place look lived in and couldn't find the motivation to make a start. Hank would be angry when he got home this time. He had been patient so far but they were into their third week. He would soon want to host his own barbeque and invite colleagues over. She tried to make a start that morning and paced the room several times, thinking of colour schemes and furnishing but it only fuelled her anxiety. She thought about asking Hank if they could find a different place but it was only a smokescreen for not having done anything to this one and he would see through it.

She checked her watch again. In another three hours she could pick up the girls from school. They would keep her occupied until she put them to bed then it would be back to gloom and boredom before it was her turn to climb the stairs and end yet another day. Hank was going to have to make some kind of a compromise with her. She thought about negotiating her stay to a year. It wouldn't do his career any harm. They could always say her mother was ill. A year apart might even do them some good. She would talk to him about it as soon as he got back. She needed something to look forward to, something less than seven hundred and fifteen days to go.

She glanced at the phone, debating whether or not to plug it in and call one of her friends in Virginia. Most of them would be up and about and getting their kids ready for school. She had spoken to most of them several times each in the past week, racking up hours of long-distance charges. Without that contact she felt she would go nuts a lot sooner. She still deliberately left the phone unplugged in case one of the wives called. Joan had telephoned three times and two other wives once each the first week, inviting her to tea and offering to show her around the shops in Bournemouth. After some hastily contrived excuses that must have sounded lame she had decided to avoid contact altogether. There was the risk that shutting off the phone might prompt one of them to call around. In fact someone had the evening before but she didn't answer the door. After a minute she heard them walk back to a car and drive away. But having the phone turned off also meant Hank couldn't call. The truth was she didn't much care to talk to him either. All he talked about was the damned job; how the SBS do this and we do it just as well and maybe better but we could learn this off them and so on and so on.

It did worry her, the way she was feeling about Hank these days, or the lack of feeling. Most times she didn't care if he came home at night or not. She put it down to the frustration of being stuck in England. It wasn't this bad back home. The only thing stopping her from packing up and taking the kids back to Virginia was the certainty that it would cause a serious turn in their relationship and she wasn't ready to face that. Not yet anyhow. She sighed heavily and got up and plugged the phone into the wall socket.

She sat back down on the couch, reached for the receiver, and then paused to decide who to call first and what to talk about. Her friends had heard in great detail every complaint she had to offer about her current life in England and she was concerned her constant negativity might be turning them off. She would not mention it unless specifically asked and keep the conversation about their own daily lives. As she reached for the phone it rang.

She snatched her hand back and watched it. It rang for a long time, far too long to be polite. It had to be Hank. They had not spoken for several days. He normally called every day when he was away if he could, which meant he had not been able to. He knew how much she hated answering the phone. The longer it rang the more certain she became that it was him. As she reached for it, it stopped. She immediately regretted not picking it up and felt guilty. It wasn't Hank's fault she was unhappy. This wasn't about him. He was just doing his job and did not deserve her petulant moods. The phone rang again. She picked it up but then said nothing, just in case.

'Hello,' a man's voice said. It wasn't Hank's and she did not recognise it. 'Hello,' he said again.

'Who is this?' Kathryn asked.

'Is that Mrs Munro?' the man asked. He had an American accent.

'Yes,' Kathryn said.

'This is Commander Phelps, spec ops. I'm calling from Washington DC.'

The name meant nothing to her and she relaxed knowing it was for Hank. 'My husband's not here,' she said. 'He's at work – at the base.'

There was no reply but she could hear his muffled voice, talking to someone in the background, as if he had his hand over the phone. 'Hello,' she said, but he did not reply right away. She was miffed by his rudeness. 'Hello,' she said again.

'Mrs Munro. I'm sorry . . . em. No one's called you . . . the Brits . . . from the base?' he asked. There was a hint of trepidation in his voice. Kathryn could detect it. He sounded unsure of what to say or how to say it. As a result a mild flutter of alarm kindled in the pit of her stomach.

'Called me? About what?' she asked. Again he did not answer right away reinforcing her fear.

'I'm sorry that we're having this conversation on the phone,' he said. 'Someone should have come to see you by now.'

'Is there something wrong?' Kathryn asked, suddenly sure that something bad had happened to Hank.

'Can I first stress that we believe your husband is okay.'

'What do you mean?' she asked. 'What's happened? Where is he?'

'Mrs Munro. I can't really talk about it over the phone.'

'What can't you talk about? I don't understand?'

She heard him say something to the other person in the background again. It sounded like 'Shit,' and then, 'What do I tell her?'

'Hello,' she said, panic beginning to mingle with the fear.

'Mrs Munro,' the voice came back. 'Someone's going to come around and see you right away.'

'If something has happened to my husband please tell me,' she demanded.

'Mrs Munro,' he said, pausing a moment to compose an answer. 'Your husband is missing.'

'What do you mean, missing? How could he be missing?'

'I'm very angry that no one has contacted you,' he said. 'This is damned absurd.'

'Will you please tell me what's happened!'

'I can't. Not over the phone. I must stress that we believe he is all right, that he's alive. I'm afraid that's all I can tell you right now. I'm sorry you had to hear about it this way. You should have been told.'

His words echoed through her head, suggesting horror but making no sense. 'Told what?' she said. 'Told what?' Kathryn was growing angry.

'Mrs Munro. I want you to remain calm and stay where you are. Everything is going to be just fine. I'm going to have someone come around and see you immediately. Do you understand, Mrs Munro?'

'Are you or are you not going to tell me what has happened to my husband?' she said with finality.

'I can't. Not over the—'

Kathryn slammed the phone into its cradle and held it firmly while her mind raced. Something terrible had happened to Hank. She was flushed. Her heart was racing. Her soul felt like it had been stabbed. A thousand horrible thoughts flooded her mind. She processed a myriad questions in seconds. Was he dead? What would she do if he were? She wouldn't have to stay in England. No, it's not right to think like that. Images flashed across her mind: Hank laughing, playing with the children, saying something sweet, like forgotten photos in the attic. She took hold of herself. She couldn't stay and wait for someone to come to her. If they couldn't tell her anything over the phone then she would go to them.

The phone started to ring again but she ignored it, grabbed her car keys and a coat, and hurried out of the room.

Kathryn slammed the front door and hurried to the car. She climbed in, nearly bent the key trying to push it into the steering column, and started the engine revving it wildly as she crunched it into gear. The car screeched down the steep drive, the sump thumped into the sidewalk, she turned sharply on to the road and accelerated down it.

Kathryn's mind was racing as hard as the engine. Her subconscious had taken over the driving and navigating while she dealt with the situation.

The fifteen-minute journey to the camp seemed to take an age. It was as if every slow driver in Dorset had been waiting to pull out in front of her. She honked her horn and cursed everyone who impeded her progress. It was not until she turned the corner at the bottom of the hill leading up to the camp that the road cleared of traffic and she could put her foot down. She took the final corner to the camp entrance much too fast, her screeching tyres drawing the attention of the main gate sentry. He stepped from his cubicle in his camouflage fatigues and green beret, his SA80 assault rifle cradled comfortably in his leather-gloved hands, and watched her speed towards him. She jerked to a stop at the barrier a few yards before him and wound down her window. The sentry casually walked to her without any haste.

'I need to see the commander of the SBS,' she said quickly. 'It's urgent.'

The sentry appeared not to have heard her and peered into the car, checking the front and rear seats.

Kathryn exhaled tiredly. 'Did you hear me?' she said. 'This is an emergency.'

'Do you have a pass?' he asked casually.

She started to search automatically then stopped, realising she had nothing. 'My name is Kathryn Munro. My husband is Chief Petty Officer Munro, US Navy SEALs.'

'Do you have a pass?' the sentry repeated like a robot.

'What kind of pass?'

'One that gets you into the camp, miss.'

'I don't know anything about a pass.'

'I can't let you drive into the camp without a pass.'

Kathryn gritted her teeth, snapped open the glove compartment, and searched it. She found nothing that looked like a pass amongst the logbook and bits of paper. She flipped open the compartment between the front seats and rummaged through that. 'I don't have a pass . . . My husband must have it. Look. This is an emergency. I need to see the commander of the SBS immediately.'

'You see that lay-by over there,' he said, pointing to the other side of the road before the barrier. 'Park your car there, then pop into the guard room just there and see the guard commander, all right?'

Kathryn searched over her shoulder to identify the lay-by. She turned back to the sentry but he was already walking back to his cubicle. She mumbled a curse as she crunched the gears into reverse, looked over her shoulder, screeched back a few yards, found first gear and turned sharply into the lay-by, her front wheel mounting the kerb. She stopped sharply, ripped up the handbrake, stalled the engine and climbed out of the car slamming the door shut. She walked smartly past the barrier and up a couple of steps to the single-storey guardroom not much bigger than a volleyball court. There was a small alcove with a ticket-style window and she peered in to see a soldier seated at a desk the far end of the narrow room reading a newspaper. She rapped on the window. 'Hello?' she said.

He looked up at her, casually put down the paper, got to his feet, straightened out his combat jacket as he crossed the room, and slid open the small window. 'Yes, ma'am?'

'I need to see the commander of the SBS.'

'What's this about?' he asked, with a little more feeling than the sentry, but not much.

'My husband is Chief Petty Officer Munro, US Navy SEALs. He's posted here. I have to talk to the commander of the SBS. It's very urgent.'

'Is he expecting you?'

'I doubt it but I promise you he'll see me. Can you get someone to take me to him.'

'Do you have a pass or ID?'

'I've been through that with your guy over there. I haven't got a pass.'

'You can't get into the camp without a pass, miss.'

'So it would seem. But I need to see the SBS commander. It's urgent. I have a right to. Will you please take me to him. I'm not a terrorist, okay. I don't have any bombs or guns on me, I promise.'

'I'm glad to hear it, miss. I'll call the headquarters building and let them know you're here. What's the name again?' he asked as he took a pencil and licked the end.

'Chief Petty Officer Hank Munro . . . '

'*Your* name, miss,' he said.

'Kathryn Munro. Look, I received a call, and, well, I know they'll want to see me—'

'I can't let you into the camp, simple as that,' he interrupted and walked over to his desk and picked up a phone.

She reined in her frustration and held herself in check while she watched him talk into the phone. A minute later he walked back to the window.

'Someone will be up to see you shortly.'

'How long will that take?'

'They'll probably be coming from HQ block.'

'So how long will that take?' she repeated irritably.

'It's on the other side of the camp. If he walks, about ten minutes, if he drives, a couple.'

She sighed deeply and held herself as if she were cold.

254

'You can wait inside if you want to,' he said.

'No . . . ' then changing her mind. 'Yes. I'll wait inside.'

He walked to the back of his office, through a door into the hallway, and to a door the other side of the alcove and opened it. She stepped inside. He led her to a room where half-a-dozen Marines sat in chairs and on bunks watching a television. Rifles were stacked in a rack near the door and fighting orders hung on hooks along a wall. The Marines, all dressed in combats as if ready to leave at a moment's notice, glanced at her for a few seconds before going back to the television.

'Is this the only place I can wait?' she asked the guard commander.

'You can wait in there if you want,' he said, pointing to a small room across the hall. She walked to the room and stood in the doorway. It was a cell. There was a simple cot in one corner, a blanket folded neatly at one end of its stained mattress, with a clean pillow squared away on top of it. A sink was fixed to the wall in another corner and bars covered the tiny window near the ceiling. She looked back but the guard commander was already heading down the hall into his office.

She walked in to the immaculate cell, sat on the edge of the bed and put her face in her hands, holding it there as if trying to shut everything out for a moment. Hank remained at the forefront of her thoughts. She could not begin to imagine what might have happened to him. The night he left he had mentioned going on an exercise but she had paid no attention. She remembered him saying he didn't know much.

The sound of the main door opening made her look up. A man was standing in the hallway looking at her, a Royal Marine officer in lovat trousers, woolly-pully and green beret. He was wearing the expression of someone who was uncomfortable with what they were about to do. She stood up as he approached.

'Mrs Munro,' he said with a sincere, warm smile as he stepped into the cell. 'I'm Lieutenant Jardene.' He held out his hand to her. There was something pleasant about the man. He was strong and forthright in manner. She offered her hand and he shook it.

'I'm sorry we haven't met before now. My wife tried to call you last week to invite you to a get-together but you must've been out. She called several times in fact. I've been trying to phone you myself. I drove to your house yesterday evening but I missed you again . . . I'm Hank's team commander.'

'Are you the commander of the SBS?'

'No. I'm in charge of training. Hank is in one of the training teams.'

'I want to see the commander.'

'I'm afraid that's not possible. He's in London at the moment.'

'What's happened to my husband?'

Jardene looked back into the office where the duty corporal was looking up at them from his desk. Jardene closed the cell door, not completely, and stood opposite Kathryn in the confined space. 'Mrs Munro. Your husband is missing.'

'So I've been told,' she said, starting to raise her voice. 'Where is he?'

Jardene raised his hand in a calming fashion. 'I'll tell you everything I can. Before I do you must understand one thing. What has happened is of a very sensitive nature. It is highly classified.' He took a moment to consider his approach. 'Your husband was involved in an operation.'

'Operation? What operation?'

'I'm not at liberty to discuss those details right now.'

'Hank didn't come here to get involved in any operations. He never said anything to me.'

'Hank wasn't meant to be on the operation. He was there as an observer.'

'Where?'

'I can only tell you what I'm allowed. Unfortunately something went wrong.'

'Why can't you tell me where?'

'Because I can't, Mrs Munro. Please try and understand. Everything will be revealed in good time.'

'Has he gone to the Middle East? Is that where you sent him?'

'No . . . '

'Where then?' she insisted.

'Please, Mrs Munro . . . Something went wrong and Hank was taken.'

'Taken?'

'Kidnapped.'

Kathryn couldn't believe her ears. 'Kidnapped?

Jardene gave her a moment to digest the news.

'By whom?'

'I'm afraid—'

'By who, goddammit?' she shouted, her voice almost painful in the concrete room.

'Please, Mrs Munro. You have to show calm.'

She suddenly became as calm as he asked, but it was a dark, calculating calm. 'Now you listen to me,' she said. 'If you don't tell me where my husband is, what happened to him, who's kidnapped him, I'm gonna walk out of here and go to the police, I'll get a lawyer, I'll go to the damned newspapers. I'll kick up such a ruckus between here and the

257

US you'll have to tell the whole goddamned world what happened to him, not just me.'

'Please, Mrs Munro. That wouldn't be wise.'

'What are you gonna do to stop me? Lock me up in here?'

'No one is going to lock you up, Mrs Munro. If you go public with this it can only worsen matters for your husband.'

'Bullshit! Tell me where he is!' she shouted. 'Tell me!'

Jardene was not equipped to deal with this kind of situation. Give him a battlefield, an enemy, exploding shells, raking machine-gun fire and he would feel confident, but a hysterical woman was another matter.

'Mrs Munro—'

'Would you step aside please. I'd like to leave now.'

Jardene remained blocking the doorway.

'I said I want to leave now.'

Jardene was in an awkward situation to say the least. He had to deal with this here and now. It was his responsibility but Kathryn did not appear to be in any mood to negotiate. 'Mrs Munro—' he started again, but she cut him off.

'If you're keeping me in here against my will I want that soldier outside to tell me. Guard!' she shouted. 'Guard!'

'Mrs Munro,' Jardene said, raising his voice, trying a touch of male domination as a last effort. The door pushed open gently and the guard commander stuck his head in.

'Is everything okay, sir?' he asked.

'Yes, Corporal, thank you.' Jardene reinforced his comment with a look that conveyed the woman was being difficult but he could handle it. The corporal nodded, glanced at Kathryn, then withdrew. Jardene closed the door completely this time. Kathryn looked at him defiantly.

'Okay,' Jardene said, sighing deeply. 'Will you assure me that you'll keep this in confidence. I'm serious when I say it could harm your husband if it got out.'

'I'm not going to do anything that will hurt my husband.'

'Your husband's been kidnapped by people who, well, people I would have to describe as terrorists.'

Kathryn listened quietly, absorbing every word.

'They obviously thought he was one of ours,' Jardene continued. 'Hank found himself in a situation he should not have been in. It was as much our responsibility he was in that position. He ended up isolated and was abducted. Now, we fully expect that when the kidnappers realise their mistake they'll let him go. They have no reason to hold an American. It doesn't serve them any purpose.'

Jardene felt he had revealed more than enough and waited for her reaction.

'That's it?' she asked.

'I can't tell you more than that I'm afraid. Perhaps in a day or two . . . '

'Well, I'm sorry but that's not good enough. If you can't tell me, then perhaps you'll tell a lawyer or the newspapers.'

'Mrs Munro—'

'Where was he kidnapped?'

Jardene was being outgunned and he knew it. 'A European country,' he said.

'Eastern Europe?' she asked.

'Western.'

That was a surprise to her. 'What were you guys doing?'

'There are some things that lawyers and newspapers will never be told.'

'Who kidnapped my husband?'

'I'm putting myself on the line by telling you as much as I have.'

'You put my husband on the line,' she said coldly. 'You owe me something for that . . . You said he was taken by terrorists. What terrorists?'

Jardene wondered for a moment if he should just lock her in the cell, then quickly dismissed the thought as preposterous despite its attraction.

'Irish Republican terrorists.'

'The IRA?'

'Probably not the official IRA but, yes.'

Kathryn mellowed. For reasons that were not immediately obvious to her, it didn't seem quite so bad as it first seemed. 'Has someone seen him? Have they contacted you?'

'No. We've heard nothing yet . . . There has already been a significant investigation and we believe it is not in their interest to harm Hank, and, as I said, once they realise he's American, well, hopefully things will get sorted out quickly.'

'Hopefully?'

'Hopefully sooner rather than later is what I meant.'

Kathryn finally calmed herself. There was nothing else she could think of asking, nothing that he might know or would tell it seemed.

'Can I trust you to keep what I have said to yourself?' he asked.

She didn't appear to have heard him.

'Mrs Munro? You'll be kept informed. If there is any news, I'll call you immediately.'

Kathryn felt very tired all of a sudden. 'I'd like to go home now,' she said.

'Of course.' He opened the cell door and stepped out. He paused in the hallway for her to join him. As she passed the television room all the Marines turned to watch her leave, having heard the raised voices. Jardene opened the door and they stepped outside into the crisp air. She didn't say goodbye and walked to her car. Jardene watched her climb in and drive away. He was not looking forward to telling the boss how much more he had told her. Hopefully he would understand that Jardene had to do it to avert exposure, but it would be another black mark in his report. This whole thing was a nightmare and one he could expect to last for a very long time, and far beyond its conclusion.

Kathryn was calm as she drove away from the camp, her mind focused on dealing with this quandary. This situation had changed everything. She could deal with it in England or back home. It wasn't a difficult decision to make. All she had to do was justify going back Stateside. The unexpected feeling about this was that she was suddenly in charge. She now had the power to solve the most burning issue in her life – other than Hank of course – and that was getting back home. There was nothing to stop her. When Hank was released she would fly back to England immediately. The SEALs would no doubt fly her. This was no small thing that was happening to her. It could even mean the end of Hank's UK assignment. As the British officer said, it didn't make sense that the IRA would hurt Hank since he was American. And when they found out he was Irish American they'd probably treat him first class.

Kathryn turned into a cul-de-sac and pulled to a stop by the kerb at the entrance to Rushcombe school. She was almost surprised to see she had arrived. It was as if her subconscious had brought her here without her knowing. She climbed out and looked over at the playground where a class was playing rounders. Helen and Janet were not amongst them. Kathryn headed up the flagstone path to the main entrance, stepped inside and walked along the corridor, pausing to look in each room through the small glass window in the door. She found her daughters seated at their desks in the last classroom at the end of the corridor. They were following a passage in their books as another girl stood by her desk reading out loud. Kathryn opened the door. The girl stopped reading and all the children, including the teacher, a rotund grey-haired woman, looked up at her.

'I'm sorry for interrupting,' Kathryn said. 'I've come to collect my daughters: Janet and Helen Munro.'

'I'm sorry,' the teacher said, quite unhappy with the interruption. 'And you are?'

'I'm their mother,' Kathryn announced as if it were obvious.

'This is most irregular,' the teacher said. 'Have you spoken to the headmistress?'

'No.'

'There are rules, Mrs . . .'

'Munro. As in Janet and Helen Munro. Come along,' Kathryn said to her girls. 'And get all your things – your sweater, Janet.' The two girls collected their sweaters and backpacks and made their way to their mother, both looking embarrassed.

'Could you tell the headmistress that they won't be back,' Kathryn said to the teacher as she ushered the girls into the corridor. And then as an afterthought she added, 'I'm sorry for interrupting your class. Please tell the headmistress that it was urgent.'

She closed the door, leaving the teacher looking exasperated.

Kathryn walked briskly along the corridor and out the main doors. Janet and Helen had to run to keep up.

'Where we going, Mommy?' Helen asked.

'Back home. America.'

'We can't go home yet, Mommy. We haven't finished school,' Janet said.

'It's can't, not carn't,' Kathryn said, opening the rear door of the car for the girls to climb in. 'Stop speaking in an

English accent. You're Americans. Buckle up your seatbelts.'

Kathryn climbed in and started the engine. 'Mommy, the sleeve of my jumper's caught in the door,' Janet said.

Kathryn climbed out, opened Janet's door to let her pull the sleeve in. 'It's not a jumper, honey, it's a sweater. Kangaroos are jumpers.'

Kathryn climbed back in and they pulled away.

'We going home to America right now?' Helen asked.

'First flight we can,' Kathryn said. Then it dawned on her. She'd forgotten. They couldn't go to Norfolk. Their home was rented out on a two-year lease. And she couldn't impose on any of her friends, not at such short notice and to stay for weeks.

There was only one option, which did not appeal to her particularly, but it was better than staying in England. Boston, New England. Her mother's house. Whatever spark of relief there was to be had from leaving England was significantly reduced by the prospect of moving back to her childhood home. Having her mom visit them in Norfolk was bad enough, but to stay with them at her house would be hell. Mind you, the kids liked Grandma. That was something at least.

'Mommy,' Helen said, 'if we're going home, where's Daddy?'

Kathryn had been so consumed with her own problems she hadn't even thought about what she was going to tell the children.

'He's going to come along as soon as he can, honey.' Of that she was strangely confident. Kidnapped. It probably sounded a lot worse than it was.

16

Quincy, Boston Massachusetts was wetter and colder than England had been that month. Kathryn's mother lived in a spacious New England-style house built in the twenties and just within reach of the spray from the bay during a strong south-westerly gale. The neighbourhood had not changed much since Kathryn was a child apart from the cars parked in the thickly tree-lined street where mothers still let their children play. Every house squatted on its own plot, a small garden in front, a larger one in back, with none of the inhabitants apparently obsessive about gardening. The wooden siding that covered the exterior of the house had seen a new coat of paint in recent years but the detached garage in the far corner of the back garden could have done with a lick and a new layer of felt on the roof. A wide porch cluttered with retired lounge furniture took up much of the front of the house and the front door in the centre of it was wide enough to march a generous dining table through without too much manoeuvring. It all had a lazy, old feel to it.

The ground floor was a sprawling living room, which the front door opened directly into, and across a short hall, where a staircase led up to the second floor, was a spacious kitchen, the centre occupied by a solid wooden table that Kathryn used to play table tennis on with her brothers.

Upstairs were half-a-dozen bedrooms and one large bathroom; the wooden floors creaked in all of them. Dusty, tired rugs covered most of the old carpeting. The house was evidently occupied by an old person but filled with memories of youthful, bustling times. Framed pictures had claimed a piece of just about every level surface and were evidence that several generations of the same family had lived in the house.

Kathryn stood in the kitchen looking through a window at Janet and Helen playing in the back garden. They were pushing a small wheelbarrow around collecting bits of rubble, pretending to be construction workers. They reminded her of her own childhood when the house was also home to her sister, two brothers and four adults. Now her mother lived alone, the children all grown up and gone, and her father, aunt and uncle all in St Mary's church cemetery.

A car pulled into the drive and stopped in the back garden in front of the garage. The heavy driver's door creaked open and a sprightly woman in her sixties, wearing a well-tailored dress suit and a new brittle hairdo, climbed out.

'Grandma, Grandma!' Janet and Helen shouted as they dropped their tools and building materials and ran to her. A broad smile spread comfortably across the woman's craggy face as she embraced the girls.

Kathryn didn't move from the window as she watched her mother open the trunk and pull out several bags stuffed with groceries. Janet and Helen took a small item each and flanked their grandma as she headed for the back door. They walked under the window, where Kathryn looked down on them, and then up a short flight of steps to the back door.

Kathryn's mother led the way in, puffing under the load and put the bags down heavily on to the kitchen table. She took the items from the two girls and rested her hands on her knees to catch her breath and also to look into their little faces. 'Thank you,' she said, squeezing them on the cheek one at a time. 'At least someone around here is kind enough to help an old lady out,' she said dryly in her thick, Boston accent.

Kathryn didn't react. It was an old record. Her mother was a habitual critic as far as Kathryn was concerned. Kathryn had built up a kind of immunity, although it was rather like being in a tank: the bullets bounced off harmlessly but the sound was still psychologically discomfiting.

'I need a cold drink,' her mother said as she took a glass from a cupboard. 'The air's dry today.' She opened the icebox and removed a bottle of fruit juice. 'You haven't washed the plates from breakfast.'

Kathryn remained quietly staring out of the window as her mother poured the juice into the glass.

'Two days you've been here and you've not lifted a finger to help with the housework. I'm not the maid, you know.'

Kathryn watched a seagull land on the garage roof. It reminded her of the times her brothers used to lie in wait in their bedroom overlooking the garden, clutching loaded catapults and a supply of ammunition in readiness for just such a target. She would wait and watch with them, stealthily crouched, nose level with the window ledge, fascinated, but never enough to want to take a shot herself. In that regard she was quite the typical little girl. Her fun, as she remembered it, was dolls, playing mommy and dressing up for pretend parties.

'I have enough to do by myself,' her mother continued. 'You could help out, you know.'

'Mom, leave it alone. The house isn't exactly falling down around your ears.'

'Is that what you're waiting for before you do anything?'

Kathryn rolled her eyes. 'I have a few things on my mind. Just cut me some slack will you, please?'

Kathryn's mother could drift from one mood to another with surprising ease. Not that a shift meant the original mood, or subject, was necessarily closed for the day.

'It's been a while since I came out of the store with this much produce. Mrs Franklin asked me if I had an army moved in . . . Must be five years since Mark left home. Boy, could they eat, his wife and those three boys of his.'

'Seven,' Kathryn corrected.

'What?'

'Seven years. They left seven years ago.'

'Can't be more than five.'

'They left before Helen was born and she's six and a half.'

'He's had another baby, did you know that?' her mother continued without further debate, but leaving the impression Kathryn was wrong. 'Another boy. A terror just like the others. He lets those kids do whatever they want. What can you expect from a Polish wife, I guess. At least they're Christian. I suppose that's something.'

'She's not Polish, she's American.'

'She's as Polish as you are Irish. You know what I mean. Why do you have to be so argumentative all the time? You can't just have a normal conversation. You always have to be awkward.'

Kathryn's mother took two popsicles out of the freezer and gave one to each of the girls, who had been standing between them listening. 'There you go. That's for being such good little angels. Now go on and play.'

'Say thank you,' Kathryn said.

'They don't need to say thank you. It's theirs to have.'

'Thanks, Gramma,' Helen said anyway and the girls left the kitchen and headed upstairs.

Kathryn felt her mother was the most irritating dichotomy. She was so incredibly annoying, and at the same time so generous, especially with the children. Kathryn had thought she might be able to bear it for a few months at least, but even that was now looking impossible.

'Mrs Franklin might come around to see you later,' her mother continued. 'She couldn't believe it when I told her what happened to Hank.'

'You told her?'

'And why not? It's not every day we have a kidnapping in the family.'

'Mom, I don't want everyone knowing.'

'She's practically a friend of the family.'

'I don't want anyone knowing.'

'Why not?'

'I told you. Because the publicity won't do Hank any good.'

'Baloney. The British have fed you a load of horse manure. The publicity would be good for everyone except the British. If you don't believe me ask the Father. He agrees with me.'

'You told him?' Kathryn asked, growing angry.

'Of course. The Father is the one person who could make some good out of this.'

'I can't believe you told him.'

'For God's sake, girl. Your husband's been kidnapped by our own people. There's no one in a better position to deal with it than the Father. Sure, he probably even knows who did it.'

Anger flushed through Kathryn, making her face redden. 'Now just hold on one goddamned minute—'

'Don't you swear at me, young lady.'

'You are not going to treat Hank's kidnapping as some kind of political tool.'

'For the sake of Christ, will you listen to yourself? Are you blind, deaf and stupid, girl? Anyone who's kidnapped becomes a political tool.'

'He's my husband! Your grandchildren's father!'

'Some things about you never change, do they?' Kathryn's mother said, shaking her head. 'Always stubborn and thinking you know everything. The Father will make sure no harm comes to Hank and he'll make the most out of it at the same time. The Brits have to be made to suffer for what they did and he'll make sure they do.'

'I don't want Father Kinsella getting involved in this,' Kathryn said, vexed.

'He's more than just a priest, young lady. I know.'

Kathryn rolled her eyes in frustration. 'I know what Father Kinsella is, Mom. I'm not stupid. I knew when we were kids that he recruited boys for the IRA.'

'Then you'll know not to say that out loud,' she said in a hushed tone.

'Mom, everyone knows Father Kinsella works for the IRA. He used to collect for them in every bar in the neighbourhood and also the church, for God's sake. He used to take Mark and I along on Friday nights to help carry the bags of coins. I've seen you give him money hundreds of times, in this house!'

'And a fine job he does too. I only wish I could have done half as much for the cause myself.'

'You're such a hypocrite, Mom. Why didn't you let him recruit Mark and David if you felt so strongly about it?'

Kathryn's mother continued packing away the groceries as if she had not heard.

'When the boys were older you used to discourage them from going to Father Kinsella's confessionals, didn't you?' Kathryn continued. 'That's how he recruited the young men.

He used the confession box to get inside their souls.'

Kathryn's mother threw her a warning glance and went back to packing tins of food into cupboards.

'Why wouldn't you let the boys get involved? Come on, Ma, tell me that.'

'They were not suitable for that kind of a life. Mark was an artist.'

'He's a plasterer, Mom . . . And what about David?'

'David wasn't very strong.'

'And so you sent him to a military academy in Vermont. Give me a break.'

'He wasn't strong in the head. He'd have done something stupid.'

'Who are you trying to kid, Mom? You didn't mind other mothers' sons joining in the fight, but you didn't want your own.'

Kathryn's mother slammed a can on to the table and glared at her. The seagull left the garage roof and flapped into the air. 'Your grandfather did his part, and his father before him,' she said. 'Your great grandfather on your father's side, God bless him, was shot by the British just for standing in the road in defiance. There are families out there, in this very street that have given money to the cause but have never spilt a drop of blood for it. This family has done its bit.'

The old woman took a moment to gather herself before carrying on with her unpacking. Kathryn sighed, hating the argument.

'Mom, I'm not saying you should've given them Mark and David. I'm glad you didn't, obviously I am. I'm just saying, well . . . I wish you hadn't told Father Kinsella about Hank.'

The phone rang. Kathryn's mother went to where it hung

on the kitchen wall and picked up the receiver. 'Hello,' she said into it. 'That's right.' She nodded. 'Yes, she is,' she said, looking at Kathryn, who was suddenly curious. 'That won't be a problem,' Kathryn's mother continued. 'That'll be fine then . . . Goodbye.' She put down the phone and went back to her work.

'Who was that?' Kathryn asked.

'The *Tribune*.'

'The newspaper? What did they want?' Kathryn asked, already suspecting the answer.

'They want to talk to you about Hank.'

'You told the newspapers?'

'No. The Father did.'

Kathryn shook her head in utter frustration. This was spinning out of control.

'Tell Father Kinsella from me he is wasting his time. I'm not going to talk to them or anyone about Hank.'

Kathryn's mother stopped what she was doing and stared coldly at her daughter. Kathryn could not remember the last time she saw such an uncompromising look in her mother's eyes and it froze her. 'Since when did you become sympathetic with the Brits?'

'Don't go down that road, Mom. You know I have no love for the Brits. Your ambition is to further the cause. Mine is my children and their father, and it starts and stops there.'

There was a knock at the front door. Kathryn's mother glanced towards the lounge then moved to the sink and started cleaning up the dishes. 'Go answer the door,' she said in a way that telegraphed she knew who it was. Kathryn didn't move, suspicions flying in from all directions.

'Who is it, Ma?'

'I said go and get the door.'

The knock came again. Her mother turned to stare at her. Kathryn started to look defiant, but she could not win. She never could against her mother.

She left the kitchen, walked through the lounge and paused at the front door. The figure behind the frosted glass was a large one. She opened the door.

Standing on the porch, blocking out a lot of light and smiling like a snake-oil salesman was Father Kinsella. Kathryn wasn't surprised.

'Kathryn, Kathryn, Kathryn,' he said, beaming. 'You look as beautiful as ever.'

'Hello, Father Kinsella,' Kathryn said somewhat demurely, standing back to let him in. And in he strode.

'Well, well. It's been quite a few years since these tired old eyes have settled on your pretty face. I've missed you, so I have. How long's it been?'

'I don't remember.'

'Your mother told me your children are here.'

'That's right.'

'You know, I've always been disappointed you never brought them home and let me be the one to baptise them,' he said, still smiling, but there was a shadow behind his pale blue eyes. Kathryn forced a smile and began to mouth an excuse, but she couldn't and stopped herself from trying. He unnerved her.

'Where are the little ones, anyway?' he said, letting her off the hook and looking around the room.

'They're upstairs. Mom's in the kitchen.'

'Well, I tell you what. We'll bother them later. It's you I'm here to see anyway. Sit down, sit down,' he said, as if it were his own house.

Kathryn obeyed. There were two people in her life who withered her courage like a straw in a furnace and both were in the house with her. Father Kinsella had a similar effect on most of the community and for as far back as many could remember. Rumour had it that in his younger days, before he got the call of the church, he made his money in illegal street fighting. There were even stories that it was the church or jail for him after some dubious goings-on involving the Irish gangs that were behind a lot of the organised crime in those days. It may have been many a year since he swung a punch at someone, but he still had the look of destruction in his eyes when he was displeased. As he looked at Kathryn, his smile faded, a warning of a more serious topic of conversation to come.

'First of all, I'm here to say how sorry I am for what has happened to your husband.'

Kathryn gave a perfunctory nod of appreciation.

'How do you feel about what's happened?'

'Feel?' she asked, unsure as to his meaning.

'Yes. How do you feel, about what's happened to Hank?'

'I feel like I want him to be released and come home.'

'And so he will be,' Father Kinsella said. 'So he will . . . What I mean is, where is your soul in this matter, not your heart?'

'My soul?'

Father Kinsella seemed to be having a bit of trouble getting Kathryn to see his point, which was unusual for him, but in this matter he felt it was worth taking a little time over. He knew Kathryn, at least her basic sensibilities. He had formed his opinion about her when she was little, which is why he had a lot of time for the young. Adults were more difficult to figure out and therefore harder to manipulate. It was his experience that a person's fundamental character changed little with age, and those that did could be revitalised with a little gentle persuasion. 'You didn't like having to go to England, did you?'

'No.'

'And not just because your mother told you the English are our enemies.'

'Father. I'm not seven years old any more, sitting with you counting coins.'

He burst into sudden laughter and slapped his knee. 'Ah, those were great days, weren't they? Seems like only the other day. That was your first job for the cause. And you were paid handsomely if I remember. At least an ice cream or chocolate bar a time.'

'A nickel was a bullet and a dollar was a bomb,' she said, smiling herself. 'That's how we used to total them up, in bullets and bombs.'

'Yes, those were fine old days. Bullets and bombs.' He grinned a while before growing sombre once more. 'I suppose the world was a lot easier to figure out then . . . I need your help, Kathryn.'

'You need *my* help?'

'Yes. What's happened to Hank affects a lot of people, not just you. But you're in the best position to help all of us, not just yourself.'

This was what she had been expecting. 'And how's that?' she asked.

'You can be a voice.'

'A voice? And what would I say?' Antagonism was slowly starting to surface in her. Father Kinsella could see it in her eyes and played her carefully.

'Kathryn. I'm not asking anything of you other than to let people look at you. Let them know what's happened. Your husband, Hank, the father of your two beautiful little girls, was used by the British as a political tool, and you're both paying a price.'

274

'They said it was a mistake. Whoever kidnapped him thought he was a Brit.'

'Then where is he? Why haven't they let him go? Listen to me, Kathryn. I know what I'm talking about. Don't be surprised if the Brits even find a way of turning it around and making it Hank's fault.'

She wasn't worldly enough to argue this with him.

'Look at it from another point of view for a moment,' he went on. 'The IRA are not terrorists. They're freedom fighters. That's not just a play on words. Terrorists want to destroy a way of life. All we want is our country back. We don't want to destroy the Brits' way of life. For God's sake, it's our way of life too. But the Brits want to deny us our freedom and so they play name games and call us terrorists. The whole world is against terrorism, and me included, I might add. And so if you want the world against someone, call them a terrorist. And to make the Brits' case even stronger it would suit them nicely if the Americans were seen to be helping them against the IRA because it would make them look all the more like terrorists. The Brits have duped the Americans, the Irish and you. They sacrificed your husband. Do you see what I'm saying, Kathryn? Doesn't it make sense?'

Kinsella had taken the fight out of her but he had not pushed her far enough, not yet, not as far as he needed to.

'I don't know enough to argue against anything you've said, Father. And you could be right. But I don't see what I can do.'

'You mean to say that if you believed the Brits had used Hank as bait, risked his life for a political manoeuvre, that wouldn't make you angry?'

'Of course but—'

'Then there's one thing you'd better be clear about,

275

Kathryn. And if nobody has suggested it yet, then I'm sorry to be the one to have to say it, but you had better be prepared for the possibility that you may never see Hank alive again.'

She looked into his eyes searching for the lie, but, surprisingly, all she saw was sincerity.

'Why would they . . . why would anything happen to him?'

'It's a game they're playing, Kathryn, but not a child's game.'

'But surely, being American, the best thing the IRA could do is to send him home.'

'Yes, they could do that. But that might not be the most advantageous way to play the card that's been dealt them.'

'I don't understand.'

'There's a lot you don't understand.'

'Explain it to me,' she suddenly snapped, wanting him to get to the point.

'I'm not saying executing Hank is what they're thinking of or what they plan to do. I'm just making you aware of their options.'

Her glare remained fixed on him, inviting him to explain.

'Struggles like the one in Ireland need support, and not just local support and a bit of help from patriotic Irish Americans. It needs to be shown to the world. The more the world hears of the injustice, the louder it will call for its end. Britain doesn't care what Ireland thinks, but it cares what the world thinks. A situation like this, Hank being kidnapped, is something the world would take notice of. They have to take advantage of that interest before it goes away. That's why Hank hasn't been released yet and why he's not likely to be in the immediate future.'

'But you said he could be killed.'

'I'm getting to that . . . At the end of the game, when all the publicity has been had out of the kidnapping, when the world is getting tired of the news, to make the most of it, to squeeze the last drop from it, there has to be a change in direction, and a dramatic one. It can't go on for ever. And so the question has to be answered. Will Hank come home or not?'

'You make it sound like a TV soap.'

'Sadly, the entertainment industry has taught us a lot about selling a story.'

'But I don't see why it would be an advantage for the IRA to kill him. Surely they'd look good if they let him go back to his family.'

'It would seem that way, but history has taught us something else. The happy ending might be the best way to end a movie, but in the real world, sadly people only sit up and take notice when all they are left with is horror. Mercy does not live as long in memory as does horror. And the world will call even louder for the Troubles to end . . . The IRA won't back down, so it will be up to the Brits to. History tells us they will. They've already started. Now they need to be pushed back even harder.'

It was as if Father Kinsella had been talking about another world. Kathryn was suddenly overcome with fear for Hank and loathing for everything else to do with the British and the IRA. She had never seriously considered that Hank would not return alive. Now all of a sudden, looking at it through Father Kinsella's eyes, it seemed certain he was going to die.

'You think they'll kill him,' she said, a tremor in her voice. It was not a question.

'No, Kathryn. That's why I'm here. If we can provide the IRA with the grandstand they want from this it will satisfy them. Don't you see? If we point the finger at the Brits, and the American government too, tell the world they're playing with the lives of our loved ones, making them pay the price for their political games, trying to paint a grand body of freedom fighters as terrorists, then the godfathers will benefit more by releasing Hank. Do you see it, Kathryn?' He reached out and squeezed her hand. 'Now do you see why we can't just sit back and do nothing?'

She pulled her hand away and looked at him coldly. 'Is it them telling you or you telling them?'

The priest dropped his gaze, but more in an effort to control his anger than hide any guilt. He then looked at her. 'Whatever you think of me, or my beliefs, or how I deal with the rights and the wrongs of the world, I came here to help you save your husband. I'll tell you straight, Kathryn Munro, I don't think it will be easy, but I'm willing to try.'

He stood up and straightened out his jacket. 'Now,' he said, 'before I walk out that door I want to know one thing. Are you going to help me save Hank's life or not?'

She did not trust him, but he had her trapped. She despised him more that moment than ever before.

'Well. What's it to be?' he demanded.

'What do I have to do?' she asked quietly.

'Nothing more than what should come naturally to you. Whoever asks, newspapers or anyone else, just say you miss your husband and want him to come home to his family, and that you don't trust anyone from the British or American authorities. We'll talk further tomorrow.'

Father Kinsella walked to the front door and out of the house. It was only after he had closed the door behind him that she remembered he had not seen her mother or children.

She sensed eyes behind her and looked around to the kitchen door where her mother was watching her. Before she stepped back into the kitchen, Kathryn thought she detected a look of guilt on her face.

17

Hank sat on the floor of a dark, damp room with his hands tied in front of him around a pipe running vertically upwards. A grubby hessian hood was over his head, tied loosely around his neck. He had been there long enough to discover the walls were metal, as was the floor, and added to that, the constant hum of engines and the occasional gentle bump of the entire room made it obvious to him that he was inside a boat of some kind, and not a small one either. The air was thick with the odour of diesel fuel and rotting garbage, competing occasionally with the smell of his own shit-filled and urine-soaked trousers. His captors had been less than considerate regarding his personal hygiene.

The hood filtered the light from a dim bulb that shone constantly in the centre of the ceiling. If there was a port-hole in the room it was covered, but it seemed likely, consid-ering the high temperature and close proximity of the engines, that the room was at or below the waterline.

Hank had explored with his legs in all directions and found what felt like a piece of heavy rope, a plastic bucket, a chunk of wood and a solid metal support welded to the floor, which was probably holding up a shelf somewhere above. He estimated he had been on board a day or so but it was hard to tell without a change in light. He had dozed off several times but for how long he wasn't sure. He had kept an accurate count of the number of days for the first seven, until his only source of timing, daylight, was taken from him. The old garage filled with junk they had first kept him in had a hole in the roof. 'They' being the French people: Henri and the two apes who kidnapped him. Then after a drive inside a box for an hour or so he found himself in a dank room, which he presumed was a basement without any light other than the one that was switched on whenever someone came into the room. He estimated he had been in that place for three days but if he had been told six he would not have been surprised. A few years back he had taken part in an interrogation exercise in Fort Bragg, North Carolina, and was kept in a dark cell for two days with just food and water. Light and darkness were alternated, anything from minutes to hours between them, and when the exercise was over he thought he had spent three days more in the cell than he actually had.

Figuring out his surroundings was his only pastime. The thought of escape was always on his mind of course, but the opportunity had not yet presented itself. Not that he had a life-threatening, burning desire to escape. He would if he could, if it didn't endanger him. His captors were very thorough and attentive though. The bonds they tied his hands and feet with were strong and whenever he was visited they were checked and if loose, retied. They had not removed his hood since he regained consciousness on day one, even when feeding him, which was a handful of bread, cheese or meat shoved under it and into his mouth, followed by a squirt of water from a plastic bottle. No one had spoken to him. Not a word. He'd heard voices on occasion but they were in another part of the building and muffled. When he was in the basement there were Irish and French voices. There was a woman's voice once. English she sounded, but she could've

281

been Irish. He thought she had fed him a couple of times. She wasn't as rough as the others and her hands were soft. If he guessed correctly she was the one who had given him a piece of chocolate.

After the basement came the long drive in the back of a grimy van to his present location. They had carried him in a box from the van and rolled him out into the metal room and secured him to the pole. Those were all Irishmen, or at least the only ones who said anything were.

Hank felt low in energy, kept deliberately so by his captors no doubt. He was constantly hungry but his stomach had shrunk enough so that just a small amount of food would satisfy him for a while. The only plus side to not eating was that he didn't need to take a shit, which he hadn't done the last three days.

Oddly enough, being held captive had been one of Hank's daydreams; however, he always saw himself in a cell and able to exercise every day and maintain his fitness. But being constantly tied up and hooded was not as bad as he would have imagined. There was something about Hank's generally easy-going temperament and his ability to live within himself that helped him through the endless hours sitting in silence with only his thoughts for company. He had covered just about every aspect of his situation and the endless combination of outcomes. Kathryn had figured greatly in his thoughts, of course. He expected Helen and Janet had been told he was away on a long exercise. It was Kathryn he was most worried about.

A door opened and what sounded like several people stepped into the room. Hank wondered if it was feeding time, or better still, a trip to the toilet perhaps. The only positive thing about the shit in his pants was that it offered some insulation against the cold floor, once it had dried out a bit, even though most of it had worked its way up his back and over his thighs. A shower would have been unbelievable. He might have forgiven them for everything had they let him clean up and put on fresh clothes. It sounded like they were carrying something heavy as they shuffled across the floor. They dumped it unceremoniously a few feet from Hank. He could not make out the rest of the sounds accurately, but someone was doing something energetically enough to make them a little out of breath. Then the group made its way back through the door and it was closed.

No food, Hank decided. No toilet. And definitely no bath. He became annoyed. Fear had initially dominated all of his emotions, but as the days went by it melted into the background, for the most part, and he began to feel anger and impatience. It was not so much at being captured but the way he was being kept. In a strange way he had accepted being a prisoner almost immediately. He was a soldier and incarceration by the enemy was always a potential hazard of that occupation. He was annoyed at the way they treated him like an animal and decided the next time they came in he was going to voice his complaints. If the IRA considered itself to be a contemporary army, and indeed if it expected its enemies to think of it as such, it should act in as many ways as it could like one. That included the proper treatment of prisoners. What they were doing to him was torturous and uncivilised. Hank would try and make them see things that way the next chance he got. Then he heard something, close by, across the room. He wondered if it was a rat. Then he heard a sigh. It was a person.

Hank's senses stretched to maximum sensitivity as he scanned for the slightest sound or movement. He moved his head, trying to get a glimpse of any change in the light. Another sigh, or was it a moan? Something scraped across the floor, like the heel of a foot, a leg straightening out, as if the person were sitting on the floor like Hank. It then went silent.

Hank waited an age for whomever it was to make another move. It seemed as if the person was asleep. The breathing had become rhythmic, quite loud, but it also sounded congested.

Some time later, as Hank was beginning to doze off, he heard the person start to cough and hack, trying to clear their throat.

'Ah, Jesus,' a voice moaned. It was a man.

Hank listened quietly, wondering when the man would acknowledge him.

'Ah, God,' the man said again. 'Bejesus . . . Focken bastards,' he cried out weakly.

It was obvious that the man was in pain. Hank wondered if he was a prisoner like himself. The man would surely be able to see Hank, unless he also had a hood over his head.

Hank deliberately scraped his foot across the floor. The man went silent. He'd heard him. Hank did it again. When the man spoke it was with a croaking sound, as if he had painful chest problems. 'Why don't you get the focken thing over with, yer bastards.'

He was Irish, Hank could tell that much, and he obviously thought Hank was one of them. That confirmed the man could not see him. Hank was about to say something but was suddenly suspicious. What if it was one of them? What if they were trying to trick him into talking? The first rule of imprisonment for a soldier is to say nothing other than name, rank and serial number.

'Say something, you bastard,' the man said. 'Focken beat me up again if it makes yer feel any better.'

It seemed an extreme length to go to just to interrogate

him. There was nothing he could think of that would be of any use to the IRA anyhow. Hank decided talking would be okay as long as he asked the questions.

'Who are you?' Hank said.

'What do mean, who am I, you eedjit? You know who I am or I wouldn't be here.'

'I'm sitting on the floor with my hands tied to a pole and a hood over my head,' Hank said.

The man was silent for a moment. When he spoke again the aggression had gone from his voice, although suspicion remained.

'You a prisoner?'

'Yeah.'

'Is that an American accent?'

'Yeah.'

'And you're toid op with a hood over your head?'

'Yeah, I'm tied up.'

There was a long silence again, both men trying to figure out the other.

'What's an American doing a prisoner with these people?' he asked.

'Case of mistaken identity,' Hank said.

'That right?' the Irishman said sardonically. 'Let me guess,' he said. 'You must be FBI or DEA. You were doin' one of yer arms deal stings and the boyos caught yer.'

'Nope,' Hank said.

'Then it's CIA, or maybe you're INS?'

'Nope.'

'Ah, it don't make a dick of a focken difference what you tell me, fellah. I'm for the focken tip anyway.'

'Tip?'

'You're talkin' to a focken dead man,' he said. 'They're gonna focken clip me, so they are.'

The comment filled the small space and the air took a while to clear.

'What are they gonna do with you?' the man asked.

'Don't know.'

'I shouldn't think it would be the smartest thing in the world for the IRA to clip a Yanky fed. Last thing they'll want to do is make it personal with your people.'

'I'm not a fed.'

'Oi give op then. What are yer?'

'I'm not law enforcement,' Hank said tiredly.

'Then what the fuck are yer doin' here?'

'I told you. Case of mistaken identity.'

'Bollocks . . . Look, if you don't want to tell me that's fine. Like oi give a focken shite. Got me own focken problems anyhow. Just makin' conversation . . . You're probably the last focker I'll talk to, that's all.'

Hank wanted to talk to the man, find out about him, but a lifetime in Special Forces was urging him to be cautious.

'Why're you here?' Hank asked eventually.

The Irishman didn't answer.

'Hey, you were the one who said it didn't matter and wanted to talk,' Hank said.

'I'm a tout,' he said.

Hank knew the term. 'You IRA?'

'Well, now that's an interesting question . . . Since I'm a tout I s'pose I'm focken technically not IRA.'

'You work for the British?' Hank asked.

'Brits? Fock off. I work for meself.' He cleared his throat and nose, hacking loudly, then groaning with pain immediately after. He took a moment to recover, undoubtedly in a bad way.

'Focken bastards gave me a good pasting last night. I

thought that was it. Kicked me focken stupid they did. What I'd give for a focken aspirin. Me head is focken splittin'.' He cleared blood and mucus from his nose and throat again and held his breath to ease the stab of pain the effort caused him. 'Focken bastards,' he said softly as he exhaled. 'So what the fock you doin' here then if you ain't nothin' to do with law enforcement?'

Hank kept silent.

'Oh, roight. I forgot. Mistaken identity. Excuse me focken brain but it's a bit loike mashed potato at the moment . . . So who is it they mistook you for then? Prince focken Charles, was it?'

Hank expected his captors knew who he was. In two weeks or whatever, no one had asked him. If they weren't curious that suggested they knew. If they never gave a damn, why were they keeping him? They would've searched him when he was unconscious and found his US Navy ID card. That would've surprised them, especially if they thought they had a Brit spy in the bag. In two weeks he would've expected the IRA to be able to find out who he was. Perhaps he was already in the newspapers as a missing American serviceman.

His thoughts went to Kathryn again and how she no doubt went ballistic when she found out. He wondered if they had told her it was the IRA holding him. That would confuse her already confused politics. He was going to get an earful when he got home no matter what. Hank fully expected to be repatriated once the Brits and Americans had sorted the mess out between them. It would be an embarrassment for all concerned, and the IRA had no use for him surely. What the hell, he decided. He wasn't giving anything away they didn't already know. 'I'm US Navy,' Hank said.

'US Navy? Navy intelligence?'

'No.'

'Oh, for fock sake. You're doin' my head in, man. What the fock would the IRA want with an American focken sailor?'

'I was working with the Brit military . . . observing. Something went wrong and I got snatched by these guys who thought I was a Brit.'

'Is that right? What were you observing?'

'It doesn't matter.'

The Irishman started laughing gently and then winced with the pain it caused him for his troubles. 'The American sailor got picked up watching the Brits watching the IRA. That's focken sweet, that is. You tell a grand tale, so you do, Yank.'

'How'd you end up here?' Hank asked.

'I got shopped . . . The snitch got snitched on. It was the Brits, I know that much. Focken IRA didn't have a clue about me. They're nothin' but a buncha focken eedjits. It had t'av been the Brits. I was too bloody careful.' The man took a moment to get through a stitch of pain. 'I know why they did it though,' he continued after a moment. 'It was me own fault. You went a wee bit too far this time, Seamus, so you did,' he said. 'Too bloody tempting though it was.'

'What was?'

'I shoulda got out a year ago,' he said, ignoring Hank's question. 'Got a wife and a kid, yer see. That makes yer push it, you know. When yer single you push it for the crack. When yev a family you push it for the money . . . I sold guns to the IRA and I sometimes sold the people I sold them to to the Brits, when I knew I could get away with it. And a good living, so it was.'

The Irishman went silent, then there was a sniffling sound,

softly with each intake of breath. He was crying.

Hank let him to himself and they sat in silence for a long time. The man seemed genuine enough and he wasn't unusually interested in Hank.

'Where do you think we are?' Hank asked, breaking the long silence.

The Irishman cleared his throat, bringing something up, blood or mucus, and spitting it into his hood. 'Fock. I can't cough any more. The pain is murderous. I must have at least half-a-dozen broken focken ribs,' he said, adjusting his position carefully. 'Either the Med or the Atlantic. If we're on a river we're not far inland. I heard seagulls as they brought me aboard. They picked me up in Munich and we must've drove ten hours at least but not much more. It was loit when they picked me op and loit when I got here and I didn't sleep on the journey. That's the best I can make of it for yer. Not that it makes a flying fock of a difference.'

'What were you doing in Munich?'

'About to get focken paid,' he said.

'Paid for passing information?'

'No. Running weapons. At first I thought the fockers were stitching me op, trying to take me goods without paying. When they started beating on me they explained the real reason and that me time was op . . . Bastards.'

'You really think they'll kill you?'

'Oi'll be the first focken tout in four hundred years to walk free if they don't. Oi've a sneakin' feelin' oi'm not going to be that locky,' he said. 'Anyhow, I recognized one of the voices when I came on board. A murdering bastard called Brennan. The Executioner is one of his nicknames. Bastard gets a kick out of it. Likes to take his time too. Taunting bastard, so he is. Brennan'll have some fun with me before he does the business.'

Hank believed him. The man certainly sounded like it was going to happen. It suddenly felt strange, being in a room with a man about to die.

'What did you mean earlier, when you said you went too far?'

'What?'

'You said you went too far. You think that's why the Brits shopped you. You were greedy.'

'Oh, yes,' the man said, then took a while to answer again, and this time not just because of his discomfort. Hank could almost hear him thinking. 'Do the Aral Sea labs mean anything to you?' he asked.

'No.'

'It should. The Aral Sea is in Kazakhstan. It's a big lake really, mostly dried op. The other soide of it is Uzbekistan. In the middle of it is an island, and on that island are the labs that used to churn out some of the deadliest biological weapons the world has ever heard of. That was back in the Cold War days . . . If yer know the right people, for the right price yer can buy a pint a pure death . . . Did yer know eight kilos of a chemical that oi don't even know the name of could kill two and a half million people in a city as big as London?'

'You saying you tried to buy some of that stuff?' Hank asked.

'Not troid. Oi'm sayin' oi bought some . . . "Virus U" they call it. About two cupfuls for a hundred grand. The so-called experts talk about how much damage some a these biological weapons can do, but for the most part they don't have a focken clue. A Pepsi can full could wipe out a small town and then spread and wipe out several cities. Oi don't know what two cupfuls of Virus U'll do, but oi wouldn't want to be within a thousand miles of it when it's released.'

290

'Who did you buy this stuff for?'

'Who do yer bloody think?'

'The IRA?'

'They're me only client.'

'And they have it?'

'A course they have it.'

'Would that be the IRA or the Real IRA?'

'What's in a bloody name?'

Hank was suddenly stunned as the implications of what he had just heard sunk in. 'Are you out of your friggin' mind?'

The Irishman didn't answer. Hank wondered how out of touch he was with the IRA situation. He never would have believed they would be into biological terrorism.

'Have the IRA ever bought anything like this before?' Hank asked.

'Not as far as oi know. This was a special request. It took me a year to set it op.'

'What do they want it for?'

'They don't exactly include me in their top-level mission briefings. Tell you the truth, oi wasn't going to let it happen. Oi'm tellin' the truth. Dead men don't tell lies . . . I was going to shop them to the Brits soon as oi got paid the money. It would've been me last job sure enough. Oi'd've got a few sheckles for that kinda information. The joke is the Brits've shot themselves in the foot by shopping me. You can't expect me to feel sorry for 'em. They've focken killed me and that's that.'

'The Brits don't know?'

'Sure they know. I'd made me contact and said as much as the boyos have a bottle of bio . . . I think it was a case of the left hand not knowin' what the right was doin', I mean in British intelligence. Obviously they would've wanted to know where that stuff was. They were gonna give me a fortune for the information. Some eedjit shopped me before I could complete the transaction. Maybe it was that focken IRA mole they're always talkin' about. Now that oi think of it, that would make more sense than anything else.'

It was this last comment that flicked a switch in Hank and made him realise he was very much a part of all of this and not just an observer. It was the RIRA mole they were after in Paris. 'Where is this stuff now?'

'Don't know. But they've got it. And some of the mad bastards I know in the Real IRA'll use it too. They're just as fanatical as the focken Muslims. They won't lose any sleep over killing a few hundred thousand Brits, I can tell yer that much.'

Hank could only think of one thing. He had to escape and tell someone.

Suddenly the engines revved hard and the entire boat shook. There was a jolt, as if the boat had been pulled by a tug, and then a sense of floating movement.

'We're off,' the Irishman said. 'Soon as we're out to sea that's me for the chop.'

Hank no longer cared about the man's future. He had committed an ungodly act by providing a handful of terrorists with the means to kill hundreds of thousands of people. Hank twisted his hands inside his bindings. They were firm and impossible to wriggle out of. He was going to have to do something more than just wait for an opportunity to escape. He was going to have to create one.

Kathryn walked into St Mary's church and looked about. It was quiet. The single great room was bright in the centre but the many alcoves and corners were dimly lit and shadowy.

No service was taking place. A handful of people knelt or sat in silent prayer, a couple placed candles on a rack where dozens already burned and one lady stared blankly ahead as she sat outside the confessional box, situated against the far right wall under a row of stained-glass windows.

Kathryn felt an urge to genuflect as she moved across the centre aisle, even though she had not done so since her mother used to practically drag her here most Sunday mornings all those years ago. She chose not to and walked slowly behind the back benches and to the side wall, subconsciously hiding in a corner.

The church had not changed much as far as she could remember. The altar was clean and bare and the wooden tabernacle unimpressive. The candleholders looked cheap and plastic flowers in their plastic baskets adorned a nativity scene set up on one side of the altar. Anything of value that had not been stolen over the years was locked away. The church continued to be a target for thieves until it was well known there was nothing of value left in it. The police told Father Kinsella they thought it was the act of drug addicts. Kathryn remembered how shocked she was then. It didn't seem so shocking any more. The evil was a part of life now.

The confessional box opened and a young boy stepped out and went towards the woman waiting in the pew close by. Kathryn watched as Father Kinsella, dressed in a black cassock, stepped out the other side of the box to have a chat with the pair of them. He smiled and patted the boy on the shoulder, shook the woman's hand warmly before she and the boy turned and walked away. Father Kinsella followed them with his eyes until his gaze fell upon Kathryn watching him.

His smile remained and he headed towards her.

Kathryn watched the boy as he passed by, memories of

her younger days and her visits to Father Kinsella's confessional flooding back. She wondered if he was still recruiting young warriors for the cause.

'Kathryn, Kathryn, Kathryn,' he said quietly as he approached. 'Good of you to come and see me so quickly.'

The boy paused in the entrance and waved back at the priest before leaving. Kinsella returned the wave.

'Good lad that,' he said, after the boy had left. 'He wants to join the British SAS. I've got me work cut out for me there, so I have.' He faced Kathryn, still smiling. 'Did you manage to avoid the press when you left the house?' he asked.

'Yes. There were a few reporters hanging around out front, but the shortcuts through the back gardens haven't changed.' She smiled at the memory of finding those childhood escape routes almost exactly as she remembered them, but the nostalgia was quickly swept away by the growing dread of the media interviews the priest had spent the previous evening preparing her for. She had lost track of the number of newspaper and television journalists that had called at the house, only to be turned away by her mother with the promise Kathryn would speak to them soon. And it wasn't just the media hounding her. She'd had calls from various military personnel in Washington DC, and also from the SEALs in Norfolk, Virginia; the commander of Team 2, Hank's former boss, and another officer whose title escaped her, all offering moral support and assurances that everything was being done to get Hank back home. And then there was the guy from the State Department who was coming by in the week for a chat on national security and modern terrorism, and the welfare union was sending a psychiatrist over to evaluate her and the children for post-traumatic stress disorder.

Father Kinsella had said she would be ready for the press by this afternoon, after one last coaching session, but Kathryn had had more than she could take already. On receiving the priest's message that he wanted to see her, she decided to tell him she was going back to Norfolk that evening, before meeting any of the press, and then prepared herself for the inevitable verbal onslaught on how important her work was and how she had to stick with it and 'feed the press' as he put it. But she was determined to stand up to him this time, although, she had to admit, to her surprise, he had been unusually kind and understanding since he first came to the house to see her. He spent many patient hours schooling her on what to say to the news media, and how to act, rehearsing her for specific questions, and even how to ignore or circumvent subjects in order to push prepared statements. She had lost count of the number of times she had quoted: 'I don't blame the IRA for holding my husband captive. They're only fighting for what they believe in. I know they'll set Hank free once the British Government admits its guilt in abusing my husband the way they did . . .' Instead of bolstering Kathryn's confidence the preparations only fuelled a feeling it was all some kind of ridiculous pantomime. It was clearly a propaganda campaign for the IRA and she was nothing more than another tool.

'The truth is I can't do the press interviews, Father,' she admitted, cringing in preparation for the eruption. 'I can't stay here any more. I'll go mad if I have to talk to all those people. I don't care what you say. I won't be able to do it.'

'I know, I know,' Father Kinsella said with great sympathy as he took her arm and walked her towards the church entrance. 'It's okay,' he said.

She was suddenly wary. This was not the reaction she had expected from him. Suspicion immediately set in. He was up to something. He could never be this understanding. As they walked outside the sun shone brightly in a cloudless sky and they headed along the stone path that went down the side of the church towards the car park. She wondered if he was guiding her somewhere private where he could shout his head off at her, but he seemed calm.

'I agree that you should get away, Kathryn,' he said sincerely.

Kathryn glanced at him. There was no sign of anger. 'I thought you were going to be mad at me.'

'No. I want you to go away, Kathryn … I want you to go back to England.'

She stopped in her tracks and stared at him in disbelief. 'England?'

'Well, there's no point in going to Norfolk. The press would soon find you there.'

He was wearing the look of a dealer who knew the cards he was laying even though they were face down. A trip to England certainly wasn't intended for her benefit. She could kick herself for even presuming for one second that the man had as much as an ounce of concern for her, or anyone for that matter.

'But England?'

'You'll need to be leaving tonight.'

'I don't understand … Why?'

'You're going to meet someone who can help you.'

'Who?'

'I can't tell you who right now. But it's very important. He'll be able to help you. You'll be well looked after.'

'I don't want to go back to England.'

'Kathryn. Trust me. Now would I be sending you all the way over to England if it was a waste of time?'

'Can't they come here?'

'Not this person, darling,' the priest said. 'He's very high up, if you know what I mean.'

Kathryn was only just beginning to understand. 'IRA?'

'Ay . . . It'll take but a day or so. That's all. You'll do just fine if there are any interviews.'

'I have to meet the press?'

'You'll find out everything when you get there. Depending on how you get on might decide Hank's future. He called me this morning and asked if you would go. That's a great privilege, Kathryn. Now, is that a good enough reason to go or not?' he said, beaming as if he'd solved the mystery of life.

Everything in Kathryn's soul wanted to cry out, NO! But she could not find the strength to say it. She had to do whatever it took to get Hank free. Even go back to England and meet the IRA itself. When she'd left England she'd vowed never to return, and now here she was, only a few weeks later, on her way back.

'What about Janet and Helen?' she asked.

'They'll be fine here with your mother.'

Kathryn gave him a look that must've conveyed some sign of trepidation.

'Don't you worry about them,' he said. 'A couple days aren't going to do them any harm. And I'll be here to look out for them . . . Then, when you get back, you can take them off to Virginia with you.'

She closed her eyes and sighed.

'I've got your air tickets organised. And guess what? Business class no less. It's not all for bullets and bombs, you know. And I've got you booked into a nice hotel in London with all expenses paid.'

Kathryn nodded, none too happy, but resigned. 'Will this be the last of it?' she asked.

'I've a feeling this will all soon be over. You please them in England, it'll all work out in our favour. Just keep telling yourself Hank will soon be home. That's all you need to think about,' he said. 'I haven't let you down yet, have I?'

They arrived at her mother's car. 'Look,' he went on. 'I know you find me a hard taskmaster, Kathryn, but I get the job done. Now, off you go. Pack some warm clothes, enough for three days. Keep it simple looking. No bright colours. No need to look too cheerful. I'll be around tomorrow morning at ten o'clock to pick you up and take you to the airport and tell you everything else you need to know. Okay? Oh, and one more very important thing. You tell nobody where you're going. I don't care who it is. No one. Not your mother, children, friends, nobody. I've told your mother you're away and that's that. She knows enough not to ask you anything. Do you understand me, Kathryn?'

'Yes,' she said.

'Good, because this trip is most serious. Most serious. If they think anyone is following you, for instance, the meeting will be off, and it'll not go well for Hank. I can't emphasise that enough. Now off you go.'

Kathryn climbed into the car and started the engine. She looked at Father Kinsella before pulling away. He smiled at her with one of his more saintly looks. Something about this trip was already troubling her. The past few days she had begun to think better of him than she ever had in the past, and wondered if perhaps she had misjudged him. Now, the old feeling that there was something very dark and dangerous about him, was back and stronger than ever.

18

Hank made an effort to stretch his legs much further around himself than he had tried previously, searching for anything he could use as a tool to remove his bindings. He gingerly got to his feet, his back and thigh muscles aching with the exertion, and slid his hands up the pole until his bonds reached a pipe connector and could go no further. There was nothing to be had that was of use. The block of wood on the floor a few feet away was quite substantial but useless for anything other than clubbing someone and for that he needed his hands free.

He leaned his head around the pole, gripped the side of his hood with his fingers, and pulled it up as much as the tie around his neck would allow so that he might see out of the bottom, but the view was limited and strands of hessian got into his eyes. He could make out a pair of legs flat on the floor, in trousers but without socks or footwear. Seamus's, he assumed.

The door opened and at least two people walked in.

'What the fock you doin'?' said a man. 'Going for a walk, are we?'

Hank's legs were kicked repeatedly until he dropped back down on to his backside.

'For God's sake,' Hank cried out. 'Why are you guys treating me this way? I haven't given you any trouble. I'm a prisoner of war and I expect you to treat me like one.'

'Shot the fock op,' the man said and slapped Hank on the back of the head as if he were a naughty child. Hank had begun to say his piece as planned and received a whack for his troubles. The man's shoes creaked as he crouched and Hank could hear his breathing close to his ear. 'Ay, yev been a model prisoner for sure,' said a man.

'Then why don't you treat me like one?' Hank said, his voice betraying his anger.

'Do yerself a favour,' piped in Seamus. 'The man you're talking to is Brennan. Sure I told you about him. The Executioner? You're wasting your focken breath.'

'That wasn't very nice, Seamus, tellin' the man me name,' said Brennan. 'You might've just signed his death warrant. It could go against him at the tribunal . . . I s'pose you told him about our little package?'

'Ay. The Yank's not stupid. He knows he's as dead as I am.'

This was news to Hank.

'He may well be, but you're first, Seamus,' said Brennan. 'Are you ready, or shall we play a game first?'

'Fock you, ye sadistic bastard,' Seamus said.

'You're the one who's focked, Seamus me ole' pal . . . Get his hood off.'

The men obeyed. Hank tried to visualise what he heard. Seamus hacked and groaned as they treated him roughly, and then their efforts stopped. The hood was obviously off and they were waiting for the next command. Then he heard a noise he knew very well – the double-de-clutch clunk of a pistol being cocked and then the snap and chink as the return spring threw the top slide forward to pick up a bullet and punch it into the breach where it settled snugly, ready to be exploded out of the barrel.

'It's a watery grave for you, Seamus,' Brennan said. 'You know what the Bible says goes well with water, don't you? Fire. Fire goes well with water . . . There's nothing I hate more'en a tout, Seamus. We'll have some fun with you before we set you in the water.'

'You're focken mental, you know that, don't you, Brennan.'

'Take him away. Make sure you give his bollocks a good soaking in petrol before you loit him op.'

There was a great deal of shuffling and moaning as they hauled Seamus to the door. 'Ya focken bastard, Brennan!' he cried out. Then they were gone. Hank could hear Seamus's shouts grow fainter as they carried him down the corridor.

It fell gradually silent as they climbed a stairwell.

Hank clenched his fingers to control the slight tremble in them. Nothing could prepare a person for this. No exercise the military could devise. He played Brennan's words over in his head, trying to clarify them. Something about a tribunal, and Brennan's name, and a package, obviously the virus. Hank was no longer confident about his survival.

'Hank,' a voice said inches from his face, making him flinch. It was Brennan. 'Hank the Yank . . . I lied when I said there was nothing I hated more 'en a tout. There is one thing. A Pink. I hate Pinks more 'en anything . . . Rumour has it those were Pinks in Paris. Was it Pinks you were working with, Hank?'

'I don't know what you're talking about,' Hank said, which was true. He had never heard the term before.

'Any friend of a Pink is an enemy of moine,' said Brennan. 'If I can't have a Pink, I'll have his friends.'

Brennan's shoes creaked as he stood, turned and walked across the room and closed the door.

Hank could feel his heart pounding in his chest above the throb of the engines. He was more scared at that moment than at any other time in his life. Then came a sudden shriek of a human in utter agony. It was far away, up on deck, but so shrill it penetrated the very bowels of the ship. Hank tried to cover his ears and leaned his head into a shoulder to block one at least, but it was not enough. He could still hear Seamus as they set him on fire. It lasted only a few seconds but his mind kept replaying it, pure agony. And then it ended with a single gunshot. Hank realised his hands were aching where he had been squeezing the pole too tightly.

Stratton looked up from his desk at several monitors in the corner of the administration room situated on the top floor of the SBS headquarters building. One of them showed a van pulling into the HQ car park. He watched as the doors opened and out of the back climbed three men, all short haired, well built and fresh faced. He would have guessed they were Americans even if one of them had not paused to pack a handful of chewing tobacco into his mouth between his lower lip and gums.

Stratton made his way out of the room and down a flight of stairs.

He walked across a hall and out through the main entrance, passed a large chunk of rock shipped all the way from Gibraltar – a memorial to fallen SBS operatives – and into the car park. He approached the men as they removed the last of their large kitbags from the van.

'Lieutenant Stewart,' Stratton said to the taller of the men, guessing he was the team leader. There was something about officers, Brit or American. Most of them looked like officers no matter what they wore. It took a long tour as an undercover operative to sand off the idiosyncrasies. This one had obviously not yet had that experience.

The man looked at him dryly. 'You Stratton?' he asked.

'Yes,' Stratton said, ignoring the sir out of habit, but aware offence might be taken. The Americans were big on rank respect, even in Special Forces.

Stewart let his eyes linger on Stratton's long enough to convey his displeasure, but it was not just because of Stratton's omission. The SEALs would have been briefed in detail about Hank's fate and Stratton's part in it.

'Pete 'n' Jasper,' Stewart said, indicating the other two men, who reflected their boss's attitude. Stewart would have offered his hand under other circumstances, being a well-bred Texan, but he wanted to convey his sentiments in no uncertain terms. Jasper released a long, brown streak of spit on to the ground as he stared at Stratton.

Stratton was not intimidated by the display. He understood. He might have felt the same, although personally he wouldn't have made it so obvious under the circumstances. He had learned the wisdom of keeping his thoughts to himself and his options open, especially with strangers. 'You have a good trip?' he asked, acting as if he could not read the signs.

'Great,' said Stewart, wondering if Stratton was really that thick skinned.

Stratton took out his cell phone and dialled a number. He listened for a few seconds then answered a prompt. 'Stratton. The SEALs are here . . . Okay, I'll bring 'em down.'

He put away the phone. 'We're going straight into the brief,' he said to Stewart, who nodded.

'You can leave your kit there,' Stratton continued, about to turn back towards the HQ.

'We're just gonna leave it here?' asked Stewart.

'The driver will stay with it until you come back.'

'I don't think so,' Stewart said.

Stratton squared to him. 'Why not?' he asked.

'Maybe we've got some sensitive equipment with us.'

'What sensitive equipment?' Stratton asked.

'I can't tell you.'

Stratton looked the officer in the eye and allowed his natural coldness to surface. 'Three things,' he said. 'You can't bring your equipment into the HQ building for security reasons. Second. You don't bring anything on to this op that I don't clear. Third. If you don't trust us, get your fucking arses back in the van and the driver will take you back to the airport . . . sir.'

The two men stared at each other, weighing temperaments and options. Stewart was not easily rattled. He considered his alternatives in a logical manner and went for the simplest, considering the situation. 'Lead on, Colour Sergeant,' he said. Stratton turned on his heels and walked on towards HQ block. Stewart glanced at his men, flicked his eyebrows. 'Attitude,' he said for their ears only, and they followed.

In the SBS HQ anteroom an armed receptionist inspected the SEALs' ID. Stratton led the way across the lobby, the walls of which were covered in memorabilia both old and recent: awards, photographs and plaques from various military related organisations from all over the world. Stratton opened a door leading to a staircase that went underground. The walls either side of the stairs also boasted the display of memorabilia, which the Americans snatched glances of as they passed.

At the foot of the stairs Stratton walked along a short corridor to a heavy steel door but the Americans had stopped to look at the last display. Hanging in a glass case was a pale blue ribbon with five tiny stars staggered along it, two on top, three below. It was the American Congressional Medal of Honour, presented to an SBS operative for valour in Afghanistan.

'I didn't know they got this,' said Jasper.

'He saved a CIA operative's life at the prison breakout . . . Does that mean we're even now?' asked Pete dryly.

Stratton heard it clearly enough. 'Don't bury Hank just yet,' he said.

Stewart eventually nodded in agreement.

Stratton punched a code into the lock and pushed open the steel door.

The Americans filed into the operations room, which was much larger than the narrow entranceway suggested.

Inside, the surrounding walls were covered from end to end and top to bottom in black roller blinds, all except two pulled down to hide what was behind them; one rolled-up blind exposed a map of Europe and another of the east side of England and Scotland. In the room were five other men, who turned their attention to the newcomers as they entered. The shortest and oldest of the five men, wearing a politician's smile, stepped forward.

'Colonel Hilliard, CO SBS. Lieutenant Stewart from Dev Group,' Stratton said, introducing them.

Hilliard extended a hand that appeared, to just about everyone who ever took it, a little too large for the rest of his body. He was short but his weight was substantially above the average for a man several inches taller. It was the extreme length of his shoulders that implied his broadness of chest and back were not fat, and also somewhat forgave the size of his hands, although overall, it had to be said, he was unusual looking. Hilliard was of the old school and reputedly the finest hooker the corps had in his day.

He was famously abrupt when he wanted to be, especially to those he had little or no respect for. More than once during his career he had been warned about his diplomacy, or lack of it. One of his more famous examples took place some months after the Falklands conflict when the camp was to be visited by the commanding officer of the Welsh Guards. Everyone knew the Welsh Guards were infamous for their shameless pilfering of Marines' equipment on board various ships while the Marines were on the ground. Hilliard had the visit advertised on every company notice board under the heading 'warning', with a footnote advising all personnel to secure their equipment until the Welsh CO had departed. The sign did not go unnoticed by the visitor.

Hilliard extended his hand. 'Good trip, Lieutenant?'

'Fine, thank you, sir,' Stewart said to the man a good twelve inches below him, noting the hand, possibly larger than his own.

Hilliard faced Jasper, who was suddenly uncertain as to whether he should extend his hand or salute. He chose the hand. 'Chief Morris, sir,' he said, wishing he'd dumped his chewing tobacco outside.

Pete took Hilliard's hand last. 'Chief Lexon,' he said coolly.

'Good to have you all here, I only wish it was under brighter circumstances. This is our intelligence officer,' Hilliard said, introducing Sumners. 'Captain Jardene, our ops officer Major Tanner, and Captain Singen, OC M squadron.'

All nodded on introduction.

'Can I get anyone a cup of tea or coffee before we start?' offered Jardene.

'I'm fine,' Stewart said. His men also declined.

'A cup for you to spit in perhaps, Chief?' Hilliard asked Jasper. Jasper shook his head and then swallowed the entire mouthful, aware he might well suffer for it later. 'Sorry, sir. No thank you, sir.'

'Right, well, let's get you up to speed,' Hilliard said. 'Then you can get yourselves sorted in the mess.'

'Before we kick off though,' he said, addressing the room, 'I would like to clarify some ground rules for the American presence here. As you know, an unusual step has been taken in "accepting" the US Navy SEALs offer to assist us in this operation on our home territory. There's no need to emphasise the reasons for that.'

'Our taking part would include the first wave assault, sir,' Stewart said, eager to set some of his own ground rules sooner rather than later.

'Yes, Lieutenant,' Hilliard said. 'And you understand that if you or any of your men suffer anything of a serious nature, even a fatality, the fact will be considered confidential. It will not have happened while working with British military forces within the United Kingdom or its waters.'

'We've already been briefed and we understand, sir,' said Stewart.

'What you won't have been told is that those risks have significantly increased since you and your men left Virginia, Lieutenant.'

Pete and Jasper glanced at each other, wondering what that could mean.

'Recent developments have put this operation into a very high-risk category for the assault teams. In plain language, it is possible the entire assault team could be lost . . . You will seriously need to reconsider your position in the operation.'

Hilliard then looked over at Sumners, indicating he could start his brief.

Sumners took a moment to gather his notes and thoughts

and clear his throat. 'Up until recently the focus of this operation has been to locate and retrieve Chief Munro, either by force or negotiation. To that end we have been unsuccessful in locating his whereabouts, or bringing to the negotiating table those in a position to do so. We think we now know why the IRA, or Real IRA I should say, have been stalling . . . Some weeks ago we received a communiqué from a reliable tout. This tout is an arms dealer and services both the provisional IRA and the Real IRA. He has provided us with reliable information over the years. He informed us he had purchased a biological weapon for RIRA. Based on his previous method of operation, he would have sold the weapon to RIRA before offering to sell the information on its whereabouts to us. We should have heard back from him a week ago. We have not. We have reason to believe RIRA has discovered his identity, and perhaps his purpose, and disposed of him. That leaves us with a very serious situation: RIRA may have a biological weapon of mass destruction. We're assuming this to be fact. We don't know where it is. We know they have the will to use it. We can assume they know that we know they have it, and they will therefore be doubly cautious.

'Three days ago the French Counter Intelligence service picked up the man responsible for Hank's abduction, one Serjo Henri, in Tilburg, Holland.'

This was news to Stratton.

'Here's Tilburg,' Sumners said, pointing to the map. 'The French say they have known about Henri's activities for some time. This could just be a face-saving comment since they appear to know nothing about Henri's connection to RIRA other than the information he has given them in his recent interrogations. Henri has admitted to abducting Chief Munro and handing him over to Irish terrorists.

'Now, why am I talking about Hank's abduction and the procurement of a biological weapon of mass destruction in the same brief? Well, it appears, for the present at least, that their immediate futures are entwined. By that I mean their route or journey from mainland Europe to the British Isles or Ireland. I'll explain why we suspect this may be true . . . Henri has admitted that he delivered Chief Munro to his RIRA contacts near Antwerp—'

'Did Henri say anything about his RIRA contact?' Stratton interrupted, aware he was jumping ahead; if Sumners wanted him to know, he would have said as much. Hilliard glanced at Stratton, conveying his irritation at the interruption, choosing not to vocalise it. But Stratton burned to know who the mole was and wanted to look into Sumners's eyes as he answered the question.

'No,' Sumners said definitely. The Americans had not been told about an RIRA mole in MI5 and Stewart was aware something was being discussed above his head.

'The CIA has told us they believe our tout purchased his consignment from sources in Kazakhstan. According to them the biological consignment was six fluid ounces of "Virus U". Six ounces of Virus U is a considerable threat to hundreds of thousands of lives in a densely populated city such as London . . . Our tout's message came from Holland; RIRA will want to move the weapon from Europe as soon as possible. Our conclusions? We believe the virus and Chief Munro could be on the same vessel. Other than putting all their eggs in one basket it would make sense since RIRA's transport resources are limited and two separate operations would increase the risk of being found out.

'Now. If RIRA wants to release the weapon in England it would also make sense to transport it directly to this country rather than to Ireland first, where they run an equal risk of being caught and would then have to repeat that risk when transporting it on to England. So. We will be acting on the assumption that a single vessel will transport Chief Munro and the biological weapon to England, that's if it isn't already on its way or has already arrived. However, our estimate of timings suggests it may not yet be on the British mainland . . . That's all I have for now,' Sumners concluded.

Hilliard looked over at Major Tanner, the operations officer. 'Two teams from M squadron are on immediate standby to move,' Tanner said. 'Since we don't know what part of England the boat will arrive at, if it does, we'll remain in Poole ready to go. Lieutenant Stewart. We'll go over our SOPs as soon as this briefing is concluded and decide your team's role as and when the balloon goes up.'

'We have no idea what this ship is?' Stewart asked. 'Assuming it is a ship,' Sumners reminded him. 'We are concentrating every available resource on that one task.'

'Ideally we would like to take the ship at sea for a number of obvious reasons,' Major Tanner said. 'But we're preparing for just about every scenario.'

'Sir,' Stratton said. 'As a back-up, can I request a team from the Northern Ireland detachment? Since we could be dealing with Real IRA players known to them, and surveillance may be required, they could be a useful support.'

Hilliard looked at Sumners, unsure. Sumners thought on it a few seconds, then nodded. 'I think that's a good idea.'

'Okay,' Hilliard said. 'Can you take care of that, Stratton?'

'Yes, sir.'

Hilliard checked his watch. 'Right. I have to get going . . . I don't need to tell you that the priority now is the biological weapon. It's beyond the lives of anyone aboard that vessel.'

Hilliard looked at Stewart to see if his words had sunk

in. Stewart nodded. It was clear to him. 'We'll still be going along with you, sir,' he said.

Hilliard nodded to him, then left the room with Jardene.

Stewart and his two chiefs joined Captain Singen and Major Tanner at a table. Stratton went into a glass office cubicle in a corner of the room, which contained a bank of various phones and communications devices. He reached for a red receiver, picked it up and dialled a number.

The phone rang in the detachment operations room and Graham the bleep, sitting back in a chair reading a book, picked it up. 'Ops room,' he said lethargically, still reading.

'That you, Graham?' Stratton asked.

Graham sat up immediately on hearing the familiar voice. 'Stratton?'

'Yeah.'

'How's it going? Didn't think I'd hear your voice again.'

'Can't tear myself away from you,' Stratton said. 'Is Mike there?'

'Yeah. One sec.'

Stratton looked through the glass at the Yanks discussing weapons and equipment. Sumners was making notes in a file and looked up at Stratton. They stared at each other a moment; it was as if they knew something about each other that no one else in the room was privy to.

'Mike here,' came the voice over Stratton's receiver.

'Mike?' Stratton said, turning his back on Sumners.

'Stratton. How's life treating you?'

'Not so bad.'

'This isn't a social call, I take it?'

'Go secure,' Stratton said.

'There was a strange sound over the line, then when Mike's voice returned there was a very slight metallic ping

311

in the background. 'I'm secure. Go ahead.'

'You guys busy?'

'No.'

'I need a team,' Stratton said. 'Four will do.'

'When for?'

'By the time you get them to the standby chopper it will be waiting to fly them to the mainland.'

'Where they going?'

'Poole first, but that could change at any time. It might involve water. Tell them to bring their own comms. Channel 4 will work in UK.'

'Understood,' Mike said.

'I might need a female op,' Stratton continued. 'Is Aggy around?'

'She should be in London. She volunteered to take a car over for exchange. Be back tomorrow.'

'I'll give her a call. Soon as you can, Mike.'

'Will do. Can you tell me what it's about?'

'The Yank that was kidnapped. We may have an in. Your ears only.'

'Understood. Good luck.'

'You too,' Stratton said and put down the phone. He couldn't tell anyone about the bio threat. That was going to be top secret as long as they could keep it that way. As for his request for a female operative, he didn't really think he'd need one. It was a spontaneous request. As soon as he thought of the det he had thought about her.

Kathryn climbed from a taxi outside the three-star Cumberland Hotel in Kensington and paid the driver. She read the instruction sheet Father Kinsella had given her, checked the address, pulled her bag on to her shoulder, and walked up the steps and into the hotel.

A receptionist greeted her at the main desk with a broad smile. 'How can I help you?' she said.

'I believe I have a room booked.'

'What's the name please?'

'Mrs Munro.'

'One moment.' The receptionist checked her computer screen. 'What's your first name?'

'Kathryn.'

The receptionist's smile disappeared as she tried several options to find the name without any luck. 'I'm sorry, but you don't seem to be booked. Oh. Mrs Kathryn Munro. There's someone here to see you.' The receptionist pointed to a quiet reading area the far side of the lobby.

Kathryn looked towards it; plants and a partition obscured much of the area.

'There are rooms available. Would you like one?' the receptionist said, the professional smile back on her face.

'One moment,' Kathryn said.

She picked up her bag and walked over to the reading area. Only one person occupied it, a man seated in an armchair reading a newspaper. She walked up and stood in front of him. He ignored her and turned a page.

'You want to see me?' she asked him.

The man looked over his paper and studied her, confirming who she was. He was a hard-looking individual with a face that appeared unused to smiling. He folded the newspaper methodically and indicated the seat beside him. 'Sit down,' he said in a soft Irish accent.

She obeyed. Kathryn had thought of little else on the journey than about whom she was going to meet. She wondered if this was the all-important terrorist leader. Father Kinsella had told her she was not to speak to her contact unless asked.

She had felt quite calm about the whole thing during the flight, although she hadn't slept, but since climbing into the taxi at Heathrow she had started to feel nervous. During the drive into London it crossed her mind that what she was doing, meeting with terrorists, was illegal. She toyed with the pros and cons, and finally reasoned that she could not know if the person she was to meet was actually a terrorist. They could be a representative, which was like meeting a criminal's lawyer. Not that it mattered. She would meet the devil himself on this matter, even if just to prove to herself that she was a good wife and mother.

Whenever she thought of Hank she pictured him stuck in a dark and dirty cell, but in truth she remained as confused as ever about her feelings for him. They were tested a few days before when her mother asked her what insurance Hank had and if it covered abduction by terrorists. Kathryn found herself thinking about it on and off the rest of that day. She was pleased to be able to at least say she never actually tried to find out if she was covered and for how much; to do that before Hank's fate was known would have been very low in her estimation. Her mother had also said a good lawyer could sue the US Navy for millions. Kathryn had done her best to rid her mind of such thoughts, but despite her best efforts they had helped dull her misery. In fact for one moment she saw herself moving into a big beautiful house on the water. She tore the thoughts from her mind, but could not help acknowledging that they did bring into question her true feelings for her husband. She was determined to do everything physically possible to save Hank if for no other reason than were something bad to happen to him she could look herself in the face without feeling guilt.

The man handed her an envelope.

'Listen to me carefully,' he said. 'Inside that envelope are train tickets and a hundred pounds. Open it and check it.'

She put down her bag and opened the envelope. The contents were as he described and included an itinerary and instruction sheet.

'Read and follow the instructions to yourself as I explain them to you.'

She unfolded the piece of paper.

'The hundred pounds is for taxis and general expenses. You'll catch a taxi outside this hotel to King's Cross railway station. You'll go straight to platform 9 and catch the first train to King's Lynn. Platform 9b to be exact.

'Make sure you're on the right train. Ask someone. King's Lynn. Go to the far end of the platform. Make sure you're in one of the front four coaches or you might get left in Cambridge. The journey takes about an hour and three-quarters. Do you understand so far?'

'Yes,' she said, intimidated. She could feel his strength, his resolve.

'King's Lynn is the end of the line. The train doesn't go any further. Get off the train, go outside, and get a taxi. The station has a taxi rank. If there are none left, wait for one. Don't go anywhere else. Do you understand?'

'Yes.'

'Tell the taxi driver you want to go to Burnham Market and a hotel called the Hoste Arms. He'll know where it is. Read that back to me.'

'The . . . Burn-ham Market, the Hoste Arms.'

'Burnham. One word. The H is silent. Not burn ham.'

'Burnham,' she repeated correctly.

'Go in the front door and find a seat in the bar. Someone will meet you there. They'll say, *what's the weather like in Boston, Kathryn?* Say that back to me.'

'What's the weather like in Boston, Kathryn?'

'When your business is concluded, ask the hotel to call you a taxi and you will do the exact same journey in reverse. Is that clear?'

'What business?'

'Were you not told, don't ask any questions?'

'Yes. Sorry. It's just that—'

'I'm here to talk. You're here to listen and do what you're told. Do you understand?'

'Yes.'

'When you get back to King's Cross, platform 9, you will walk directly out of the station. If the train does not stop at platform 9, you will walk to platform 9 as if it had, and then walk directly out of the station. When you are outside, that's in the open air, as opposed to being under the roof of the station, you will turn right and move out of the flow of pedestrian traffic, just a few feet. That means you will still be by the entrance to platform 9. Do you understand?'

'Yes.'

'Someone will meet you there. At the bottom of the instruction sheet is a number. It's a mobile phone number. You will call that in the event of an emergency only. Do you understand?'

'Yes.'

'That's it then.'

'Can I ask you one question?'

He sighed. 'What is it?'

'Am I staying in this hotel?'

'No.'

'Do I have time to freshen up, I—?'

'No.'

'But I didn't sleep on the plane.'

'No. You'll leave your bag with me. You'll get it back when you return to London tonight. Now go. Outside.

Catch a taxi to King's Cross railway station . . . Go,' he said with finality, staring into her eyes.

Kathryn stood, looked at her bag, changed her mind about asking to get something from it, and turned and walked away.

She stepped out of the hotel and looked up and down the road for a taxi. She saw one and waved, then realised she was waving with the envelope and money in her hand. She folded them and put them into her coat pocket as the taxi pulled over to the kerb. She paused to look at the hotel; there was no sign of the man – or her bag. The level of her nervousness went up a notch as she climbed into the cab.

'King's Lynn railway station, please.'

'King's Lynn? You sure, luv?'

Kathryn had a flash of panic and quickly took the envelope from her pocket and checked the instructions. 'Sorry. I mean King's Cross.'

'That's more like it,' the driver said as he pulled away and headed up the road. 'King's Lynn is bloody miles away. Nice place though, parts of it. It's on the coast. Me an' the misses used to keep a caravan up there. Up the coast a bit. Nice place. Ain't been there for years though. Yeah, don't you get King's Cross mixed up with King's Lynn for Christ's sake. Cost you a pretty penny by taxi that would . . . '

Kathryn hardly listened to a word he said.

Aggy sat in her bedroom at her dresser, looking at herself in the mirror. She wanted to do something with her short hair but couldn't think of anything she liked. Her eyes fell on the perfume bottle on the dresser. It was the only one she had. No one had ever bought her perfume before.

She picked it up, removed the top, sprayed a little on her hand and smelled it for the umpteenth time. What the hell, she thought. Got to start sometime. She sprayed some on her wrists and rubbed them together then gave a little squirt to either side of her neck. She then had a mischievous thought, hiked up her skirt and sprayed some on her inner thighs, high up and close to her panties. She went to her bed, where she had laid out a selection of possible clothes to wear. She held up two blouses, looked from one to the other several times, and settled for the tighter one. She picked a bra up off the bed and tossed it into an open drawer and pulled off her shirt. She inspected her breasts in the mirror from one side and then the other, cupped them in her hands and pushed them up and then smoothed them over, as if putting them back into place gently. She pulled on the blouse and adjusted it. Sexy was definitely the word that came to mind.

Her door opened and her mother leaned in holding a cordless phone.

'Call for you,' she said, then put her hand over the phone and mouthed playfully, 'It's a man.'

Aggy smiled and took the phone as her mother raised an eyebrow at the blouse, suggesting it was cheeky. Aggy playfully shooed her out and closed the door.

'This is Melissa,' she said. There was only one man she was expecting a call from, and he knew her as Melissa. She was happy that he'd called even though she was due to meet him late that afternoon to spend the rest of the evening with him – and perhaps the night too.

'Aggy,' the voice said.

All cheery images of her and Bill Lawton together fled from her mind. She knew who it was and he was the last person in the world she had expected to call, even though for a long time he was the only man she hoped would. She had long since given up that daydream. Now here he was.

'Stratton?' she said.

'How you doing?' he asked.

'Fine. You?'

'Not bad. I asked your mum for Melissa by the way.'

She'd thought Bill was the only person in NI who knew her real name. But then, nothing about Stratton surprised her, except a telephone call from him.

'What are you doing?' he asked.

She couldn't believe it. Now that she was seeing someone he was calling her. Nevertheless, she was torn. Bill had started to win her heart the past few weeks, but it was obvious Stratton still had a place in it.

She and Bill had somehow managed to cultivate their relationship secretly by meeting a few times in Ireland. The credit really went to Graham the bleep. Aggy was permitted to leave the compound to go out in the evenings only if someone from the det accompanied her. It was the same for all the operatives. But she could hardly meet Bill if she was with one of the others. But on one shopping trip in Lisburn with Graham, they had bumped into Bill. It all seemed coincidental but Aggy remained suspicious that Bill had engineered it. By the time all three had finished lunch together it was obvious to Graham there was something between Bill and Aggy. Instead of spilling the beans, Graham actually suggested how he might be of help; he and Aggy would leave the det together for an evening out and while Aggy spent the time with Bill, Graham would happily hang out in a bar and wait for them to be done.

Even though Aggy could not be disloyal to Bill, something deep within her hoped Stratton was finally making his move. She would not be able to accept, not now at least, but she would be pleased. But letting Bill go didn't seem right either. Her heart was, in a word, confused. It was certainly not something that could be figured out right there and then anyway.

'I was just about to go out,' she said, aware that it was essentially deceptive not to admit it was with a boyfriend. She expected Stratton might suspect as much anyway and wondered how that might affect his interest. She would come clean if he asked, although she would not tell him who it was.

'You're going to have to cancel,' he said. 'You're working.'

'I've got to go back?' she asked, surprised as well as disappointed on several levels.

'No. You're on immediate standby to move. Sorry if it's inconvenient . . . This is big, Aggy.'

Aggy's heart sank. She had not for a second considered he might be calling about work, since he had left the detachment.

'You don't have a mobile, do you?' he asked.

'No.'

Stratton expected as much. She was on leave for a couple of days to take a car back to the mainland and therefore would not have been permitted to take any operational equipment with her such as communications or weaponry. It would also be highly unusual for an operative to have a personal cell phone since they were not permitted to carry one on the job for security reasons, and operatives were home little enough to warrant owning one.

'Then you're gonna have to stay home and wait for my call. Sorry.'

'Is this happening in London?'

'I'll let you know soon as I do. Later,' he said, and hung up.

Great, she thought. Not only did he not ask her out, he

320

screwed up her evening to boot. The bastard. She sat back down at her dresser and looked at the phone in her hands. Despite the disappointment it had been nice to hear his voice. She began to wonder what the important job could be, then her thoughts went to Bill. Dear Bill.

19

Bill Lawton climbed out of the shower, grabbed a towel and walked into his studio flat to dry himself off and pour a glass of whisky. He was feeling in a fine mood. Life was looking pretty good, all things considered. This feeling wasn't based on anything tangible, although recent events had a lot to do with his optimism. It was more a suspicion that things were heading in the right direction after so many years of being in a kind of limbo. Since Henri had been blown, a vital link between Bill and his handlers had been broken. It was beginning to look as if this might work in his favour and assist his plans to remove himself from the tyranny of his obligations. It had all seemed to fall into place quite nicely. He wondered why he hadn't seen the advantages earlier. All he had to do, while in this zone of silence and confusion, was quit the military, and as soon as he could. His excuse to his handlers, whenever they eventually made contact again, would be that he thought he was blown after the Paris incident, or at least was about to be, and that he felt he should get out while he still could and avoid incarceration. There was a possibility also that, once he was a civilian, even if MI5 did discover he had been the mole they might do nothing about it. That was not necessarily a pipe dream; they would not want the negative publicity it would bring, and these were not good times to shake the people's confidence in the country's intelligence services. As for his own people, once he was a civilian there was little he could do for them any more. He had provided them with some quality information over the years and it was inevitably going to come to an end one day. He was not so naïve to believe it would turn out as smoothly as this simply because things never did, but it was without a doubt the way forward. Anyway, he had already set the wheels in motion by asking for an interview with his boss when he got back to Lisburn. He was going to make an official request to terminate his Queen's commission as soon as possible.

The other reason for his happiness was Aggy. He had never expected to feel the way he did about her. His initial attraction had been purely sexual and he honestly never expected it to be anything more. It was a pleasant surprise when she turned out to be so much more fun than he imagined. She was more mature and complex than she appeared; she kept a lot inside and he found it rewarding each time she revealed a little more of herself to him. He could tell she was learning to trust him and, strangely, he was enjoying being trusted – and being trustworthy.

And by God her body was every bit as beautiful and exciting as he had imagined. Those fools back in the detachment had no idea what a woman they had in their midst. He could not get enough of her. They had slept together only once, on their second date, the night after their first evening together. The memory itself was almost as exciting as the actual event. Even looking at her naked body afterwards was pure joy. When she got out of bed to leave him that night he could not take his eyes off her, revelling in every second of her flesh until she pulled her clothes on. He swore that if the only pleasure he were to be allowed for the rest of his life was to run his finger from her neck, down her back and along the parting of her buttocks, he would be more sated than most.

A loud knock startled him out of his daydream and his eyes flashed to the front door. He wasn't expecting anyone. In fact no one but a handful of his workmates in NI knew he was home. He'd sneaked back from over the water just to see Aggy, having lied to his boss that it was a family emergency. She was of course the one person in London who knew he was home and the thought brought a smile to his face; she obviously couldn't wait until their date later in the day.

He went to the door and paused as a mischievous thought crossed his mind. He discarded the towel. The knock came again. He stood naked at the door, his hand on the latch. If it was someone who had the wrong apartment they were going to get a shock.

He flung open the door, arms spread, in all his glory, and couldn't have been more horrified if it was the grim reaper himself standing there. In Bill Lawton's estimation the visitor was a fine candidate for the job. Father Kinsella stood in the hallway in a well-tailored tweed suit and hat, a small briefcase in his hand, his eyes fixed on Bill's, and he wasn't smiling.

'You,' Bill said, plainly shocked. He kept his composure and retrieved his towel, wrapping it around his waist. Father Kinsella walked in and closed the door.

'Just a wild guess, but by any chance were you expecting someone else?' the priest said.

'What the hell are you doing here?' Bill said angrily as he took his shirt off the bed and pulled it on.

'It makes me sad that you're not happy to see me, Bill me lad.'

'You know what I mean.'

'I didn't think you'd be home.'

'You're not supposed to come here. No one is.'

'Things don't always stay the same way, do they, Bill?'

Bill pulled on a pair of trousers and discarded the towel, already fearing dark reasons for Kinsella's arrival at his home.

'I was worried about you,' Father Kinsella said. 'There's been no secure way to get hold of you since the Paris thing. You never made any effort to contact me, so I had to come and make sure everything was okay.'

'You were the one who said I would always be kept isolated.'

'I'm just a harmless priest from Boston, remember? And we're old friends.'

Bill was finding it hard to suppress his hostility, but warned himself to push it to one side and remain calm. This was not the time to lose his composure, nor the person to lose it with. He could be shooting himself in the foot. Dealing with Father Kinsella was going to be the most difficult part of seeing his plan through and ultimately setting himself free. Bill had to remain cool if he was going to be the manipulator, a role he usually played well. But this was Father Kinsella, he reminded himself, the master of manipulation.

Bill mellowed. 'I'm sorry . . . It was a bit of a shock seeing you, especially since I was wearing nothing but a smile.'

'I can understand that, son. She's not on her way up, is she – I take it you were expecting a lady?'

'She was the only person who knew I was home but I'm not expecting her for a few hours . . . Well, now that you're here, would you like a drink, Father?'

'I don't normally mix alcohol with daylight, but to be sure it's dark enough where I live right now, so I will.'

Bill poured some whisky into a glass, handed it to Father

Kinsella, and picked up his own. They raised their glasses and took a sip, both glancing at the other over the rim.

'Good stuff,' Father Kinsella said. 'Good stuff . . . How long is it since we've seen each other, Bill? It's been a few years, hasn't it? Time does indeed fly.'

'It does,' Bill agreed.

'So tell me, how are things going with you?'

'What things?'

'You know what I mean. Since Paris.'

Bill had to be careful how he handled this conversation. He couldn't give anything away about his plan to quit, but at the same time he wanted Kinsella to see, if he hadn't already, that it might be time for him to move on. At least Bill could try and get a sense of how Kinsella felt about the possibility.

'That was a close shave,' Bill said. 'At first I thought they were coming for me. They had an entire surveillance team on the ground, surrounding my hotel.'

Father Kinsella didn't say anything and took another sip of his drink.

'I don't mind admitting it scared the hell out of me,' Bill went on. 'Still does. I've been looking over my shoulder ever since . . . I'm worried they might be on to me.'

Bill couldn't read any reaction in Kinsella.

'The French have Henri, you know,' Bill said.

'Henri won't tell them about you. He'll tell them a lot of things, but not about you. He's a canny French fox and was well chosen.'

'Nevertheless, I'm warm. That's a fact.'

Kinsella didn't give any indication he agreed. 'So what are you thinking?' he asked after a moment of silence.

Bill decided to go for it, but one careful step at a time. 'I'd like to back off, for a bit. Go cold. If they've got me, they've got me. But if they haven't, they'll be laying traps for me.'

Father Kinsella walked across the room and looked out of the window and down on to to the street. 'This is a well-chosen apartment,' he said. 'You've a good view of the street. Can you get on to the roof?'

'Yes. And from there you can get into the apartment block next door and down the stairs.'

'Were you thinking about escape routes when you got this place?'

'At first maybe. But I've learned enough over the years to know that if they were to send anyone for me, running out of the building isn't going to do me any good.'

'That's true,' the priest said as he continued watching the street. 'You'd need your friends for sure if they came after you.'

Bill wondered why Kinsella had made that comment. Perhaps he did see that Bill's future as a spy was no longer tenable after all, unless it was a set-up for something else or a cleverly disguised warning.

'I thought you were going to tell me you wanted to quit for good,' Father Kinsella said.

Bill looked at the priest's back, wishing he could read his mind the way the man seemed to be able to read his. The truth was the priest was the only person he needed a blessing from if he wanted to get out. If Kinsella gave him the okay, then the godfathers would no doubt agree. Bill was, after all, Kinsella's protégé. He sometimes wondered just how far up the ladder the priest went; he might even be a godfather. That would explain a few things.

'And what if I did?' Bill ventured, trying to make it sound as if he wasn't all that serious.

Father Kinsella turned to look at him. 'I was right then. You want to quit.'

Bill cautioned himself. He had to be most careful now. 'I wasn't suggesting that.'

'Were you not?'

'Obviously I've thought about it. Especially after what happened . . . What do you think about me going cold for a time?' Bill said, immediately regretting it. It gave the priest room to manoeuvre in that direction. Bill didn't want to go cold. He wanted out for good. 'You're a man of many experiences,' he went on, since Father Kinsella had kept quiet, 'but I don't think you know what it's like to live in constant fear of being found out. First I might ever know about it is a bullet to the back of my head.'

'Would you like to get out, Bill? Is that what you're asking me?'

Bill studied him, deciding whether or not to just go for it. The danger was telegraphing any actual intentions. He was aware Kinsella could just be fishing. 'I wish I knew if MI5 had any suspicions about me,' Bill said, weaving around the question. 'Of course it's possible they're not even close to me.'

'Make your mind up, Bill. A moment ago you sounded as if they did know.'

The attack made Bill strike back. 'I don't want to go to prison for the rest of my life. Or end up getting executed by one of their assassins . . . I've been useful, haven't I? I've given the cause some valuable information over the years.'

'So you have, Bill. So you have. No one's ever said anything less than what a blessing you are for the cause. You're probably the greatest spy we ever had. You're a living hero, Billy. When the war's over yours will be one of the names that'll be remembered for hundreds of years. They might've forgotten the likes of Thomas Meagher but they'll not forget you. Sure you might even get your statue put up one day.'

'Are you making fun of me now?'

'I couldn't be more serious. In fact that's what I'm here to offer you. Not a statue, lad. I'm here to offer you a chance to get out.'

The comment couldn't have been more laced with suggestion and innuendo. Father Kinsella had used the words offer and chance. It was obviously not going to be as simple as packing a bag and leaving.

'What do you mean?'

'I mean I agree with you. If you think it's time you got out, then I have to respect that.'

Bill remained prepared for the catch.

'Just do one more thing for us, and we'll call it a day.'

There it was. One more thing. The way Kinsella said it so casually was enough to get him worried. 'What thing?'

'A job.'

'A job? I'm not an operative, Father.'

'I haven't told you what it is yet,' the priest said.

He didn't need to. Bill always suspected his career as a spy would not end in a whimper but a bang if Kinsella had anything to do with it. That was his style exactly.

'Well?' Kinsella asked.

'Well what?'

'Is that the way you want to proceed?'

'I don't understand. If you think I'm burned, then I should go. I shouldn't have to buy my way out.'

'That's just the point. I don't think you're burned. You're the one who does. If you want to leave, that's up to you. But even in the British Army, if a soldier wants to leave before their time is up, they have to buy their way out.'

Bill couldn't believe this man. After all that he had done, the bastard was asking him to trade for his release. But Bill knew it would be pointless arguing with Kinsella. There was something else to this. Kinsella didn't just come here with a job offer to barter Bill's release. The mission itself was Kinsella's prime reason for coming to see Bill. If Bill hadn't said anything about the possibility he was compromised and wanted out, Kinsella would still have set him up for it. Bill was trapped. His career as a spy for the IRA was clearly at an end and Kinsella wanted one last shot from him. If Bill refused he could find himself out in the cold. Or even worse. Bill could only pray that the job wasn't going to be a bad one.

'What do I have to do?' Bill asked.

'That's the way, Bill.'

It was the only way. Bill had to keep some friends in high places. He had nowhere to run otherwise.

'Before you say what it is, Father, I'm asking you to consider who I am, and what I've done for you.'

'Bill. Do you think I'd ask you to do anything I didn't think you couldn't do in your sleep and get away with? You're the only one who could do this job.'

'What is it?'

'You're going to deliver something,' he said, picking the briefcase up off the floor and putting it on the table. Bill had wondered what the case was for – it didn't look like Kinsella's style – but he'd forgotten about it once they'd started talking. He wondered if it was a bomb of some kind. This was already looking very bad.

'It's a bomb?'

'There's not one piece of metal on or in this case,' Kinsella said. 'The whole thing's made of plastic.' He opened it. Inside was a sponge mould with a piece cut out of the centre, nothing else, no components, no wires, no explosives. 'You can get this past any metal or explosives detector in the world.'

'I don't understand,' Bill said.

'It's not complete, of course. There's a component that fits snugly into here,' he said, indicating the gap in the sponge.

'What?'

'A piece of glass with a liquid in it,' Father Kinsella said. 'All you need to do, when the time comes, is lay the case down on its side and stand on it, right in the middle, your weight fully on it. The glass will break and release the liquid.'

'And what's the liquid?' Bill asked, his mind going into overdrive, producing possibilities he prayed were not even close to the truth.

'It's a message that will tell the world in no uncertain terms that we want our freedom, we want our country back, and we are prepared to go to any lengths to get it. You do this, Bill, and we believe we will win the fight that has taken centuries and cost thousands of lives. The Brits are on the fence. This will shove them over. You'll be an even greater hero, lad.'

'What's the liquid?'

Kinsella knew Bill would work it out if he hadn't already, and even a wrong guess in the right direction was the same as him knowing the truth. 'It's a chemical.'

'Now we're into biological warfare? You must be mad. That's not the message we want to send out to the world.'

'Hold on to your horses for just one minute, me lad. Hear me out. It's a virus. It needs to be transmitted by people. It's not a nerve gas or anything like that. When the bottle is broken, as long as they contain it, it won't harm anyone. If you leave it the second it's broken, you'll be safe. But where you're going to *put* it will shock them to their very foundations. We're not looking for lives here, Bill. We're looking to convey a message. That message is we have the will and the means to take the fight to them at any level.

That's all they need to learn. You take it into the building. You crush the glass. You leave. They get a phone call telling them where and what it is. It'll be up to you where you place it. Put it somewhere safe. As long as it's inside that building. That's the message . . . I know it wouldn't serve us to kill thousands of people, but it would serve us to scare the living hell out of them. Do you understand, Bill?'

'What building?'

'You'll be told later.'

Bill could see the point as Kinsella described it, even though he still believed it was crazy. But he could not reveal his concerns to Father Kinsella. If this man was capable of releasing a deadly virus into a city as populated as London, he was capable of anything. He wondered why he had never noticed how mad the priest was before this moment. It would seem that Bill had underestimated Kinsella as much as Kinsella had overestimated Bill.

'Where is this virus?' Bill asked.

'You're going to collect it. I'll call you as soon as I have the details. Don't go anywhere. Stay here and wait for my call. Is that clear?'

'When is this going to happen?'

'Tonight. I'm sorry, but you'll have to cancel your evening,' Kinsella said.

'I'll have to leave the country right away?'

'It's all taken care of.' Father Kinsella put a hand on Bill's shoulder and squeezed it like a father would his son. 'It's equally important to us that you get clean away. I'll look after you, Bill. Your escape will be another slap in their faces and almost as much a victory as the attack itself.'

Bill nodded. 'It makes sense,' he said, wondering how the hell he was going to get out of this one.

'Good lad,' Father Kinsella said and left the briefcase on

the table and went to the door. 'You'll receive full instructions in a while. Just remember: King's Cross, platform 9.' The priest opened the door and looked about the hall, checking it was clear. Before leaving he looked back at Bill. 'You're my greatest victory, Bill. I could never have dreamed that day when we first met in the cemetery that you would win the war for us. I'm proud of you, Bill.'

He closed the door behind him.

Bill felt suddenly weak and sat down. He took his drink and held it in his hands. They were surprisingly steady as he drained the glass into his mouth.

Hank estimated it had been at least an hour since the engines had suddenly reduced power, followed a few minutes later by a jolt as they came alongside. The boat was perfectly still now and the only sound was the throb of the generator that ran the lights and pumps.

No one had visited him since Brennan had left and Seamus had been taken away. That seemed like five hours ago, more or less.

Hank had worked out a loose plan of escape, very loose in fact, since it all depended on his acting ability to open up an opportunity, then his jailers' reaction and, of course, fate. No matter how much the odds were stacked against him, he knew he had to try; there was no point just sitting and waiting to find out if he was to be executed. It was Brennan's parting words that had convinced him of the uncertainty of his future; as Brennan had pointed out, Hank knew his name.

And then there was the virus. Hank had an obligation to alert the authorities in case they didn't know. And wasn't this the opportunity he had been waiting for all his life, the chance to do something truly heroic? Perhaps this was his destiny. He had considered all these things in the peaceful solitude of his dark and dingy cell and had fully motivated himself. Now he waited for the opportunity.

Since making the decision he had been exercising as best he could. He had remembered a lecture from a former Vietnam War prisoner during a survival training exercise years ago. The man had been held in a confined space for years and had kept himself fit using isometrics. It was quite simple and apparently very effective; Hank had felt the difference after just a few hours. It consisted of selecting a muscle group and pulling or pushing against an immovable force or one's own body and holding the tension until exhausted. For instance, his hands were tied together, so he straightened them and tried to pull them apart. After a while, he could feel the pain in his shoulders as the burn set in. It was more tiring than Hank could have imagined, and even enjoyable. After a few experiments Hank decided to work from the bottom up, isolating as many muscles as he could. Since each muscle had an opposite, the challenge was finding a way to exercise them both. He pulled himself towards the bar, stopping himself with his feet, and held the tension. This exercised the biceps. Pushing away worked the triceps.

The door to the room opened and someone walked in. Hank relaxed.

Whoever it was sounded like they were searching through some tools or a box of nuts and bolts on a shelf.

'Hello,' Hank said. There was no reply. 'Look, I need help. I've gotta go to the toilet. I'm in agony here.'

There was still no reply and whoever it was continued their search.

'For God's sake,' Hank said. 'Is it so difficult to be just a little humane? Why do I have to be in agony? Is torture part of everything you guys do?'

The person stopped searching and went still.

'What's your problem?' an Irishman eventually asked. He sounded young.

'I haven't been to the toilet in a week. I'm bunged up sitting here on the cold floor. I'm in a lotta pain. I don't know if you're aware, but a person can die of something like this. I'm a medic. I know. If that's what I'm supposed to do, die like this, then forget it. But do me a favour. Can't you just shoot me? This ain't a nice way to go.'

Hank was laying it on a bit thick but he couldn't think of anything else. The young man seemed to be considering his request.

'I'll have to ask someone,' he said.

'Yeah, you do that,' said Hank. 'But don't take all day.'

The man left the room. Hank took a deep breath and then began to tighten and release his buttock muscles, each time holding them in tension for a count of ten. His target was a hundred.

Kathryn climbed out of the taxi in the village of Burnham Market and looked at the front of the old building, which had several wooden picnic benches outside. The sign read 'Hoste Arms Hotel'. As the taxi drove away she double-checked the name against her instructions. This was the place.

Before going to the front door she paused to look at the village. It was like a picture she had seen in a magazine, or was it a movie? This was her first idyllic English village. The roads the taxi had driven along the last few miles were so narrow that the driver had to pull up on to the verge and stop to let oncoming vehicles squeeze past. She had never seen a live pheasant up close before and by the end of the journey had seen so many she was almost tired of them. And what with the deer, hares and rabbits, and countless types of birds, the children would have loved it. The view in parts had been so beautiful it had almost distracted her from her bizarre mission – whatever it was – particularly the glimpse of the sea in the distance, a golden sliver of sand separating the grey blue water from the green fields. On entering the village the narrow road gave way to a broad centre surrounded by quaint little shops, two greens fat with trees and a brook running through it all. Idyllic it was, but all she wanted was to be back home in Norfolk, Virginia, and this was just a bad dream she would wake up from any second.

She faced the hotel and walked in.

Immediately inside the front door was a small entrance hall with another door directly ahead. Through the glass she could see the bar and people inside. She opened it and stepped in.

A log fire burned in a large brick fireplace the other side of the room. There was a dozen or so people; a couple were seated at the bar and the rest at some of the old wooden tables. No one gave her any more attention than a brief glance as she walked to the bar. There a short, stout bartender, almost as broad as he was tall, asked her for her order. She asked for a glass of white wine and after paying for it took it to a corner table near the fire, from where she could see everyone in the room and the front door.

She sat down with her back to a bookshelf stacked with old hardbacks, took a sip of wine and tried to compose herself. She was tense, her neck and shoulders were aching. She suddenly felt eyes on her and glanced at a couple sitting by the large bay window that looked out on to the front of the hotel. It was not the couple watching her, but some-one outside looking in, a man, in his fifties, in a well-tailored coat. She stared back at him. He walked away and a moment later the door to the bar opened and he stepped inside. He was carrying a hatbox tied with a decorative twine and walked directly to the bar and ordered a drink. She watched as he placed the box on the bar, took a wallet from inside his coat pocket, paid for the drink, and replaced the change in the wallet and the wallet back inside his coat. He turned at the bar to face her, took a sip of what looked like a whisky, picked the box up off the bar, and walked over to the fireplace. He put the box down to warm his hands and glanced over at her.

'What's the weather like in Boston, Kathryn?' he said.

She said nothing and just stared at him. He picked up the hatbox and sat opposite her, placing the box on the floor between them.

The man was known to the Northern Ireland detachments as O'Farroll, RIRA's quartermaster. This was only the second time he had stepped outside of the Republic of Ireland in the past six months. The last time was to visit a church in County Tyrone to put on a little pantomime in order to draw the attention of a man hidden inside the boot of a car.

'You must be tired,' he said.

Kathryn was uneasy in his company. Something about him reminded her of Father Kinsella. He too looked like he had once been a street fighter. 'I'm okay,' she said.

'Good. Well, it'll all be over soon and you can go back home.'

'What about my husband?'

'He's fine.'

'When can I see him?'

'Soon. By the time you get to London he'll be starting his journey to you. You've just got one little thing to do for me, and that'll be that.'

He glanced around casually to make sure no one was

within earshot as he took a sip of his drink.

'Under the table, between us, is a hatbox. You saw me carry it in. I'm going to get up and leave in a moment. When I've gone you'll pick up the box, walk over to the bar and ask the barman to call you a taxi. You'll take the taxi back to King's Lynn train station and follow your instructions to London.'

She leaned back to take a look at the box.

'Don't worry. It's not a bomb. It's just a small inconsequential package. You'll be met at King's Cross station by a man who'll ask you if the Hoste Arms was crowded. You'll hand him the box and he'll tell you where you can go and pick up your bag. Is that simple enough?'

She nodded.

'Don't talk to anyone else, and don't let the box out of your sight. That's all you have to do to get Hank back,' he said with a thin smile. 'You have a good life, Kathryn. Sure I wish I were taking a trip to America myself. I haven't been there for ages . . . Good day to you,' he said as he finished his drink, stood and walked out of the bar and the hotel.

She could not be more pleased with his comment that the sooner she got going the sooner it would be over. She took a long sip of her drink and got up. She reached under the table and picked up the box. It was surprisingly light for its size, as if all it did contain was a small hat. If it was a bomb it was a very small one.

She went to the bar and asked the bartender to call her a taxi.

No one paid her any attention as she left the hotel and stepped outside. There was no sign of the man she had met. She placed the box on one of the picnic tables and waited for the taxi. There were quite a few people in the village centre, passing in and out of the little stores and looking in the windows of estate agents and antique shops. Not even a trained surveillance operative would have noticed the car parked the other side of the village green with two men in it watching her. The one in the passenger seat was Brennan.

20

Stratton sat in the ops room with his feet up on a table, lost in thought. Sumners was studying the maps while sipping a mug of tea. Tanner was going over equipment lists and options with Captain Singen. The three Americans had left to take their kit to the mess and grab a meal. It was late in the afternoon and Sumners had mumbled more than once how they should've heard something by now. Coastguards along the entire west coast of Europe had been alerted, through circuitous means involving various foreign intelligence agencies, to be on the look-out for a boat possibly smuggling weapons into England. No one knew that the weapon was biological. That had to be kept secret. MI5 had issued a report that the occupants were highly dangerous and under no circumstances was any suspicious boat to be boarded and searched. It was to be left to run its course after its position had been reported. That suited the various European law enforcement agencies, who did not particularly want to get involved in a gun battle at sea with desperate terrorists. They would happily let the Brits deal with it.

The phone rang. Sumners snatched it up. 'Sumners here.'

He listened for a second then put his cup down quickly and signalled the others. 'That's good enough for right now,' Sumners said into the phone then hit the hold button. 'Get in the air,' he said to Tanner, then depressed the hold button again and put the phone back to his ear. 'Names, names! For God's sake, man!' he said as he grabbed a pen and started scribbling. '*Glory Bird*, *Wind Dream*, *Alpha Star*. Why three so close together? . . . What?' he exclaimed. 'Which was the first? . . . *Alpha Star*. When for God's sake? . . . This morning! Before first light! What's the type and tonnage?' He scribbled it all down, then put the phone back in its cradle and addressed the others. 'The Dutch Coastguard monitored three ships heading out from Den Helder.'

'That's Dutch Navy ground, isn't it?' said Tanner.

'Yes, and you could hide a bloody supertanker in those waterways. The *Alpha Star* is the best possible to start with because she's got no cargo registered and left before last light. She was last sighted heading due west.'

'Why's this info taken this long to get to us?' asked Singen.

'The report's been lying on some idiot's in-tray all bloody day. She could be on our east coast by now,' Sumner said as he stuck a pencil on the map and drew a line due west across from Den Helder. 'Twenty-eight thousand tons. What kind of draught would that be?'

'Two, three metres maybe. Depends what kind of boat it is,' Stratton said.

'Hull to Ipswich,' Sumners said, marking the map.

'Big area to cover,' Tanner added.

'Your teams should head for somewhere central to start with.'

'What's exactly due west?' asked Stratton following a line. 'North Norfolk. Great Yarmouth to Hull.'

'Split the difference,' Sumners said. 'Head for Lynn. You can go either way from there. We've got a Nimrod somewhere in that area. Get going. Hopefully I'll have something for you before you're halfway.'

Singen and Stratton headed for the door and were gone.

Sumners picked up the phone as he stared at the map, as if hoping it would tell him where the boat was. 'Twenty-eight thousand tons, two metre draft, Yarmouth, Lynn or Hull,' he mumbled to himself. 'Unless they stopped off the coast and transferred to another boat, or went north or south along the coastline to another port.'

'Or it's a boat load of Afghans,' Tanner said.

'That would be a good one to tell the local authorities,' said Sumner. 'Time to bring them into the game, I think.' He dialled a number. 'Sumners here. Time to alert the port authorities . . . All of them from Cornwall to Edinburgh. Start with Ipswich to Hull.'

On the camp rugby field the twin rotors of a Chinook helicopter beat the air. Two vans pulled up near the rear ramp and a dozen men in black assault gear, equipment harnesses and carrying weapons, climbed out. Most were equipped with the reliable H&K SD silenced SMGs, two carried bags containing a selection of sniper rifles including 22.250s and 7.62 Barking Dogs, and everyone wore a Sigmaster 226 9mm semi-automatic pistol in a holster strapped low on their thigh. They trooped into the techno-cave interior of the CH47 where equipment boxes were already stacked and a loadmaster was making final pre-flight checks. Stratton arrived carrying a bulky black kitbag, with Singen close on his heels. He took a seat near the forward door while Singen plugged his headset into a communications socket across from him, then looked over at his team leaders, who gave him a thumbs-up.

'Whenever you're ready,' Singen said to the pilot via his headset.

The loadmaster started bringing up the ramp.

'Wait up!' Stratton shouted. 'Where are the Yanks?'

'Are those them?' asked the loadmaster, pointing towards three men emerging from the trees, running as fast as they could under their heavy kitbags.

'Yeah, that's them,' Stratton said.

As the men bounded up the ramp the loadmaster continued closing the back.

Stewart dropped his kit bag on to the floor and slumped into the seat beside Stratton almost completely out of breath. 'Wouldn't be trying to leave without us, would you?' he asked.

'Don't you read the newspapers? We can't do anything without our American cousins these days,' Stratton shouted above the noise of the engines.

Jasper and Pete dropped into a couple of seats, both sucking in air as the helicopter screamed and shuddered and slowly raised its awesome weight off the ground.

'Where we to?' Stewart asked, removing the tie he had put on for his meal in the mess.

'Norfolk mean anything to you other than in Virginia?'

'Nope.'

'Well maybe it will by the time this day is over,' Stratton said.

Stewart nodded and was quickly lost in thought. On the surface the American was blasé, cool, laid back, which was his style and he wore it well. But deep down he had concerns he'd been unable to shake since the briefing. He'd pushed to the front of this operation, got his boss to bully the Brits into allowing him and his two chiefs to take a point responsibility on the assault, since it was the Brits' fault Hank had been kidnapped. That the Brits had allowed them to take part was actually a compliment. They wouldn't have done so a few years back, but his unit had since reached standards the Brits considered high enough to play with them, the arrogant bastards. But now it was suddenly real.

He'd gained a lot of experience over the years – perhaps more in the last four than most SEAL officers had in the thirty or so since the end of Vietnam – but nowhere near that of these guys. They were still way ahead of every Special Forces unit in the world when it came to small team, water-borne assault ops, the undisputed champs, with a dozen successful operations to their name over the last decade. Shit, they were still the only people in history to have captured and sank a ship after landing on it from the air – and that was twenty years ago.

They were a tough act to join but the past five or six years had been good to the SEALs. They had gained a lot of experience around the world and had no major cock-ups to be embarrassed about. He knew he was up to this job. He'd had the training and enough combat experience to know he was confident and reliable in a firefight. But assaults of this kind were not ordinary. Boarding a boat occupied by armed terrorists with the view to capturing it and rescuing a hostage without losing any of the team required pure surgery. Stewart and his team were amongst the most qualified in the SEALs to mount a ship assault – having led most of the rehearsals over the past year, boarding a dozen different types from small merchants to super tankers – but no one in the training or ops team had ever done one for real apart from a couple of drug boats, which didn't really count. The Brit operators surrounding him in the helicopter knew that. They would all be wondering if these Yanks could cut it. There was more at stake here than just Hank and the virus. By pushing his guys to the frontline Stewart had made a statement: that they were as good as the best. Stewart was one of the finest officers the SEALS had, an 'A' student, smart, fit and had never screwed up in his career.

But he knew that record was not just down to ability. Luck had played its part. This business was often like that of a trapeze artist's; sometimes you had to leap blind, trust in fate as well as your teammates, and hope the bar was where it should be when you reached for it. He'd been lucky. He just hoped it would stay with him for this one.

'What's your sensitive equipment?' Stratton shouted into Stewart's ear, snapping him out of his reverie.

'What?'

'The sensitive equipment you're carrying. What is it?'

'Nothing too sensitive really,' Stewart admitted. 'I was pissing on your tree a little.' He reached for his bag, unzipped it and took out three small black plastic hexagonal shapes, each half the size of a cigarette packet, and also a small electronic device. He handed one of the hexagons to Stratton. 'I was gonna give 'em to you guys anyway. It's our new super explosive remote-door charge. The initiator's good up to a hundred metres line of sight, fifty in a built-up area.'

'I've heard of this stuff. Is it as good as they say?'

'Don't know what you've heard, but it's good. Faster burn rate than C4 or PE, higher temperature, lighter; down side is it's harder to shape, which is why it comes in pre-moulds, otherwise great . . . Take 'em,' he said, handing Stratton the other two and the detonator. 'I've gotta bunch of 'em.'

Stratton nodded a thanks, then studied the devices. Super 'X', a nice addition to anyone's arsenal.

Kathryn was seated in the second to rear carriage of the train as it sped through the countryside towards King's Cross. Beside her on the seat was the hatbox. A ticket inspector came through the connecting door to the rear carriage calling for all tickets to London. She produced hers and he stamped it and moved on. The last ticket he checked before stepping through to the next carriage was Brennan's, who was seated where he could catch a glimpse of Kathryn if he leaned into the aisle.

As the ticket inspector disappeared through the connecting door Brennan had a quick check on Kathryn and then sat back and looked out of the window, hardly interested in the view, but it was better than staring at the back of the seat in front.

Brennan had mixed feelings about this sudden and unexpected field promotion. On the one hand he felt relief since he had feared he had lost favour with the War Council after the failure of his last operation, having not heard from them since the debriefing a week later. It was possible he was reading too much into it; perhaps there wasn't a lot of work about – there had been long dry spells before – plus his buggered leg was likely another reason the phone hadn't rang. Not that his leg was that bad. He had a bit of a limp and he might not be able to run as fast, but then he never ran anywhere anyway. Everyone knew it was not his style. Sprinting on a job showed bad planning in his books. If pursued, his MO was usually to fight, which was why he insisted on being well armed.

On the other hand, his new level of responsibility suggested that his role within the organisation had significantly altered and he wasn't sure he liked the implication. He was nominally a gun for hire, not truly an official member of RIRA.

O'Farroll's call had come out of the blue. Brennan's role was to be one of considerable importance in the most bold and destructive operation RIRA had planned to date. In fact it was greater than anything the Provisional IRA and IRA had planned in their own histories.

The initial offer was a routine abduction and execution

of a tout, Seamus. But after he arrived on the boat in Holland Brennan was told exactly what it was Seamus had acquired and that it was on board. He was shocked, although he didn't show it. O'Farroll gave him the responsibility of escorting the weapon to its final destination. Brennan liked his mercenary status but being brought closer into the fold made it more difficult to discuss his financial compensation for operations. Next thing they would be expecting him to work for the cause rather than for the money. O'Farroll, the head of the War Council, had told Brennan he would be well looked after for his services but there had been no time to talk about money. Everyone had been so tense, what with the virus on board as well as the American, and uncharacteristically Brennan had agreed to take part in the operation before the financial side had been discussed. He had to figure out a tactful way of reminding the War Council that his position as a hired specialist was unchanged.

One would expect such a key assignment to be given to a senior officer. Asking Brennan to do it suggested it was highly dangerous, but it also meant the War Council trusted him greatly and regarded him more highly than he thought, and truthfully, more than he wanted. Then again, it was also possible that they were short of clean manpower, not that Brennan was exactly pristine, but that was better than clean and green. The only new and untarnished members of RIRA who were not on Special Branch's suspect list were youngsters with no experience.

He had questioned the wisdom of having the American's wife courier the virus into London. She did not know what was in the box, but she was not trained in awareness and reaction techniques and she would not take evasive action if the need occurred. O'Farroll's reasoning was that there was something still to be gained if she was for some unexpected reason discovered. If, for instance, a RIRA member were busted carrying the virus it would go badly in all directions. But if she was discovered there was some positive publicity mileage to be had as the wife of the kidnapped American.

None of that mattered now anyway. She was on the train to the rendezvous and Brennan was her tail. He was curious about the character she was to hand the box over to. O'Farroll had revealed she was to be met by one of their people in Brit military intelligence. Brennan hadn't known they had anyone that deep, although he'd heard the rumours about the famous mole. He'd always thought these to be nothing more than wild propaganda, but it seemed they were true after all.

Brennan decided to kill some time by calculating the value of the operation and how much money he should ask for. The deeper he got involved, the more he figured he was worth. There was a limit, of course. It would all depend on how it finished. That was surely going to be interesting no matter what.

Stratton sat at the open door of the helicopter, looking out at the countryside where it met the horizon. He had been trying to clear his mind of all the recent events, but without success. He could usually manage a crude form of meditation before an operation and found the cleansing helpful when it came to refocusing on the job. But this one was too complex. His focus was being divided. He knew he should be concentrating on the virus and Hank but all he could think about was the mole. Somewhere along the line his fixation had taken on a personal element. Perhaps it was because this traitor had been behind the attempted kidnapping of Spinks, one of Stratton's team, and now Hank, who had been Stratton's responsibility. Or perhaps it was because

Stratton knew he had come close to the mole in Paris and that he should have got him. There was something about that day, a clue he'd missed that left him unsettled and frustrated. The answer had brushed past him, he was certain of that, and he hadn't seen it. Stratton's anger was fuelling a growing obsession with finding the mole.

Captain Singen tapped his shoulder and snapped him out of his thoughts.

'It's King's Lynn,' Singen said, wearing his communications headset and shouting close to Stratton's ear over the noise of the engines and the wind. 'The *Alpha Star* is a very good possible.'

'Is she alongside?'

'Been in port about two hours,' Singen said. 'Your lot from the NI detachment have already been diverted to Lynn. They'll be there before us. They've been told to put it under immediate surveillance. We're landing at Sandringham House. They're laying on transport for us. The old girl isn't home but she's given us the okay.'

Stratton gave him the thumbs-up, dug his mobile phone out of his pocket, put in the earpiece and hit a memory code. Covering his ear he could just about hear the phone ringing.

Singen squatted to unzip a bag revealing dozens of neatly folded maps. He thumbed along them, occasionally lifting one partly out to check it before moving on to the next. He found what he was looking for and pulled out two of them. The first was an Ordnance Survey of King's Lynn and the surrounding area. He found Lynn and then Sandringham a few miles to the north, then his eyes lost focus for a moment as his mind conjured up images of previous ship assaults.

This would be his fourth. The first had been an Iraqi

merchantman during the Gulf War when he was a brand new, straight out of the box, operative, one month after he'd joined the SBS. The op had been quite basic since there had been no opposition but it was a fine introduction to the art. The second ship was a drug runner heading into UK waters from Africa. There were five armed couriers on board that one, but the teams had hit the boat so swiftly and quietly the two on the bridge didn't know about it until the lads came crashing through, and the other three were asleep in their bunks. Not a shot was fired. The most notable point of that op was the strong smell of shit and urine immediately after the couriers were held at gunpoint. It was not unusual: the experience of a team of highly aggressive, swift and powerful men dressed from head to toe in heavy black fireproof material, armed to the teeth, with chest harnesses bristling with all kinds of weaponry and sophisticated devices was enough to make anyone crap themselves.

The most memorable assault was the last one he'd done, off the Colombian coast. There had been eleven armed, mostly South American, drug couriers on that one. The two men on deck, wide awake at one in the morning, had spotted the teams in their assault craft before they had actually reached the side of the ship. The couriers were either high on their own merchandise, or they were more frightened of what their bosses would do to them if they did not put up a fight, because they went immediately on the offensive with their selection of sub-machine-guns and assault rifles. Singen's team bagged three but unfortunately, because he was in the tail pair and his team were the back-up assault wave, he did not personally have the opportunity of a hit himself. Six couriers were killed and four seriously wounded within three minutes, which was as long as it took to secure the boat once on board. The only injury among the teams was a creased arm from a ricochet. That had been a good day's work.

But this boat was going to be tactically different. It was static alongside, which meant the first phase would be as if for a building. In theory it should be much easier, and normally Singen's concerns would be only along the lines of the overall success of the operation since, being an officer, he would never take point on the assault and so his chances of taking a hit were similar to those for him getting a kill. But this bio thing was a different story. This was a first for everyone. They were going into the record books once again, but he wondered how it would read this time. It had to be treated like any other ship assault and they would just have to hope to God luck was on their side when it came to the bio itself.

He tapped Stratton on the shoulder and handed him the other map.

Bill Lawton was at the window of his apartment looking down onto the street. It was quiet, the occasional car, but no pedestrians. He hadn't been able to get rid of the frown on his face since Father Kinsella had left. How could a day that started so well turn into such a disaster so quickly? And it was only going to get worse.

The phone rang. He looked at it. Had it not been for Kinsella's sudden and unannounced arrival he would have bet his life the caller was Aggy. There was no longer any joy or sudden expectation at the sound of its chirp. He wanted to let it ring but he could not. It might be Kinsella. If it was Aggy he would explain that they could not meet. He couldn't tell her that meant never again, which was why he had delayed making the call himself.

He picked up the phone.

'Get something to write with,' Father Kinsella instructed.

It had been too much to hope his prayers had been answered, that Kinsella had been struck by a bus. Bill found a pen and scribbled on the phone pad to check it worked. 'Okay,' he said.

'You've got an hour to get to King's Cross railway station, platform 9, and meet the train from King's Lynn. Have you got that?'

'Yes.'

'You're going to meet someone off the train. A woman. She will meet you outside the platform building. She's a pretty woman, dark hair, well dressed, thirty years old. She'll be carrying a hatbox. You will walk up to her and ask her if the Hoste Arms was crowded. Say it back to me.'

'I've got it,' Bill said tiredly.

'I'm sure you have, Bill me lad. Say it back to me anyway and keep an old man happy.'

'Was the Hoste Arms crowded?' Bill said, tiredly.

'You'll then take the hatbox and escort her away. Now this is what I want you to tell her once you're clear of the station. She's to go directly to Heathrow airport, terminal four. In the arrivals terminal there is a meeting place designated by a sign that says just that. She's to wait there and she will be met and given her next instructions. Is that all clear?'

'Yes.'

'As for you, Bill. You'll go back home to your apartment and you will open the box and carefully place the contents into the briefcase I left with you. The glass container will fit neatly into the space in the sponge mould. I'm sure I don't need to emphasise the word carefully, do I, lad?'

'No,' Bill said. There was a flutter in the pit of his stomach as the unthinkable began to take shape.

'At around seven p.m., when it's good and dark,' Father Kinsella continued, 'you will make your way to Millbank and MI5 headquarters.'

Bill's jaw dropped visibly as he heard the destination of the virus. 'You've got to be kidding,' he said.

'Do I sound like I'm in a jocular mood?'

'But MI5—'

'Listen to me,' Father Kinsella growled. 'You will enter the building with the briefcase. The detectors will not trip as I explained. Make sure you don't carry anything metallic on your person. The rest, Bill, is up to you, as we discussed. As long as you crush the vial.' Father Kinsella let those last words hang as he listened to Bill's breathing. 'Make sure you have your passport with you and nothing else,' he went on. 'You'll be going into the building as you are. When you're done you will go to Heathrow airport, terminal four arrivals and wait in the designated meeting area. Is that clear?'

'Yes . . . Where am I headed?' Bill asked.

'Now you know better than to ask questions like that, Bill. Everything will be taken care of. I'm not going to wish you good luck because you're not going to need any. Now get going.'

And with that final command the phone went dead.

Bill pushed the receiver pedals down, took a moment to collect his thoughts, and then dialled a number.

Aggy was lying on her bed staring at the ceiling. It was at times like these she liked to read a book, but she would have been unable to concentrate. She couldn't decide whether to call Bill and cancel the evening or wait until she got a call from Stratton to tell her she was to move. There was the possibility Stratton wouldn't call that night and she was toying with the idea of inviting Bill to come around and see her. He wouldn't be able to stay the night, but they could talk. But then it would be difficult to explain why she couldn't go out, and then why she had to if Stratton should call. The sensible thing to do was cancel but she couldn't think of an excuse. Bill would be so disappointed. She would too, but not as much as him judging by his comments the day before; he was going to have her clothes off before he'd even shut his front door. That hadn't sounded such a bad idea this morning, but strangely, since Stratton had called, it was no longer as attractive.

The phone lying beside her gave off an electronic ring and she picked it up. 'Hello,' she said.

All she could hear was a loud static hiss and rumble, then Stratton's voice echoed in the background. 'Aggy?' he said. 'Aggy, it's Stratton.'

'Yes,' she said, sitting up.

'You're on your way to King's Lynn railway station. King's Lynn. You got that?'

'King's Lynn,' she said.

'I'll meet you there, at the station,' he shouted. She realised he was in a helicopter.

'I'm leaving now,' she said as she stood up and took her leather jacket off the back of her dresser chair.

'Soon as you can,' he said. 'And Aggy?'

'Yes.'

'I'm looking forward to seeing you.'

'Me too,' she replied, without even thinking about it. The phone went dead.

It was odd how those few words had made her feel so good. She never expected to hear them from him. She dropped the phone on to the bed and pulled on her jacket.

As she opened her bedroom door to leave, the phone rang again. The first person she thought of was Bill. She hadn't called him and was about to leave having completely forgotten to. But then it might be Stratton again. She picked it up.

'Hello,' Bill Lawton said.

'Hi. I was just about to call you,' she said, screwing up her eyes and hating herself for being such a lying coward.

'Melissa. I've got to go somewhere,' he said. 'Would you believe my boss just flew into town. Remember I'd told him I'd come back to London because my mother was sick? He called and wants to see me, to go to dinner if I've got the time. I could hardly say no. I'm sorry.'

'That's okay,' she said, relieved. She wouldn't tell him she couldn't make it either.

'I've got to run,' he said. 'I'll talk to you later.'

'I might be out later,' she said quickly in case he did call or come around to the house. 'I'll probably go and see some old friends.' At least that wasn't a lie.

'Okay. I'll call you tomorrow.'

'Don't forget I'm heading back to the obvious early tomorrow,' she reminded him.

'Oh, right. How could I forget that? I'll call you when I can then.'

'Okay. Bye.' She was about to put down the phone when he called out her name quickly.

'Yes,' she said.

'Melissa . . . I just want you to know . . . well, I want you to know that I've gone and fallen in love with you.'

Aggy couldn't say anything, but she wished he hadn't said it.

'I don't care if that scares you. Strangely enough it didn't scare me to say it . . . I've gotta go. Have a great night.'

The phone went dead in her hand. She tossed it on to the bed. This was not the time to think about it. Fortunately she had enough to distract her for now. She had to get to King's Lynn.

She double-checked she had money and ID. Then suddenly something occurred to her: what if Bill was on the same operation? There was something odd about the way he had cancelled the evening, something in his voice, what he had said.

She closed her bedroom door and walked down the stairs. There was no point coming up with a new excuse for her mother. She'd let her continue to think she was out with Bill for the evening, and if the op went on for days she would have to wing it. Life was not this complicated a few weeks ago.

21

Kathryn listened to the announcement that the train would soon be arriving in King's Cross, London, where it would terminate. The carriage had almost filled up at Cambridge and she had had to put the hatbox on her lap to allow someone to sit beside her.

As the train slowed to a crawl and the platform appeared alongside the window she decided to avoid the press of the crowd and wait until most of the people had got off. It came to a complete stop with a jerk, and a gush of compressed air announced the opening of the doors. The passengers streamed out and when the carriage was almost empty Kathryn stood up with her hatbox and left her seat.

She was not the last person to alight from the carriage. Brennan climbed out of his seat after she stepped through the door and watched her walk down the platform. He felt a twinge in his leg where the bullet had grazed the bone and he flexed it a couple of times to loosen it up before stepping through to the next carriage. He kept Kathryn in his sights as he limped along the aisle, keeping slightly behind her.

The mass of passengers moved ahead of her, slowed by the funnel effect at the end of the platform. Kathryn noted she was on platform 9 and took her time so as not to catch them up. Her nerves started to increase again as the next phase of her 'mission' grew closer and she went over it in her head. None of it had been difficult so far but she kept dreading something might go wrong, be it her fault or anyone else's. What if this next person didn't turn up, for instance? What was she supposed to do with the box? She did have that emergency number. She told herself not to think about any of that unless it happened. There was no need to add to the stress she was already under.

As she stepped outside the platform she followed her instructions precisely and turned to the right, walked a few paces so that she was out of the flow of human traffic, and stopped.

She looked at almost every man that came into view even though for the most part she saw only the backs of their heads since more were leaving the platform than entering it. She hoped to find a pair of eyes looking at her. Then her peripheral vision picked up movement on her right, a lone man crossing the road, heading directly towards her.

At that precise moment Aggy walked out of the alleyway that connected the main station to the entrance to platforms 9, 10 and 11. She slowed as she saw Bill walking directly across her front at an angle that would put him on a collision course with her if she continued towards the platform entrance. She stopped, not wanting to meet him, even though it appeared they might well have the same destination. This was too much of a coincidence otherwise.

Someone walked out of the alleyway behind her and bumped her in the back without offering an apology. Aggy flashed him a look and might have snapped a remark about his bad manners. Instead she stepped aside to allow the flow of passengers from the alleyway and watched Bill. She started to move off, slowly, giving him time to get ahead and for her to decide whether to catch him up. She had to keep with the possibility he was not on the op and it might therefore be wiser to leave him be. After his parting comment on the phone it would all be a bit strained anyway. Then he stopped to talk to a woman standing outside the station. Aggy stopped. If he turned to look in her direction, despite the people moving between them, he would see her. She should have turned around and walked back into the alleyway, but remained where she was.

'Was the Hoste Arms crowded?' Bill asked Kathryn.

Kathryn felt awkward. Not being given anything to reply suddenly seemed odd. She held out the box to him, eager to be rid of it anyway. 'I think this is for you,' she said, feeling as if she ought to say something. He took it from her.

'Walk with me, will you?' he said, and turned to indicate a direction away from the platform entrance, back the way he had just come.

Aggy watched them walk in front of her. Thankfully, Bill didn't see her.

The woman was pretty and quite sophisticated. It suddenly struck Aggy there was something vaguely familiar about the woman. She couldn't begin to think where, but she was certain she had seen her before. Aggy had only been inside the Lisburn HQ briefly a couple of times on errands for the det. It was possible she'd seen her there, a passing in a corridor perhaps, but she could not recollect. Bill hadn't kissed her on meeting, which was a clue the relationship was a professional one since Bill kissed just about every woman he met on the cheek whenever he said hello or goodbye. He kissed Aggy's mother the first time they met and when she blushed he apologised in his charming way, explaining it was a habit he'd picked up in Europe. Apart from a brief exchange of words and the hatbox, Bill and the woman didn't speak as they walked away.

Aggy watched until they were out of sight and then continued on her way to platform 9. The one thing niggling her was that Bill's boss was a he.

She entered the platform and walked down to the far end and stepped into the last carriage.

The Chinook circled the Sandringham estate once to identify the landing point before starting on its descent glide path over the dense conifer woods to an open, manicured green. To one side of the touchdown point, near the trees, was a collection of civilian vehicles.

The rear ramp of the helicopter was already opening as it landed. Singen was first out of the side door and hurried over to the vehicles to talk with several gentlemen waiting to greet him. After a brief exchange Singen looked back at his men coming down the ramp carrying their equipment boxes. 'The two vans,' he shouted as the rotors started to wind down. The men shuffled their equipment to the vans and started loading them, the three Americans equally energetic and helping where they could. 'We're moving straight out,' Singen added.

Stratton stepped from the helicopter carrying one end of a large box, an operative on the other, and put it down outside a van, whereupon it was immediately hauled inside.

'Stratton,' Singen called out as he walked over to him. 'That's your vehicle there,' he said indicating a plain white four-door. 'Keys are in it. Superintendent,' he called out to the group of gentlemen. A man in a black suit left them and briskly came over.

'This is Superintendent Allison,' Singen said. 'He's up to speed on the boat, Hank and the bio.'

Stratton shook the man's hand and faced Singen again. 'I'll head off and do a recce and check on the det people. Let me know as soon as you've found a mounting area.'

'Will do,' Singen said, checking on the vans.

Stratton faced the superintendent. 'Where exactly is the boat?' he asked him getting out his map.

'I've got a map already marked out for you,' the police officer said as he took it from his pocket and opened it out on the bonnet of the car. 'The boat's tied up alongside the town quay. Do you know this area at all?'

'No.'

'This is exactly where the boat is.' The Superintendent indicated a mark circled on the River Ouze that ran north/south along the west side of the town.

'We're going to need a noose around the boat, at least four hundred metres radius,' Stratton said. We need to be able to close down the entire area in a second if the situation requires. That's every road, alleyway, back door, wall, fence, sewer. Airtight.'

'I understand,' the officer said confidently.

'And they'll need to be armed,' Stratton added.

'The armoury's being emptied as we speak.'

Stratton nodded, taking a moment to study the map and make sure he'd covered all his immediate needs. 'Good to have you aboard, sir,' Stratton finally said to the superintendent as he folded the map.

The police officer was suddenly flushed with pride, ready to fly to the moon if this lot asked him to. 'Anything you need, just ask,' he said.

Stratton looked around. Everyone was wearing black assault gear under civilian coats, except for him and the three

Americans. 'Lieutenant Stewart,' he called out. Stewart was helping load a box into one of the vans and looked up to see it was Stratton calling him. Stewart walked over to him.

'What's your first name?' Stratton asked.

'Tom.'

'Tom. Get your two guys into black and tooled up. You come with me. We're gonna do a recce of the boat,' Stratton said as he grabbed his bag and put it on the back seat of the car.

Tough as Stewart was, he couldn't help but feel somewhat jazzed at being invited to accompany Stratton on the initial recce. Not only was it a compliment, it communicated that he and his boys were every bit a part of the team. It was becoming obvious Stratton had a way with soldiers.

'Superintendent. Do you have a card?' Stratton asked.

The Superintendent reached into his pocket and found one. Stratton checked it. 'I can get you on this mobile number?' he asked.

'Any time.'

Stratton climbed into the car. Stewart returned from instructing his men and climbed in beside him. Stratton handed him his own map that he had folded to show the area. 'We're there,' he indicated. 'Sandringham House.'

'Yeah. Place looks great. Wish I'd brought my camera.'

'We can probably wangle a discount on the tour later. I want to get on to this road, the A149. We'll take it down to this roundabout here. Knight's Hill. Then find our way to here, where the boat is. You all set?'

'Yep.'

'Tooled?'

Stewart opened his coat to reveal a regular cannon: a black, long-barrelled, 20-round 45 Magnum semi-automatic with dewdrop nose recoil stabiliser tightly secured in a quick-release shoulder holster. 'Fucking Yanks,' Stratton said, shaking his head with a smirk. 'Don't fire that thing at the boat or you'll sink it.'

'Just let me know,' Stewart said, grinning for the first time since arriving in England. Stratton started the car and drove across the green on to a road that led to one of the huge ornate gates. Behind him the vans were already starting their engines as the last operative climbed in.

Twenty minutes later, Stratton and Stewart were standing on the cobbled stone quay, with the old customs house at their backs as they looked towards the southern end of the quay where the *Alpha Star* was moored. Stratton took a small, flat radio from his pocket, stuck a wireless earpiece inside his ear and clipped a microphone to his sweatshirt, hiding it under his jacket. 'Let's see who we've got with us.'

He turned on the radio, set the channel to 4, and put it inside his breast pocket. He faced Stewart and looked at him as if he was talking to him. 'All stations, this is Stratton. Who've we got?'

There was the familiar sound of the secure communications system kicking in, his words being scrambled, then a voice unscrambling back to him. 'Hello, Stratton. This is Ed, 'ere.'

'Good to hear you, Ed,' Stratton said. 'Where are you?'

'South of target, three fishing boats. I'm on one of 'em.'

'What have we got?'

Ed was sitting back on the deck of the deserted fishing boat, hidden from view with a pair of binoculars pressed up against his eyes. 'It's a good possible,' he said. 'I've seen one face I think I recognise. Sean McKennen?'

'Of the Warrenpoint McKennens,' Stratton replied.

'That's right. He was out on deck just for a moment. 'Ad something bulky under 'is coat. Wouldn't be surprised if it was an SMG.'

'Any movement on or off the boat?'

'Not since I got 'ere 'bout twenty minutes ago, but the boat 'ad been alongside a while, I think.'

'Who else we got?' asked Stratton.

'Bobby's up on the roof of the corn exchange. Says 'e's got a good view of the boat deck.'

'Bobby,' Stratton said. 'You hear me?'

'Loud and clear, Stratton. This is a good location for a sniper. Can't see faces too clearly.'

'Roger that. Who else?'

'Take a guess,' Ed said. "E's on the west bank, in the water, under a fuckin' sewage pipe covered in shite.'

"Allo, Stratton,' came a voice.

'That you, Spinksy?'

Spinks, wearing a dry-bag and facemask, was tucked into the opposite bank to the boat, in the water up to his chin, some flotsam arranged nicely in front of him, with a dripping sewage pipe above him. 'It's me,' he said.

'What's that location like?'

'Fuckin' 'orrible. No one'll find me 'ere. Got the water side of the boat covered. Nothing'll come off or on it without me seein' it.'

'Anything?' Stratton asked.

'I'm pretty sure that was McKennen too. Saw a bloke on the bridge who looked like he 'ad an SMG. 'Ard to say 'ow many on board. Seen five or six different blokes so far.'

'How long you good for there?'

'Fuck it. All night if you want. Got me flask and a bag

a sarnies. 'Ad a piss already. Me right leg's a bit cold. Might need a shit in a minute, but I don't need to go anywhere for that, do I? I'm in a sewer.'

Stratton shook his head.

'When are the super soldiers gettin' 'ere?' Ed asked in his usual sarcastic manner.

'Soon. You'll have at least one in each of your positions, except you, Spinks. You're on your own.'

'It's the way I like it,' said Spinks, as a large, black slimy something or other fell out of the pipe and landed in the water in front of him, splashing his face. He wiped a piece of muck off his facemask and maintained his vigil.

Stewart did a fine job of acting as if he was in conversation, with a nod here and there.

'We need the police cut-offs and the guys in position asap,' Stratton said. Lieutenant Stewart nodded automatically, but his mind was on the boat as he studied it over Stratton's shoulder. 'I'm talking to you, Tom.'

Stewart snapped out of his trance-like stare. 'Right.'

They started back towards the car when Stratton's mobile phone vibrated in his pocket. He checked the caller, hit a button and put it to his ear. 'Yes,' he said. It was Singen telling him they had located a mounting area in the back of the corn exchange not more than a hundred yards from the boat and that a police officer was waiting for Stratton at the church to guide him in. Stratton told him the police could go ahead and start laying in their invisible cordon.

Stratton climbed into the car, Stewart the other side. 'I'll drop you off at the church where a cop'll take you into the mounting area,' Stratton said.

'Where you going?' Stewart asked.

'The train station. Nothing's going to happen here for a while and one of my det operatives should be arriving there now.'

Stratton pulled up in front of King's Lynn train station and Aggy climbed in.

'Hi,' she said, offering a slight smile but unable to control a sudden awkward feeling.

'Good trip?' Stratton asked, at a loss for any other words of greeting. Their previous comments about looking forward to seeing each other hung thickly in the air.

'So, what's this all about?' she said, getting down to business.

'A RIRA weapons boat,' Stratton said. 'It's in the town. You know about the Yank who was kidnapped in Paris?'

'He's on it?'

'Not confirmed but it's a good possible.'

'And weapons?'

'Unconfirmed,' he said. Stratton chose not to tell her about the bio. It was still need to know and she didn't need to. Hank was enough for her to do her job, for the time being at least. If the situation changed she was cleared to hear all the facts, but it was not necessary at the moment.

'Ed, Spinks and Bob are on target. One of our assault teams is in a holding area close to the boat. It's the usual sit, wait and watch sketch.'

She nodded. The routine was certainly a familiar one. They drove along a road that wound through the town and led to the quay. Stratton slowed a little as masts came into view in the distance. He noticed two police cars parked in a side street. A glance the other side of the road and he saw another. Aggy was staring ahead and didn't notice.

'See the fishing boats on the left?' he asked her.

'Yes.'

'They're left of the target. Ed's on one of those. We'll turn right on to the quay and do a pass. The building to the right, at the end, is what we're calling the corn exchange. M squadron are in the back.'

They approached the quay and the road turned right on to it. There was only one ship alongside.

'That it?' she asked.

'The *Alpha Star.*'

They drove at normal speed along the quay, passing the boat on their left. Aggy took a quick look, taking in as much information as she could in a few seconds, enough to see there was no sign of life on deck. Until she caught a glimpse of movement on the bridge.

'Spinks is in the water the other side. Bob's on the roof of the exchange,' he said as they left the boat behind them and headed along the quay.

'Is the green light up to the ground commander or the gods on high?' she asked.

'The gods are calling this one. There are complications.'

She glanced at him. That meant there was more to it but she wasn't in the loop. That was unusual. It was obviously big. 'What's my job?'

'For the moment, hang tight with me. If anyone goes foxtrot from the boat you'll take 'em. We've got an armed police airlock in place.'

Stratton reached the end of the quay where he and Stewart had stood earlier. He turned the corner, parked out of sight from the boat and killed the engine. The sun had already dropped beyond the horizon and lights were coming on in the surrounding houses.

Pedestrian traffic was light but constant; the main shopping area of Lynn was nearby and the northern end of the quay was a convenient place to park.

This was all too familiar for them both, parked up in a car, waiting for something to happen, a wait that might last hours. There was almost a skill involved in killing time like that, for hours on end, without looking unnatural. It was obviously much easier for a man and a woman together to remain unnoticed as opposed to two men, if they played the role comfortably, that is. Although a man and woman sitting in the front of a car staring ahead and not talking or touching looked just as conspicuous.

Stratton placed his arm over the back of Aggy's seat and leaned closer to her. She leaned a little towards him, his chin close to the side of her face. She could hear his breath and feel his strength, and was reminded of the last – and only other – time they were this close together. How could she ever forget it?

They were in a car they had backed up a farm track just off a main road that led into Cookstown, Country Tyrone. They were there for most of the night, until three a.m., while a team changed the batteries to a bug the det had placed in a house a couple of years previously. All that time the bug had yielded little information, and now that it was dying, the occupants, who had originally suspected a device of some kind, had seemingly forgotten about their fears and were starting to become chatty. Aggy was the driver on that occasion. If they got wind from the operatives inside the house that something suspicious was happening outside she was to head into the town and drop off her warrior.

Up until that night she had not thought about him in any kind of amorous way. Indeed, she had found him attractive but he was one of those super soldiers, highly professional and leagues above her mere status of undercover operative – and a green one at that. And besides, everything about him said 'loner'. But that night something happened to drastically change her feelings towards him, or waken them.

A car had driven slowly past their front along the road from the town and Stratton put his head close to hers and nuzzled his face into her neck, playing the game. She watched the car slowly head on up the road; but as it moved out of her vision, she was suddenly aware of Stratton in a way and with a sensitivity she had never experienced before with anyone. She inhaled his smell, felt his cheek against her ear, his hair against her face. Something was happening to her. Without warning, she quivered and drew in a slight, sharp breath.

She remained frozen, refusing to respond further, but her body was screaming out for him to touch her more. Her wish was immediately granted, as if he'd heard, and he moved his other arm around her to hold the side of her face. She was aware he was looking behind her neck, out of the window, monitoring the vehicle's progress, but still she felt small in his powerful arms, protected. She did not know how long they stayed like that; it might have been minutes or barely seconds. Then the car turned around in the road, its headlights flashing across their front, and headed back towards them. Stratton took Aggy's face gently with his hand, pulled it towards his, their noses touched and he put his lips against hers. The car slowly passed. They held the kiss, their mouths opening, their tongues finding each other's. It was only when the car's lights were almost out of sight and he gently pulled his lips from hers to check it had driven off did she realise her eyes were closed and she'd been holding the side of his face.

'That might've been a pass,' he said, meaning they had

possibly just been checked out by the enemy. They stayed close for a while longer, Stratton looking for the car, and Aggy looking at Stratton. She wanted the car to come back.

She would never forget that moment he kissed her, certain she had felt him quiver as she did. He had been tender and gentle in a way it was hard to believe Stratton capable of. The way he slowly parted his lips from hers at the end of the kiss was as if he too wanted the moment to continue. But when they returned to the detachment in the early hours, before the sun had yet risen, it was as if nothing had happened. He went into the ops room to write his report without even saying goodnight.

For the rest of his time at the det he hardly spoke to her other than when work required it. Her only hint that there was something between them was the times she sensed him watching her, from the other side of the room, and their eyes locked as she looked up. The day he left she was on the ground on an op. She didn't know he was leaving. It was all quite sudden, to do with the run over the border when he rescued Spinks. The det was an empty place from that day on in many ways; gone was that special added attraction at meals, briefings and piss-ups, because he would no longer be there.

She had thought she had moved on from there, but now she was close beside him again and could smell him and feel his strength around her, all her feelings came flooding back.

Aggy would have been surprised if she knew how often Stratton thought of that night outside Cookstown. Had it not been for the kiss she might have remained just another pretty girl to him, one who perhaps had something alluring about her, but never finding out just what it was. The kiss was like nothing he had felt before. At least he had never thought about one so much after. He put it down to the moment. 'Love' in action was like a holiday affair; more shouldn't be squeezed out of it than it had to offer. But either he had not squeezed enough or it was more than just a moment brought about by unusual circumstances.

But the unexpected arousal was all the more reason for Stratton to walk away. His position within the world of special operations was complicated enough without bringing a love affair into it. In a trade that required heartlessness it was unwise to cultivate emotions. Stratton had worked hard at suffocating his feelings since those early days, his childhood, cherishing what little love he received, always wanting more. He'd had none passing through adolescence to manhood and had turned his apparent reclusiveness to his advantage, weaning himself off the need for affection. Perhaps one day in the future, if he survived this ridiculous occupation, he hoped to find love, if he was able to recognise it by then. But not now.

Now, almost a year after that night outside Cookstown, close to her again, the temptation to kiss Aggy was strong. But he sensed something was different about her now. He didn't know what, but she had changed in some way. For instance, he didn't remember her wearing perfume before.

'When did you start wearing perfume?'

'Today.'

'Why today?' As soon as he said it he wondered if she had worn it for him.

'I put it on before you called. I wouldn't have had I known I was working.'

She felt guilty at hiding the truth from him. She'd already lied to one man today – her lover. She didn't want to lie to the one she hoped one day to be in love with. 'I had a date tonight.'

Stratton found himself feeling disappointed to hear the perfume was for someone else.

'A guy?' he asked, then realising his *faux pas*, 'I didn't mean it to sound that way.'

'Yes, a man,' she said. 'And no offence taken.' She was used to it. She'd hoped at least Stratton might have understood why she played down her looks in NI, but it seemed he wasn't as all-knowing as she thought.

'When this is over I'll arrange for you to have a few days off,' he said. Her private life was none of his business and he shouldn't have shown interest. She was with someone else and that was for the best. But a part of him saw her as his. These feelings grown men often had for women were so bloody irritatingly childish.

Aggy felt she was starting to figure Stratton out, well, an aspect of him at least. She was certain he liked her but suspected that, as far as women were concerned, he needed a wide open door with a big welcome sign above it before he could walk through it. Strange for such a tough guy. She should come clean and tell him how she felt.

'Stratton,' she said, and then suddenly realised he was not the only one who needed some encouragement. Perhaps this was a mistake.

'What?'

'Um . . . Nothing.'

Stratton was curious about her relationship but at the same time annoyed at himself for being so. For someone who didn't want a relationship he was sure acting like someone who did. Whatever, he had to know.

'This a serious relationship?' he asked.

'No. Not really.' What the hell, she decided. She was going to get this out into the open here and now. 'You know him,' she said.

Stratton looked at her. 'One of the det guys?' he asked. 'No, well, kind of . . . Bill Lawton.'

'The LO?' He was so surprised he almost turned in his seat.

She didn't think he would be quite so shocked. 'It just happened . . . We met on a flight to London.'

'How long ago was that?' Stratton asked, wondering if it was while he was in the det.

'Three weeks.'

Stratton was relieved in some small way. He didn't know much about Lawton. He was MI5, pure int and Stratton was SF. Their paths crossed only when Lawton came to the det to hand over intelligence. He never rated Lawton as a particularly good liaison officer. An LO's job was to bring in information pertinent to the detachment's needs, create operations, provide key pieces to puzzles. But it wasn't just a case of going around and plucking the information off desks. At this level of the game, quality int was closely guarded and not given up easily, even to those on the same side who needed it most. Information was often bartered and exchanged. Special Branch officers and those who ran intelligence cells had to be coaxed, unless they offered it first, which meant a favour or an exchange. A good LO had to have certain qualities. He needed to be charming as well as manipulative, be able to party hard, especially with Irish Special Branch officers, but not forget his objective. Lawton just never seemed to come up with the top-quality intelligence that the det needed. Occasionally he plucked a cherry, but not often enough. And he had yet to come up with the big one, which was every LO's dream, but apparently not his.

'He bought me the perfume,' Aggy said.

'It's nice,' Stratton said. 'Can I suggest you don't put so much on?'

Bastard, she thought. 'It's supposed to be very good. The best they had on the flight.'

'I didn't know they sold perfume on the flight between Aldergrove and London,' he said, wishing he wasn't having this conversation any more.

'They don't.'

'You went on holiday together then?' he asked, deciding he was going to drop the subject. He was beginning to sound jealous even to himself.

She rolled her eyes, but was nonetheless encouraged by his jealousy. 'No. He'd been to Europe for the night.'

A tiny ding went off in his head, not quite suspicion, but the natural machinery inside an intelligence operative's brain moved a single cog. 'When was that?'

'Three weekends ago.'

Another clog clunked forward, this time with a little more resonance. Stratton would have been interested in anyone who had been to Europe three weekends ago. An MI5 operative got his attention.

'He told you he'd flown to Europe?'

'No. But I told you he'd bought the perfume on a flight.'

'How do you know?'

Because it was written on the back of the bottle. British Airways.'

'How do you know it was Europe?'

'Because it wasn't duty free.'

'What day was that?'

She could sense the change in him. He'd gone from matter-of-fact mild irritation to a more intense curiosity. 'What day was what?'

'What day did he fly to Europe?'

'Well. We flew to London from Aldergrove on the Friday morning. He said he wanted to take me to dinner that night

374

but couldn't. We met Saturday evening and he gave me the perfume.'

'The twenty-third?'

'Yes.'

The day Hank was lifted in Paris. Stratton's mind was reeling.

'I know he's not a man's man,' she went on, 'but he's a lot of fun. You don't like him very much, do you?'

Stratton's earpiece suddenly buzzed to life. It was Singen. He touched a button on the radio in his pocket.

'Send,' he said.

'We're moving the snipers into position.'

'Roger that,' Stratton said and opened the car door.

'What is it?' Aggy asked.

'The snipers are moving up . . . I'll just be a minute.'

'Stratton?' she said as he started to climb out. 'I don't know what Hank looks like. Might be useful.'

'In my bag. There's an ops file. Be careful rummaging around in it.'

As he climbed out she leaned over the seat and opened the bag. Inside were several guns, magazines, boxes of ammunition and things that looked like explosives, which she did not want to touch. 'And they talk about women's handbags,' she muttered as she found the file and pulled it out.

Stratton had got out of the car to put his thoughts in order. Lawton knew everything about the Spinks operation a week before it took place. It would also explain why the Paris op went tits up. The team was rumbled by Henri at the meeting place not because they had cocked up the surveillance but because the mole was watching the café. The mole telephoned the café and told Henri the meeting was cancelled because he saw something that alarmed him, an operative. Stratton was near the café. It was Stratton the mole recognised. If they could put Lawton in Paris the morning of the 23rd he was their man.

He pulled his mobile phone from his pocket, hit a memory button, and held it to his ear. A few seconds later it was picked up the other end. 'Sumners here,' the voice said.

'It's Stratton. Do you know a Bill Lawton?'

'Bill Lawton,' Sumners repeated. 'Can't say I do.'

'He's an NI detachment LO, South det, also MI5. It is possible he was in Paris on the twenty-third.'

Sumners knew exactly what Stratton was suggesting. 'Spell the name,' he said as he grabbed a pen.

'L–A–W–T–O–N.'

'Okay,' Sumners said. Stratton put the phone back in his pocket.

He looked at Aggy in the car reading the file. He didn't suspect her of being involved. If Lawton was his man he didn't need her to gain information about the dets. He knew more about them than she did. And she wouldn't have told Stratton what she had if she was aware Lawton was the mole. But she was guilty by association. It would mean the end of her career. In the intelligence world no one took chances they didn't have to. When the question came up about Aggy, as it most definitely would, she would be discharged from the intelligence world, because nothing would be gained from not doing so, but there was a million to one chance something could be lost if she remained. It would follow that she would be kicked out of the army. The blemish would follow her through her life. Even those associated with her, boyfriends, lovers and whatever else, would be highlighted. If Stratton told Sumners now, he would order her pulled from the op, and from the detachment too. But she would not know why, not until it was all over, and perhaps not even then.

He climbed back into the car feeling anxious. He wanted this op to get going, assault the boat, find Hank, the bio – and then get on with Lawton. He would protect Aggy as best he could but it would be difficult, perhaps impossible. He looked at her innocently concentrating on the file, unaware her life was in such turmoil, and he was filled with an urge to look after her.

Aggy looked up from the file, something troubling her. 'Is Bill Lawton on this op?'

Stratton wondered where that question came from. 'Why do you ask?'

'I'm sorry,' she said. 'I shouldn't have. Forget I said anything.'

'Why? Tell me.'

'I was out of order. I should know better than to ask questions like that.'

'Tell me.'

'I saw something I shouldn't have and you know the rules about that.'

He took her arm strongly. 'I want to know why you asked that question,' he said.

She wondered if this was a more intense kind of jealousy, and then saw something far darker in his eyes. She showed him the file, a photograph of Hank and his wife, filling the page.

Stratton glanced at it.

'If I wasn't supposed to see her meet him at King's Cross I did, that's all.'

Stratton couldn't quite believe, or assimilate quickly enough, what he had heard. 'Are you certain?'

'Pretty much. King's Cross, platform 9 to King's Lynn, where you told me to go. I saw Lawton meet her.'

'You saw Bill Lawton meet that woman in King's Cross?'

'I'm pretty certain.'

'How certain?'

'It's what I do for a living. Watch people. They virtually walked right past me.'

'Was he on the train with her?'

'No. She was standing outside the platform waiting. He came from across the street. They met. She handed him a hatbox, or what looked like one—'

'When?' he interrupted brusquely.

'Just before I caught the train here.' She checked her watch. 'Two and a half hours ago.'

Stratton took a moment to think the possibilities through, trying to pull together all the information.

'How sure are you it was them? I know the business Aggy, I know it isn't always easy to match a photograph to a real person?'

'So do I,' she said, not offended by his cross-examination. 'Bill, obviously, I know. The first profile I had of her was almost the same as this photo. She has the same hair. Same eyes. She's pretty, and she had the same expression, a little sad maybe, as if she was listening to the answer to a sad question. You know what I mean? I wouldn't stake my life on it, but I'd call out a team.'

Stratton had a lot of confidence in Aggy. She might not be the best driver in the unit but she was good on the ground, good at surveillance. The other operatives made fun of her in camp but they believed her on the ground. They would all admit to that.

He started the car and accelerated hard to take the corner sharply and speed up the street. Aggy grabbed the door handle and dash, surprised by his sudden activity.

'Did he see you?'

'No.'

'You sure?'

'What is this all about?' she asked.

'Did he see you?' Stratton shouted.

'No!' she shouted back.

Stratton pushed a button on his radio. 'Zero Alpha?' he called out as he took the next corner sharply, sliding the back end a little.

'Send,' came the reply.

'I'm heading for London. I'll explain later.'

'Em, roger that,' said Singen.

Stratton disconnected and turned on to a main road. 'Check and see if there's a blue light inside the glove compartment.'

Aggy was experienced enough to switch into high gear even though she had no idea why. The glove compartment was empty.

'Try the back, behind the seats.' Aggy stretched over the seat as Stratton went through a red light. When she came back she was holding a blue police light with a long lead from it. She plugged it into the lighter and it started to spin and flash. She opened her window and placed it on the roof, where the base magnets held it firm.

'You know where Lawton lives?'

'Yes,' she said. Her eyes flashed between him and the road ahead, hoping he'd tell her what this was about.

Stratton weighed all he had so far: Aggy, Lawton, the growing implications. He was going to need her help with whatever was coming up. She wasn't a spy for RIRA. She was on his side. Time could be short, and perhaps there were other things she knew about Lawton that would be meaningless to her unless she knew the whole story. She'd learn about Lawton soon enough anyway. She needed to know.

'I believe Lawton's a spy for RIRA,' he said. 'A mole.'

They hit a major roundabout, ignored several more red lights, caused a bus and a car to emergency stop, and belted off down a road signposted to London. Aggy hardly noticed the near misses, dumbstruck by what she had just heard.

Stratton took out his mobile phone, hit a button, and waited for the call to be picked up.

'Sumners? Anything on Lawton yet?'

'I've put it into the system but it's not the hottest priority right now.'

'You might be wrong. Two and a half hours ago he met Chief Munro's wife at King's Cross station outside platform 9, where a train from King's Lynn had just arrived, and she handed him a parcel.'

There was a moment's silence before Sumners answered. 'Holy mother of God.'

'I'm heading into London. Be there in two hours plus. I'm gonna need a team on standby.'

'I'll get on it right away.'

Stratton was just about to hang up when he heard Sumners call his name. 'Stratton? Wait! How did you come by this?' he asked.

'Luck. One of the det operatives on the way to Lynn for the op happened to see Lawton and recognised Mrs Munro from the ops file.'

'We needed some luck; hope this is it.'

Stratton pocketed the phone and dropped a gear to overtake two cars on a sweeping bend. As he passed them he knocked back up into fifth and gained speed along the straight. It might take Sumners a while to figure out that Stratton had asked about Lawton being on a flight to Paris before he told him he was seen at King's Cross. It was probably going to be impossible to protect Aggy but he would continue to explore the options for as long as he could. Of course, it didn't mean Lawton had the bio but the implications were huge and irresponsible to ignore. Besides all else, it gave Stratton the excuse he needed to go after him. This was a bigger fish than the boat assault.

Aggy felt dazed. She couldn't believe this was happening to her. She had figured her way through all the implications, what it meant to her career, her life and to her relationships in the military. It was all too horrible to contemplate. Her world had turned upside down. She suddenly felt a long, long way from Stratton.

22

Lawton sat on his bed staring across his apartment at the glass vial on the coffee table, the opened hatbox on the floor. It was a clear liquid with a strawberry tint and was surprisingly refreshing looking. One microscopic spec could turn a human body into an incubator that within days would produce a virus so virulent it could be transmitted on a breath or by contact with the smallest imaginable droplet of perspiration. From the moment of infection a fit, healthy adult could expect to live five to seven days. Only during the last few hours, before an agonising death by internal drowning, would that person be unable to walk; just twenty-four hours prior to that they would have felt as if they had nothing worse than a bad cold. That meant for three to five days that person was a walking virus dispenser, moving amongst the living like some kind of grim, deadly crop duster on permanent spray.

Using a conservative estimate, if an infected person took a twenty-minute journey across London during rush hour, by Underground for instance, and infected a hundred people, and then another hundred on their way home, by day three those two hundred people would have infected forty thousand others. By day five, when that first person started showing signs of illness, four million would have been infected. Day seven it could have claimed twenty million people around the world ... Lawton dropped his head into his hands, his brain aching from the effort of calculating the horror he would be responsible for.

It was no longer a case of self-preservation. He couldn't let innocent people die just to save himself, and he would be just as guilty if he allowed someone else to do it. What he needed was a plan that would allow him to safely neutralise the virus as well as survive the wrath of the RIRA and the authorities. Achieving all three was probably going to be impossible.

To survive RIRA, he had considered the feasibility of Father Kinsella's suggestion, putting the virus somewhere in the MI5 headquarters where no one could get near it before the authorities were warned of its location. But it didn't take long to decide that was going to be unworkable. In his capacity he only had access to about fifty per cent of the building, along with a few hundred other people. There wasn't a room he could just lock it inside. He couldn't guarantee any office or closet would not be opened within five minutes of him leaving it. The building didn't exactly empty out for the evening. MI5 was busy 24/7. It would be totally irresponsible even to take a chance like that. Only one person needed to come in contact with the virus for a split second to start the deadly chain reaction. Even leaving it without crushing it was a risk that was not worth taking, and that would work against him with RIRA anyway. Whatever was to happen, he decided he was not going to go down in history as the man who wiped out London.

He played with the thought of just running off with it, but then what would he do with it? He had no idea how to get rid of a deadly virus. Burying it somewhere was out of the question. He even thought about flushing it down the toilet or throwing it in the River Thames but he could not be certain that would kill it rather than spread it everywhere.

Then it came to him. It was really his only option and the simplest of all. He would leave it in his apartment and get as far out of town as he could. When he was well on his way he'd call the authorities and tell them where it was. The virus would be made safe and he might get away. All he had to figure out was where to go and how to get there.

He got up off the bed, pulled an empty holdall out from under it, and set about packing a few things while he tried to think of a place on this planet he could hide, not just from MI5 but from RIRA too.

Hank had stopped exercising after a drop in his energy level was made worse by an irritating thirst. It had been half a day at least since he'd been given a drink and a day or more since he'd eaten anything. He wasn't feeling well at all. It was bad enough that he was not allowed to use a toilet, but now it seemed they were trying to starve him to death. Keeping him weak was no doubt an added measure of securing him, but it was also increasing his desperation and determination to make a break for it.

The door opened and someone came in. This was what he had been waiting for the past few hours. He immediately started to moan and slouch as if delirious. Whoever had walked in crouched beside him and untied his hood but did not remove it. Hank pulled away, moaning.

'I'm trying to give you some food and water.' It was the young man from earlier.

Hank accepted the water and choked on it a little. 'I . . . I need help. I'm in pain. My stomach. I can't empty my bowels . . . can't shit. Please, help me.' Hank acted as if he had hardly strength enough to hold his head up. 'Please,' he moaned. 'Don't let me die like this.'

The young man stayed beside Hank for a moment, no doubt considering the situation. He then stood and walked out of the room. Hank could hear him call out to someone in the corridor. A moment later he was joined by another man.

'I think he's in a bad way,' the young man said.

'What's wrong with him?' the other one said, sounding none too sympathetic.

'I don't know. He says he's in pain and can't shit. Maybe he's bunged op.'

'What do you mean, bunged op?'

'Bunged op, for fock's sake. He can't take a shite. Let's put 'im on the pot at least.'

'Brennan said to leave him be.'

'Brennan didn't say he was to focken die. What if somethin' happens to 'im? We'll get in focken trouble . . . And you know what that bastard's like . . . Come on, man. It's only a visit to the pan, for fock's sake.'

Hank decided to give the other man some encouragement and let out a moan. 'Please. Help me . . . Please.'

'Come on,' said the young man. 'I'm not into this torture lark. Brennan's not here . . . He's not even a focken Brit. He's a Yank, for Christ's sake.'

It seemed to be enough to convince the older man. 'Okay,' he said. 'Let's get him to the pan.'

Hank could feel his hands and feet being untied. This was it. He cautioned himself to choose the moment carefully. He would only get one chance. The main deck was his immediate goal. From there his best bet was the water. It was doubtful any of these people could swim half as well as Hank, even on his worst day. He could probably do the first thirty yards underwater in case they started shooting at him. He could manage fifty with ease in swimming trunks and healthy, but thirty yards in clothes, unwell and desperate was feasible. A duck-dive for a gasp of air and he might tack on another twenty yards. Then it would be a fierce breaststroke to wherever. If it was dark he had more than a reasonable chance of escaping. His biggest problem was going to be his initial break and then finding his way out on to the deck. That attack was going to have to be swift and positive to give himself a few yards' head start. If he ended up in a wrestle with the two men he was lost. Or a wrong turn once he was off and running could leave him trapped. What he was going to need was a lot of luck.

'Who the fock tied this op?' the older man asked, struggling with Hank's hands. 'You got a knife?'

'No.'

'I'd better get a knife. That knot wasn't tied by any focken sailor.'

Hank heard him leave the room. The young man untied Hank's feet and then had a go at his hands. He pulled at one of the lines and it gave. Hank felt the rope go loose. 'Eedjit,' the young man said. 'Couldn't untie his laces that one.'

Hank let his arms fall limply from the pole as the rope was removed and he leaned heavily against it. He was completely untied, the hood was loose around his neck, and there was only the one man in the room. He debated whether to go for it right there and then, or wait until they took him to the toilet, which might produce a better opportunity. But what if this was his best opportunity? What if that Brennan character suddenly returned and ordered them to tie him back up and leave him alone? Before Hank could consider it further he had pulled off the hood. For the first time in weeks he could see clearly. The young man was kneeling in front of him wearing a bright yellow waterproof, the nose of a sub-machine-gun poking from it where it was, hanging by a strap around his neck. They stared at each other for a second. The young man was bright-eyed, fresh-faced, with curly orange hair. Hank's face was pale and covered in a short beard, and his eyes were red.

'You're not supposed to do that, pal,' the young man said and reached for the hood in Hank's hands. Hank grabbed his wrist, twisted it harshly into a lock, bent the arm at the elbow with all his weight, and threw him forward until the man's face slammed into the floor. Hank fell with him and twisted himself over so that he landed on top of the Irishman's back, holding him firmly in an arm lock. The young man let out a heavy moan as Hank's weight forced the air from his ribcage. The block of wood Hank had felt with his feet several times was inches away. He grabbed it awkwardly because of its rugged shape, raised it high and brought it down with every ounce of strength he could muster on to the back of the young man's skull. The force of the blow not only tore open the flesh on the man's head, it also broke his nose and jaw against the floor. But there was fight in the young man yet and he brought his free hand around and started to push himself up with it. He was having little success but Hank raised the chunk of timber again and brought it down with equal force. The young man shuddered under the blow but continued to push as if he suddenly knew his very life depended on this last great effort. Hank raised the wood and this time brought it down on to the man's hand, cracking several bones in it. The young man wavered. Hank slammed him on the head again and the man started to sink. Another blow cracked his skull and took all the effort out his struggle. Seconds later he ceased to move.

Hank remained on top of him, breathing heavily, exhausted. Then as if a fire had ignited beneath him, he scrambled to his feet, the adrenalin dulling the aches in his joints and muscles. He went to the door, looked out, and darted back instantly. A man was heading down the corridor, rubbing the blade of a knife across the palm of his hand.

Hank grabbed up the block of wood and went to the side of the door. His foot hit something and it clanged noisily as it fell. It was a length of pipe. Hank quickly put down the wood, grabbed the pipe and raised it with both hands as the man stepped into the room. The man paused at the sight of his colleague lying still on the floor but that very second the pipe slammed on to his cranium so forcefully it nearly split his skull in two. Hank raised the pipe to smash him again but the man crumpled to the floor like a puppet with its strings cut.

Hank dropped the pipe, grabbed the man's SMG and unclipped it from its strap. He checked the corridor in both directions. It was clear. He looked over the weapon, unsure what type it was, not that it mattered. He identified the cocking lever and safety-catch. He pulled at the magazine, pushed in the release button and it popped from its housing. The magazine had bullets in it. He pushed the rounds in against the return spring. They didn't travel more than a few inches, indicating it was full. He pulled the cocking lever back and tested the trigger. The mechanism worked and he knew all that he needed to fire it. He pushed the magazine into the weapon, pulled the cocking lever all the way back, where it clicked into position, and gripped it firmly in both hands. A touch of the trigger would release the breach block to pick up a bullet, shove it into the breach and at the same time fire it, then return to pick up the next bullet.

Hank held the gun up vertically by his head and checked

the corridor once again. There was no sign of life. A combination of success and the weapon in his hand gave Hank a shot of confidence. Luck had indeed been on his side, so far. He was halfway home. But if these two were armed it was safe to assume others he might encounter would also be. He decided to spend a valuable moment or two to think whether there was a way of improving his chances of getting safely off the boat.

He pulled the older man away from the door and closed it.

First thing first was to disguise himself as one of them. It might only give him one second of an edge in an encounter, but that was better than nothing. He knelt by the young man, who was more his size, and rolled him over. There was a lot of blood on his face. His eyes were half open and it didn't seem as if he was breathing. He'd killed him. Hank could hear the young man's voice in his head. He'd been alive and talking only seconds before. It felt strange. Hank had never really considered them the enemy, least of all this young man, who was the only one who had tried to help him. And yet here they were, the young man Hank's first confirmed kill. One thing was for sure: there was no giving up now. He'd killed one of theirs. Hank glanced at the older man who was not moving either. Perhaps two.

Hank put down the gun and started to take off the young man's yellow coat.

Stratton backed into a space between two parked cars and turned off the lights and engine. It all went very quiet in contrast to the haste and roar of the last couple of hours. They were in a narrow residential street in south London, with small terraced houses tightly packed on either side.

'First right,' Aggy said, indicating ahead. 'There are two new-looking three-storey apartment buildings about a hundred metres along from the corner. His is the second building.'

'Let's take a look,' he said, and just as he was about to open his door his mobile phone vibrated in his pocket. 'Wait a sec,' he said and reached for it, pushed a button and held it to his ear. 'Yes.'

'We can't confirm that Lawton was in Paris on the twenty-third,' Sumners said. 'But he did take three days' leave then, *and* he took two days' leave to go to London the week before Spinks was lifted. The dates coincide with the meetings with Henri. We're taking the lead. You're to proceed.'

'I'm around the corner from his flat, a couple hundred yards from Wandsworth Road and Queenstown Road. Where's my backup?'

'Bit of a problem, I'm afraid. A4 has two major ops going on. Everyone's either up north or in bloody Cornwall. They've been called off and are on their way back but that could take a few hours. Meanwhile we're trying to find anyone off duty to help you until the teams get here.'

Stratton went silent for a moment as he considered the options. Lawton could be home with the virus, or not, and then the possibilities were dark and endless.

'I can have a police special weapons unit with you in five minutes,' Sumners said, aware Stratton was holding it all together by himself.

Stratton considered the offer for a second or two. 'No.'

'I can't keep the lid on this any longer, Stratton. It's becoming too risky. I'm aware of the dangers of turning this over to the police too soon but they're starting to be outweighed by the dangers we risk if we fail to corner these people right away.'

'I understand. Let me find out if Lawton's home and if he has it.'

'How long do you think that will take?'

'Give me twenty minutes.'

'Twenty minutes then,' Sumners said.

'One more thing. How can I destroy it?'

'What?' Sumners said.

'If I have to. Can it be flushed down the toilet for instance?'

'I'm not an expert on that. I'll have to find out.'

Stratton ended the call and put the phone back in his pocket. Aggy wondered what on earth that conversation was all about – if Lawton had what? Flush what down the toilet?

Stratton reached over to the back seat and pulled his bag on to his lap. He took out the three black hexagonal blocks and initiator Lieutenant Stewart had given him and put them on the dashboard while he searched for something else. Aggy, ever curious of technological things, picked up the initiator to examine it.

'Easy with that,' Stratton said as he searched. 'Or those,' indicating the black blocks, 'will make a very nasty mess of this car, not to mention you and me.'

She put it back as Stratton found a small leather case with a zipper around three sides, put it in one of his pockets and the black blocks and initiator in another.

He opened his door and got out. She climbed out of her door and they both instinctively closed them quietly by pushing them shut one click. He went to the boot, opened it, and put his bag inside. Before closing it he took a look at her.

'Does he know that jacket?' he asked.

She thought a moment. 'I can't remember. I've worn it over the water. Maybe.'

Stratton dug into his bag and pulled out a tightly rolled

piece of green and brown clothing. 'Put that on,' he said.

She unravelled it. 'It's a camouflage jacket,' she said.

'No one will see you then, will they?' he said.

She regretted it as soon as she said it. A lot of civilians wore camouflage clothes. She pulled it on and they walked along the pavement together. He put his hands in his jacket pockets and stuck an elbow out towards her. She looped her arm through his and they fell into step.

'Can I ask something?' she said.

'What?'

'What were you talking about? How to destroy something and flush it down the toilet?'

'Just keep your mind on the business in hand.'

She had been scolded, but she couldn't tell if it was Stratton's usual hard-arse attitude or peevishness at her relationship with Bill. They turned the corner. Up ahead, on the right side of the street, were the two apartment blocks. 'The second one,' Aggy said.

Her eyes drifted up the building as they approached it, looking for Bill's only window on the front side. 'Top floor, far end flat. Lights are on.'

Stratton looked up and saw a shadow pass the window.

'Looks like he's home,' she said.

Stratton scanned the street, nearby cars, doorways, expecting the place to be watched if the grand prize was inside. There was no sign of anyone.

'Keep an eye open for caretakers,' he said. Aggy wondered why but she wasn't about to ask him any more questions.

They continued to the next junction and turned the corner. Stratton looked ahead for a place to duck into, found somewhere and crossed the road. He led her up a path that divided a row of terraced houses and they stopped midway in the darkness.

'I need you to go up to his flat,' he said as he peeled the camouflage jacket off her shoulders. 'You have to get him out of the apartment. I need at least fifteen minutes inside. Okay?'

She looked distracted as she took off the jacket and handed it to him.

Stratton wondered where she'd gone. 'Aggy?'

'I'm thinking,' she said.

'What about?'

'How to get him out of his apartment.'

'Do it while you're walking there,' he said, folding the jacket up neatly.

She frowned. He was such a bastard if people didn't do what he said right when he said it. She wondered why on earth she had looked forward to being with him. If her romantic side had not sidetracked her she might have remembered what a demanding sod he was to work with. On the other hand, a RIRA arms shipment and a Brit mole uncovered constituted a fairly big deal as operations went. If her senses were anything to go by there was even more to it than Stratton was letting on. Calm as he was, there was something about the way he had acted when she told him Lawton had met Chief Munro's wife, and the way he had talked on the phone to whomever. He also looked more tired than she'd ever seen him, and it was not a tiredness from lack of sleep. Something deeper.

'Get going,' he said. She was about to step off when he took her arm lightly and looked into her eyes. 'Aggy. Be careful . . . Be as natural as you can. Okay?'

There was an intense sincerity in his words. She was touched, but at the same time it unnerved her. He would not have warned her like that if it weren't dangerous. She nodded.

'I shouldn't tell you this,' he added, 'because I don't want it to distract you, but I have to. Things have changed for Lawton. Yesterday he was a mole, just a spy. Today he's something far more sinister. Whatever he was like before, he isn't the same person. He can't be. I'm saying he could be dangerous . . . Be careful.'

She nodded again and walked away, out of the alley and back along the street towards the apartment block.

Stratton watched her go. He could see her slender prettiness even in the near darkness and his heart ached a little, fearful for her.

23

Hank strapped the SMG under the yellow coat and took a few seconds to practise grabbing it and bringing it up on aim. Neither of the Irishmen had a pistol, or even a spare magazine for the SMG. The young man sat limply on the floor, propped against the pole, his head hooded and hands and feet tied up as Hank's had been. The other man was stuffed in a corner hidden under a tarpaulin and some ropes. He was still breathing faintly when Hank covered him, but if the guy ever did come out of it he would probably have brain damage. The image of himself beating the men kept flitting into Hank's head, the brutality of it. He had never done anything remotely like that before in his life although he had imagined pounding a man to death on more than one occasion, such as the time Kathryn came home upset because a bunch of hooligans had harassed her outside a mall while she was loading her shopping into the car. Helen and Janet had been with her and Kathryn thought the thugs were going to rob her, or worse. For hours after Hank's mind fed on the images of him finding the guys and beating them to a pulp. This day on the boat he had lived out what could have been just another of his daydreams: a persecuted individual, outnumbered, unarmed, his life threatened. But he had beaten one guy to death and the other as good as. Hank wondered if perhaps the daydreams had actually been a preparation for this day. He found a chocolate bar in a pocket of the coat, unwrapped it and bit into it greedily.

He readied his weapon and opened the door carefully as he munched. The corridor was clear of life in both directions. One end was a metal watertight door that looked like an entrance to the engine room. The other end of the corridor appeared more promising: a flight of stairs went up into light.

Hank remained in the room and closed the door again to take a moment to think it through once more as he stuffed the rest of the chocolate into his mouth. He was growing confident and having second thoughts about his options. It might just be the adrenalin, but he was feeling a lot better physically than he had been earlier. His plans of action were becoming grander. Freedom was obviously the primary aim, but he wondered if there was more to be gained from this escape attempt. There didn't appear to be many people on board. Judging by the size of the boat he figured there was no more than a dozen crewmembers. Hell, a super tanker, ten times the size, had just over two dozen men. And since the boat was alongside it was more than likely some had gone ashore. No one had been along the corridor for ages. It was an opportunity he should at least explore. It might just be possible to take over the boat by himself. He could always go back to the original plan at any time and leap overboard.

That made up his mind. The first thing he needed to do was a recce. He would take a look around and assess the ship's manpower and location. Based on what he found he'd decide whether or not to have a go at securing the boat or to slip over the side.

He checked the weapon once again, made sure the safety-catch was off, firmed his grip and pulled it out so that the strap was taut. He opened the door, checked up and down, and stepped out into the corridor, pulling the weapon in close to his body and keeping it central so he could swiftly turn and engage targets front or rear. He reminded himself, on engaging the enemy, to keep his bursts to three shot maximum if possible. Distract, destroy was the principal – first round in the chest to distract, then in the head to destroy.

He moved his feet easily along the corridor careful not to cross them over as he was taught and maintain his balance, like a boxer, ready for anything. He came to the bottom of the stairs and looked up to the first landing, where a corridor crossed port and starboard and then continued up to another deck. The corridor was brightly lit, electric lights, not natural, and there was still no sign of life. Hank could feel a cool breeze coming down the steps, a strong indication the deck led to the outside. It was fresh with a chill to it and felt good.

Hank placed a foot on the first rung. He was committed. The feeling that whatever was about to happen would change the course of his life for ever suddenly washed over him. He took another step, aimed the barrel at the doorway above, and moved carefully up.

Bill Lawton zipped up his holdall, which looked as if very little more could have been squeezed into it, lifted it off the bed, and placed it near the front door. He selected a jacket from several hanging on coat hooks, his favourite black leather one, and pulled it on. He went to his sideboard, opened a drawer, took out his passport and buried it in the inside pocket of his jacket. He checked the contents of his wallet – almost a hundred pounds and two credit cards – and put it in his pocket alongside his passport. He looked around the apartment to see if there was anything else he needed. He was suddenly gloomy at the thought he was seeing it for the last time. It had been his London home for more than four years and held a lot of memories, some of them exceptional. A few very beautiful women had graced it . . .

This was the end of London for him. If he survived, perhaps he could come back one day, twenty or thirty years from now. Who was he kidding? he asked himself. He could never return if he wanted to be sure of staying free. RIRA might give up after a while, but if the Brits decided to go after him there would never be a time, if he lived to be a hundred and fifty, when he could relax and think it was over.

He suddenly thought of Henri, in a cell somewhere no doubt, never to sit in a café again and sip a glass of wine, or walk along the banks of the Seine on a perfect evening. Bill's chances of getting away were fair as long as he had an early drop on both the IRA and the Brits. He would leave the flat just as it was. Once out of the country he would call the police and tell them where to find the virus. The flat would soon be filled with people from every imaginable department of military intelligence. Dozens upon dozens of them would troop through this room before it was over. Every single item would be inspected and taken apart, every minutia of his life pored over. Everyone he ever knew or met that there was a record of would be scrutinised. Every number he ever called from his home or mobile phone would be run through a computer, every recorded purchase logged.

On a table was a picture of his mother and father, his natural parents, a gift from Father Kinsella a few weeks after that first meeting in the cemetery all those years ago. At the time he was overcome with appreciation at the gesture as Kinsella knew he would be. Kinsella never told him how he came by it. Only in recent years, when things began to look jaded to Bill, did he start to doubt the authenticity of the picture. He wondered if MI5 knew about that part of his life, his true beginnings. It was probably in a file somewhere. The picture would be a clue otherwise. Bill picked it up and looked at it, as he had a hundred times. There was something in the woman's eyes. Perhaps they were Bill's. He wanted then to be. He took the picture out of the frame and put it in his pocket.

His eyes then fell with finality on the vial of liquid on the coffee table. It stood alone, simple and unadorned, innocent and attractive, yet capable of wiping out all of humanity if allowed. He wondered what kind of mind could think of creating something like that.

The knock on the door was like a cannon going off in Bill's head. He stared at it in disbelief. Perhaps Kinsella had come back to escort him on this, his greatest triumph. Or perhaps it was his own people, MI5. Bringing a bottle of deadly virus into the country was perhaps too ambitious for RIRA and it had been traced to Bill. His heart pounded in his chest.

Bill went to the window and looked down on to the street. There was nothing out of the ordinary, no unfamiliar vehicles, no one visible. The knock came again. Bill couldn't ignore it. If it was Kinsella or MI5 he wasn't going anywhere else. His plans to escape evaporated.

Instinctively, as a precaution, he put his holdall behind the bathroom door and went to the coffee table and picked up the virus carefully. He opened a cupboard, put the vial in the back between some blankets, made sure it was safe and closed the door. The knock came again. He closed Kinsella's briefcase, put it down beside the empty hatbox, went to the front door, and opened it.

Aggy stood there, framed by the doorway, looking as though she was trying to hide some embarrassment behind her slight smile. His heart fluttered as it always did on seeing her. No memory of her image was equal to the sight of her in the flesh.

'Hi,' he said, unable to hide his confusion.

'I should've called,' she said. 'I was with a friend just up the road and decided to pop round. I know you said you had to go out but I took a chance . . . Is this a bad time?'

'No. Just got back actually. He didn't want to go to dinner in the end . . . I was just about to call you.' Under normal circumstances he would have been more than just delighted to see her. He would have dragged her in and be ripping her clothes off within seconds of closing the door. All he could think of now was how to get out of inviting her inside. What he would have given for a surprise visit from Melissa any other time. She no doubt wanted to stay the night or she wouldn't be here. It was what they both originally expected to do that night. What a cruel world this was. He would have to let her in, but just for a minute. He did not have the heart to turn her away and never see her again. Perhaps that's what this was. Providence had intervened to allow him one more look at her, one more embrace, before it was all to end. He stepped back from the door.

'Come in,' he said.

She remained outside on the landing as if the threshold to his flat was a landmine. 'Would you like to go for a walk?' she said. 'It's a nice night. Maybe we could go to the pub . . . I fancy a walk.'

There was something different about her. He could sense it. Something was on her mind. Why didn't she want to come in? It suited him perfectly, but it disappointed him at the same time.

'Sure,' he said smiling. 'Let's go.'

Then he suddenly considered the wisdom of leaving the 'stuff' in his apartment. Then again he was going to walk away from it in a very short while anyhow. He stepped through the door and closed it behind him, ensuring it was locked. He winked at her as he went ahead and led the way downstairs. Both their smiles disappeared as he turned his back on her.

On the landing, across from Bill's apartment, a grey fire door with 'ROOF EXIT' written on it was wedged slightly open by an empty cigarette packet. Someone in the darkness behind it was looking through the narrow gap. The door slowly opened and Brennan stepped on to the landing and looked down the stairwell that zigzagged to the ground floor.

He regarded Bill's front door. His brief had been to stay with the bio, but something about the woman's arrival tweaked his curiosity. They'd left empty handed so the bio was safe enough in the apartment. He made his way down the stairs.

Bill and Aggy walked out of the apartment block and up the street. Bill placed his hands in his pockets as they walked along together in silence. Aggy was aware of her awkwardness when Bill opened his door and hoped he'd put it down to shyness. She was warming to the show, trying to act natural, as Stratton had told her to, but it was a different kind of undercover work than she was trained for. The dets for the most part observed, listened, photographed, recorded and followed. They mingled but never adopted false identities or attempted to penetrate society. That was unjustifiably dangerous, difficult, and arguably unnecessary. But Aggy was now mingling with the enemy, only because of her unique circumstances perhaps, but nevertheless. There was something exciting about it. On the other hand, it felt unreal because it was Bill. He was, essentially, still her lover. In many ways she didn't know this man beside her, but she didn't feel as if Bill had cheated her. He'd never used her to gain intelligence. He knew or could find out more about the operations she was involved in than she. And she still believed him when he said he had fallen for her.

She put her arm through his. Even though Stratton had warned her Bill was now dangerous she felt sad for him. She looked at him and he glanced at her. They both smiled and walked on.

Brennan looked out of the apartment entrance to see Bill and Aggy walking up the street arm in arm. He waited until they were a good distance on before walking out of the building, crossing the street and following them.

Stratton remained around the corner in the alleyway where Aggy had left him. He checked his watch. Sumners would be getting agitated. If Lawton was in his apartment, Aggy might find it difficult to get him out of it, especially if he had the virus. What was his plan if she didn't show? He would have little choice but to go to the apartment himself and take it from there.

He decided to give Aggy another five minutes. Then she appeared with Lawton.

'Ata girl,' he said to himself as he watched them cross the street and continue out of sight towards Wandsworth Road.

Eager though he was, he forced himself to wait a moment and give them time to get some distance from the apartment. When he stepped out of the alleyway he quickly ducked back into it. A figure was walking up the road in the same direction as Aggy and Lawton. The person was the other side of the road and Stratton couldn't make out any features. He could see it was a man with a limp but not much more. Stratton waited for the figure to move on before leaving the alley, crossing the road and heading for Lawton's apartment block.

As he turned the corner he checked Aggy, Lawton, and the other figure were still walking away. Then he entered Lawton's building and jogged up the stairs. When he got to the top floor he was a little out of breath, a reminder he had not been working out much lately because of all that had been happening. A month ago a couple flights of stairs would have been nothing. He needed to start putting the miles in again, just one more reason he wanted to see the back of this operation.

He stopped on the landing and paused a moment to survey the scene and listen. There were four doors on this top floor: three apartments and a grey door marked 'ROOF EXIT'. He walked over and opened the grey door. A flight of stairs led up to another door. He quickly went up the steps and tried the handle. It opened on to the roof. That would be useful if anyone came.

He returned to Lawton's door and took the small leather case from his pocket and unzipped it. Inside were several finely crafted tools that could easily be mistaken for a dentist's travel set, each in its own little sleeve. He examined the lock. It was a Yale dead bolt with a fixed collar and several years old. The older the better. He selected a tension spring, a slender piece of flat metal bent at one end, and inserted the short end into the keyhole, bending the other end to apply pressure to the tumblers. He decided to rake the six tumblers first. If that didn't work he would have to choose a fine pick and push each individual tumbler up until they all cleared the revolver. He slid the rake in, teeth upwards, and pulled it out swiftly while maintaining the spring pressure. He repeated the action without a result. He then raked it back and forth swiftly and suddenly the lock turned under the pressure from the spring and the door opened.

Stratton moved inside and closed the door behind him. He replaced the tools in the case and put it back in his pocket.

Lawton had left the light on. That meant Stratton had to be careful moving around or he would be seen from the street. First rule of searching was to stand and look, divide the room up into quadrants and furnishings and search each section in turn with his eyes before moving from the door. He looked in the bathroom beside the front door and noticed the holdall. He checked it. It was full of clothes. He closed it and took another look at the room. On the floor was a hatbox that fitted Aggy's description. Beside it was a small briefcase. He'd seen enough and it was time to physically search.

Keeping low he moved to the case, put it on the coffee table and opened it. He noted the two halves filled with sponge one of which had a bottle-shaped cut-out. If he had had any doubts about Lawton's involvement with the bio this quickly eliminated them. He checked the hatbox. In it was a polystyrene mould that had a similar sized cut-out in the centre. The most cynical intelligence expert would have to concede this was damning evidence. The briefcase obviously didn't come with the box since there wasn't enough room in it with the polystyrene, therefore it was quite likely intended to supersede the hatbox as a carriage for the bio. But where was the bio? There was no time to search the entire flat before Aggy and Lawton returned. If he knew for certain the bio was in the building he could close the operation there and then, take care of Lawton, and leave the rest up to a search team. But the bio could be anywhere, hidden outside in a garden or in a car. And so the op would have to go on until they could pin it down. He couldn't afford to be caught in the apartment or leave any sign he'd been there.

Stratton had to get going, but something was holding him back. He needed some kind of insurance. He just about had time for that.

He took one of the sponges out of the briefcase. There was plenty of it and it was a snug fit. Using a pocketknife he cut a piece out of the back of the sponge and put it in his pocket. He took the three small black hexagonal blocks from a pocket and pulled off the magnets that were stuck to the back of each. They were even lighter now. He flicked a tiny switch on one, arming it, placed them snugly into the sponge, and fitted it back into the briefcase. He weighed the case in his hands to feel if it was noticeably heavier. A person would have to be supersensitive to detect a difference. If it was discovered the game was up but his need for some kind of contingency outweighed the risk he was taking. He put the case back on the floor as it was.

After a quick double-check to make sure he had everything he left the apartment.

He walked down the stairs to the glass entrance, paused to see if the street was clear, and walked out of the building and away.

He pulled out his mobile phone, hit a key and put it to his ear. 'Sumners? Stratton. No bio but wait. There's a briefcase with a bottle-sized sponge mould in it. The hatbox is there. All signs indicate the bio is close and that Lawton still has it. I'm pretty sure we can close this down here.'

'Okay,' Sumners said, thinking as he listened. He trusted Stratton, but if anything went wrong it was on his shoulders, and there was another set of shoulders above him. And after all, Stratton was just a ground operative. Sumners respected his opinions and usually went with his recommendations, but Stratton would never know the whole picture. And Stratton had his own views on the outcome, and his own politics, which were not always shared by those above. Then there was the operation value, the price one was prepared to pay to have an op succeed. It varied from op to op. Usually the value just referred to equipment and money, but sometimes the price was higher. A ground operative could not be expected to give his life for an operation, but someone else could give it.

'The wheels are in motion and going as fast as they can,' Sumners said. 'We're setting up a chemical hazard centre about a mile from you. Every biohazard team within two hundred miles is on its way to that centre. The police have been prepped that something big could be going down, though they don't know what yet. All leave is cancelled and they have literally hundreds of teams earmarked to move to any area in London and seal it off.'

'And my teams?

'I understand some are already on the way to you. The others are still on the outskirts of London. When they get to you the package will include an eye in the sky and a link into the traffic camera surveillance system.'

Stratton hoped they would get to him soon. 'There's something else,' Stratton said. 'I've mined the case.'

'You've what?' Sumners said.

'I'm flying by the seat of my pants here.'

'If they find it they'll know we're on to them.'

'If we lose them or the bio we lose everything.'

'You don't even know if an explosive charge is enough to destroy the bio.'

'That's right. But I should by now.' Stratton was politely scolding Sumners. Fortunately, in this business, rank was not in your face. Everyone was a professional working their own part of the complex game and it was not inconceivable to ball out the boss if he did something wrong.

'What kind of charge?' Sumners asked. He sympathised with Stratton. He was out there on his own and, given the circumstances, the charge was not a bad idea.

'American Super "X". Their new lightweight door charge.'

'I'll find out and get back to you asap. Don't use it unless I tell you to, no matter what. It's possible all it will do is spread the damned virus into the air.'

'I'm aware of that,' Stratton said as he approached a major road. A couple turned the corner towards him. 'Get me my team,' he said quickly and killed the phone.

All things considered, he felt the balance of control was in his favour, despite the fact he was without a team. His gut feeling was things were okay. He needed to stay lucky; although that was not a good place to be – an op of this magnitude being dependent on luck.

24

Hank was in the corridor that ran port to starboard, standing at the top of the stairs that led down to the deck where he had been held captive. The door at the far starboard end was closed but the port side door was open. Hank made his way towards it. Holding the SMG close to his chest, the end of the barrel inches from his face, he paused halfway along the corridor outside a cabin door to press his ear against it. There was no sound above the gentle hum of the generator that vibrated the entire ship. He continued on to the port door and peeked out on to the brightly lit deck without extending his head through the doorway. Whatever was beyond the rail and the bright lights of the boat was in complete blackness.

He heard someone outside on deck and pulled back behind the door and out of sight. His immediate question was if he should capture them as they stepped into the corridor or let them pass. If he was going to take this boat, dealing with the crew one at a time was the perfect solution and a gift from God if he could have them all that way. He decided not to pass on this opportunity, especially since the target would have his back to him. He would shove the barrel into the back of the man's head and take him somewhere where he could secure him. Hank gripped the weapon tightly, clenched his jaw, determined and ready to be ruthless.

But whoever it was continued along the deck past the open door. Hank released the chest full of air he had been holding and relaxed his grip on his weapon to let the blood flow back into his fingers.

He stepped out from behind the door and looked outside once again, this time poking his head out enough to look left and right. There was no sign of life. Up to a few metres out from the side of the boat the water was bathed in light. Beyond that it was black. He could just about make out the far bank, a dark line a good hundred feet or so away. There were clusters of lights up and down the river but none directly opposite other than in the far distance, perhaps a mile or so away.

He stepped back into the corridor and walked along it to the opposite end to explore the other side of the boat. The door was not fully closed and there was a gap large enough for him to see through. The edge of the quay was a couple of feet higher than the rails and there was a gap of a few feet between it and the boat. Hank would have to climb on to the rail and scramble on to the quay, which didn't present a problem other than he would be in full view of the deck above and the bridge. The quay itself looked quite open, the nearest building at least thirty yards away. There wasn't a soul in sight. If a lookout wanted to take a shot at him as he ran they would have a fair amount of time to do so. Where he headed to depended on the country he was in. The Med or Atlantic, Seamus had said. Hank suddenly thought of that poor bastard and where he was right now. No doubt at the bottom of one of those seas.

He gleaned nothing about the country from the few silhouettes of buildings he could see. There was a sign on the warehouse or factory opposite but not enough light for him to make out the letters. His confidence in being able to escape increased yet again and he therefore decided to stick with the plan and recce the rest of the boat. It was time to check the deck above and then perhaps get a look into the bridge.

He moved back to the centre of the corridor, where the central staircase ran up another two flights, and made his way up to the next deck. He peeped through the open doorway into the corridor and counted four internal doors, cabins most likely, and noted the heavy doors either end of the corridor that led to the outside were closed.

He decided to ignore that deck for the time being, moved back into the stairwell, and cautiously climbed the last flight of stairs until the bridge door came into view. There was no glass in it as he had hoped but he could hear men's voices. It sounded as if they were speaking English but he couldn't be sure. Only for a second did he think about rushing in on them, but since he did not know the layout of the bridge or the number of people in it, it was not the wisest idea. Even if he survived unscathed, a gunfight would bring others and things might then come unstuck. The risk was more than he was prepared to take. This was about survival first and being a hero second. He had every intention of going home to his wife and children in one piece. Taking the boat was a bonus, not an essential. But so far, the option was still open. While he had the advantage and the freedom he would continue to test its feasibility.

He went back down to the corridor and stepped inside. He ignored the four cabin doors and headed to the heavy metal door at the port-side end. He released his weapon to hang by its strap and carefully unclipped the six dogs that surrounded the door and then gave it a little shove with his shoulder to open it an inch. He paused to listen. There was nothing unusual. He opened the door enough to step through and shut it behind him, turning one of the dogs to hold it closed.

The water shimmered below as he stood on a platform with stairs running down to the main deck and up to the bridge wing, a larger platform outside the bridge.

Hank focused his attention above and climbed the steps, high enough to be able to see the bridge over the lip of the bridge wing. The bridge itself was surrounded on three sides by plate glass from the ceiling down to rail level. It was slightly darker inside than it was outside making it difficult to see. Hank took another step up and could then make out three men and possibly a fourth on the far side.

'Don't fall off there, Pat,' came a man's voice from below. Hank almost did exactly that as he fumbled to turn and level his gun. When he looked below a man, wearing a red work jacket and blue bobble hat, was heading casually along the deck to the bows. He had obviously mistaken Hank for the young Irishman, the owner of the coat. Hank quickly climbed back down the steps and into the corridor. This was becoming risky, he warned himself. The more he moved about the greater the chance of bumping into someone, and the longer he took increased the odds on someone becoming curious about the whereabouts of the two men he whacked. The ship-takeover was becoming less of an option. If he sneaked off right away all signs indicated he could manage it without anyone noticing.

Spinks had maintained a running commentary on his radio, describing the activity he had seen on the boat in every detail. He had counted eight different persons since he moved into his OP and had become familiar enough with four of them to differentiate. The man in the red coat and blue bobble hat had been given the name Red. He was the most active on deck and probably the duty crewmember since he was the only one who seemed to be doing any work. There were two who wore yellow waterproof jackets, known as Yellow One and Yellow Two and Spinks had confirmed that both carried SMGs under their jackets. Yellow One was about six foot and Yellow Two, dark-haired, shorter and stockier than his mate, had not been seen for a while. A new crewman, also in a yellow coat and carrying an SMG, had appeared on the main deck level a short time ago and Spinks named him Yellow Three. The most recent movement was Red passing along the main deck while Yellow Three climbed the superstructure staircase halfway to the bridge seemingly looking for something. After a brief word with Red, who carried on aft, Yellow Three went down and back into B deck superstructure.

Bob, on the roof of the corn exchange, shared his space on the ledge with an M squadron sniper and another operative holding a directional microphone aimed at the bridge. They had a good view of the top of the boat and the starboard side and Bob confirmed or added to Spinks's commentary when appropriate. The combined observers and listeners updated every movement on board so the assault teams could establish routines, habits and most importantly pinpoint the whereabouts of each crewman, information that would be useful when they got the 'go'.

In the makeshift ops room behind the corn exchange Captain Singen and the team leaders pored over blueprints and plans of the boat that had been faxed from London. Everyone was dressed and ready to go at a second's notice. Over their Kevlar assault suits they wore biological warfare suits, a one-piece outfit made of absorbent material and a neutralising agent. It had a hood designed to fit completely over the head and snugly around a gasmask. The suit generally made things more cumbersome but no one complained or considered going in without one. Each man was aware what could be on board and what the consequences might be if it were released. The possibility that the bio might even be thrown at one of them had been considered and so each man carried a decontamination spray as well as a bag of absorbent powder. There was nothing more they could do to prepare themselves.

Most of the men sat back and waited, keeping movement to a minimum to avoid overheating. Their faces were already wet with perspiration just sitting still. Not that they cared much at present. Each was thinking of his own role in the upcoming assault. They had been told that there was a very high chance they would be going in hot. That was as good as it got in this job. When the signal was given it would be a simultaneous multi-pronged attack. Snipers would take aim as three teams sprinted from the shadows of the corn exchange. When the teams were halfway to the target the snipers would take out anyone in view using the silenced, high-velocity 22.250 rifles, more ideal for this scenario than the Barking Dogs. It had been decided not to use incendiaries, percussion devices or entry charges for fear the bio, should it be in a glass container or similar, might not take kindly to the shockwaves. All weapons were suppressed, meaning they were virtually silent but for the metallic clatter of the breach mechanism as it shunted back and forth like a piston, picking up and firing bullets. Speed and stealth were the watchwords. The most difficult order to interpret was that if a target was even suspected of holding the bottle he was not to be shot unless he was an absolute threat to life.

'Red from aft to stern-port side,' came Spinks's voice over each man's earpiece.

Lieutenant Stewart flexed his back and stretched his arms to test the movement in his extra large bio-suit. He was the biggest operative on the assault although everyone looked like a giant in the outfits. He looked over at Jasper, who was quietly staring into space, chewing his tobacco. Pete was the other side of the room studying a copy of the ship's blueprints. The three Americans had been divided up into the three teams. They would have preferred to stay together as a single team but that had been overridden. Since they had not trained with the rest of the men the variation in two standard procedures was considered a danger in such a confined space. They could live with that though and had not argued. It was after all the wisest choice and at least they were going in.

Captain Singen checked his watch. In this situation he would not have the power to give a 'go' under any circumstances, even if Hank were dragged on deck and hung by his neck from the cargo winch. The priority was the virus and the decision to charge on board, guns blazing, to capture it was going to have to come from on high. That might happen in the next second or days from now.

Bill opened the door to the apartment building and held it open for Aggy. He still hadn't worked out how he was going to tell her she couldn't come in. They had hardly talked on their walk. He thought they might pop into a pub for a drink but she didn't suggest it and he didn't feel like it either, so they kept on walking the streets in a large square until they ended back at the building.

Because of her strange attitude he had suspected she was looking for a way to tell him it was over between them; that would have upset him even though he knew it was over anyway. But when he asked her if everything was okay she smiled and apologised for being so distant and explained that she had family matters on her mind and her silence had nothing to do with him. That only made him wonder if he should announce the end of the relationship himself, but that would only lead to questions and explanations he was not in the mood to create. What bothered him most was how she would think of him when she eventually learned he had been the IRA mole. He wanted to find a way of saying goodbye that would contain some sort of hidden message, something she would understand the meaning of later. It would take something special to convince Aggy he had not been her sworn enemy. But as proud as he was of his gift for the gab he couldn't find the words in the twenty minutes they had been walking.

He followed her up the stairs and when they arrived at his front door she stood back from it.

'Well, then,' she said. It was a clear message that this was to be their parting point and that she was not coming inside. Once again Bill was hurt by the rejection even though it saved him doing the same to her.

'I understand,' he said, lying, curious as to why she did not want to come in. He began to wonder why she had come to see him in the first place.

'I don't think you do,' she said, stepping closer and putting her arms around his neck. She had already decided she would remain affectionate towards him, not because of any urge to but it was the least suspicious thing she could do. She was compensating for her inability to act natural with him earlier, worried that he might be wondering why she had come over. But her task was complete. It didn't really matter after she left. She had given Stratton his twenty minutes. This would be all over soon anyway, and Bill would be arrested.

Bill held her tightly, wanting her terribly, knowing this was the last time he would hold her.

'I suppose I'll see you over the water,' she said.

'Yes . . . Maybe we can hop down to the Golden Harp next Friday. That band last week was good, wasn't it?'

'They were,' she said.

'Remember you have that op Tarquin coming up next week. I hear they're going to let you plan that one. Your first op.'

'Seriously,' she said. 'The weapons cache in Omagh?'

'Team leader. I heard the CO give it the nod himself,' Bill said with a wink. Deep down, behind the smile, he was suddenly missing his job in Ireland too. It had become so much more fun since he started seeing Aggy. 'You'll be running the detachments before you know it,' he said.

She smiled with difficulty. His comment only served to fuel bitterness towards him. Not just because of his deceit but every op Bill had anything to do with or could conceivably know about would be cancelled. And anyway, her career was over, even after this little job. She had always wanted to run her own op. Now, just as that was about to happen, it was all over.

He moved a strand of hair off her brow, an excuse to touch her and look at her face, her eyes, her perfect lips. 'You are so beautiful,' he said.

She was going to have to kiss him goodbye, and on the lips, deeply, her tongue inside his mouth, the way they had last said goodbye. She would rather not. He did not repulse her. On the contrary, she still found him attractive, liked him even. It was a strange place to be. He gently put his lips on hers and held her tightly. Their mouths opened and their tongues explored inside each other's. He suddenly grabbed her more tightly and held her close to him, as if afraid she would escape.

Then the moment was over and he had to let her go. He released her and she stepped back, her hands on his arms for a moment, and then they were gone, like the string of a balloon ascending out of reach.

'See you,' she said as she turned and went to the top of the stairs.

'Melissa?' he said. She looked back at him. 'There's something I want you to know. There are many reasons why I'm not going to do what they want me to do tonight, but the most important one is you.'

'I don't know what you mean,' she said, genuinely curious.

'You will. I can't explain more than that . . . I regret a lot in my life. Some things you get into and can't get out of.'

She knew what that was supposed to mean but she didn't know how to respond.

'I love you very much. That's never been a lie,' he said.

She felt suddenly very sad for him, more than she did for herself. She knew how much he loved life and that it was over for him, but only then did it dawn on her how horrific it was going to be for him. He would be in jail for the best part of his life if not all of it. And he would be alone, as spies were kept, so that they could not pass on information that might still be useful to an enemy. She found herself moving into his arms once more and holding him. Poor Bill.

He was surprised by her sudden move and could feel her tremble ever so slightly. She had been different all evening, and now this, as if there was something wrong between them, as if she was saying goodbye also. And then it all fell into place. She knew. Of course she knew. That was the only explanation. She had come to see him to get him away from his apartment. That's why she was acting so strangely. He held her shoulders and gently moved her back to look into her eyes.

Bill opened his mouth to say something just as the grey door to the roof opened and Brennan stepped out holding a gun.

'I can't stand any more of this focken tripe,' he said. 'You'll have me in focken tears if you go on any longer, so you will.'

Aggy and Bill snapped their heads in his direction and froze at the sight of the gun.

'Open the door to your apartment, Billy,' he said. 'Nice and easy. And you, you focken bitch. I'll blow your focken brains out if you so much as twitch in a way I don't fancy.'

Aggy slowly released Bill. If the Irish accent wasn't enough to warn her who this man might be, everything else about him demanded respect. 'That's a handy route you've got there, Bill, from one building to the other across the roof,' Brennan said with a grin. 'The door, Billy boy.'

Bill took his key from his pocket and opened it.

'Now. Both of you put your hands on your head, link your fingers together, and walk inside.'

Aggy and Bill obeyed and entered the apartment. Brennan pushed her forward into Bill's back, shut the door, and stayed by it, keeping a good couple of yards between him and the two of them.

'First things first,' Brennan said. 'Are you armed, Billy?'

Bill shook his head.

'Take your jacket off anyway and toss it over here.'

Bill did as he was told. Brennan felt the pockets and dropped the coat. 'Raise your arms and do me a little twirl,' he said.

Bill raised his arms and slowly turned so that Brennan

could see he was unarmed. 'Raise your trouser legs.'

Bill bent down and pulled up his trouser legs, one after the other.

'Fine,' Brennan said. 'Keep your hands on your head . . . Now you, little missy. Come 'ere.'

She walked over to him with her hands on her head. 'Turn around and face Billy,' he said like a schoolteacher. She obeyed. 'That's a good girl. Now let's see what weapons you have on you.'

He shoved the barrel of his gun into her neck with one hand while the other moved round to her front and started to frisk her all over, slowly. 'Nice tits,' he said as he squeezed them gently, one after the other. He felt all around her waist. 'Got a crotch piece by any chance?'

She shook her head.

'Mind if I feel anyway? I like to be invited.' He moved his hands down to the front of her trousers. Aggy tensed. He found her zip and pulled it down. As he slid his hand inside Aggy looked away from Bill, not wanting to see him watching. Brennan slipped his hand under the elastic of her panties. Her every instinct was crying out to react, to lash out, but she kept control. He pushed slowly down and as he reached the top of her vagina she was almost unable to contain the pressure to spin on him and tear his face off. Then, as if he sensed it, Brennan jammed the gun into her neck, reminding her it was there. It was enough to make her take hold of herself. There was no point in committing suicide just because this scumbag was feeling her up, and the lessons she had learned in the past year about Brennan's type were enough to leave little doubt he would pull the trigger.

Bill tried to keep his eyes on Aggy's, even though she would not look at him, but he couldn't help glancing down

419

at Brennan's hand violating her. Brennan's eyes were on Bill's, a dark smirk on his face, as if inviting him to make a move. Brennan was slightly taller than Aggy and had to drop his shoulders to push down further until his fingers went between her legs.

Aggy was suddenly aware that there was no sign of any emotional change in Brennan, no indication that he was actually turned on by what he was doing. She jerked as he slipped his fingers inside her, the gun jamming tighter into her neck at the same time. It might have pushed her over the top had she sensed any arousal in him, but there was none. He was trying to terrorise her and Bill. That was a different kind of challenge in a way. It was intimidation, not rape. The selection course had in some way prepared her for this challenge, conceptually. Brennan was playing with her mind. She could handle that, as long as he didn't go any further.

'I can see why you like this one, Billy. She's tight as an arse,' he said. He pulled out his hand and licked his fingers. 'Tastes good too,' he grinned. Planting his hand on her back he pushed her harshly towards Bill. She caught herself on a chair and arrogantly straightened to face him while she did up her jeans.

'I think I must've heard all your conversation out there, the best parts of it anyway . . . Well, well, well. My luck is changing. A focken Pink, and a girly one at that. I'll be famous now for sure . . . So, Bill. You said you weren't going to do what you were told to do tonight. Is that right?'

Bill had made up his mind. He had accepted the price of such a decision, though he had hoped it might be a while longer before they collected. Surprisingly, he had no qualms about remaining committed to his decision, admittedly made easier with Aggy beside him. 'Apart from being

420

a huge mistake politically, it's wrong,' he said.

'And you came to that decision all by your lonesome, did you?'

'You must see it. It doesn't make sense, killing thousands of people. Omagh was a mistake. This is a thousand times worse.'

Aggy didn't know what he meant.

'Omagh was a success, say what you like,' Brennan said. 'There's nothing we could do wrong now. Every pain we inflict on the Brits, we push them closer to giving us what we want. They can't say no. We've beaten them and they know it. The peace treaty's a load of bollocks. We even give them crap weapons we wouldn't use any more as part of the decommissioning deal while we get new ones in the back door. They know it but still say thank you and have a nice office in Parliament if you want to, why don't you. They're ready to give us it all, Billy boy. This will speed them along a wee bit . . . Christ, I'm even beginning to sound like I'm runnin' for focken election meself now.'

Aggy was trying to piece together what she knew about this attack they were referring to. Stratton had talked about destroying something, obviously a bomb of some kind. Bill was supposed to put it where it would be hugely destructive to human life and had changed his mind. That's what Bill was referring to when he said he was not going to do it. Besides all that there was something familiar about this thug. Aggy had seen him before, or perhaps it was a photograph. She couldn't place it.

'I only heard about you a couple of days ago,' Brennan said to Bill. 'I never knew we had a mole in Brit intelligence. And MI5 too. I'm told you've done some great work for the cause.'

Bill glanced at Aggy. She hadn't flinched. It confirmed that she knew.

'So, what do you think?' Brennan asked Aggy. 'Pretty smart of us.'

'I don't know what you're talking about or what's going on,' she said. She might as well take that tack. She had nothing more to lose. This arsehole was itching to kill her anyway.

Brennan chuckled. 'Not that it matters. The most important thing is that you're here, that's the main thing, and him being in love with you and all that soppy stuff. You see, I'm going to need a bit of incentive here for Bill to do his little job. I figured the threat of a bullet in the back of his head might do it, but then again it might not. He might just tell me to go fock meself. But since he's declared his undying love for you it makes it all so much more simple for me . . . Billy, if you don't do the job, I'm going to kill her, then you. What about that then? Is that incentive enough?'

Bill stared at him, his mind racing, searching for a plan, anything.

'Tell you what,' Brennan went on. 'If you say no, I'll kill you, then I'll rape her, since I've already got a taste for her, if you know what I mean, then I'll kill her. Does that sound any better?'

Bill's only choice was to comply and move the game along. An opportunity might present itself. It had to. There wasn't one here.

'Tell you the truth,' Bill said, with a subtle smile on his face. 'I was only on the fence about not doing it. Threatening my life alone would be enough to convince me the job's a great idea.'

Brennan grinned. 'I was told you were a smart one. Just don't get too smart,' he said, his grin fading. 'There's a reason they sent me to look after such an important prize. I'll get the job done if I have to do it myself. You'll both be dead if it comes to that . . . So, where is it?'

Bill didn't move. Brennan levelled the gun. 'If you tell me you don't have it I'll focken shoot you right here and now.' It was not an idle threat.

'In that cupboard,' Bill said.

'Go get it then. What am I, your focken servant?'

Bill went to the sideboard opened it, and reached in among the blankets. When he pulled out his hand, it held the large vial of rose-coloured liquid. Brennan was fascinated.

'Amazing how one tiny bottle could kill so many people,' Brennan said. 'I'm humbled by whoever invented it.'

Aggy realised this was no explosive. And Bill held it with such care and respect. There were a limited number of explanations.

'Where's the case?' Brennan asked.

'There,' said Bill.

Brennan saw it on the floor, recognising the hatbox beside it. He lifted up the case, placed it on the table and opened it. 'Put it inside,' he said.

Bill placed it carefully into the space cut out of the sponge.

'Shut it,' Brennan said. Bill closed the lid and fastened the two clips. Brennan picked up Bill's jacket and tossed it at him. 'Put it on.'

Bill pulled on the jacket.

'Now. We're going for a walk, then a little ride, all three of us. I want you to remember this. Ultimately, it doesn't matter where that stuff ends up broken in this city. It's going to end up somewhere. Personally, I'd take it down to the nearest busy pub and just pour the stuff into someone's pint and that'll be the start of it. But the powers that be, God bless 'em, want to make their point, and so we're going to

Millbank. If at any time I think you two are intending to fock with me I'll not hesitate to blow both your focken heads off and pop down the pub with the stuff meself. The result'll be the same in the end. In fact I'd like the excuse to do that.'

Brennan studied them both, looking for any sign of a challenge. Both appeared to have understood, although the girl looked at him coldly. 'You,' he said to Aggy. 'Pick up the case.'

She'd heard enough by now to know that the liquid was a seriously toxic poison or chemical. Stratton obviously knew. She could understand why he never told her. It would have dominated her thoughts. She would obey everything this mad bastard told her to do. Stratton was out there somewhere and he would have a plan. She wondered what it was.

Stratton was crouched in the front garden of a terraced house, in the bushes just beneath the bay window, through which a family could be seen on couches watching television. It was the ideal position from which to observe the front doors of the apartment building. He wondered what was taking Aggy so long to get out of there. It had been a good five minutes since he saw them enter the building. Shadows moving across the ceiling indicated someone was in the apartment. While he had been sitting silently he had thought about Aggy and Lawton's relationship and wondered how serious it had become. Perhaps she had fallen in love with him. Stratton had no concerns about her loyalty, but people in love were capable of irrational things. He chased the thoughts from his head to stay in keeping with his own rules. Too much hypothesis was unhealthy in this business.

He went through his plan again, which was, as he liked

to put it in simple military terms, straightforward until it got complicated. Whenever Aggy eventually came out he would allow her to walk away without alerting her to his presence. It didn't matter where she went or ended up, she was out of the game, her job done. If there was surveillance to be done she would be of no use because the target knew her. If Stratton could he would tell her to go home. Since she had no mobile phone hopefully she would come to that conclusion herself.

He had boiled his options down to essentially two. If Bill came out with the briefcase, Stratton would move in and take care of that situation by himself. If Bill wasn't carrying the case then Stratton needed some fresh faces to carry on with the task. Sumners should have called him by now with news of his back-up and also the answers to some of his 'what if' scenarios. If Bill didn't have the bio it could mean several things: he'd left it in his apartment for some reason; someone else now had it or was going to collect it; he was going to pick it up from somewhere; or he was baiting any would-be followers away from RIRA's real intentions. This is where it could be made to look more complicated than it was if cool minds didn't prevail. It was Stratton's MO to keep scenarios simple, even when there was a plethora of possible options. Most operations fell apart at this phase, trying to figure out what the opposition might do and prepare for every possible eventuality. That's why so many ended in a gun battle, and why so many were ultimately designed to end in an ambush, which was just a gun battle on the ambusher's terms.

When all else failed Stratton's overriding consideration was governed by 'the price plan', the value of the operation, or in more plain language, who or what could be sacrificed to succeed. This one wasn't difficult to value since the cost could be the population of London and a lot more. Basically, every bastard involved, on both sides, was expendable.

The door to the apartment building opened and Stratton watched Bill, Aggy and, to his surprise, another man walk out; the man with the limp who had appeared behind Aggy and Bill when they went for their walk. They passed him on the other side of the street. Aggy was in the middle and it looked like she was carrying the briefcase. The light was too poor to make out any other details.

And that, Stratton said to himself, was what they called Murphy's Law. Had he come up with a scenario such as this it would've been way down on the list. It highlighted another important philosophy, which was 'be flexible'. This was going to require a combination of both options. The bio was there, almost certainly, but Stratton couldn't risk taking it alone. Not yet anyhow. He didn't know who this third person was and there was still the possibility it was all a piece of bait. He felt the electronic initiator in his pocket. All he needed to do was remove the safety lock, push the arming switch, hit the red button, and boom. But two things were very wrong with that choice. One was that the explosion would kill Aggy. He was capable of sacrificing an operative if that was within the price plan but only if there was absolutely no choice. And this was, after all, Aggy. To date, he had never lost an operative on one of his own planned ops, except Hank of course, but hopefully that wasn't over yet. The second and far greater consideration was that it still had not been confirmed if exploding the briefcase would kill the virus. If Sumners gave him the all-clear it would then just be a matter of getting Aggy away from it. He would happily extinguish Lawton, which would suit everyone perfectly, and this character with the limp, whoever he was.

Stratton put the initiator away, got to his feet, climbed over the squat wall and headed along the street, keeping a good distance from the three figures but not letting them out of his sight. They were heading for Wandsworth Road only a couple hundred yards away. He would have to close up as they approached it or risk losing them in the busy street. He wondered if they had a car. This could all get very desperate very quickly. Where the hell was Sumners?

Stratton took out his phone and hit a memory dial as he walked. It rang.

'Ops here,' said the operations officer.

'Stratton. Give me Sumners.'

'He's not here, Stratton.'

'Where the hell is he?' Stratton asked, unable to control his annoyance, which was unusual for him. It was a warning that the pressure was building. Secure phone lines were probably ringing all over the country by now. The PM was no doubt already pacing his office or on his way to a safe location out of the city. And Stratton was holding this whole thing together. Where were his operatives? They should have been arriving in their droves. Stratton wondered if Sumners hadn't screwed up. The fine line between need to know and telling everyone was sometimes a difficult one to call. Stratton was glad he didn't have to make those decisions. On an op like this Stratton should have just about every force available at his disposal, including stealth helicopters, a link into London's video surveillance camera system, which literally covered the entire city and all the highways and motorways leading in and out of it, and cohorts of operatives tripping over each other. Instead he was alone. It was ridiculous.

'I think he's gone to the loo,' the ops officer said.

'Tell him the bio is foxtrot, that I have no idea where the fuck it's headed, and if I don't some get backup in the next two minutes I'm going to blow it to hell because I'll have no fucking choice.'

'I understand,' the ops officer said calmly. 'I'll go and find him.'

Stratton killed the call and pocketed the phone. You do that, he said to himself. This was bullshit. The operation was at the most crucial stage and the wheels were about to fall off it.

Aggy, Bill and Brennan reached Wandsworth Road and turned left on to it. Stratton speeded up then slowed as he reached the junction. He was hoping there would be a shop or something he could use to get a reflection off, but there was nothing. He peeked around the corner and darted back like an amateur. They had been right there, all three, yards away, climbing aboard a crowded double-decker bus, and Aggy still had the briefcase. Stratton's mind raced. He couldn't get on board, Bill would see him. He was going to lose them. He felt the initiator in his pocket. Blowing them up along with a bus full of people was well within the price plan, but there was still another option he could play. There was always another option. It was all about figuring it out in time.

He watched them move along the bus and Bill lead upstairs. The stranger with the limp paused to look behind him and out of the window. It was a warning to Stratton that the man was experienced and aware. By the stark lights of the bus Stratton got a look at his face. He knew him. A photograph perhaps? The man headed upstairs. Then the limp brought it all together.

'Brennan,' Stratton muttered to himself. A few weeks after the failed operation to snatch Spinks, Special Branch had come up with the identities of the players in the crashed van. Three had died; one shot through the chest and the other two killed by the impact of the crash. The one that got away, even though he had been shot through the thigh, was Brennan.

Stratton watched as they headed towards the front of the upper deck and the bus started to pull out into traffic.

He stepped out from his corner and watched it crawl away into traffic. Number 77A. He touched his jacket under his left arm, feeling his gun beneath, and moved to the street, scanning cars, looking for a candidate. A single occupant was wisest. The hard part about hijacking a car was finding a driver who didn't look like they would put up a heroic fight or crash the car at the first opportunity. Women were not always an obvious choice. Stratton preferred to go for someone who actually looked hard. Chances were they weren't. And if they were, then they might appreciate the consequences more graphically if the person doing the threatening looked serious enough. He saw a gum-chewing, tattooed skinhead in an old RS2000 that looked in good condition. This was his man.

The car had slowed in the traffic as a direct result of the bus pulling out. Stratton opened the passenger door, pulled his gun out of his shoulder holster under his coat, and climbed in beside the skinhead, who was about to say something until he saw the weapon. Before he closed the door Stratton thought he heard his name being called. 'Stop the car a sec,' Stratton asked the skinhead calmly, who obeyed instantly.

'Stratton?' came the voice again. Stratton looked back along the pavement to see a chubby man in his early thirties in grubby clothes walking briskly towards him. There was something familiar about him.

'Wilks,' the man said as he approached the car. 'We worked togever couple years ago in Birmin'am.' Wilks saw the gun in Stratton's hand, ignored it and looked in at the skinhead. 'Awright?' he asked the skinhead, assuming he was an acquaintance of Stratton's. The skinhead nodded quickly, wide-eyed.

Stratton remembered Wilks. 'A4?' he asked.

'Yeah. We got a message to 'ang aroun' Wandsworth and Queenstown Road. Said you'd be abart.'

'You got a car?' Stratton asked quickly.

'Yeah. Over 'ere.'

Stratton put his gun away. 'Sorry, mate,' he said to the skinhead and climbed out and shut the door.

'That bus,' Stratton said to Wilks, indicating the only one in the street. 'Our target's upstairs.'

Wilks was a pro and instantly switched up gears. 'This way,' he said and they hurried towards his car. 'I was on me way 'a Brighton wiv me missus and two nippers when they called me. Did she kick up a stink or what? Gave me merry 'ell.'

At the wheel of Wilks's car was a young black guy wearing a grin that turned out to be a permanent feature. Stratton climbed in the front and Wilks the back. 'Chaz, Stratton,' Wilks said by way of quick introduction. ''At bus, me old mate,' he pointed.

Chaz also picked up on the urgency, started the car and bullied his way into traffic with practised ease.

'Seventy-seven A?' Chaz said in a Scouse accent. 'Goes to Vauxhall, across the bridge, Tate Gallery, Parliament Square. Can't remember where it goes then. Victoria or Trafalgar. One of them.'

Stratton thought about that a moment. 'Do you know what this is about?' he asked them.

'Not a clue,' Wilks said. 'All we know is there's a right flap on, everyone's at abaat ten thousand feet, an' 'at whatever it is is real 'eavy.'

'You armed?' Stratton asked.

'Yeah,' said Wilks. Chaz nodded.

'On the bus is a woman and two men. One's a RIRA hitter. Extreme. Undoubtedly armed. Give him one sniff you're not Kosher and he'll take you out. The other's MI5, but he's a spy for RIRA. The woman's one of us and she's a hostage . . . '

'Fuckin' 'ell,' said Wilks, seriously impressed. 'It don't get much 'eavier 'en 'at.'

'They're carrying a biological weapon that could wipe out London,' Stratton added.

Chaz gave him a quick glance. Wilks was temporarily speechless.

Stratton's phone vibrated. He put it to his ear. 'Yes.' It was Sumners. 'I'm with two but I need at least four more cars,' Stratton said. 'Two snipers would be useful.'

'Three teams should be with you in twenty minutes,' Sumners said. 'I'll have two police snipers RV with the team commander asap.'

Too much too late, Stratton thought. 'Target's on a bus that goes through Parliament Square. That's Lawton, a RIRA hitter named Brennan and Aggy from South det. She's a hostage. I used her to get Lawton out of the apartment for my recce and then Brennan entered the plot.'

'I see. And the bio?' Sumners asked. He didn't need to know any more at this stage. The only time you lived in the past on an op was at the debriefing when it was all over. The bio was the only thing of importance, where it was and where it was headed towards. Sumners would ask about Aggy's part in all this later.

'They're carrying the briefcase. I'm certain the bio's in it,' Stratton said.

'We should soon know if it's on the boat or not,' Sumners

431

said. 'They'll be hitting it any time now.'

'What about the explosives?' Stratton asked.

'The boffins have been in touch with the Yanks and they're still calculating. It's not something anyone wants to take a guess at. For God's sake, Stratton, don't even think of blowing it until I let you know for sure. And one last thing. Lawton must not live through this. That's from the top. Understand?'

'Don't I always?' Stratton said and shut down the phone.

'Twenty minutes to Parliament?' Stratton asked Chaz.

'Twenty, twenty-five,' Chaz replied.

'We need to get the advantage back,' Stratton said, thinking out loud mostly. Right now they were just waiting for an opportunity. He had to create one. 'We have to get everyone off the bus,' he announced.

The other two didn't quite understand.

'The bio's in a briefcase,' he explained. 'So's a chunk of explosive.'

'They've got a bomb as well?' asked Chaz.

'The bomb's mine.'

Wilks was trying to keep up with Stratton but finding it hard. 'We gotta get everyone off the bus wivout the targets knowin',' he said.

'Right.'

''Ow we gonna do that?' Chaz asked.

'We take it over,' Stratton said. 'They're upstairs. We should be able to clear the bottom at least.'

'And then you're gonna blow the fuckin' thing up?' Chaz asked, a bit shocked at the thought.

'Don't get ahead of yourself. First let's catch us a bus.' He looked to Chaz for a physical response. 'That means we've gotta get in front of it, find a bus stop, and flag it down as normal.'

'Right o,' Chaz said as he dropped down a gear and simply powered out into the oncoming lane and floored it.

Wilks gripped the back of both front seats.

Cars braked, screeched and swerved to avoid them as Chaz overtook one at a time, cutting back into gaps just long enough to let an oncoming vehicle pass then pushing out again and hammering forward.

As the bus drove under a railway bridge Chaz moved out to overtake it. Its windows strobed past, the passengers bathed in orange light. The bus driver swerved towards the curb and blasted his horn in frustration as he swung back out into his lane. The road opened up ahead of the bus and was clear enough for Chaz to accelerate to over ninety.

'Nine Elms Lane,' he shouted. Stratton and Wilks were busy concentrating on his driving and looking out for a bus stop.

They approached the broad intersection that led into Vauxhall.

'Bus stop just before the bridge!' Wilks shouted and pointed.

'Got it,' Chaz said. 'I know where to put the car.'

He drove directly across the intersection, over the pavement the other side, down a grass verge, and on to a piece of waste ground close to the river. He braked hard and before the vehicle had come to a complete stop the doors were open and they were all clambering out.

Stratton led the run back up the grass verge in time to see the bus heading for the intersection. Chaz arrived at the top of the verge and Stratton quickly faced him, his back to the bus. As Wilks arrived out of breath he saw the bus and was about to bound off ahead of it.

'Wait,' shouted Stratton, grabbing Wilks's jacket. 'Wait for it to pass.' He didn't want the front upper deck to see them running. But that meant they were going to have to sprint as soon as it went by. Wilks was aware of that and, being far too overweight, was already dreading it. He was not given time to think about it. As the bus passed Stratton was off with Chaz alongside him.

The bus came to a halt at the stop to let a handful of people on and off. It was still a good hundred yards away and it was touch and go as to whether they would make it. Chaz turned on the afterburners and moved ahead of Stratton. The driver punched out a ticket and counted out the change for the last new passenger. Stratton ran as hard as he could, suddenly filled with the fear he had miscalculated the distance and how long it would take to cover it. The passenger took his ticket and started to head down the aisle. The doors gushed with air as they started to close and the bus crept forward. Chaz reached out and flung his arm into the closing gap. The driver saw a hand come through to grab the inside of the door and quickly braked. He gave Chaz a stern look and shook his head as he opened the doors.

Chaz stepped aboard, regaining his breath and Stratton climbed on behind him.

'One . . . more,' Stratton said to the driver, standing in the doorway so it couldn't be closed.

Wilks staggered up and virtually fell into the bus. Chaz helped him inside and the driver closed the door.

'Is it that important?' the driver asked Chaz, shaking his head as he pulled away and on to the bridge.

Stratton went to the bottom of the stairs and looked up and then around the lower deck to get an idea of numbers. Chaz and Wilks joined him. The bus looked about a third full, with seven people in the lower deck.

'You clear upstairs,' Stratton said to Chaz. 'They're near

the front. The girl's pretty, short hair. If the older guy eyeballs you, you quit and get off. You take no chances.'

Chaz nodded and made his way upstairs.

'Let's get everyone off,' he said to Wilks. 'Not all at once. And don't let anyone on.'

'Not a problem,' Wilks said.

Stratton went back to the front of the bus and reached into his breast pocket. The driver glanced at him and indicated a sign that instructed passengers not to hang around the driver and not to talk to him. 'Go and find a seat, please, sir.'

Stratton held open a small leather wallet in front of the driver's face. It was a very official-looking photo identification of Stratton with the words 'Ministry of Defence' embossed boldly across it.

'Can you read that?' Stratton asked.

The driver frowned, glanced at it long enough to read it, then nodded. Stratton flipped down the picture to reveal a sparkling metal badge with an ornate white enamel face that had the Royal Crest finely crafted on it along with the inscription, 'MI5'.

'And that?' Stratton said.

The driver nodded again, a little slower, his frown disappearing.

'And this?' Stratton said as he pulled his jacket aside to reveal his pistol in its shoulder holster. The driver's final nod was enhanced by a facial expression that was most convincing.

'What's your name?' Stratton said, hiding his weapon.

'Burrows. Robert Burrows.'

'They call you Bob?'

'I prefer Robert.'

'Listen carefully, Robert. On board your bus, upstairs, are

435

some very dangerous criminals. What we need to do is get everyone off without them knowing. Do you understand?'

'Yes,' the driver said, nodding, a little nervous, but in control.

'I need your help, Robert,' Stratton continued. 'I want you to stop at the next bus stop and get out of your seat. I will drive. You will then help my colleague behind me. Don't tell anyone the real reason they have to get off or they'll panic. Understood?'

The driver nodded and swallowed heavily. 'I understand,' he said.

Stratton looked into the distance as they came over the hump of the bridge. 'You're going to stop at that bus stop, right?'

The driver nodded.

'Act natural. Take it easy . . . The people on this bus are in your care, Robert. This is your ship.'

That was exactly what the driver needed to hear. This was his ship and he was the captain, and the passengers were his responsibility. They made movies of this kind of stuff and it was happening to him for real.

'Nice and easy,' Stratton said as they pulled to a stop. 'Don't open the front doors.' Two people were waiting to get on. The driver left the doors closed and climbed out of his seat. Stratton noticed the driver's jacket on a hook behind the seat. He removed his leather jacket, dumped it behind the seat, and pulled on the jacket that had ample room around the front if a little short in the sleeves. He sat in the driver's seat and looked at the mirror that reflected the images caught by the convex mirror upstairs. Brennan, Aggy and Lawton were all there at the front. He studied the controls. 'Middle doors?' he asked and the driver indicated the lever. Stratton activated it and the doors opened. 'Remember, no one on, Robert.'

436

'I understand,' the driver said. He waved at the two people waiting to get on and indicated they could not. Meanwhile, Wilks went to the three young women nearest the middle door, showed them his badge, and asked them to get off. Surprisingly, they did so without making a fuss. Movies and current events had made the average person far more co-operative in such situations these days. The driver went over to an elderly couple and decided the best way to deal with them was to explain that the bus was stopping where it was because of engine problems and another one was right behind. The old couple got off quite quickly. He repeated the same story to a couple behind who had overheard and they obediently followed.

Stratton checked the rear-view mirror, saw Wilks give a thumbs-up, shut the door then slipped it into drive and slowly accelerated away, leaving the people who had been ushered off as well as those who had been waiting in the street somewhat bemused.

Chaz sat down on the top deck and took a moment to get a look at the targets. He picked out the only short-haired, pretty girl at the very front of the bus and it was easy to see who the two men were. The younger one was beside her and the older one behind them both. No one was seated the other side of the aisle to them.

Chaz turned around and faced two middle-aged couples in the two seats behind him. He showed them his badge, told them in a low voice he was with the London special security services, and asked them to quietly and calmly get up and go downstairs. They looked at each other, wondering if this was some kind of a joke. He repeated his command, making sure they could see his picture clearly on the MoD identity badge, and further explained he was a form of police officer and that they were quietly to go downstairs where a colleague would explain the situation to them. They were eventually convinced enough to get up and go to the stairs. Chaz kept an eye on Brennan, who remained looking forward.

As the four passengers reached the lower deck they started talking and asking what was going on. Wilks gave them a quick shhh, put his finger to his lips, and reinforced the command with a flash of his badge. They obeyed this new stranger.

Stratton was anxious for the next bus stop. He wanted everyone off as soon as possible. He took the right turn off the bridge and drove along the riverbank. The road curved slowly to the left and then a stop came into view. As he started to slow, the driver came alongside him.

'This is the wrong stop,' the driver said clandestinely.

'You mean none of those people waiting at the stop will want this bus?' Stratton asked.

'That's right. We don't stop 'ere. Ours is around the corner a bit further.'

'Perfect.' Stratton brought the bus to a stop alongside the bus stop and hit the lever that opened the middle doors with a gush. Wilks ushered the people off. Stratton closed the doors and moved the bus on its way.

Chaz got up and walked to a seat opposite the last couple upstairs, who were one seat back from Brennan. Brennan was aware someone had arrived close by and glanced back. Chaz avoided Brennan's eyes and looked out the window until Brennan faced the front again. Chaz reached a leg across the aisle and tapped the young man on the foot. The man looked at him strangely and then saw the badge in Chaz's hand by his knee. Chaz made a motion for him to move back. The man frowned, wondering what Chaz wanted. Brennan started to look around but was seemingly interested in something across the river and went back to facing ahead.

Chaz suddenly started to feel the pressure. It dawned on him that he had never been in such a dangerous position in his life. He was used to following foreign diplomats mostly, Russians, East Europeans, Middle Easterners. He'd worked against the IRA loads of times but never like this, never close to a killer who was prepared to waste him if he made a mistake. Chaz looked at the young man with eyes so intense it was if he was trying to burn the message into him. He made another, more severe jerk with his head towards the stairs. The young man's girlfriend was suddenly aware of her boyfriend's distraction and looked past him to see Chaz holding his badge. Chaz thought about showing them his gun, but changed his mind for fear it might scare them into a negative reaction.

The girl was more switched on than her boyfriend and took a look at the people in front of her, evaluating why the black guy was being so secretive and cautious. As if Brennan had sensed something he turned and looked at her, into her eyes. It was as if she saw something in him that scared her. Brennan looked ahead again. She nudged her boyfriend to get up. He was resistant. She nudged him again, harder. Chaz put his fingers to his lips, the young man gave in, and they got up.

Brennan looked back just as Chaz was getting up to leave. Chaz caught his eyes, just long enough to see the beast in them, then followed the couple down the stairs. Brennan looked ahead again, but this time niggled by something. He looked back to see the upper deck was empty.

On the lower deck the couple had joined the last of the

passengers herded together at the centre doors as Stratton slowed the bus to a stop at a set of traffic lights. He decided to go for it and opened the doors.

'Everyone off,' Chaz said quietly, keeping an eye up the stairs. 'You too,' he said to the driver.

'But this is my ship, I mean my bus,' the driver said.

'You've done your job, mate. You've got to get off now, please.'

The driver glanced over at Stratton in his seat, accepted it was all very much bigger than he was, and stepped down off the bus. Stratton shut the doors and as the traffic lights turned green he drove on through the junction.

Wilks and Chaz glanced at each other, at Stratton, and upstairs. Now what?

Wilks took a seat on the bench behind Stratton, nearer the stairs, while Chaz made his way to the back and sat down.

Stratton pushed on along the riverbank taking it as slowly as he could without alerting suspicion, every few seconds flashing a look at the upper-deck mirror. Parliament was a mile or so further on; he needed to drag the journey out as long as he could. There had been no call from Sumners yet, no support team, no plan. It was beginning to look as if everything was going to be down to him. With Brennan, it could get messy. He wondered if the bus could be the best place to end it. He could stop the bus, walk upstairs, and take his chances on shooting Brennan before he could react, and then Lawton. If the virus was somehow released they would have to stay on the bus. It could be sealed off where it was by the biohazard teams and they would take it from there. Not the best end to the day Stratton could imagine, but it might have to do. Then came a loud ding that made Stratton flinch.

It took a split second for him to realise it was the stop request bell.

Stratton looked at the upper-deck mirror to see the backs of Brennan, Lawton and Aggy on their feet. He looked at the mirror showing the lower-deck interior, at Chaz and Wilks who were looking up at the sound of footsteps above moving to the top of the stairs.

Stratton saw a bus stop up ahead and started to slow. The footsteps clomped down the stairs. Lambeth Bridge was several hundred yards away, still a fair distance from Parliament Square. Then it hit Stratton like a slap. Of course. MI5 headquarters. A perfect place to put the virus, and Lawton the perfect person to deliver it there.

Aggy was first to step from the stairwell on to the lower deck, followed by Lawton carrying the briefcase, then Brennan who kept an arm's length from the other two in case he needed to draw his weapon.

As Chaz saw Brennan he felt a sudden flush of anxiety. Brennan had looked at him upstairs. If he saw him again he might become suspicious.

Aggy didn't know where Brennan and Bill were headed with the virus. She wasn't familiar with this part of London and was feeling numb with helplessness. Attacking the thug would be a losing start. She was no match for him. Grabbing the briefcase wouldn't gain her anything more than a bullet in the back. Bill might help her if she started it; she could grab the thug as the doors opened and Bill could run with the case. But that would probably end with a bullet for both of them. He might not even run. Bill looked as helpless as she felt. She believed he would not let the virus be released, not if he could help it. He had assured her as much on the stairs outside his apartment. But how much was he protecting her, and where would he draw the line between saving her and everyone else? The thug wasn't going to let her walk away at the end of all this no matter what. She was only alive so far to keep Bill in line. As soon as they reached their destination she was dead. Bill must know that.

Aggy looked around the bus, which was now almost empty and saw the chubby bloke who was looking directly at her. There was something in his eyes. He seemed tense. She took a look at the other guy seated at the back and felt her senses tingle ever so slightly. Were they who she thought they were? She looked towards the front of the bus, at the driver, and her reaction was almost visible but she held it in check. He wasn't looking at her, she couldn't see his face, but she'd know that head and straggly hair anywhere. His presence was like an emergency chute after the main one had failed as she plummeted to earth. He was here and suddenly there was hope. She had to be alert now. Whatever his move was going to be she had to be ready. She hoped she could figure it out seconds before and be of help, or, if not, avoid being a liability.

Stratton assessed the situation and concluded they were all well and truly screwed. If he drove on without stopping Brennan would figure it out pretty quickly and go nuts with his gun, etcetera, etcetera. If Stratton stopped the bus and let them off he would have to act. It was now or never.

He brought the bus to a halt at the stop and opened the doors. One way or another it was going to be party time very soon.

When Wilks saw Aggy look at him he knew he had to somehow communicate she was not alone. He couldn't play it too strongly and when she looked away he wasn't sure if she'd sensed it. Brennan had held back and Wilks briefly considered making a grab for him, but could not see how that would do much good. The briefcase was the focus and the other man had that. Chaz was too far away to help, and Stratton was driving. This was not the time to take matters into his own hands. Anyway, he wasn't prepared for that kind of heroics. It wasn't something he ever thought of and didn't have the confidence he could carry it out without screwing up, and that would mean the end of him and the others too quite likely. He had a wife and two kids who needed him as much as he wanted them. He would stick to what he was good at and that was being led. Stratton would have to make the move and he would do his best to follow.

Lawton stepped off the bus feeling completely useless, as he had from the moment Brennan had surprised him and Aggy outside his apartment. There was nothing he could think of that could even begin to get him out of this problem. Every scenario he ran through his head ended with Aggy dead or as good as, him dead and the virus in that maniac's hands. However, time was fast running out and it was beginning to look more and more as if he should accept the inevitable and throw himself into the arms of fate. He could not allow the virus to be released. He would be damned for ever if he did that. Aggy's usefulness would soon be at an end. He had to act at his first opportunity and hope luck had not deserted him. He stood with his back to the bus, waiting for the inevitable growl from Brennan to get going. If Brennan got close enough he would make a grab for him. Perhaps Aggy would grab the case and run for it.

Aggy stepped off the bus beside him. He felt her look

at him but could not return it. He wanted to let her know he was ready to do something, but how?

Brennan moved forward to step off the platform and, as his instincts demanded, he checked his flanks. To his right was a fat guy on the bench looking at Aggy. Brennan glanced at the driver, found his eyes in the mirror staring at him, piercing eyes, enough to hold Brennan's gaze for a split second. Brennan continued forward as he turned his head to look in the other direction and saw Chaz, the black man from upstairs. As his foot hit the pavement his mind was screaming a warning at him. The combination of the burning eyes in the mirror and the black man was an alarm bell so loud he reached inside his jacket for his gun. He heard the doors shut behind him as he took another step. No one had gotten off. If they had he would have drawn his gun and been shooting as he turned. He kept his hand on his gun and pushed Aggy forward into Bill's side.

'Go on,' he said. They walked across the pavement and angled towards the large building on the corner. Brennan's eyes were forward, but his senses were all aimed to his rear.

Bill looked up at the front of MI5 headquarters. Ahead were the steps that led up to the main doors through which he could see the lobby and the perspex tube turnstiles, hollow pillars that a person stepped into and waited for the sensors to permit them inside.

Stratton watched them reach the steps. Something was vibrating in his pocket. His phone of course. No doubt it was Sumners, or perhaps it was the new ground leader wanting to know where to deploy his teams or needing an update. Whoever it was they were too late.

'What do we do now?' asked Wilks.

'When we get off, spread out. Wait for me to start.'

Stratton's phone stopped vibrating for a moment then started again. He ignored it as he watched Brennan, counting the seconds, calculating when to make his move.

Brennan was aware the bus had not moved. He no longer had any doubt the men on board were the enemy. Then he heard a gush of air that told him the bus doors were opening again. He pulled his gun from its holster and kept it under his coat.

'Go on,' he said in a raised voice as he pushed Aggy forward to follow Lawton up the steps. He glanced over his shoulder long enough to catch sight of figures moving from the bus. Now was the time.

Stratton's gun was in his hand. Wilks and Chaz held theirs and moved apart.

Brennan pulled his gun from his coat as he surged up the steps to overtake Lawton and Aggy to put them between him and the men.

'Freeze,' Stratton shouted, aiming his gun.

Bill froze just before the top. Aggy stopped beside him. Brennan grabbed Aggy and spun her around to face Stratton, with his gun at her head.

'One more step,' Brennan shouted, 'and I'll blow her focken head off!'

'And I'll blow your head off, Brennan, as I should've done on the border.'

Brennan focused on Stratton. He cast his mind back, replaying the events of that day. He could see the chopper, the man inside it leaning out of the cab holding a rifle aimed at him. 'Pink,' he muttered, gritting his teeth with utter hatred, his leg throbbing from the short sprint. It was a standoff, and not the first time he'd been in such a situation. Four years earlier in Cork, after robbing a building society, a plain-clothes cop happened to be on the street outside and drew his weapon. Brennan grabbed a woman who was in front of him and put his gun to her head. After a brief exchange of words he took the initiative and shot through the woman's head, sprinkling the cop's face in blood and giving Brennan the precious split second he needed to shoot him too. But this was not going to be as easy. The Pink was too far away, and anyway, the man was no street cop. He was a killer like Brennan, that was obvious just by his manner. The eyes told the rest. There was going to have to be another way out of this situation.

'If you were gonna give her up, you'd have done it by now,' he shouted.

'You can take things only so far,' Stratton replied. 'But time's run out. It ends here.'

'There's always enough time for negotiation,' Brennan said.

'There's always time for that,' Stratton agreed. 'Her life for yours.'

But both men knew they were simply playing for time and an opportunity to take the other out. Both were the key to winning or losing this fight.

'Well, I tell you what, Pink. I trust you about as far as I could throw that bus.'

Aggy stared at Stratton, his gun levelled at her in one hand, the other hand down beside his body. It moved, ever so slightly and her eyes flicked to it. He was holding it for her to see what was in it. The initiator. She knew immediately what it signified. That's what Stratton was doing in Bill's apartment. He couldn't find the virus; Bill had hidden it. So Stratton mined the briefcase. He was warning her to

446

get clear. This was his move, his plan. There was only one problem. Brennan would shoot her through the head if she so much as twitched.

Brennan was like a rock, hands steady, his glare determined, his mind spinning like a fruit machine trying to work out his options. 'Lawton,' he growled. 'Put the case down on the floor by my foot.'

Lawton didn't move.

'I said put it down, Billy boy.'

Bill still didn't move.

'You've got five seconds, then I shoot the bitch, and you, and probably get a chance to hammer that case before those bastards get me. It's your call.' He shoved the barrel of the gun hard into Aggy's head. 'On the ground, now!'

Bill turned and held up the case towards Stratton. 'Shoot her and I throw him the case,' Bill shouted.

Brennan's finger froze on the trigger. He had pushed Lawton to the brink and now he was prepared to sacrifice himself and the girl.

Chaz watched all of this as if from the front seats at a bullfight. He was a part of it and yet he wasn't. All the cards were being dealt in front of him but he had none to play himself. His gun was up on aim but he would only fire when the maniac or Stratton starting shooting. It all had to end here one way or another but he couldn't start it. His phone suddenly chirped in his pocket. The 'Ode to Joy' was his ring tone, a merry melody for such a moment. No one else appeared to notice. He ignored it himself, but it kept on ringing and was almost becoming an embarrassment. Wilks was a few yards away with his gun levelled. Chaz carefully slid the phone from his pocket and put it to his ear.

Bill Lawton was looking into the abyss. It was all he could

do. 'I swear, the second you shoot, I'll toss the case to him,' he said to Brennan. He had gone past the point of no return, his choice clear. This was the only chance he had to save Aggy and the virus, small though it was. It was up to Brennan now. He knew Stratton needed just one slender window of opportunity and he'd take it. Stratton was obviously trying to save Aggy too otherwise he would have wasted them all by now, even if that meant getting to Brennan through Aggy. Bill was surprised. He didn't think Stratton had this much heart. Perhaps Aggy had been wrong about him. Perhaps he did feel something for her.

Brennan knew his options had run out. Bill had turned completely and played his final card. 'You fool,' he said. 'She's the only thing keeping the both of us alive.'

'This is the last time I ask. If you don't let her go, I'll toss the case to him anyway.'

'Then she's dead for sure and so are you,' Brennan said with finality.

Lawton slowly moved into a position that suggested he was going to throw it.

'Put the case down and I'll let her walk.' Brennan said.

Lawton held himself in check. Was there still a chance? 'Let her go first,' he said.

'Lower the case to the ground then,' Brennan bartered. Lawton took a moment to decide and then lowered the case but without releasing the handle.

Chaz's eyes moved to Stratton's hand by his side as he listened to the voice on his phone and he seemed to understand the worst. 'Stratton,' he called out. 'Stratton. I've got a message for you.'

'Not a good time,' Stratton said, his gun rock steady and aimed at Brennan's head or what he could see of it behind Aggy's.

'It's someone called Sumners,' Chaz persisted trying to keep his voice low. 'It's important. That thing you asked him about. He said it won't work.'

Stratton instantly knew he was referring to the explosive device. His only ace had just been taken from him and his options were suddenly boiled away to one. It had come down to shooting Brennan at the first opportunity even if it meant losing Aggy.

'Go, Aggy,' Bill said.

'Let go of the case first,' Brennan said. He didn't trust the spy. Not that it mattered. The key was taking out the bastard Pink at the bottom of the steps and to do that he needed one fraction of a second.

Aggy realised it was all down to her now. She was the key to Lawton's next move and Stratton's too. She was going to have to move and give Stratton the shot he needed. She felt suddenly weak as if her legs could no longer support her weight. She wanted to run but she was frozen to the spot. Everything felt as if it had slowed to a crawl. And that's what it would be like if she ran. She would be too slow. Brennan only needed to move his finger half an inch and she needed to move her whole body ten times as far in the same instant. Her mouth trembled and she closed her eyes. She was going to do it.

But it was Bill who made the first move. 'Brennan,' he said. 'Here.' And he tossed the briefcase at him. Brennan saw it coming out of the corner of his eye. Aggy ducked and spun, her arms flailing, the split second distraction enough to move her head from the barrel of Brennan's gun. But Brennan was already traversing the weapon, his subconscious focused on the virus.

Brennan fired a shot into Lawton then dropped a little to engage Stratton. But he was no match for the man who had far more battle experience, and many more kills. Stratton fired two quick shots into Brennan's body and a third at his head as Brennan fired at him, missing by inches. The head-shot took the side of Brennan's head off exposing his brain.

Lawton dropped back on to the steps, his chest on fire, his legs unable to support him. Brennan dropped to his knees. There in front of him, in the haze, was the briefcase. The pain in his entire body was excruciating but the throb-bing in his head was unbearable. His throat was filling with blood and he could no longer breathe. The pain started to subside and he began to feel euphoric as his brain starved of oxygen. As he fell forward on to the case Brennan pulled the trigger of his gun. The Super 'X' explosion was thun-derous sending a shockwave through everyone and tossing them like standing corn in a blast of wind.

The entire scene was being watched through a pair of binoc-ulars from the highest point on Lambeth Bridge. Father Kinsella saw the explosion and the bodies on the steps scat-ter, one of them flying into the air and landing a distance away from where it was launched. The crack and boom echoed across the river and bounced off buildings, and fright-ened birds took flight. The ripple of sound gradually disap-peared. The area was filled with smoke and it then went completely silent. He lowered the binoculars. He didn't need them to see any more. Most of the cars on the bridge had stopped and the handful of people crossing it looked towards the source of the sudden boom as drivers climbed out to look.

Father Kinsella lifted the thin leather strap of the binoc-ulars over his head and tidily wound it around the centre hinge. He watched a moment longer then tiredly walked away towards the south side of the river. As he walked he took a mobile phone from his pocket and pushed in a series of numbers. He held it to his ear and listened to it ring. It continued to ring and ring. He looked at the face of the phone to check the number, cancelled it, then tried again.

25

The phone buzzed on the bridge of the *Alpha Star*. 'Phone ringing on the bridge,' announced the operator with the directional microphone, situated on the corn exchange roof, over the assault team's secure communications network.

Two four-man assault teams stood in silence in a line along a dark corridor inside the exchange, the hoods of their bio-suits tied tightly around their gasmasks, their SMGs in gloved hands, not a spec of flesh visible. The first team leader stood at the slightly open door that led directly out on to the quay across from the *Alpha Star,* watching it, finalising his route to the boat now that he could actually see it. The third assault team was huddled near the fishing boats just south of the target.

Captain Singen watched from a window above the grain silo, the Squadron Sergeant Major beside him. The phone was perfect. London had given him the green light only a few minutes earlier and he was waiting for the best opportunity in the five or so minutes he allowed himself to choose a window to 'go'. The best opportunity was defined by the greatest number of enemy that could be pinpointed at a given moment, preferably a visual pinpoint so that snipers could take them out of the game at the onset. Out of the eight probable targets on board – three in the bridge, Red on deck, Yellow One and Two below, Yellow Three possibly in the accommodation block or superstructure, and one below – only one target was visual and that was Red. The three on the bridge were fifty per cent visible, which was not ideal, but since the sniper knew where the phone was, now that it was ringing, all he had to do was sight it and wait for someone to walk over and answer it. That would give Singen a twenty-five per cent target lock, which was, for ship assaults, high.

The sniper watched a figure walk across the bridge and stop by the desk. 'Phone picked up,' said the directional mic operator. Had there been time MI5 would have provided a listening team to monitor the ship's communications, giving Singen far more data on crew whereabouts. But the situation at present would do him just fine.

'Standby . . . standby . . . Go!' Singen said into his throat-mic.

The two teams snaked out of the door and moved from the building as if pieces of the brickwork had melted off and formed into stealthy black shadows. Team three moved briskly in file along the edge of the quay from the fishing boats.

Team one headed north of the corn escalator towards a large steel derrick on the edge of the quay that overlooked the boat. Team two headed for mid-ships. Team three went for the aft main deck. The sniper on the nearest fishing boat had Red in his sights.

As the first team broke darkness to be illuminated by the ship's lights a bullet passed soundlessly through Red's head. It entered his eye blowing out the back of his skull and he was dead before he hit the deck. The sniper hit him with another round just to make sure.

The sniper with the man on the phone in his sights did not fire immediately. He was waiting for team one to mount the exterior stairs and the leader to reach the bridge deck. If he took his shot too soon the other men in the bridge would be alerted and go for their weapons, giving them a chance of returning fire before the team could enter the bridge.

The three teams leapt on to the ship simultaneously and team one ran up the steps soundlessly in their high-adhesion footwear. The sniper kept one eye on the team leader and the other on the man talking on the phone. Team two's leader paused by the main deck starboard entrance into the superstructure just long enough to look back and make sure his men were bunched behind him ready to go in, then he grabbed the edge of the partially-closed door, faced his partner, nodded once, and opened the door, rushing in at the half-crouch, gun-barrels pointed forward, taut against harnesses and levelled just below their faces. From that point on the team worked in pairs, clearing the main deck interior level before three men headed up to the next deck where they would clear no further and go secure, unless of course their support was requested.

As the third man in team one scaled the steps, he caught a glimpse through the small window in the external 'B' deck door of someone in a yellow coat at the far end of the corridor. 'Target, "B" deck, port side, inside heading out,' he said as he continued with his team to the bridge – he would not engage since he had his own job to do. That target belonged to someone else. As his team leader and the number two operative reached the starboard bridge wing something zipped over his head and slapped through the window of the bridge deck, making a single tiny hole in the toughened glass, and the man on the phone lost the front of his forehead. It took a moment for the rest of his body to get the message that he was in fact dead, and he dropped the handset a good second before his legs gave way. His two pals sitting in the corner of the bridge sipping tea saw him crash to the floor like a felled tree and got to their feet, but the reason for his collapse was not immediately apparent to them. By the time one of them caught sight of the dark figures closing in outside and went for his gun, bullets spat in through the windows and shredded him and his partner. As they hit the floor the starboard door slid open and the team issued in.

Team three ran across the aft deck to the rear door of the central superstructure that led down onto the lower deck and eventually into the engine room. As they approached the door they heard the short message describing the target on 'B' deck port side heading out. It was followed by another short message. 'I confirm, Yellow Three on "B" deck starboard outside staircase.' It was Spinks who could clearly see the target from where he was in the water.

The team leader moved to the port aft corner of the superstructure followed by his partner and they looked around it. The figure in the yellow jacket was coming down the steps.

Hank had stepped outside onto the starboard stairwell to check around. There was no sign of the guy in the red jacket and he decided to make his move. A gentle mist was coming off the water, a fair indication it was pretty cold. The thought of swimming was no longer appealing. The swim itself might be doable, but if he had to continue his escape in soaking wet clothes in this weather he could end up with pneumonia and he wasn't exactly at his healthiest in the first place. The quay it was to be then. He would climb off the boat and walk away. The crewman in the red jacket had already mistaken him for someone else and so he might not have a problem even if he was seen.

He walked down the steps and paused at the bottom to decide which way around the superstructure to go. He didn't want to bump into the red jacket. Hank took his SMG in his hands and turned back on the stairs to head aft. He hardly had time to blink when the figure in black that stepped out in front of him fired. It happened so fast his mind didn't have time to register what had happened until the second bullet hit him like a hammer blow to the side of his head. The first struck him in the chest close to his left shoulder. He spun back, grabbed for the air as his balance went and his legs buckled. Something hit him in his side or he hit it and the world spun and turned upside down. A second later he plunged into the icy water. The shock served to realign some of his senses, but only barely. He had no idea what was up or down. His arms and legs flailed automatically but he had nothing to aim for. It was so black he could have been blind, and his head throbbed as if nails were being driven into it.

Team three leader stepped to the rail to look below and check on Yellow Three's progress in the water. He watched for as long as he could spare, seconds was all he had, but the man did not resurface. He was satisfied.

He rejoined his team with his partner by the open door where a ladder inside led directly to the deck below and they hurried down.

The team moved swiftly forward through a dark storeroom to a door. The leader squeezed his partner's shoulder once, twice and on the third they hurried through the door followed by the others and spread out in a corridor, pausing long enough to compare it with the area they had studied endlessly on the blueprints. A flight of stairs led up to the main deck that team two was clearing. They ignored it and moved down the corridor, checking a door on the left first, an empty room, then pausing outside another on the right. The team leader opened the door quickly and moved in splitting left, his partner right. They paused, guns up on aim at a man on the floor with a hood over his head and tied around a pole. The other two team members carried on down the corridor to clear the engine room while the leader quickly scanned the room as he moved to the prisoner. His partner found another man in a yellow jacket lying under a tarp.

Two dull thuds came from the engine room bulkhead, silent bullets that had passed through the target inside to strike the wall. 'Engine room clear,' came a voice over the radio.

The team leader removed the prisoner's hood and pulled his head back to get a look at the face. He then removed his own hood and gasmask. It was Lieutenant Stewart. He scrutinised the dead man in front of him. 'This isn't Hank Munro,' he said.

The team on the bridge paused long enough to be certain nothing else was alive within their target area. Both side doors were open and the bridge decks were being covered. 'Bridge clear,' said the team leader into his throat-mic.

'Main deck and "B" deck clear,' came a voice over the air. 'Engine room and lower deck clear,' came another voice.

The team leader then noticed the bridge phone swinging by its cord over the edge of the table. He picked it up, pulled his hood back to expose his ear, and placed the phone against it. It was silent, and then after a moment, the line went dead.

Father Kinsella wasn't sure what he had heard. One moment he was talking to the captain of the *Alpha Star* and then there was what sounded like a short gurgling sound followed by a thump, as if the phone had been dropped. He said hello a couple of times, wondering if he had lost the connection and then he heard more strange sounds, like furniture being moved and things being knocked over. It went silent again for a moment and then he was sure someone had picked up the phone. But no one said anything, and then he thought he could hear breathing, strained, as if through a mask.

Father Kinsella disconnected and wondered if he should try calling again, and then had a horrible feeling something had happened. Considering what he had just seen outside MI5 headquarters it was a distinct possibility. If something had gone wrong he wouldn't be able to find out just yet. He had done all he could anyway. His best bet was to get back home. In fact leaving England as soon as he could was probably a wise decision, all things considered.

He looked around for a taxi without luck and decided to walk to Waterloo station where he would get one for sure. Things had not gone as he'd hoped or indeed expected. Not at all.

Stratton pushed himself up on to his knees and took a moment to reorganise his senses. If there was one thing he hated it was losing control of his mind and motor functions. He was dazed but otherwise seemed to be okay; a quick scan of his limbs and torso confirmed that all the main bits were still attached. The blast had thrown him back a few feet but nothing other than the expanding gases appeared to have struck him. His gun was on the ground a few feet away and he stretched for it and took it in his hand. He focused through the swiftly clearing smoke and saw Aggy on her knees on the steps looking shaken. As he got to his feet so did she. She checked herself quickly for any damage then looked around and saw him standing and looking at her.

Stratton looked for the others in his team. Wilks was sitting shaking his head as if his ears were ringing and gave a thumbs-up to Chaz, who was walking over to check on his partner.

Aggy looked over at Lawton lying still on his back at the top of the steps and made her way to him. She knelt by him thinking he was dead until he took a sudden breath and opened his eyes, blinking hard. 'Aggy?' he asked, full of panic and fear, his voice dry and raspy.

'I'm here,' she said.

He moved a hand towards her and she took it.

'You okay?' he asked.

'Yes,' she nodded, wishing she could say as much for him. Blood was seeping out from beneath him and pooling on the step. Her immediate thought was to get some aid or call for an ambulance but she decided to stay with him in case he didn't have very long. Someone would be calling the emergency services by now anyway.

Stratton walked up the steps and loomed above them. Lawton focused on him and, surprisingly, appeared to smile.

'Stratton,' he croaked with difficulty. 'Always . . . survive . . . don't you? And . . . I bet . . . you're . . . the only one of us . . . who doesn't want to live for ever.' He found his comment amusing but could barely manage a laugh before the pain cut it off.

Stratton hoped the man would die from his wounds very soon otherwise he'd have to end it for him, preferably before anyone arrived. He didn't want to have to do it in front of Aggy. He'd heard the Mick had always been a good-humoured sort and now that he was all busted up and dying he wasn't whingeing and whining but trying to be entertaining. If a man was likeable in his last moments before death, he was likeable in life. Aggy obviously liked him. That said something for the man.

Lawton looked at the gun in Stratton's hand and seemed to know what Stratton had in mind. It wasn't a surprise. 'I don't think there'll be a need for that somehow,' he said.

Aggy glanced at the gun then up at Stratton. Of course. How stupid of her. There was every reason for Lawton to die and not one for him to live. She looked at Lawton; he was probably right. At that moment she truly hated the business she was in.

Stratton wanted to tell them it didn't matter anyway. According to Sumners the explosion wasn't enough to kill the virus; they were all covered in it, inhaling it, and therefore also dead. He chose not to say anything if for no other reason than to save Lawton the anguish of knowing he had failed Aggy in his final hour. It was obvious that Lawton's motivation for doing what he had was to save her.

Chaz and Wilks walked up the steps to join them. They didn't look as if they'd sustained any damage, not physically, but Wilks's eyes betrayed a deep concern.

'We fucked then, are we?' he asked Stratton. 'Chaz said according to your bloke the explosion wouldn't be enough to burn up the bio.'

So much for sparing Lawton. 'I guess not,' Stratton said.

''Ow long we got?' Wilks asked.

'Don't matter,' Chaz said. 'We're gonna have to stay right here until they come and take us away in big plastic bags and then keep us isolated until the end. Isn't that right?'

'Something like that,' Stratton said.

Wilks lowered his eyes. The thought of never seeing his wife and kids again was like a knife in his heart.

'Focking bang seemed big enough. Another pound and

I reckon old matey there would've made the river,' Chaz said, jutting a chin towards the road where Brennan lay, still smoking from his short flight. 'If only you'd used two,' he added.

Stratton found the comment curious. 'What exactly did Sumners say?' he asked.

'He said it wouldn't work, that the boffins said one Super "X" charge wouldn't work, but two would be enough. If you'd put two in, it would've killed the virus.'

'I used three,' Stratton said matter of factly.

Wilks looked up at Stratton with an expression not unlike that of someone who'd just had an execution order reprieved. 'You serious?'

Lawton started to spasm and choke. Aggy held his hand, frustrated that she was unable to do anything for him.

'Kathryn,' he said. 'Kathryn . . . Munro.'

Lawton's pain was increasing but he was determined to speak through it.

Stratton knelt beside him to hear him better.

'Term . . . terminal . . . f . . . four,' Lawton said. He gripped Aggy's more strongly, as if he had more to say. 'K . . . Kinsella . . . priest. Father . . . Kinsella.' The effort was too great for him and he nearly fell unconscious. He gripped her tightly again, unfinished. 'Godfather,' he said with his last gasp of breath and his hand went limp in Aggy's. She kept hold of it, gripping it. No matter what Bill had done, his last act had been generous; she owed her life to him. A tear rolled down her cheek but she kept her head down, hiding it from Stratton.

Stratton stood and put his gun back in its holster as several police cars arrived, their lights flashing. People began to step cautiously out of the MI5 building. Chaz turned to head down the steps towards the police.

461

'Chaz,' Stratton called after him. Chaz stopped and looked at him. 'No mention of the virus.'

Chaz nodded and walked over to the police, holding his badge out to them.

Stratton started down the steps and stopped to look back at Aggy. 'We have one more stop to make,' he said.

She didn't look at him. He took it as a message to go away. He understood. It was obvious she had felt a great deal for Lawton – and little for him. It wouldn't have worked anyhow, he reminded himself again. But losing her to a dead spy was an irony. His eyes lingered on her a while, knowing it would be for the last time.

He turned and walked away.

'Stratton,' Aggy called out. He stopped and looked back to see her stand and walk down the steps towards him. 'I was saying a prayer for him. Where are we going?'

He wanted to smile but it wouldn't have been appropriate. He would never understand women. 'You pray?' he asked, sounding every bit as surprised as he was.

'Not usually. It was for him. He said he used to pray until a priest put him off the church.'

Stratton removed the bus driver's jacket as they walked over to a police car and he showed an officer his badge. 'We need to get to Heathrow,' he said.

26

Hank gently broke the surface like an ailing porpoise, more by luck than judgement, and took a gasp of air, the fresh intake of oxygen making his head throb harder. He struggled to keep a toehold on consciousness as he drifted in and out of awareness. His left shoulder ached like a son-of-a-bitch but he could not avoid using the arm, along with his other limbs, to keep afloat, which he was only just achieving. A thin mist surrounded him, hovering just on top of the water, and through it, much higher than he was, he could make out a long line of orange lights dispersed at regular intervals. Everywhere else was in darkness.

Hank could remember the last few moments on the boat, coming down the stairs and on to the main deck. What happened then was patchy and confusing, with flashes of light, thumps, pain and then the sudden cold. It was unclear how long he had been in the water. He couldn't concentrate long enough to make sense out of the muddle of information his mind was throwing up; a mixture of images from his past combined with others from inside a hood and beating a man to death. The water lapped over his face. He knew he should be trying to get to land but he had no clue which way to go.

Tiny blurred white lights above him slowly came into focus. They were stars. He stared at them, the only things he could see that his mind could make sense of. He recognised the Plough that led to the North Star and then to the crooked 'W' that was Cassiopeia. He wondered how he knew the formations so well; they were not something he had ever taken much interest in. Then he remembered the lecture file in the SBS training team office. But moments after focusing on them they became blurred again. He thought his vision was failing but that wasn't why he could no longer make them out. He had sunk beneath the surface and was slowly going down. The line of bright orange lights also began to fade. He beat with his arms and legs to get back to the air but it was useless. His cheeks bulged and he increased his efforts to swim back up from the darkness that was now all around. He saw Kathryn and Janet and Helen, and his father who had died when he was ten and all the pain left his body except the desperate urge to keep his mouth closed against an even more powerful force to open it and suck in anything, even the water.

Then something grabbed him and he felt a sharp tug followed by a series of rhythmic jerks until he broke the surface. He took in an enormous breath and flailed weakly to stay afloat as the hand that tightly gripped his jacket continued to pull at him. Something hit him in the back of the neck but not painfully. It was a wall of soft mud and a second later he felt himself being hauled out of the water and on to land.

'Not a watery death for you, me old matey,' Hank heard an out-of-breath man say in an English accent. He remained still on his back, unable to muster the strength to move, and tried to focus on the stranger, who appeared to be wearing a black rubber suit.

Spinks removed his diver's facemask and emptied his nostrils noisily. 'You're an 'eavy bastard you are, mate,' he said spitting debris from his mouth and squeezing the water from his eyes. 'Trust me, if you 'adn't a been on the end of my first duck-dive you weren't gettin' another one.'

Spinks finished dealing with his own minor discomforts and leaned over to take a closer look at his catch. 'Can you 'ear me?' he asked.

Hank nodded and tried to move but the pain in his chest and left shoulder was suddenly intense.

''Ow bad are you 'urt,' Spinks asked, checking him out. ''Ow many shots you take? Do you know? . . . They got you good, didn't they? Teach you to screw around with the boys, wone' it.'

Hank moved his right arm slowly and hovered it over his left upper chest. Spinks moved it away and took a look. 'Yeah, I see an 'ole in your jacket.' Then Spinks noticed the wound on the side of Hank's head. 'That don't look too good either . . . Cor, bet that fuckin' 'urts.' Spinks scrutinised Hank's face and moved his head over to get a better look. 'Wait a minute. You ain't a boyo. You're the Yank, ain't you? You Hank Munro?' he asked loud and clearly.

Hank nodded.

'Holy shit,' Spinks said as he quickly struggled to locate his communications prestel. 'This is Spinks,' he said adjusting his throat-mic. 'I'm on the west bank north of the boat. I've got the Yank. Munro. He's got a few bullet holes in 'im but he's alive, just about anyway . . .'

Hank felt suddenly tired and his eyelids grew heavy. Just before he closed them he was certain he had seen Orion's Belt directly above him but couldn't be bothered to open his eyes again to check.

Kathryn was seated under the 'meeting place' sign in the arrivals lounge of terminal four, Heathrow Airport. Tired as she was she had not been able to sleep and not just because of the uncomfortable seats and half-dozen cups of coffee she'd had from the Starbucks conveniently located a few yards away. She had been waiting for more than five hours and was wondering what she should do if nobody came to meet her. Surely Father Kinsella didn't expect her to sit there throughout the night? Everything else about her trip appeared to have been meticulously planned and executed but perhaps something had gone wrong.

For the first few hours she kept hoping Hank would appear from the stream of people that at times seemed to fill the building but her expectant glances for him had become less frequent as the evening dragged on and the passengers and visitors in the terminal were gradually outnumbered by those who worked in it. She felt grubby and unclean and yearned for a hotel room with a deep bath and a large bed with crisp, clean sheets. The first deadline she set herself for leaving if no one turned up had passed and she was determined to stick to her next one at midnight, although she doubted she would have the courage to leave even then. It would be terrible if Hank turned up tired and hungry while she lay in a comfortable hotel nearby. And then there was Father Kinsella. He would probably be none too pleased either.

'Kathryn,' a voice said from behind as her bag was placed on the seat beside her. She whipped around to see Father Kinsella and got to her feet, expecting to find Hank too. When there was no sign of him her eyes rested on the priest's.

'It's not been the best of days,' he said. 'Don't ask me any questions, Kathryn. I've just come to tell you to go home.'

'You expect me not to ask about my husband?'

'No, but I don't have an answer for you, that's all. You

466

have your return air ticket. Get a hotel for the night and go back to your children in the morning.'

'That's it?'

'Yes. That's it.'

A dangerous blend of rage and frustration began to percolate in her. 'And you expect me to just walk off and do as I'm told and not even question what the hell is going on just because you say so?'

'I do, Kathryn,' he said with an assertive look.

'Well, damn you!' she said, raising her voice.

Her ire did not appear to have any effect on him.

'It's a war we're in, Kathryn.'

'I'm not at war with anyone.'

'Sure you are. You were born into a family at war. You hate these people as much as I do, you always have.'

'I hated them because I was told to. It wasn't my hate. It was my mother's, and yours. Mostly yours . . . You're an evil man.'

'Evil, am I? Because I'm a priest at war? Go home, Kathryn, you don't know what you're talking about.'

'I always thought you were evil, even when I was a child. That's why I was always scared of you. I grew up with this stupid war and you know something, I don't have a clue what it's all about. And the reason I don't have a clue is because what you've all been saying to me all my life doesn't make any sense. Not today. I think it's only people like you keep it going because you enjoy it. That's why Hank isn't here. That's why you're evil.' She picked up her bag and stared into his eyes. 'I don't know what it was I did today, but I have a feeling that was evil too . . . If you don't tell me where my husband is, right now, I'm going to find an English police station, walk in and tell them everything that I did and your part in it.'

467

'Is that right?' he said with a threatening look. 'Are you sure you want to be playing those kind of games with me?'

'Try me,' she said just as defiantly.

Instead of being angry, he broke into a chuckle as he surreptitiously looked about to see if anyone was watching. He walked around the seat row to get closer to her.

'Ah, Kathryn, Kathryn, Kathryn. For a moment there I was foolish enough to take on that Irish temper of yours—'

'I'm not Irish, Father Kinsella,' she said, cutting him off. 'I'm American.' She turned to leave and he grabbed her arm brutally.

'Now you listen to me.'

'Get off me,' she shouted.

'If you ever want to see your precious children again—' and then he froze. Kathryn was staring at him in utter horror because of his threat, but Kinsella's peripheral vision had picked up something that shut her out of his mind as warning bells rang in his head. Still holding Kathryn's arm, he jerked his head around to see a man standing, watching, a few feet away. He didn't know the man but he identified the eyes: they were as cold and malevolent as his own.

Kinsella weighed him in an instant and knew it was the enemy. In all of Kinsella's years as a primary antagonist in the fight against the English he had never actually confronted the enemy himself. He had met many English, of course, and seen soldiers and police, but never had he actually come face to face with those who took part in the fight. He noticed a slight cut on his cheek and knew that he had seen him before, from a distance, that very evening, outside the MI5 headquarters. The man watching him like a predator was undoubtedly one of their dark forces and Kinsella had immediate respect for him if nothing else.

Kinsella let go of Kathryn's arm, all the while keeping

his eyes on the man, and noticing a pretty girl a few feet away watching him.

Stratton had been studying this large man in a tweed jacket talking with Mrs Munro as he walked across the hall, but it was not until he saw him grab her arm and utter what sounded like a threat to her children and then turn to look at him that he noticed the dog collar. It might not be too much of a wild guess that this man was the priest Lawton had referred to.

'Father Kinsella,' Stratton said, more of a statement than a question.

'And who might you be?' Kinsella asked, hostility in his voice, an instinctive reaction since this man was obviously a fighter like himself. He might never have faced the enemy before but that did not mean he would not be up to the task. If anything, years of hatred had ensured his aggression come the opportunity.

Stratton weighed the situation. Was this American a RIRA godfather? If so, he no doubt had a great deal to do with the events of the last few weeks. It was times like this he asked himself what Sumners would want him to do. He could arrest him on suspicion under the terrorism act, but there were other games to play. That was an aspect he enjoyed about this business. It wasn't always about grabbing every-thing in reach. In fact, it was often quite the opposite. Stratton took a long look at the man. His arrogance was the clue to his next move.

'I'm here for Kathryn,' Stratton said.

'She's with me and we're catching the first flight to the States,' Father Kinsella said.

'Don't push it,' Stratton said. 'You can come along too if you want. Or you can walk away, alone.'

The priest knew he had lost this fight before it began.

But at least the man wasn't here for him. The best he could do was cut his losses and walk away. He eyed Stratton coldly for a moment then looked at Kathryn.

'You be careful, girl,' he said, softly, hoping the threat was hoisted aboard.

Kathryn stood firm and looked at him defiantly. Father Kinsella could see it in her eyes and nodded. He stepped back, took another glance at Stratton, then walked away.

'Be seeing you,' Stratton said, unable to resist the parting shot, something for the man to sweat over.

The priest paused and started to turn his head to look at Stratton, then changed his mind, clenched his jaw, and walked on.

Kathryn turned to face Stratton as Aggy came alongside him.

'Hank's going to be okay,' Stratton said.

'When can I see him?' she asked.

'Soon . . . We need to go back into London. Some people want to talk to you.'

'Am I under arrest?' she said. There was no fight left in Kathryn. She felt tired and humble but above all relieved it was all over, the kidnapping at least. She felt guilty, even though she did not know exactly what she had done wrong.

'That's not for me to say,' Stratton said.

She nodded and picked up her bag. Perhaps her feeling of guilt stemmed from her flirtation with the idea of freedom from Hank. She would live with that for the rest of her life.

Stratton indicated the exit and she walked past him towards it. Stratton and Aggy followed.

'If he is a RIRA godfather, why'd you let him go?' Aggy asked, out of earshot of Kathryn.

'The devil you know . . . This war's gonna last a long time. He's not gonna get lost. I suspect she knows him pretty well. If he did have anything to do with what went on today we'll have all the help we want from the Americans. He may be more useful on the street and we can pull him in any time. Something tells me that one will be in the fight to the bitter end.'

'Will she be arrested?' Aggy asked.

'For meeting terrorists and carrying a parcel with no idea what it contained because she thought it would get her husband back? I doubt it. She's the wife of a hero who risked his life in the fight against terrorism and helped save thousands of lives. He'll probably be decorated by the Americans and us, and her part in it will remain a secret.'

Aggy nodded, her thoughts turning to her own situation. 'And what about me?'

'I've been thinking about that. You did everything right once you knew the facts. You held it all together at one point. They'll want to keep the bio a secret; if it got out RIRA will have put some points on the board. You could play hardball with them. They'll have no loyalty to you. The trick is to get them to decide it would be better to keep you in the fold.'

'I meant with you,' she said, keeping her eyes ahead.

For a second after her question he had wondered if that's what she meant. 'I could be useful to you, but not if they thought there was something between us.' As soon as he said it he wondered why he had slammed the door in her face like that. But it was true. He could lever Sumners into batting for her. The man owed him enough favours. Back in the detachment was the best place for her.

Aggy lowered her head and put her hands in her pockets. She would say no more to him. There was no point.

471

They followed Kathryn through the automatic doors and out into the cold air.

'This way,' Aggy said to Kathryn and led her to a waiting police car.

Stratton climbed in the back beside them, next to Aggy. She looked away from him, out the opposite window, avoiding him as best she could in the confined space, wondering why he hadn't sat the other side of Kathryn.

'I should think they'll let me go back to the obvious when the paperwork on this one is all done. You lot need looking after anyway . . . What do you think?'

Aggy never moved and continued looking out the window. Only someone who knew her very well could tell that deep inside she was smiling.

As the car left the kerb and headed away from the airport, Stratton stretched his neck from side to side and rested his head back. He'd hoped the successful end of the operation would have given him some kind of relief from the darkness that seemed to surround his soul, but it did not. Now that it was over he felt nothing had changed inside. Even the decision to return to Northern Ireland had no effect. He knew what part of the problem was. The only time he seemed to come to life was in the heat of action. Or perhaps that was just a distraction. But the closer he came to death the more alive he felt. It was like a drug though; the high lasted only as long as the fight. He thought about quitting altogether, but civvy street was on the outside in many ways. There was action to be had for sure, but it had to be found. Money became a factor, and the jobs were uncertain and usually the scraps. In the service the big ones came to you.

The East was the place to be now. That's where the stakes were the highest. Perhaps he would never go back to Ireland. It would no longer cut it for him. It was a dead, or at least dying, war, and minuscule in comparison to other troubles in the world. The bio had been serious enough, but that card had been played by the RIRA and was more than likely now out of their deck for good. The crusades were always the ultimate. That fight would last for ever. The people and the terrain were fiercer and that made it much more interesting.

The East it was to be then. He would ask Sumners in the morning.

He glanced at Aggy. As he had always said, it was never meant to be.